THE DRAGONS OF ANDROMEDA

THE IMPERIUM CHRONICLES
BOOK TWO

W. H. MITCHELL

Cover design: Steven Novak (NovakIllustration.com)

Published by: Willbot Books, 2020

ISBN-13: 978-1-7351189-1-8

Works by W. H. Mitchell

The Imperium Chronicles Series

The Arks of Andromeda, Book 1 (2017)

The Dragons of Andromeda, Book 2 (2018)

The Robots of Andromeda, Book 3 (2020)

Humor

A Little of Me Goes a Long Way (2015)

To my wife, who makes sure I put on
pants before leaving the house.

Special thanks to Brad Snyder and Judy Veatch.

Additional thanks to my beta readers:

Chris Buckland

Ward Lenz

A character list and glossary are located at the back of the book.

PROLOGUE

The Imperial Astronomical Society surveys the night skies, mapping the stars and the spaces in between. At the farthest reaches, well beyond the edges of the Imperium and the Magna Supremacy, the charts are blank, not because these places are empty, but because they are devoid of our understanding.

These are the areas of the great unknown where dangers may lurk and the darkness is at its darkest. As the ancient cartographers would say, *"Here there be dragons…"*

CHAPTER ONE

On the planet Aldorus, outside the city of Regalis, a sanitation robot roamed the grounds after the park had closed for the night, emptying the rubbish bins of trash left by people during the day. On a set of six wheels, the trashbot rambled along from one bin to another, lifting each with a pair of robotic arms and dumping it into a hopper.

Near midnight, the trashbot was checking bins by the lake when sounds began drifting in from the dark, somewhere off the main trail. Unlike the animal noises common during the night, these were different, faint and rhythmic.

As the compactor in his body pressed a clump of paper cups and a small raccoon into a tidy cube, the robot rambled over the carefully cropped grass to a cluster of bushes. Peering through the branches, he noticed an outcrop of rock and the entrance to a cave. The drumming clearly was coming from inside.

Organics, the robot thought, *are always up to mischief.*

He entered the cave.

Inside, a group of seven people sat around a fire, the flickering light casting shadows on the walls.

This doesn't look like a picnic, the robot thought.

In sackcloth robes and with hoods over their heads, each person also wore an amulet in the shape of an eight-pointed star, a black pearl in the center.

One of them pounded a large drum in his lap while the others chanted:

> FROM THE VOID
> THE OLD ONES COME.
> THE END IS NEAR,
> AS HEARTBEATS DRUM.
>
> BOW YOUR HEADS;
> RECEIVE YOUR FATE.
> CHAOS REIGNS;
> THEIR LOVE IS HATE.
>
> BURNING FIRE
> FROM SKY WILL FALL.
> PRAISE THE GODS!
> THE *END* FOR ALL!

On the wall at the back of the cavern the image of a door was carved into the stone. Around the edge of the door were letters from some language the robot didn't recognize.

The rhythm of the drum grew faster and louder.

The letters started glowing until the center of the doorway faded, the edges falling inward like a waterfall seen from above.

When the beats of the drum reached a frenzied crescendo, long tentacled arms flew from the doorway, thrashing about the cavern like flailing vines. The arms coiled around the hooded figures, dragging them back toward the portal.

The trashbot expected to hear screams, but the chanters made no sounds at all. Like sacrifices accepting their fate, they disappeared through the doorway. When the last one vanished, the portal closed and the doorway and the letters returned to lifeless rock.

Someone appeared beside the trashbot. Like the others, he wore a robe, but the hood was down, revealing his face covered in black soot and white ash like a skull. Around his neck hung the same amulet, an eight-pointed star.

Seeing the empty chamber, the man's face changed to a disappointed frown.

"Aw," he said. "They started without me!"

In the heart of Regalis, the Imperial capital, the VOX News headquarters building rose like a shining steeple capped with antennas. Besides beaming broadcasts across the planet Aldorus, VOX News used a network of communication drones that autonomously spread reports far and wide across the Imperium. Of their stable of anchors, Sylvia Flax was the most popular. In her early thirties, her bright, azure hair hung past her shoulders.

Her studio on the ninetieth floor was normally a simple desk with a holographic background on which images of floods and disgraced politicians appeared. Tonight, however, both were gone and replaced by a stage with spot lighting focused on three chairs and a glass coffee table. Flax sat in the first chair, facing two others, a man and a woman, seated across the table. The woman wore a fashionable dress, typical of a noblewoman, with her dark hair up in a bun. The man's clothes were more utilitarian, a plain shirt and casual pants. Compared to the woman's olive skin, the man's complexion was darker.

The fact that he was currently one of the most important men of the Imperium seemed completely lost on him, Flax noted to herself.

"Thank you for agreeing to this interview," she said.

"You're welcome," the woman replied.

"My pleasure," the man said, his smile tucked behind a full beard.

"No, the pleasure's mine," Flax went on. "It's not every day I get to interview the first new royal houses in the last seven hundred years..."

The woman smiled broadly, but the man's grin disappeared as he adjusted his position.

On a monitor, out of view of the cameras that hovered around the set, a timer slowly counted down. When it reached zero, the intro music played and credits for the show appeared on the monitor, superimposed over Flax's face.

"Good evening," she said, staring into the camera. "I'm Sylvia Flax and tonight I have two important guests, Captain Andre Santos of the colony ship *Merope* and Captain Sheba Nasri of the *Sterope*."

The camera cut to the guests before panning out to include all three in the frame.

"I doubt there's anyone in the Imperium," Flax continued, "who hasn't seen your faces by now. Certainly, the exploits that led to the discovery of your long-lost ark ships are well known. Until now, however, no one's had a chance to really hear what the captains of those two ships had to say."

Santos laughed, pulling on his beard mischievously.

"Not publicly," he said.

"Of course, I assume the Imperial government has debriefed you both..." Flax said.

"Oh, yes," Santos said. "To no end!"

Giving the other captain the side eye, Nasri interjected, "After hundreds of years in cryosleep, naturally there's a lot to get caught up on."

"Absolutely," Flax said. "It must have been quite a shock."

Nasri nodded.

"We've missed out on a great deal," she said, "but I feel fortunate we've been presented with such a rare opportunity."

"I'll say!" Flax said. "Seven ark ships set out from Earth, but only five arrived safely, or so we *assumed*. The Five Families descended from the captains of those five ships. Now, all of that's been turned upside down!"

Flax felt herself getting too excited. She took a breath.

"Not to mention the rest of your crew," she went on, "who are considered nobles in their own right, and the thousands of settlers who were also on board."

"It's a lot to take in," Santos deadpanned.

"Well, speaking for myself at least," Nasri said, "I consider this a great responsibility. I had no idea when we left Earth so many centuries ago that I might someday be the head of a royal household."

Santos rolled his eyes.

"I don't know about all that," he said from the side of his mouth. "It seems crazy to think I went into cryosleep a captain and woke up a *lord*!"

"It's been rumored," Flax said earnestly, "that the government will be giving you both a large stipend in keeping with your new status."

"Frankly," Nasri replied, "it would be hard to wield the power of a noble without the proper funds."

"That's the other thing," Santos said. "Why should *I* get a king's ransom? That money should go to my crew and the colonists from my ship. We were in it together as far as I'm concerned."

"It's what we deserve," Nasri said.

"For what?" Santos replied. "We didn't do anything."

"To Captain Nasri's point," Flax said, "your new status reflects the importance the Five Families place on their lineage to those other five ship captains. In some ways, you were robbed of your proper place in the Imperium and, certainly, the place your descendants would have enjoyed."

Santos leaned toward Flax.

"For me, it's like this," he said. "I signed up to bring the colonists to a new land so they could build a new society. When I woke up, I found a new society, but it's not what I expected. There's no democracy or rule by the people. Far from it! I don't want any part of that!"

Flax cleared her throat and tried to smile convincingly.

"Well, we have the Imperial Senate..." she said.

Santos shrugged.

"No system is perfect," Nasri spoke up, "but being part of the system helps us make it better. If I can serve humanity in my new capacity, I'm willing to try."

Off camera, the director made a cutting motion across his throat.

"Well, I'm afraid that's all the time we have," Flax said, turning to face the camera hovering a few feet away. "I'd like to again thank the two of you for coming."

Captain Santos and Nasri thanked her in reply while the monitor behind them slowly faded to black.

The streets of Regalis were mostly empty when Sylvia Flax strolled down a darkened sidewalk, her high heels tapping with a steady cadence. She probably should have taken a grav taxi, but the transmat station was only a few blocks away and she was still exuberant from the interview.

Sylvia's stylish dress, cut just above the knee, rustled against her legs as her long hair swayed with each passing step. She listened to the rhythm of her heels repeating *tip tap, tip tap.*

She became aware of another sound with a different tempo, *clump clump,* like a pair of heavy boots.

Not many people are out this late, Flax thought, and he seemed to be getting closer.

Even with the occasional lamp filling a puddle of light, the street was dark, but Flax could still make out the shape of the person approaching.

Tip tap.

Clump clump.

He was definitely not a woman, she realized. He was short, but not feminine in any way. His shoulders rose and fell like the pistons of a poorly maintained machine. Not a robot either, although that would've been a relief. Robots rarely attacked people.

The man wore baggy pants and a sleeveless shirt. He looked like he came from the Underclass, Flax concluded, the lowest of the low except for non-humans. He wore goggles, hiding his eyes.

Tip tap. Clump clump.

He was nearly abreast now. Flax couldn't tell if he was looking at her. His eyes were hidden behind those terrible goggles. And his lips. They were painted black, a sharp contrast against his sickly white skin.

Tip clump tap clump.

She could smell him as he passed. She tried not to look, at least not directly. And those goggles. What were his eyes doing? Were they looking at her?

Clump clump. Tip tap.

He went by without a word. Flax released a long breath, not realizing she had been holding one in the whole time. Then, something like metal flicking across metal snapped behind her and she instantly felt the edge of a switchblade scrape against her neck. It was him, his body pressed against her back.

"Step out, Magnus!" he yelled down the street. "I know you're there!"

Further up the sidewalk, a different man stepped out from a doorway concealed in the shadows. Lamp light reflected off his closely shaved head and stubbly face. Intricate tattoos at the base of his neck poked out just above the collar of his shirt. The rest of him was covered by a long, brown coat.

"There's a contract out on you, Tokai," Magnus said. "And I'm here to collect."

Tokai, still holding the knife at Flax's throat, shrank behind her. "Come any closer and I'll cut her!"

"Do what you like," Magnus replied. "She's nothing to me."

Flax didn't like the sound of that.

"You can't just let him hurt me!" she shouted.

"Sorry, lady," Magnus said. "I'm a hit man, not a hero."

"I'll pay you ten thousand credits," she offered.

"Twenty thousand."

"Fifteen."

From her vantage point, at least twenty feet from the hired killer, Flax detected a nearly imperceptible grin at the corner of Magnus' mouth.

"Deal," Magnus replied, effortlessly drawing a weapon from a holster beneath his coat.

Tokai, the situation perhaps dawning on him, yelled out "Wait!" but a blast of orange light had already charred a hole in his forehead, exiting the back of his skull.

Flax stood in stunned silence until Tokai's body landed with a *thud* behind her. Then she got angry.

"You could've killed me!" she screamed.

"No," Magnus replied calmly. "Then I wouldn't get paid."

"Are you crazy? I'm not paying *you*!"

Just as calmly, Magnus pointed the gun at her.

"Yes, you will," he said, and he was right.

A cool wind on an otherwise warm day blew in from the sea. Lady Rebecca Veber, along with two of her aides, waited on the transmat platform. Draped in a long gown of aqua and white taffeta decorated with a scallop shell pattern, Lady Veber was in her early forties with a wide face and blue eyes, her blond hair worn in an intricate braid. The platform jutted out over a cliff, high above the white beaches and turquoise waters typical of the planet. The Veber family owned the planet *Lokeren*, a world of island chains and vast, tropical oceans. Of the many estates built on the planet, this particular one was Lady Veber's favorite due to the gentle breezes that blew just after dusk.

"He's transmatting now," an aide said, holding a finger to his earpiece.

At the center of the platform, the air sizzled like burning oil as a golden haze materialized into a man. Lady Veber and her two staffers bowed.

"Prince Richard!" she said, raising her head. "Always a pleasure."

The first son and eldest child of the Imperial emperor, Prince Richard was ten years Lady Veber's junior, with a primly trimmed mustache and wearing a gold and red tunic. He smiled graciously as he walked stiffly toward her. He took her outstretched hand and kissed the back of it, just above a ring encrusted with diamonds.

"Of course, the pleasure is all mine," he said.

"I must admit I was somewhat surprised the Imperial palace could spare you for a personal visit," she said, withdrawing her hand.

"We live in interesting times."

"Do we? I hadn't noticed."

"Perhaps we could talk inside," the prince suggested. "This is more fresh air than I'm used to..."

The group walked away from the cliffs toward the palace, a series of cube-shaped buildings with clay walls painted white and domes of light blue. Once inside, the two aides left them alone in a large room with a vaulted ceiling covered in byzantine tiles with the same shell motif as Lady Veber's dress. She and the prince sat on a bench covered in satin pillows.

"You really should get out more, Richard," she said, feigning concern. "A little fresh air never hurt anyone."

"No, but sound travels," he replied. "I wanted our conversation to be more private."

She sighed.

"Very well," she said. "Why *have* you come all this way?"

"I assume you've seen the interview with Lord Santos and Lady Nasri?" Richard asked.

"Well, I don't think Captain Santos would care for the title *Lord* being used."

"Exactly," Richard replied. "How do you react to a man who turns up his nose to wealth and fame? It's unnatural..."

"At least Lady Nasri is more... agreeable?"

"Yes, but they're a package deal."

"Are both really necessary?"

"What happens when we need to choose our next emperor?" Richard asked. "With six families, we could have a hung decision, three votes for and three against. The turmoil would be a disaster! With seven, a majority is guaranteed."

"I suppose," Lady Veber replied skeptically.

"Perhaps more importantly," the prince added, "our society is built on each family's prestige being directly tied to the captains of the colony ships. It's our birthright."

"Yes?"

"But if Captain — I mean *Lord* — Santos denies the inherent importance of being such a captain, it calls into question the status of the other Five Families, not to mention the lesser families who descended from the rest of the ships' crews."

Lady Veber considered this for a time.

"Indeed," she said finally. "I see your point."

"We need Santos on board," Richard said, "or people will start questioning the foundations of our authority and the very fabric that holds the Imperium together."

"I presume you're here on the Emperor's behalf to prevent that from happening?" she replied.

Prince Richard nodded with a sly smile.

By evening, Prince Richard had departed as he came, in a crackling of electrons disappearing into nothing. The air was still warm and gently brushed through Lady Veber's hair as she returned inside to consider what the prince had said. However, her mind was preoccupied with other business far closer to her heart.

Passing through the estate's long corridors, Lady Veber was scarcely aware of those she happened upon. She heard their voices and vaguely registered what they said before disregarding it as unimportant. Whatever they needed could wait.

She entered her son's quarters but didn't knock, knowing it was unnecessary. In the main room, a man in a white coat with buttons down the left side waited for her, but Lady Veber passed him silently and went into the bedroom. Her son Philip lay in the bed while one of Lady Veber's handmaidens stood watch beside him.

Philip was nineteen, with brown, deep-set eyes. His hair was matted and damp from a cold compress on his forehead.

"How is he?" Lady Veber asked.

"His fever is the same, ma'am," the handmaiden said, an older woman with a round face.

"Has he eaten today?"

"No, ma'am."

Lady Veber, scowling angrily, returned to the outer room.

"They told me you were the best physician in the Imperium," she said, trying not to shout, "yet my son keeps getting worse and worse!"

"His illness isn't responding to treatment," the doctor replied. "I can order another battery of tests..."

"More tests?" she scoffed. "You've scanned and pricked him a hundred times and you're no closer to curing him!"

"So far, his condition has defied diagnosis. We simply don't know what's causing this."

The handmaiden cried out, bringing Lady Veber and the doctor into the bedroom where they found Philip shaking violently.

"It's another seizure!" the handmaiden yelled.

Lady Veber and the other woman held the boy down while the doctor injected a sedative. Within a few seconds, the boy's convulsions subsided, allowing them to release their hold on him.

"Get out," Lady Veber told the doctor.

The man, his face reddening, moved toward the door but stopped.

"Should I run the additional tests?" he murmured.

"Just get out!" Lady Veber shouted.

The doctor turned and left. Lady Veber rearranged several blond hairs that had come loose and hung haphazardly around her face.

"Ma'am," the handmaiden said meekly.

"What is it?" Lady Veber said, mopping beads of sweat from her forehead.

"I know you're convinced conventional medicine will help—"

"I'm not convinced of anything right now..."

"It's just there's something I want to show you."

From around her neck, the handmaiden removed an amulet hanging on a long, black chain. The ornament was an octagram, an eight-pointed star, made from a strange, dark metal. A black pearl was set in the center.

CHAPTER TWO

On Aldorus, sub-basement 31 was over three hundred feet below the Regalis starport. Magnus Black found this useful for two reasons. First, it was too deep for someone to transmat in or out, including transmatting Magnus without his permission. Second, it was too deep for orbital bombardment to reach, even if someone wasn't timid about destroying the thirty floors above sub-basement 31 and whatever happened to be sitting on the starport surface.

It was also dimly lit. Magnus liked that most of all.

Positioned in the shadow of a rusted storage container, Magnus waited. His head and face were shaved to a mere stubble and he wore a dark leather coat. Inside the coat, a blaster pistol hung by a shoulder holster.

Farther down the line of containers, an elevator door opened with a cheerful *ding* and a man in uniform stepped out. His name was Colonel Hugo Grausman, a man Magnus knew very well.

In his fifties, the colonel wore a green uniform with black, spit-shined boots. His brown hair was cut high and tight, revealing a large scar running along the side of his head.

Colonel Grausman held up his hands and turned completely around, showing that the holster at his hip was empty and no other obvious weapons were visible. Magnus let him stand there for a full minute before saying anything.

"I didn't expect to see you again," Magnus said, "unless I was going to kill you."

Following the assassin's voice, the colonel took several steps in that direction before stopping.

"I get that a lot," he said.

"I hope this isn't just the Intelligence Service luring me into a trap," Magnus said, emerging from the shadow.

"They're still looking for you?"

"If I'm still breathing, they're still looking for me."

"Maybe I can help you with that..."

"Is that why you're here?" Magnus asked. "To do me a favor?"

"Not exactly."

"I'm hurt," Magnus replied.

"There's been a terrorist attack on Marakata," the colonel said.

Magnus shrugged. "That's a daily occurrence..."

"A suicide bomber got into the green zone and blew himself up, taking out half the officers' quarters," the colonel went on.

"The Draconians aren't going to stop until the Imperials leave their planet."

"I know that!" the colonel said angrily. "I've been fighting them for twenty years."

"So, why's this attack different?"

"Because my wife and kids are dead! They died in the explosion!"

Magnus arched his eyebrow, but said nothing.

"We killed off the terrorist cell responsible," the colonel continued after collecting himself, "but the leader's still at large."

"Who is it?"

"Do you still remember General Ekavir?"

Magnus glared. "You know damn well I do."

"Then you won't mind going after him for me."

"He's not my problem anymore," Magnus replied.

"A lot has changed since you were there," the colonel said. "Ekavir's lost most of his people from reprisal raids. The rest don't want to be anywhere near him. They say he's lost his *honor*."

"I guess killing kids will do that for a person."

"The two of you have unfinished business. This is your opportunity to finish him off once and for all."

"Are you sure he's still on Marakata?" Magnus asked.

"The planet's been under blockade since the attack," Colonel Grausman replied. "I haven't allowed anyone off the planet except myself to come here. He's got to be in the jungle somewhere. It's just a matter of finding him."

"On a world covered in jungle. That shouldn't be hard..."

"Some of your old contacts are still alive. I've made sure of that."

"What about payment?"

"Five hundred thousand credits," the colonel replied.

Magnus shook his head slowly. "Not enough."

"Like I said, I can get the IS to stop looking for you."

"Now, how would you do that?"

"I've made new friends," the colonel said. "They might do me a favor if I ask nicely."

"The IS was pretty pissed when I quit," Magnus replied. "It didn't help that I killed their agent on my way out the door..."

"Is that a *yes*?"

Magnus considered for a long minute but finally nodded. "Okay."

When the expansion of the Imperium reached the Draconian home world Marakata, the humans found a race of fierce warriors who, even without advanced technology, resisted all attempts to subdue them. Taller than humans, these large reptiles were covered in thick green scales with wide, bone-like protrusions around the crown of their skulls. Although they had claws on both hands and feet, they were masters of bladed weapons including what the natives called the *Draconian Battlestaff*. At the end of a long pole, the head of the battlestaff combined a pointed side for stabbing and an axe side for slashing.

The Draconians did a lot of both.

Two hundred years and several revolts later, Marakata was a police state with Colonel Hugo Grausman as the military governor. Even with Imperial soldiers manning checkpoints throughout the main city of Sucikhata, attacks by Draconian separatists occurred so frequently that most governing offices, both civil and military, were located in an area of relative safety called the *Green Zone*.

Although the inhabitants of the city enjoyed all the modern amenities one would expect, the architecture of Sucikhata gave it an ancient appearance. Instead of concrete and plasteel, the buildings were constructed of stone blocks carefully fitted together without mortar or cement. Since most buildings were only a few stories tall, the city grew outward, forming a sprawling labyrinth of narrow alleys paved with large, flattened stones. Like everywhere else on the planet, vines and vegetation were prevalent throughout the city as the jungle attempted to take back what was rightfully its own.

Magnus checked into a hotel where he found his equipment waiting for him, courtesy of Colonel Grausman. Magnus lifted the blinds and stared at the jungle visible just outside the city. In the haze of the afternoon, a volcano rose from the leafy sea of green.

As a new recruit, barely in his twenties, Magnus learned all about Agniparvata, the name of the Draconians' revered volcano. According to their legends, a two-headed dragon named Bonamalum lived inside the mountain. One of the heads, Bona, was good while his brother, Malum, was evil. One day, a hero climbed the mountain and challenged Malum to combat. The evil side agreed, attacking the hero, but after a battle lasting seven days and seven nights, Malum's head lay severed on the ground. As the hero rejoiced in his victory, he noticed that Bona was bleeding to death from the wound that killed his evil brother. Powerless to help, the hero could do nothing as the good dragon collapsed and died.

Over the last two decades, most of the soldiers Magnus served with had either died or been transferred off-world. He hadn't made many friends among the locals, because he was killing them most of the time. The few native contacts Magnus did make were usually uncovered by resistance groups and executed as traitors. Even so, there was one Draconian he was confident still lived. A quick search of the business registry confirmed it.

Despite the tropical heat, Magnus pulled on his leather overcoat and made his way down the streets of Sucikhata. Military checkpoints blocked most major arteries, but Magnus avoided them, preferring the narrow side streets. A group of Draconian children playing with a ball stopped, their jaws hanging open, as the strange human passed by. Most non-Dracs were too afraid of the dangers that dwelled in the alleyways. Besides regular gangs, thieves, and misfits, these were the passageways where true believers in Draconian freedom were found. For them, spilling human blood was a rite of passage.

Appearing oblivious, Magnus strolled undeterred except for the heavy sweat running down his face and neck.

Turning a corner, three young Draconians barred his way. Each carried a machete-sized blade.

"Lost?" one of them asked.

"You must have a death wish," said another.

Magnus opened his coat, revealing a blaster rifle hanging from a shoulder harness.

"Go home," he said.

"We're not afraid of you!" the first youth replied defiantly.

"If you knew how many Dracs said that to me and ended up dead," the assassin replied, "you'd already be gone."

The Draconians traded nervous glances, but Magnus already knew what the consensus would be. Courage was no substitute for experience, and fear trumped them both.

Reluctantly, but still with an element of haste, the three stepped back and turned, making their way down a side alley and out of sight. Magnus closed his coat and continued on his way.

The Dragon's Teeth was a shop far enough off the beaten path that only people who already knew it existed ever went there. The shop's name, by law, was written in the human language, called Imperial Standard, while below in smaller script was the translation in Draconian cuneiform.

Magnus pushed the front door open and went in. If the hit man thought the air was hot on the outside, he was unpleasantly surprised to find it like a furnace on the inside.

At least it was a dry heat, he thought. *Like sticking your head in a convection oven.*

A bell over the door alerted the owner someone had entered. A tattered curtain covering an archway parted and a Draconian, hobbling on a peg leg, shuffled in. Seeing Magnus, the old Draconian swore something in the local language. Magnus could guess what it meant.

"Hello, Daaruk," Magnus said. "How's business?"

Daaruk swung his head toward the racks of swords hanging on the walls, a blanket of dust covering them.

"About as well as my leg," he replied wryly. "The one you shot off as I recall."

"That's a shame," Magnus replied. "You're the best weaponsmith on Marakata."

Daaruk chuckled. "Only because your people keep killing my competition."

Magnus shrugged. "I guess it's good to be the last one standing."

The Draconian pivoted on his wooden leg and went back through the archway. Magnus followed.

In the next room, a forge filled the center, a well-worn anvil standing to one side. Daaruk took a pair of tongs and grabbed a piece of glowing-red metal from the burning forge. With a hammer, the Draconian struck the metal over the anvil a few times before shoving it back into the fire.

"So, you took my leg," Daaruk said. "Did you come back to finish the job?"

"No," Magnus replied. "I have a different job in mind."

"What's it got to do with me?"

"I'm looking for someone."

"Unless he's a customer, I don't know him."

"The Jade General?" Magnus asked.

Daaruk pulled the rod from the forge again, but instead of laying it across the anvil, he swung it around toward Magnus' head. Anticipating the move, Magnus thrust his hand through the pocket of his coat, firing his blaster rifle through the lining. Daaruk's peg leg disintegrated into ashes, leaving him off-balance. He fell heavily on his chest, the smoldering metal bar sliding across the floor.

Magnus removed the rifle from his coat and pointed it at the back of Daaruk's head as the Draconian lay there gasping for breath.

"Was it something I said?" the assassin asked.

The weaponsmith rolled over, rubbing his shoulder where he had hit the floor.

"Barbarian," he said.

"That's funny," Magnus replied. "That's what Colonel Grausman calls *you*."

"Humans think we're primitive because we don't use blasters," Daaruk said, "but humans are the real barbarians because you have no *honor*."

"Honor never stopped a man from dying," Magnus said.

"Will you help me up?"

"No, I like you where you are just fine."

"Are you really looking for Ekavir, the Jade General?"

"I am."

"He is also without honor," Daaruk said.

"That's what I hear," Magnus replied. "Why is that, by the way?"

"Do you know the story of the Dragon's Tears?"

"It's about the dragon, Bonamalum," Magnus said, "or at least Bona, the good one. When his evil brother Malum was killed, Bona wept and where his tears fell, Draconian warriors sprang to life."

Daaruk nodded. "They're called *Dragon Soldiers*. They pledged to always serve their people, no matter the enemy."

"What's that got to do with Ekavir?" Magnus asked.

"He forgot about the pledge. He only cares about revenge against the human invaders, even when it means Draconians die in the process."

"So, you abandoned him?"

"No, no. He abandoned *us* for his own selfish ambitions."

"Alright," Magnus said. "Where do I find him?"

"In the jungle..."

A blast of hot plasma leapt from the rifle, blowing a hole in the floor beside Daaruk's head.

"I'm going to need specifics," Magnus said.

Daaruk eyed the tiny crater, silently smoking, in the floor.

"I'll see what I can do," he replied.

The Draconian camp was well hidden inside the jungle, the huts huddled below the tree canopy hundreds of feet above. Cold blooded, the separatists might have needed a fire somewhere else, but not on Marakata where the air was heavy with a stifling, oppressive heat. Even if they had wanted to, the Draconians knew the Imperials used satellites to search for camp fires, always on the lookout for bivouacs like this one. There were stories of whole villages wiped out by orbital bombardment, simply because they looked suspicious.

These rebels were laying especially low. No electronic signals from communications or other equipment. Nothing to give their position away. They didn't want to be found, certainly not by the human occupiers.

Unfortunately, KB-8E was not a human. He was a killbot designed to track and destroy.

Covered in emitters that mimicked the surroundings, giving him near-perfect camouflage, KB-8E lurked just outside the camp, watching the Draconians through spectra far outside human or Draconian perception.

The robot knelt behind the bush-like flora. His body, the surfaces reflecting an image of the bush, was armored and capable of withstanding both projectiles and energy weapons. On a spindly neck, KB-8E's head didn't have a face except for a bundle of sensors, all different sized, used to analyze a range of inputs including visual, sound, and even smells. It was precisely the latter that helped KB-8E find the separatist camp due to the Draconians' particularly poor hygiene. Lastly, beside the bundle of sensors was a large red lens, the business end of a particle beam accelerator.

Taking aim, the killbot fired an invisible ray of subatomic particles at a separatist standing guard. The beam passed neatly through the Draconian's chest, turning his heart and other internal organs into freshly warmed soup. Not aware he was dying until he was already dead, he dropped where he stood without making a sound.

KB-8E leapt from his hiding place and landed several yards away in the center of the camp where most of the other rebels were sleeping. Starting with the closest, the killbot began punching a Drac in the upper chest. With each punch, a long bayonet blade extended from the robot's wrist, piercing the victim before retracting again as the arm pulled away. In this fashion, the killbot repeatedly skewered the Draconian until moving on to the next one.

By the time KB-8E reached the fourth rebel, the remaining three were sufficiently aware the night had gone terribly wrong that they reached for their weapons. The robot jumped over their heads, landing behind them. KB-8E drove his blades into their spines, killing them one by one. Although the emitters on the robot's frame attempted to keep mimicking the surroundings, they were covered by a thick and sticky layer of blood, making camouflage difficult.

When the last of the rebels was dead, the killbot stopped and surveyed the scene.

Although everyone was satisfactorily eliminated, the robot's scan noted his intended target was not present. This disappointment was magnified when a projectile, fired from long range, pierced KB-8E's neck, the only part of his body that was not armored with ballistic mesh. The killbot's head popped into the air before landing, upside down, at the feet of one of the dead Draconians.

Magnus Black left the high-powered sniper rifle with the rest of his gear and walked into the rebels' camp. He leveled his flashlight on each of the Draconian bodies, or what was left of them, until he was satisfied General Ekavir wasn't present.

The beam of light landed on the killbot's head, the severed neck pointing up. Cut off from the body's main power supply, the particle gun was no longer operational, but Magnus kept out of his line of fire just in case.

"Even for a killbot," he said, "that's some impressive carnage."

A light on the robot's head blinked. "Thank you."

"My contact told me General Ekavir was at this camp," Magnus added.

"I, too, was hunting the general."

"Did Colonel Grausman send you?"

"Indeed."

"Me too."

"Then why did you shoot me?" the killbot asked.

"I don't like robots," Magnus replied. After a pause, "What do they call you?"

"Unit KB-8E."

"Not a proper name like Robert or Cuddles?"

"No."

With a shrug, Magnus turned and started to walk away.

"Are you leaving me like this?" the killbot called after him.

Magnus looked over his shoulder. The light on the robot's head was still blinking in the darkness.

"I was thinking about it," he said.

"How do you intend to find General Ekavir now?" KB-8E asked.

"Well, you've killed all the Dracs that might've told me where he was, so I guess I'm not really sure."

"I tracked this group of separatists with my sensor suite. Using it again, I am confident I could find the general's new camp."

"I think your mission's over, bottle cap."

"If you repair me," the robot went on, "I can assist you."

Magnus shook his head. "Sorry, I work alone."

"As do I," the robot replied, "but a temporary partnership would be mutually beneficial."

Magnus faced the robot, cocking his head to the side so he could see the killbot roughly right-side up.

"Fine," he said.

CHAPTER THREE

Beyond the borders of the Imperium, the Talion Republic was a nation of star systems collectively settled by a race called the Tals. In one of these systems, farther out than the rest, the planet Isyium was the home of a single colony surrounded by outlying farms that took advantage of the rich soil and mild climate. On one of these farms, a young Tal left a shed where he had retrieved a sonic spanner for his father who was repairing a tractor out in the neighboring field.

Like many farmers, his family was poor and he himself was dressed in worn pants and a shirt caked with dirt. His body was covered in fine scales of a bright orange. He had deep-set eyes above high cheekbones and his pointed ears extended straight outward from the side of his hairless head. Typical of the Tals, the boy also had a long ridge running along the top of his skull.

Emerging from the darkened shed into the sunlight, the boy stopped at the sound of a sonic boom that shook the walls of the building. Several small ships, each painted in red and black, flew overhead, followed by another craft, this one painted orange. The boy recognized the latter as a Talion fighter, but the other ones were completely foreign to him.

His father was running at full tilt toward him, the dust from the field rising around his feet. He was waving his arms and shouting, even before the boy could hear what he was saying. When he got close enough, the sound resonated in the boy's ears.

"K'thonians!" his father yelled.

His father ran past him to the main house. When he returned, he held a gauss rifle they kept behind the stove. The boy's mother stood in the doorway, watching the father run back.

"Get inside with your mother," the boy's father said.

"What's happening?" the boy replied, but his father kept going until reaching a stone wall that bordered the field.

The boy's mother was calling, but he couldn't move, mesmerized by his father holding up the rifle and firing at some unseen target.

Some of the crops, golden and nearly ready for harvest, began burning and the smoke drifted back toward the shed and the house. The boy struggled to see what his father was firing at, but soot in the air stung his eyes.

From the field came a sound like lightning and the boy felt a static charge crawling over his scales. He took a step toward his father as he heard the noise again. This time, he saw a bolt of electricity, blue-white fingers branching in all directions, strike his father in the chest. His father writhed in pain and fell, dropping the rifle.

On the other side of the wall, a figure came from the field. It was tall, with dull purple skin and a long, squid-like head from which two large eyes, solid red, peered underneath heavy, angry brows. Where its nose should have been, squirming tendrils coiled and twitched. It wore priestly robes of deep purple and a sash covered with archaic lettering. Standing there, the K'thonian stared at the boy with hatred in its eyes as a pair of vestigial wings, crude and leathery, unfurled on its back.

The boy froze, his arms and legs like stone.

Staring into the K'thonian's eyes, the boy felt the creature reaching into his mind and, at the same time, he could see into the creature's own thoughts.

He saw a field of stars, each point of light dimming and then going out. When all was black, the sky became an ocean of dark water, the waves crashing over him. He sank deeper, the cold seeping into his flesh and bones, and in the murky depths, an ancient city of coral-encrusted stones appeared at the bottom. From this city, something was emerging, a shape beyond understanding except abject horror. The form grew closer and larger, but before it reached the boy, the young Tal's eyes opened into blinding light.

It was the sky.

"Are you alright?" his mother asked.

Lying on the ground, the boy sat up. Beside him, next to where his mother stood with the gauss rifle, the K'thonian's corpse lay still, purple ooze bubbling from a hole in the side of its head.

Lord Rupert Tagus II was the patriarch of the Tagus family, one of the Five Families. Living in semi-retirement in the West End district of Regalis, he was a man in his late sixties with thinning gray hair and a white beard with a few strands of black from an earlier time. Sitting in the parlor of his mansion built in the Victorian style, Lord Tagus offered a tray of cookies to the woman in the leather chair across from him. The rest of the room was dimly lit except for a fireplace burning nearby.

"No, thank you," she said politely.

"Shall I call you Captain or Lady Nasri?" the old man asked, returning the tray to the coffee table beside them.

"I think *Lady* is more appropriate these days," Nasri replied.

"You know, in the navy they would call you by both. My son, Rupert the Third, was addressed as *Lord Captain Tagus*."

"I'm probably too old for a commission," she said.

Lord Tagus laughed dryly.

"I suppose you are," he said. "Have they calculated your age, actually?"

"It's impolite to ask a woman's age," she replied, "especially when she's over fifteen hundred years old."

"To be fair, you were asleep most of that time."

"So I'm told."

A butlerbot entered and removed the tray of cookies, leaving the two humans alone again in the orange glow of the firelight.

"Have you heard much about my son?" the senior Tagus asked.

"Somewhat," Nasri said cautiously. "There was some trouble apparently..."

Tagus nodded knowingly.

"You might say that," he said, his eyes blazing for a moment. "He never accepted the fact that I wasn't selected as the emperor. You see, when a new emperor is required, the Five Families propose candidates and then vote on them. There's a lot of intrigue involved, as you might imagine, with families forming alliances and such. My house and the Groen family are often paired, while the Augustus and Montros families are as well. House Veber often casts the deciding vote."

"So, the vote didn't go your way?"

"No, indeed. Hector Augustus became the new emperor and he's ruled ever since."

"But your son didn't respect the vote, I take it," Nasri said.

Tagus sighed as if tired.

"He's strong-willed, much like myself when I was younger," he said, "and his tactics were... *unsubtle*, let's say."

"I'm told he's in exile."

"Perhaps for the rest of his life," Tagus said.

"I'm sorry," Nasri replied, looking away from the old man and at the portraits along the wall behind him. Each showed a member of the Tagus family, some from several centuries ago.

Lord Tagus leaned closer.

"Do you know why I've asked you here, Lady Nasri?" he asked.

"Not entirely, no," she admitted.

The old man pointed his finger, bony and wrinkled, at her.

"When I first saw you," he said, "I recognized someone with an understanding that most people lack. Unlike the majority who see opportunity, you have the courage to grab it with both hands! You know your place in history and want to make sure you have the power that comes with it!"

Nasri crossed one leg over the other, a slight grin in the corner of her mouth.

"I think I'd like that cookie now," she said.

At the insistence of the government, Captain Andre Santos found himself shopping for an estate in West End, something he never dreamed he would be doing.

Of mixed heritage, Santos was born in the slums of Rio de Janeiro. As a boy, the Church became his refuge and he joined the seminary as a way out of poverty. However, he left by the time he was eighteen, disillusioned with the failings, as he saw it, of God and religion. He joined the Brazilian military, ultimately becoming a captain in the air force. This, too, became tiresome as the hierarchies of command and the tyranny of one corrupt government after another pushed him out of the country entirely. When the opportunity to fly a colony ship appeared, Santos jumped at the chance to leave not only Earth, but his entire past behind.

Waking from cryogenic sleep, Santos could not believe that all the promise of their journey was gone in an instant. He recognized oppression when he saw it and couldn't believe his eyes, now that his dreams of a new reality looked too much like the one he had left on Earth.

"Of course, all of the appliances are stainless steel," the realtorbot chirped proudly. Like a flying hat box, it hovered in a kitchen larger than the shack in which Santos was born.

"Why?" Santos replied. "It'll show every fingerprint..."

The robot swept closer, balanced on its anti-gravity repulsor.

"In my experience," it said in a woman's voice, "humans are indeed a greasy people." The realtorbot continued into the dining room, adding "but you'll have cleaningbots, so it shouldn't be an issue I'm sure!"

Santos followed behind, still wearing a simple shirt and pants, similar to the clothing he had worn for the televised interview. The government told him he'd need a crest and a set of colors to represent his new royal house, but he had no interest in any of that.

"Did someone live here before?" he asked.

The robot, traveling the length of an expansive dining table, stopped abruptly.

"Yes, a nobleman from one of the minor families," she said. "He bought a larger estate."

"What for?" he asked.

"Apparently he was seeing too much of his wife and wanted something bigger."

After a pause, Santos said, "Was he descended from one of the colony ship crews?"

"Of course."

"Do you know which one?"

"I'm afraid not," the realtorbot admitted. "Would you like me to look it up for you?'

"Forget it," Santos replied with a wave of his hand. "A hundred people could live in this house..."

The robot wobbled in midair.

"I hardly think so, sir," she said. "There's only twenty-one bedrooms and ten and a half baths after all!"

"*Merda*," he sighed. "My mistake."

In the living room, on a video wall, a headline crawled across the screen:

IN NEWS FROM THE CAPITAL,
SEVEN MEMBERS OF A SUSPECTED NULL CULT
WERE REPORTED MISSING FROM A LOCAL PARK.
TUNE IN FOR MORE ON VOX NEWS!

Addressing the robot, Santos asked, "What's a Null Cult?"

He appeared, but no one knew precisely how. Above the planet Lokeren, no new ships had arrived and no gravcars or ocean cruisers had landed on the Veber's island estate. Standing in the entrance hall, he was not dressed like a local. He wore brown vestments and carried a tall, wooden staff of spiraled wood, topped with a skull. He was also not human. His skin was gray and chalky like bleached bones and his eyes blazed like fires from otherwise empty sockets. An amulet with an eight-pointed star hung around his neck.

"I am Ghazul," he said.

With her handmaiden behind her, Lady Veber took stock of the guest, not quite sure what to think.

"I'm not sure... this was a good idea," she replied, stumbling over the words.

"He can help," the handmaiden insisted.

"Perhaps," Lady Veber said, "but I'm not sure how."

Ghazul moved forward, his staff tapping on the tiled floor. Lady Veber retreated a step.

"There's no need to fear me," he said. "I mean you no harm."

"Sorry," she said. "I've never seen your race before."

"My people are called the Necronea. We are a very old species."

"Can you help my son Philip?"

"Yes."

"He's very ill and none of the doctors seem to know what's wrong with him."

"He's been poisoned," Ghazul said flatly.

"What?" Lady Veber replied in shock. "What makes you say that?"

Ghazul raised his head as if smelling the air, although Lady Veber noted that he only had a hole where his nose should be.

"I can sense these things," he said.

"You can tell if someone's been poisoned?" she asked skeptically.

"I know why someone is dying, regardless of the cause," he added.

"Do you know who poisoned him?"

"No."

Lady Veber sighed.

"Is there a cure?" she asked.

"No."

"Then how in the world can you help my son?"

Ghazul, his empty sockets fixed on Lady Veber, spoke softly.

"I will perform a ritual," he said, "that will reverse death once it comes."

"That's impossible!" Lady Veber replied angrily. "Do you think I'm a fool?"

The handmaiden tugged at her mistress's sleeve.

"The Necronea are people like us," she whispered, "but they don't die, at least not anymore."

Lady Veber pulled her sleeve away.

"My son is dying!" she shouted. "Every second I spend away from his side is time lost that I'll never get back!" Turning on her handmaiden, she said, "And now you've made me waste more time talking to this... *creature*!"

"But ma'am..." the handmaiden pleaded.

"Send him away!" Lady Veber screamed.

Turning around, she stomped out of the room, leaving her servant and the necromancer behind.

Lady Veber stormed into her son's quarters but stopped short at the sight of Philip standing in the main room.

"What in god's name are you doing out of bed?" she asked.

"Oh, mother," he offered weakly. "I just wanted a change of scenery..."

His mother went to him, her eyes showing her concern. She put a hand on his shoulder, feeling the skin and bones beneath the linen of his bed clothes.

"You feel cold as ice," she said.

"Better than a fever I suppose…"

"Well, sit down at least," she suggested, guiding him to a thickly padded arm chair. He obeyed, falling heavily into the cushions.

"You needn't look so worried," Philip said. "It's embarrassing."

"Don't be stupid," Lady Veber replied sharply. "You're my only child. What would I do without you?"

"Get out more, probably?"

His mother smiled.

"This is paradise!" she said without irony. "Why would I leave?"

"I heard through the grapevine that Prince Richard was here." Philip said. "What did he want?"

"It's not important."

"Hmmm, that's an obvious lie…"

"It's nothing you should concern yourself with," Lady Veber went on. "You need to focus on getting better."

"I know it's been hard since I've been sick," Philip said. "You haven't been able to do all the things you could before. You haven't been to the capital in ages!"

"I've got more important things to do here…"

"We're still Vebers," Philip replied. "You can't just take an indefinite vacation from being part of the Five Families…"

Lady Veber straightened her chin.

"Of course I can," she said. "They can do just as well without me anyway."

Philip laughed, but stopped, his mouth twisting in one corner.

"What's the matter?" Lady Veber asked.

"I feel funny," the boy said, his words slightly slurred.

"I'll get the doctor!" she replied, running out of the room.

When she returned with the physician, Philip was lying on the floor, his body jerking uncontrollably. The doctor pulled away the chair and rolled him on his side. When the convulsions stopped, the doctor called for a nursebot to help carry the boy back to his bed. Once back in his bedroom, Philip had another seizure as his eyes rolled back in his skull.

The nursebot, little more than an orb with thin mechanical arms extending from her body, scanned the unresponsive patient.

"His heart rate is erratic," she said in a harsh woman's voice. "And his pressure is crashing."

"I need you to step out, Lady Veber," the doctor said, nearly pushing her toward the bedroom door.

"No!" she replied.

"Lady Veber, please!" he shouted.

When the door slid shut, the last thing Lady Veber saw of her son was his face, ashen as if all the blood had drained from his body. After many minutes had passed, the door opened.

Philip was dead.

Back on Aldorus, in the West End of Regalis, Prince Richard walked through the gardens surrounding the Imperial Palace. Beside him, his father, Emperor Hector Augustus, was having trouble keeping pea gravel from lodging in his shoes. In his early sixties with a silver beard, the emperor stopped and sat on a stone bench. Removing his shoe, he dumped the contents back onto the trail. On his bald head he wore a simple gold ring as the Crown of the Imperium.

"That should do it," the emperor smiled proudly, returning the shoe to his foot.

"Maybe you should just pave the whole thing," Prince Richard suggested.

"Oh, I could," his father replied, "but then I wouldn't have an excuse to stop and sit, would I?"

"You're the Emperor, father. You can do whatever you want."

The emperor stood, testing his footing.

"Even an emperor has limits," he replied.

They continued walking as gardenbots, seeing them coming, scurried out of sight behind the high hedges that bordered the path.

"Lady Veber seemed agreeable to our proposal," the prince said.

"Was she now?" the emperor asked.

"Why wouldn't she be?"

"Her family is more powerful than you realize."

Prince Richard shrugged dismissively. "No more than any other..."

"House Veber has always acted as an arbiter among the other families," Augustus went on. "They've remained above the usual squabbling between the other houses."

"Even so," the prince said, "the Vebers have the same sense of duty as we all do."

The emperor chuckled.

"Duty has nothing to do with it!" he said. "None of the families give a damn about anyone except themselves. If it wasn't for a status quo that's made us all fabulously wealthy, any of the houses would've burned the others to the ground long ago!"

"To my point," the prince replied steadily, "it's that balance that keeps the Imperium from collapsing. It's an equilibrium that benefits us all."

The two men passed a fountain featuring a stone cherub bending to smell a flower. A narrow stream of water squirted from the angel's rear into the basin.

"My agents tell me Lady Nasri was seen at the Tagus estate," the emperor remarked matter-of-factly.

"That can't be good," the prince remarked. "Old man Tagus is dangerous; always has been."

"The head of each of the Five Families is dangerous," the emperor replied, "but the question has always been, *dangerous against whom?*"

"If Tagus is up to something, there's no question about *whom.*"

"He's clearly attempting to turn Lady Nasri to his way of thinking—"

"Against you, you mean?"

"Precisely," the emperor replied.

"All the more reason to get Lord Santos to change his mind," Prince Richard said. "If Nasri is against us, we'll need Santos more than ever."

"Perhaps, but I get the impression Captain Santos is not impressed by our little palace intrigues."

"Then he must be made to see reason!"

Emperor Augustus raised an eyebrow.

"Indeed," he said.

Lady Veber never wanted to have children. As a young girl the thought of babies, and especially the thought of one growing inside of her, made her squirm. Then, after meeting her future husband, things changed.

He was handsome and charming, even if he came from one of the lesser families. He made her laugh and he seemed genuinely interested in what she had to say, unlike the gentlemen she was accustomed to. They spent much of their time on the beaches of Lokeren, soaking up the rays and feeling the warm waters wash over their legs in the surf.

When they married, Lady Veber became aware how much her new husband wanted children. She knew he would never ask her directly or make demands of her, but she knew it was always in the back of his mind. With time, they started trying and then things became more difficult. Even with advanced natal medicine, her first attempts ended in stillbirths. She cried, late at night, feeling a sense of failure for something she never dreamed she would ever want, but now she wished for more than anything.

Eventually, Lady Veber became pregnant and it went to term. They named the baby *Philip*, a healthy boy with dark brown eyes like his father.

They were happy together, the three of them, and played in the sands below the cliffs surrounding the southern palace. Lady Veber saw the joy in her husband's eyes every time their boy ran up and down the beach, growing older and stronger with each passing day.

When the boy was twelve, his father died when his gravcar crashed into the ocean. The investigation found a mechanical part had failed, causing the vehicle to lose control, spiraling into the sea.

Lady Veber wore black for a year after her husband was buried. When she began wearing regular clothes again, white and blue with the ubiquitous shell motif, she noticed something in her son. Philip looked more and more like his father. The way he walked and carried himself was the spitting image of Lady Veber's late husband. It was uncanny, but it gave her a sense of continuity, as if her husband somehow lived on in the child they shared.

When Philip turned eighteen, he fell in the courtyard of the palace. He laughed it off and told his mother he must have tripped. A month later, when he fainted at dinner, Lady Veber called for the doctor. Philip was a strong boy and there wasn't any reason why he would be feeling so weak. The family physician was mystified so Lady Veber sent to the capital for a specialist. A parade of specialists, in fact, visited Lokeren, each with their own tests and machines.

None of them could find the reason for Philip's illness and, all the while, he grew worse.

Lady Veber withdrew from public life and her responsibilities. The other families began speaking of her in the imperial court as if she was the one who had fallen ill.

And then Philip died.

She sent away the doctors and the nursebot and her staff. Alone in her son's bedroom, Lady Veber sat beside Philip's lifeless body. She thought about the funeral arrangements and remembered the funeral of her husband when he had died. She never wanted a child, but now that was all she ever wanted. Most of all, she wanted Philip alive again.

A storm had brewed over the ocean, the waves crashing against the cliffs below the palace where Lady Veber, her husband, and her son had played. The lightning burned the sky, bright shadows cast for mere moments among the corridors of the estate.

When the door to Philip's quarters opened, Lady Veber and Ghazul of the Necronea emerged. Behind them, a little unsteady at first, someone followed. His eyes were no longer brown, more of a steel gray like the ocean when the clouds are covering the sky. His hair had fallen out and his skin was tight against his skull.

Lady Veber knew he was no longer human, but in her mind, Philip was still her son.

CHAPTER FOUR

As a younger man, Magnus Black served in the Imperial military as part of their counter-insurgency forces on Marakata, the Draconian home world. At the time, he was known as *Pitt*, but the Draconians knew him by a different name: *The Butcher of Bhadra.*

The township of Bhadra was founded at the confluence of two rivers, deep in the territory controlled by the separatists. Its location was strategic, both for the river traffic that brought raw materials out of the thick jungle and because it contained a religious site, a tiered pyramid where the native Draconians went to pray for their fallen brethren.

The head of the local cell of revolutionaries was named Ekavir, but his followers also called him the *Jade General.* Under his command, the separatists had repelled every attempt by Imperial forces to take the town. To the people of Bhadra, and even some in the Imperial ranks, the Jade General seemed unbeatable.

Colonel Grausman, the military governor, considered leveling the town from orbit, but the outrage it would cause, especially the inevitable destruction of the temple, would inflame opinions both on and off the planet. The Draconian cause, despite Imperial attempts to portray them as mindless savages, was popular among many in the rest of the empire.

The colonel decided that a team, led by Pitt, would infiltrate Bhadra and take out any hostile enemies they encountered. Pitt had distinguished himself by completing jobs that no one else could. What Colonel Grausman didn't consider was that everyone in Bhadra was hostile and Pitt was very literal about following his orders.

Wearing power armor, a carapace that covered his entire body, Pitt walked into the village along with a squad of Imperial soldiers. As groups of rebels began charging with their Draconian warstaffs, the troops opened fire with blaster rifles, cutting the separatists down in droves. Soon regular townspeople joined the fight, defending their homes and businesses against the invaders. As the civilian death toll rose, the Imperial soldiers started dying as well. Still, Pitt led his men deeper into the village. After their blaster power packs had reached zero, drained of energy, the soldiers switched to their own edged weapons. For his part, Pitt wielded a vibro-blade, a five-foot long sword with handholds along its length. Resonating at high speed, the cutting edge could slice through nearly anything and certainly the scales and bones of the Draconians.

Carving through the crowds against him, Pitt searched in vain for General Ekavir. After hours of fighting, Pitt found himself alone atop the temple pyramid. His armor, dented and scarred, dripped with the blood of those he had killed as if he had swum through a river of their bodies. Below Pitt, down the stone steps draped with corpses, the population of Bhadra lay where they had died. Like a terrible god of death, Pitt bore witness to what he had done. He felt sick, but knew each one he had killed had wanted him dead. They gave no quarter and he gave none in return.

Still, where was Ekavir? Where was the one who sent these villagers to die? Pitt continued to search but found nothing. The Jade General had vanished into the jungle.

His repairs complete, KB-8E led Magnus Black through the dense jungle. Minute amounts of organic matter, left by Draconians passing by, clung to the leaves and hung in the air, all recorded and analyzed by the sensors in the killbot's head. Following this invisible trail, the robot and the human found themselves in the remains of a town just as the sun was rising over the forest canopy.

"It appears General Ekavir came through here," KB-8E said.

"If you say so," Magnus replied, eyeing the stone buildings, the doorways and windows blackened with soot. "Do you see this damage?"

"The town appears to have burned."

"With a little help from above," Magnus remarked, pointing at the gap in the canopy. "An orbital strike…"

"It seems the inhabitants had little chance of survival."

"That's the idea."

Magnus leaned against a broken wall, taking a drink from his canteen. His feet were nearly submerged in ashes. The robot waited patiently.

"Do you have much experience on this planet?" KB-8E asked.

Capping the canteen, Magnus hooked it back onto his belt. "Yeah."

"May I ask when?"

"It's been a while," the human said. "I wasn't much older than twenty. I kinda fell into service with the Imperium and was good at it."

"Good at what exactly?"

"Killing."

"Would you say you were made for it?" the robot asked.

Magnus gave the machine a side glance. "Like you?"

"Indeed," KB-8E replied. "I was built for my function. I have no other."

"Well, you didn't have much of a choice, did you? I suppose I did."

"I sometimes wonder…"

"Yeah?"

"If perhaps I could do other things besides killing."

Magnus chuckled. "Like a hobby?"

The killbot lacked a mouth so he wasn't able to smile, although he sometimes wished he could.

"I mean whether I could perform other functions," he said, "that did not require ending someone's life."

"Hell if I know," Magnus admitted. "You're a slave to your programming, I guess."

"Indeed."

After a long pause, Magnus asked, "Why did Colonel Grausman assign you this mission?"

"Actually," the robot replied, "he sent several units like myself. However, I remain the only one still in operation."

"Serves the colonel right," Magnus said. "Don't send a robot to do a *man's* job."

"Do you resent him sending robots?"

"Like I said before, I don't like them."

"Why is that?"

"You kill a man, he stays down," Magnus went on. "Destroy a robot and they just build more."

"True," KB-8E said. "We can always build more killbots..."

When Ekavir, the Jade General, was still a young Draconian, his father told him about the virtues that made them a proud, honorable race. His father spoke of courage, wisdom, and loyalty, and how the human invaders lacked these things. The Imperium, with all its wealth and technology, was a dim spark compared to the fire of the Draconian spirit.

"They're barbarians," his father said. "Never forget that."

Ekavir was no more than a teenager, in relative terms, when he saw his first battle. A patrol of Imperial soldiers made the mistake of taking the same trail once too often, allowing the resistance fighters to set up an ambush. In the murky light of the jungle, the green scales of the Draconians blended with the leaves and branches, giving the rebels the perfect element of surprise. Armed with a warstaff, Ekavir dropped from a tree onto one of the unsuspecting soldiers. Years later, he still remembered the eyes of the human, blue like the sky, wide with the fear of his impending death. Ekavir hacked the man's head from his shoulders, the body going limp like a sack of loose vegetables. What Ekavir found most shocking was not the blood or the screaming, but the ease with which these humans died. Their skin was soft and their bones weak. They crumbled with such little prodding that he couldn't understand how they could rule an empire such as the Imperium.

It was unbelievable.

Over time, as Ekavir grew older, he developed contempt for the humans. They were not just barbarians, they were cowards. They used their weapons to strike from a distance, even from high above in orbit. He understood why. They were too fragile to face the Draconians in hand-to-hand combat, unless they wore suits of armor like robotic warriors.

It sickened him.

What really bothered Ekavir, however, was that these weaklings kept winning. The humans could be killed — that much was not debatable — but there were always more. For every soldier the Dracs killed, ten more arrived from off-planet. It was unending. No matter how many humans died, freedom for Ekavir's people remained always in the distance, never closer than the horizon.

Now grown and an experienced insurgent, Ekavir began leading attacks against the invaders. He developed new tactics, too. Instead of waiting in the jungle, he and his agents planted bombs in the places were the humans lived and worked. There were sometimes casualties among his own people, but they were the price that had to be paid for freedom. Their deaths were blood spilled for the revolution. Ekavir was confident they would have laid down their lives willingly if he had merely asked.

As the years dragged on, he never wavered or lost hope. The words of his father remained in his ears long after his father had died in an Imperial reprisal. The humans could not break Ekavir's spirit, no matter how many Draconians they lined up to be shot.

However, not everyone was as strong. Some of his people questioned his methods. They suggested negotiations, even as they lived in chains. This bothered Ekavir even more than the humans. This weakness in the face of the enemy could not be forgotten or forgiven. Those who were not for him were against him and, naturally, his enemy. They, too, must suffer the consequence of their barbarism.

Squads of his men fanned out into the jungle and the cities alike, looking for collaborators. These traitors were pulled from their homes, sometimes with their families watching. It was only right that they died within view of those they had betrayed. Ekavir took no pleasure in these killings, but he knew in his heart that only the strength of honor could lead to salvation and banishing the human invaders.

Even so, the bombing of the Green Zone, where the humans kept their spouses and children, was a miscalculation. The videos of the dead, played hourly by the Imperial propaganda machine, weakened Ekavir in the eyes of his people. The friends he knew he could trust suddenly were no longer reliable. The safe places became dangerous and the strikes from the sky became more frequent. All the while, he retreated deeper into the jungle.

With a machete, Magnus Black hacked at a particularly stubborn vine blocking their path. The jungle had grown ever thicker, slowing their progress. KB-8E considered using his particle beam but doing so, with the associated smoke and possible flames, would ruin any chance of surprising the Jade General. The killbot waited impassively as Magnus made a final swing, severing the vine in two.

"Have you worked with robots a great deal?" KB-8E asked suddenly.

Magnus wiped his face with the sleeve of his shirt. "What?"

"You said you don't like robots," the robot went on. "I wondered how much time you've actually spent working with them."

Magnus turned his eyes toward the machete in his hands as if contemplating something.

"Machines are everywhere," he said. "You can't kick a sweeperbot without hitting *another* sweeperbot."

"No, I meant working together with a robot, as we are."

"You mean, like a *partner?*"

"Indeed," KB-8E replied.

Exasperated, the human shook his head. "We're not partners!"

Without a face, KB-8E could not express emotions, provided he had any. However, the robot's blinking light stared at Magnus without the machine saying anything.

"Don't tell me I hurt your feelings?" Magnus said finally.

"I'm not programmed to have feelings," KB-8E replied.

"Good."

"In fact," the killbot added, "I believe humans created killbots to avoid feeling the guilt associated with ending another person's life."

"Is that so?"

"How do *you* deal with your emotions after killing?"

Magnus shrugged. "I don't think about it."

"That seems wise," KB-8E said. "Most of your kind seem to ruminate endlessly about their actions."

"Well, I don't."

Magnus reared back to strike the next vine with his machete.

"Perhaps you are what they call a *psychopath*," the robot said.

Magnus missed the vine, narrowly missing his own leg.

"That's a hell of a thing to say!" he growled.

"Or are you a sadist of some kind?"

Shaking the long blade in his hand, Magnus held it threateningly. "I'm none of those things!"

The light on KB-8E's head blinked several times. "If you say so."

"I'm a killer, that's true," Magnus replied, "but it's my job and I'm damn good at it."

"But you don't think about those you kill?"

"Do *you*?" Magnus asked.

"Actually, I do."

"Bullshit."

"On the contrary," the robot said, "although I assume you would consider it a fault in my programming, I do indeed consider the lives I've ended and the consequences of what those lives might have accomplished if I had not ended them."

Magnus, both his machete and jaw slacking, stared at the killbot.

"I'll be damned," he said.

Every morning at around 10 AM, when the temperature and the humidity reached the proper mix, the rain began falling and continued for half an hour before stopping again. It was like clockwork, every day. The drops fell from the heavy clouds, the water winding its way through the tops of the trees down to the jungle floor before emptying into streams and rivers. Swollen with the morning shower, one such river plunged as a waterfall into a small lake. A deluge at first but then, the surge past, abating to a trickle, the falling water revealed the entrance to a cave partially flooded by the lake.

Magnus Black, submerged in the muddy water, swam beneath the surface into the cave. He wore a dark gray bodysuit with black goggles and a breathing device clenched between his teeth. A blaster was holstered on his right leg while a long blade was strapped to his left ankle. He could barely see, but he knew that meant the Draconians couldn't see him either.

The robot had scanned the cave, giving Magnus a general idea of its dimensions. The entrance was narrow but widened into a cavern. When Magnus thought he was at the right spot, he risked a look, the top of his head and goggles disturbing the surface. He was beside a boat, woven from palm fibers, partially beached on a parcel of sand.

Past the beach, stone steps led up to a level area below the ceiling at least fifty feet above. A few huts crowded the plateau, open fires burning between them, with a larger shack on the other side.

The air was thick with the scent of wet lizards.

Hearing someone coming down the steps, Magnus pushed the boat away from the beach.

A Draconian warrior cursed, seeing the craft floating toward the flooded entrance. Wading out to retrieve it, the warrior got waist deep before Magnus drove a dagger into his heart. The body floated for a moment before sinking.

Slipping out of the water, Magnus left his goggles at the shoreline and inched across the beach, careful to tread lightly over the sand. At the foot of the steps, he listened. Sure that no one was coming, Magnus climbed the stairs until his eyes peered over the top. Several Draconian warriors, armed mostly with swords or warstaffs, were shuffling around the camp amid the huts. Like the boat, the hovels were constructed from leaves and wood gathered from the jungle outside. Under the domed roof, they looked to be more for privacy than shelter.

With one hand holding his blaster and the other his knife, Magnus crept from the steps to the back of a hut. Thinking he had made little or no noise in the process, Magnus was surprised when a Draconian came crashing through the hut wall, tackling him to the ground.

"What the hell?" Magnus said, both hands pinned.

The Draconian, within inches of Magnus' face, grinned a mouth full of teeth.

"I can smell a wet human for miles," the warrior said.

"Good to know," Magnus replied.

His right arm bent, Magnus extended it, pulling the Drac's hand out along with it. The warrior's eyes widened as Magnus contorted his left knee into the Draconian's leg, knocking him off balance and rolling him over. With their positions reversed and Magnus on top, he fired the blaster, incinerating the warrior's snout and most of his face. Magnus shook off the dead claws still holding his wrists and turned just as more Dracs came around the side of the hut.

Magnus burned holes in the first two to reach him. A third leapt over the dead warriors, making a wide swing with his warstaff.

Magnus felt a surge of pain in his hand as he watched the blaster sail over the edge of the rocks and into the water below.

This is not ideal, he thought.

He dodged the next swing, ducking under it while slicing the warrior's tendon as he rolled past. Dropping to one knee in agony, the Draconian exposed the back of his neck into which Magnus, jumping back to his feet, drove his blade, severing the spinal column.

Magnus grabbed the Draconian warstaff and buried it into another warrior's chest. Using his foot as leverage, he pulled the staff free as memories of Bhadra floated back to mind. The raw smell of their blood filled his nostrils. He killed, as he did then, by taking long swaths like a reaper's scythe through the ranks of the defenders.

He was the intruder. He was the invader. He didn't care.

Drenched in blood, Magnus stood before the large shack at the end. With both hands, he held the warstaff against his waist.

The door, driftwood lashed together with fibers, opened. Ekavir stood in the doorway, backlit by the warm flicker of a fire behind him. In his hands he held a blaster rifle.

Also not ideal, Magnus thought.

"Drop your weapon," Ekavir said, gesturing with his rifle.

The warstaff landed in the dusty ground at Magnus' feet.

"Do you know who I am?" the assassin asked.

The Jade General grinned and nodded. His scales were worn in places, the natural green faded by age.

"The Butcher of Bhadra," he said. "I recognize you."

"I don't recall seeing you there," Magnus replied.

"I was there."

"Hiding while your people died?"

"My people sacrificed themselves," Ekavir said, "so I could escape and continue the battle elsewhere."

"They paid the price so you could live..."

"So the *revolution* could live!"

"I'm pretty sure the revolution would've survived without you."

"I *am* the revolution!"

Magnus chuckled, eyeing the general with his modern weapon.

"Are you sure?" he asked. "Seems like it's already passed you by."

"No," Ekavir replied, sticking his chest out. "Long after you're forgotten, my people will sing songs about me. After the worms have spat you out, I will go on."

Magnus shook his head.

"Alright then," he said. "Anytime now."

The Jade General raised the blaster rifle, but Magnus wasn't speaking to him. The tips of two blades burst from Ekavir's chest. The Draconian gazed down at them with confusion in his eyes as blood came spilling out. When the tips retracted, only to re-emerge moments later, Ekavir roared in pain and fury. He attempted to point the rifle at Magnus, but the weapon fell from his hands, followed close behind by Ekavir himself, landing on top of it.

KB-8E stood in the doorway. The robot's camouflage emitters flickered off.

"What the hell were you waiting for?" Magnus shouted at the killbot.

"You seemed to be in the middle of a conversation," KB-8E replied.

Magnus kicked the corpse over so the general was facing up. He picked up the blaster rifle.

"The primary target appears to be eliminated," the robot said, examining the body.

"Yeah," Magnus replied slowly, "but there was always a secondary target, wasn't there?"

The killbot looked up. "Sadly, yes."

The barrel of the robot's particle beam lit up, just as Magnus rolled to the side. The material of his bodysuit charred at the shoulder, Magnus fired, a hot bolt of plasma impacting KB-8E's chest in a shower of sparks and molten plastic. The robot fell backwards, landing halfway inside the shack.

When Magnus got back to his feet, he wasn't sure if the robot was destroyed until he saw the red light blinking on his faceplate.

"Don't move," Magnus said.

"I do not think that will be possible," KB-8E replied, his voice modulating intermittently.

Magnus kept the rifle pointed at the disabled robot. "There was never any deal with Colonel Grausman."

"Affirmative," the robot said. "I was to terminate you once the primary target was killed."

"Why?"

"It is my understanding that his superior officers demanded it."

The assassin shrugged. "Yeah, that checks out."

"I regret that I can no longer work alongside you, Mr. Black," the robot said. "It was interesting."

Magnus didn't reply.

"Will you kill Colonel Grausman?" KB-8E asked.

"Oh, yeah," he said. "He's going to die."

"Before he does," KB-8E said, "please pass along my apologies for failing in my mission."

After a pause, Magnus said, "Sure."

"Farewell, Mr. Black."

Magnus pulled the trigger and swam out of the cave. He had a long hike ahead of him back to Sucikhata and the Green Zone.

CHAPTER FIVE

Oscar Skarlander didn't remember dying, or the person who killed him, for that matter. His last memory, before waking in a cloning vat, was sitting in a chair with electrodes attached to his head. He was in the headquarters of Warlock Industries, getting a neurological scan of his brain, a snapshot of his consciousness. This was a monthly safeguard against the unforeseen, like getting his head cut off on a far-flung asteroid. In case of death, the recording was downloaded into the brain of a clone so Skarlander could live again.

I'm getting tired of this shit, he thought.

Hairless and weak, Skarlander rested his arm on the edge of the vat. Technicians and medical staff passed through his cloudy vision of the room. The rest was just bright lights and green wall tiles. He tried to speak, to give an order, but the feeding tube down his throat made him gag. Someone, a woman, he thought, was reaching for the tube and gave it a firm tug, drawing it out. Skarlander choked while his lungs filled with breaths of air.

"Keep still," someone said and stuck a syringe into Skarlander's arm. He recognized the pain. That was a memory he knew well.

"What happened?" Skarlander asked, fluid gurgling out of his mouth along with the words.

"You'll be debriefed in a few hours, Agent Skarlander."

Satisfied he was too frail to do much more, he laid back against the warm ooze filling the vat and wondered what else he could remember.

After the *Merope* and *Sterope* left the Cyber Collective where they had been found and entered Imperial space, a task force of military ships escorted the two ark ships to Aldorus. The captains and crews had already disembarked, safely whisked away to a secure location where they could be debriefed and indoctrinated into their new lives as royalty. The vast majority on the ark ships, several thousand colonists in cryogenic hibernation, remained asleep, a slumber that had lasted since leaving Earth approximately fifteen hundred years ago.

Once the ships reached an orbit high above the capital city of Regalis, specialists began the arduous process of waking the sleepers, in groups of fifty at a time. Not everyone survived the trip. A percentage of the cryo capsules had failed, the people inside turned to desiccated corpses. Some colonists simply died while being revived, their bodies too weak to endure the shock of the waking process. The specialists deemed a mortality rate of twenty percent as acceptable.

Once unfrozen, the resurrected were kept in a medically induced coma for a week while electrodes stimulated their nervous systems to heal muscular atrophy. When the week was over, each colonist awoke to their new lives in a new time and a new galaxy.

Most began screaming almost immediately.

After another two weeks of psychiatric therapy, the screaming stopped and most were considered mentally stable. Those who were not were sent to a different facility, likely for the remainder of their lives, while the rest went to dormitories. This was their temporary home until faculty from the University of Regalis gave them a crash course in Imperial history and the importance of the Emperor in their new lives.

After more screaming, most came to accept this new reality. Those who didn't were sent to yet another different facility, also likely for the remainder of their lives.

Lars Hatcher was a farmer. When he signed on to the great migration to the Andromeda Galaxy, they said he would be using his farming skills to grow food for the new colonies. He expected to wake up and become a valuable part of society, one desperately needed since only a limited supply of food could be brought on the sleeper ships. Instead, Lars woke to find that agriculture was entirely automated, usually by massive robots that planted and maintained all crops until harvest, and then did the harvesting too.

Waking from a fifteen-hundred-year nap, Lars found himself obsolete before the frost on his cryo capsule had even melted.

In his infinite generosity, the Emperor endowed each colonist with a free apartment, for up to one year, in the Middleton district of Regalis. After leaving the dormitory, Lars moved into his apartment on the twenty-seventh floor overlooking a row of identical apartment buildings. On the other side were skyscrapers housing the major businesses of the Imperium including dy cybernetics, Warlock Industries, and VOX News. Somewhere beyond those, to the West, was the Regalis river and the West End.

Instead of looking out the window, Lars spent his free time, which was all of the time he had, sitting on his couch watching the video screen. The programs streaming across it filled his days since he had little else to do.

Lars, pressed into the material of the couch, was built like a rugby player with thick limbs and a wide neck. In comparison, his head looked a little too small and his eyes a little too close together beneath an overhanging brow. Typical human bias suggested Lars wasn't entirely bright, but in fact he was of average intelligence. Unfortunately, most of his intelligence focused around farming, which was limited in his one-bedroom apartment. Off the galley kitchen, in front of the window, he had filled the breakfast nook with plants that he faithfully watered. He tried to find seeds for tomatoes and other vegetables, but recreational gardening no longer seemed a common pastime. He had to settle for some potted plants he didn't recognize.

Lars propped his foot against the coffee table and opened a beer that a robot at the convenience store had recommended. It had the word *fungus* on the label but also said *genuine draft*, so Lars felt it would probably be alright. Taking a sip, he judged it acceptable and turned his attention to the video screen. At more than fifty inches, the screen was at a definition that appeared three-dimensional, perhaps more.

Lars began forming an opinion of what Imperials considered appropriate to broadcast. Ultra-violent and nearly pornographic programming was common, along with commercials that featured only text. Lars had no idea why but conjectured, as he opened another bottle of fungus beer, that it was somehow akin to plain labeling on cigarette packaging.

While he stared at the screen, an advertisement appeared:

BIGBOTS! DISCOUNT ROBOTS!
OUR PRICES ARE AS LOW
AS YOUR EXPECTATIONS!

Lars wasn't sure what a *BigBot!* was, but it sounded like a good bargain.

A woman's face appeared. She was attractive with blue hair and a nice smile. Lars recognized her from previous reports on VOX News, but couldn't remember her name. She was doing an interview, but when her guests' faces came on screen, Lars knew exactly who they were. One was Captain Andre Santos of the *Merope* and the other, Captain Sheba Nasri of the *Sterope*.

From what Lars had heard, they had both become very, very rich.

The robot read the report aloud while Oscar Skarlander, still dressed in a medical gown, lay motionless on a reclined chair in his darkened office to protect his newly opened eyes. A recent model from dy cybernetics, the robot was humanoid from the waist up, with arms and a head, but instead of legs, it floated on a pair of anti-grav repulsors.

"According to media outlets," the robot went on, "an unidentified individual used a heated garrote to separate your head from your body, killing you."

Skarlander raised an eyebrow. "He remains unknown?"

"Correct."

"Hmmm, I'd like to meet him someday and return the favor."

"The metamind who accompanied you," the robot continued, "was also killed."

"I'll need another one then," Skarlander replied.

"The process is currently underway."

"What about the captain I woke, Sheba Nasri?"

"She was taken to Regalis along with the other captain," the robot said.

"Showered with gifts, I'm sure."

"The Imperial government has transferred several billion credits into accounts in their name. Some members of the Five Families have also begun advising them on proper etiquette and their expected responsibilities."

Skarlander sighed.

"Well, that's an opportunity missed," he said, "but perhaps we can still exert influence. Even the super-rich have a price..."

"Warlock analysts have concluded that the other captain, Andre Santos, is vulnerable to persuasion based on his socio-economical background."

"Really?"

"He is considered an *idealist*."

"Ah," he said. "Idealists may be stubborn but given the right cause, they can be quite useful..." After a pause, "What about that idiot, Lord Maycare?"

The robot hesitated, its eyes flickering as it accessed information from the nodesphere.

"Lord Devlin Maycare received the prestigious *Emperor's Medal of Achievement* for discovering the lost ark ships," the robot said. "He remains firmly in the public eye due to his sporting endeavors and work locating xeno technology."

"Jackass," Skarlander remarked.

"Be advised," the robot said, "the Warlock board has expressly forbidden you from having contact with Lord Maycare or his associates."

"What?"

"Due to the violent nature of your last meeting with Lord Maycare, the board considers additional conflict with him politically risky."

"Well, well..." Skarlander said. "I suppose I could focus on other things for a while."

"To that end, our intelligence division has intercepted communications concerning an artifact of interest."

"One Maycare doesn't know about?"

"To our knowledge, he is unaware of it."

"Tell me more..."

Lars Hatcher rolled out of bed after ten, took a shower and got dressed. In no particular hurry, he ate breakfast over the sink and watered his plants, noticing they were turning brown. That was the closest he'd gotten to farming since they roused him from cold sleep. The routine of daily life, devoid of prospects, was getting him down. He wondered if meeting someone would cheer him up.

Searching the nodesphere, he found a dating app called the *Meet Market*. He registered and began swiping through the photos of available women. Eventually, he connected with a few and one, a user name *SxyPnts*, started messaging him:

[SxyPnts]: I like your profile pic.

[LarsHat]: Thanks.

[SxyPnts]: Are you really from an ark ship?

[LarsHat]: I sure am.

[SxyPnts]: How exciting! I've never met one of those before.

[LarsHat]: It's been hard getting adjusted. Everything's pretty overwhelming.

[SxyPnts]: Sry to hear that. I heard they gave you a bunch of money. :-)

[LarsHat]: Well, not really that much.

[SxyPnts]: Srsly? I heard they gave the crew millions of credits!

[LarsHat]: Yes, the *crew*, but I'm not one of them. I'm a colonist.

[SxyPnts]: WTF???

[LarsHat]: I'm sorry. I don't know what that means.

[SxyPnts]: You shithead. It means you've been wasting my time!! Screw you!!!

[[You have been blocked by SXYPNTS.]]

His other attempts were equally unsuccessful, so he gave up.

As the days wore on and failures mounted, watching TV was the only thing Lars felt reasonably confident in accomplishing. Another ad came across the screen:

HAVE YOU BEEN INJURED BY A ROBOT
PURCHASED FROM BIGBOTS! DISCOUNT ROBOTS?
THEN CALL THE LAW OFFICES OF
SCHMECKLE & SCHMECKLE;
WE'LL GET YOU THE SETTLEMENT YOU DESERVE!

That reminded Lars that he had wanted to buy a robot. Nothing too fancy. Just something to keep him company.

He shaved and showered for the first time in days. He even put on real pants and shoes instead of loungewear and slippers. This was the motivation he needed to get out of the apartment and get some fresh air for a change.

Lars stepped out of his building and walked down a pedestrian boulevard crowded with people. Lars felt self-conscious, unsure if the others around him knew how awkward he felt on the inside. However, no one seemed particularly interested in him at all. He found this strangely comforting.

Lars came to a building along the boulevard that looked like a tram station except for the word *Transmat* along the side. At this point, he realized he had no idea how to use the city's transmat system. Also, he didn't know where BigBots! was located.

A little girl wearing a pink dress and holding hands with a much taller nannybot took notice of him and pointed.

"Don't you know how to use a transmat?" the girl said overly loud.

Lars felt his face reddening. "No."

The little girl laughed.

"I thought all grown-ups knew that!" she said, looking up at her robot. "Nanny, can you help him?"

Covered in shiny chrome, the nannybot nodded. Within a few minutes, Lars thought he had the gist and thanked the robot and the little girl. The girl took the robot's hand again, waving goodbye with the other.

"Bye!" she shouted.

Inside the transmat station, Lars stepped into a booth and keyed in his destination. After swiping his credit stick, he touched a large red button and felt his insides turn instantaneously into fireflies.

Fully rematerialized, Lars was dizzy in the head and sick to the stomach. He rushed out of the station and threw up behind a row of bushes, though the branches were mostly bare and provided little in the way of cover.

When he looked up, Lars saw a large cat-like person on the sidewalk, holding the paw of a cub, a pink bow between her ears.

From his training, he recognized them as Tikarin. The small female cub pointed a claw at him and seemed to laugh before saying something in a language Lars didn't understand. The adult pulled the youngster away and continued down the sidewalk while Lars wiped his mouth clean with a shirt sleeve.

Steadying himself, Lars took a look around. Unlike the Middleton district, the trees in this area were mostly dead or dying, the leaves collecting in disorganized piles in the gutter. It slowly dawned on Lars that this wasn't the way to BigBots! at all. This was somewhere in Ashetown, the poorest district of Regalis.

He turned back toward the transmat station, but his stomach heaved.

Hell's bells, he thought. *Maybe I can find a taxi somewhere.*

Lars passed a few stores and two tattoo parlors before he got to the first intersection. Beside the curb, a gravcar lay abandoned. Lars peered through the broken window. The interior was stripped of electronics and anything of value and Lars was pretty sure he saw something furry rolled up into a ball. He stepped back, nearly colliding with a man.

"Hello there!" the man said. "You look lost, friend!"

In his forties, the man was bald except for a long mustache and eyes the color of dried motor oil. Most surprisingly, he wore a two-toned blue and green shirt and pants covered in a garish diamond pattern like a harlequin.

"I was trying to find BigBots! Discount Robots," Lars said clumsily.

"Those hacks?" the man replied. "It's a good thing I ran into you then."

"Who are you?"

"Zarro Boogs!" he said, thrusting his hand into Lars' and giving it a firm shake. "Who might you be?"

"Lars Hatcher..."

"Well, Mr. Hatcher — can I call you *Lars*? — I'm a business man in these parts and I can get a deal on any kind of robot you're looking for. By the way, what kind are you looking for?"

"Well—"

"A sweeperbot to tidy up the place? A killbot maybe, no questions asked? How about a sexbot? I'm not going to judge..."

"Actually, I needed something to keep me company," Lars said.

"A sexbot it is!"

"No," Lars stammered. "I don't want that..."

At the sound of a loud shout, Boogs jerked his head around. From down the street, a man in a leather jacket and jeans with orange flames painted down the legs motioned angrily in their direction. Lars noted the man's abundant hair was nearly the same color as the flames on his pants.

Boogs smiled even as sweat beaded around his forehead.

"I just remembered some business uptown," he said and took off in a mad sprint in the opposite direction of the other man who was now, along with a few other men, running towards them. They raced past Lars who pressed against a wall and watched them disappear around the corner.

Stepping forward, Lars glimpsed something on the wall behind him. Scrawled in green spray paint were the words *Free Marakata*. Lars scratched his head, not sure who Marakata was or why he needed to be freed. From the abandoned gravcar, something hissed at him.

Lars went looking for a cab and a way back home.

Hours later, Lars stumbled through his apartment door, his clothes dirty and wrinkled. The lights came on automatically, sensing Lars' presence, as he nearly tumbled onto the couch and turned on the TV. Face-down, he lay on the cushions while the sounds from the vidscreen filled his ears like a hive of bees. Poorly formed ideas cluttered his mind. Thoughts, only partially gestated, mutated from one to another, finding no real substance.

Since waking up from his cryo-cocoon, Lars felt like he was always a step behind everyone else, like they knew something he didn't. Lars smacked his forehead with the palm of his hand.

Idiot, he thought.

On the TV, an ad appeared:

WARLOCK INDUSTRIES IS LOOKING FOR A
SINGLE MALE HUMAN (WITH NO NEXT OF KIN)
FOR AN INTELLIGENCE STUDY.
WHAT ARE YOU WAITING FOR, DUMMY?
APPLY AT WARLOCK IND. TODAY!

Lars stared at the screen, the letters displayed in simple type across a white background. He shook his head.

It's fine, he thought. *No need for extremes. I just need a little more time to fit in. I'm sure something will come up.*

Lars roused himself from the couch, pulling down his shirt to smooth out the wrinkles. He crossed the room to the kitchen and poured himself a glass of water. In the adjacent breakfast nook, the plants were looking worse, the leaves brown and drooping. From the glass, he poured water into each pot, puzzled why the plants wouldn't perk up.

A sticker was poking out from under one of the pots. Careful not to spill, Lars set his glass aside and lifted the pot over his head so he could see the bottom. On the underside, he could just make out a label:

SELF-WATERING PLANTS.
DO NOT WATER!!
(YOU MORON)

Lars was pretty sure he imagined that last part, but it could have been true. In the back of his head, he saw the little girl by the transmat station.

Pointing her finger, she laughed.

Oscar Skarlander had grown about half an inch of new hair since his rebirth. Even his goatee had started coming in nicely. Now with hair, when he passed Warlock employees in the hallway, he saw recognition in their faces along with the accompanying expressions of terror. It was good to know his reputation had not diminished after his death.

Skarlander's robot, hovering on its anti-gravity repulsors, followed him through the corridors of Warlock headquarters, otherwise known as the *Cauldron.* Skarlander wore a simple brown suit with matching shoes. His dark eyes, landing on items in his line of vision, scrutinized each thing before moving on to the next, evaluating its usefulness or lack thereof. People were the same. He would size them up and move on, his eyes never resting too long on any single person.

"The project concerning Lord Santos has commenced per your directive," the robot said as they continued down the hall.

"Good," Skarlander replied coolly. "And the *other* thing?"

"Another group of Null Cultists has gone missing."

"At least they're getting their wish..."

"Our analytics department," the robot said, "suggests a connection with the increased K'thonian activity in the Talion Republic."

At the doors of an elevator, Skarlander pushed the call button.

"That'll be all," he told the robot.

"As you wish," the robot replied, revolving in midair before heading back down the hallway.

Skarlander took the lift down, deep below the basement levels where Warlock Industries maintained several genetics laboratories. This was where the megacorporation, not entirely in compliance with Imperial law, performed testing on human and non-human subjects. Pulling apart strands of DNA like a child plays with red licorice, the scientists rebuilt entire genomes, forming species not entirely human, or any other race that occurred naturally.

At the entrance of Lab 22, Skarlander palmed the ID pad and went in. Besides the ubiquitous smells of a lab, the room contained long tables topped with trays of test tubes, hooded workstations, and machines that Skarlander could only guess at, if he had actually cared to. He passed them until reaching a single door at the back. Once on the other side, he found himself in a room with a woman dressed in a lab coat, and a man lying on a table. The woman was in her early thirties with red hair pulled tight against her head. She looked at the new arrival with a level of disdain that Skarlander would normally have punished. In her case, he always made an exception.

"What do you have for me, Dr. Sprouse?" Skarlander asked.

Without answering, she handed him a datapad. While reading, Skarlander eyed the man on the table, covered to the middle of his chest by a white sheet. His skin, not much darker than the sheet, was sickly pale except for veins like gnarled branches. The blood vessels crept up his neck and spread across an oddly large, and completely hairless skull. The veins covered two lobes on either side of the head, both of which pulsed slightly with each heartbeat.

"He's quite a monster, isn't he?" Skarlander remarked.

"He has a name," Dr. Sprouse said.

Skarlander glanced at the datapad. "Lars Hatcher?"

The eyes of the man, sunken and surrounded by dark circles, looked up.

"What a treat," Skarlander said. "A metamind with a name!"

Abruptly, the datapad flew from Skarlander's hands, smashing against the far wall. The lobes on Lars' head throbbed rapidly.

The broken pieces clattered to the floor as Skarlander watched. Turning back to the man on the table, he smiled.

"He's *perfect*," Skarlander said.

CHAPTER SIX

His Imperial Majesty's Ship the *HIMS Baron Lancaster* was a heavy cruiser of the Imperial fleet. At over 900 yards long, the wedge-shaped *Baron Lancaster* had a soaring superstructure, like an armored citadel, rising above its surrounding hull. Inside the tower, Chief Operations Officer Lieutenant Kinnari transferred a message from her console to a datapad and walked down a short corridor from the bridge to the captain's office. As the only Dahl on a human warship, Kinnari knew she had to maintain both her appearance and professionalism at all times. Her uniform was immaculately clean and starched to a crispness that would allow it to stand at attention even if Kinnari was unconscious. Sensing a hair out of place, she tucked it behind her pointed ear.

Standing in front of the door, she tapped the buzzer while pressing the datapad tightly against her chest.

"Come in!" a man's voice shouted from the other side.

The door slid away and Kinnari marched into the well-lit office where her commanding officer was sitting behind a desk of metal and glass.

"We've received a new transmission, Lord Captain," the lieutenant said, advancing the rest of the way into the room. Two chairs stood in front of the desk, but she remained on her feet.

Lord Captain Martin Redgrave was a man in his early fifties with gray hair and deep wrinkles around his eyes. Like the lieutenant, he wore a steel-blue uniform with gold piping and a tall collar. Of noble blood, the captain also wore a cape that draped over the back of his chair.

"Give it here," Redgrave said, his hand outstretched.

Kinnari gave him the datapad and stood at attention while waiting for him to finish reading the communication. His face turned sour.

"Well, shit," he said. "The military governor on Marakata is dead."

"Colonel Grausman, sir?"

"Assassinated in his own office," the captain continued.

"Were the two of you close?" Kinnari said.

The captain looked up from the datapad. "Hell no! The man was a monster, but at least he kept the Draconians in check…"

"May I speak freely, sir?" Kinnari asked.

"If you *must.*"

"It seems the situation on Marakata is intractable," she went on stiffly. "Short of autonomy or annihilation, there's no tenable solution to the continued occupation."

"You think we don't know that?" the captain replied. "It's a damn distraction if you ask me, lieutenant. We've got better things to worry about."

Kinnari nodded curtly. "To that end, sir, we've also received a report of a Parvulian merchant ship being attacked."

"Again?"

"As before, the crew was taken while the cargo was left intact."

"Well, it's definitely not the Pirate Clans then," the captain said. "They've never met a cargo container they didn't like. I'm tempted to think it's Celadon Corsairs… those little green pricks would love to muscle into Clan territory and they're known for taking captives."

"But the cargo wasn't touched…"

"I heard you, lieutenant," the captain grumbled. "It's a mystery."

Fortunas IV, a backwater world on the outskirts of the Imperium, had no real water to speak of, but the planet's position along the trade routes made it a useful refueling stop. Over the centuries, a small marketplace grew into a sprawling bazaar containing hundreds of covered stalls where vendors, most of them not human, sold their wares to travelers passing through.

Rowan Ramus walked between the shops, his boots stomping over the hard-packed soil. Captain of the freighter the *Wanderer,* Ramus was a Dahl but, with bright red hair and silver rings piercing his ears, he bore little resemblance to his brethren. Wearing a sleeveless red shirt, exposing archaic lettering tattooed on his arms, Ramus doubted his parents would have approved. On the other hand, they wouldn't remember him anymore anyway…

A few steps behind Ramus, a silver and blue robot followed her master. A general-purpose android, she went by *Gen* for short. About the same height as the Dahl, Gen had the curves typical of a petite woman and large, expressive eyes.

"You still back there?" Ramus asked without turning.

"Yes, sir!" Gen replied enthusiastically.

Gen carried a bag stuffed with supplies, slung over her shoulder. Even if she wasn't a heavy-duty workbot, she could still manage pretty well on her own, Ramus thought. His ship's engineer, Orkney Fugg, would have preferred a more rugged robot for the *Wanderer*, although if he really got his way, the engine room would have been filled with sexbots and fungus beer.

"Are we headed back to the ship?" she asked.

"No," Ramus replied. "We're seeing a client somewhere in town. Fugg's supposed to meet us there."

"Oh, that'll be nice," Gen said.

"Well, Fugg's picking the place, so I'm sure it'll be a dump…"

"As in garbage?"

"No," Ramus said, "as in strippers…"

Life on the streets of Fortunas IV was neither glamorous nor long for many of the children who grew up there. For Storma Bane, nothing was easy since as far back as he could remember. Like all other humans, he could trace his ancestry to the first colonists who arrived in Andromeda seven centuries earlier. Since his forefathers weren't part of the crew, they didn't become part of the aristocratic class that developed over the years. Storma's family tree started with low-level technicians and mechanics that might have made something of themselves but, for whatever reason, never did. His parents ended up on the far side of the Imperium with no money and no prospects. Storma was born, discarded, and grew up on his own in the alleys and slum housing of this arid world. By age fourteen, he joined a gang and was running errands for the local mob. By eighteen, he had a gang of his own, mugging drunk tourists.

Tonight, Storma and his crew waited in a darkened alley for someone to wander by. Like coyotes in the desert, their keen eyes were always on the watch for an easy mark. Now in his early twenties, Storma crouched beside a garbage bin, smoking a cigarette.

The sound of footsteps approached on the sidewalk outside the alley. From the metallic cadence along the cement, Storma knew one of them was a robot.

This is a good score, he thought. *Robots are expensive.*

A man and a general-purpose android passed by the alley entrance. Storma recognized the man as Dahl by his short stature and pointed ears. He had some strange tattoos, but that detail faded as Storma grabbed his men and stepped out into the lamplight.

"Nice robot," Storma said, pulling a knife from his belt.

The android, blue and silver, stopped and turned.

"Why, thank you!" she said, "I was recently refurbished."

Storma glared at the Dahl.

"Hand over the bot or I'll slit your throat," Storma said.

Half expecting the Dahl to run away, Storma was surprised when he stood his ground, even taking a step closer. The tattoos on his arms were glowing with an odd, radiant blue, turning a little brighter each second. His eyes were blazing like fire.

"What the hell is this?" Storma muttered.

The Dahl was transforming, his hands and fingers growing longer. His fingernails curled into wolf-like claws and his mouth transformed into jaws full of fangs. Storma couldn't look away.

"You should be running, too!" the creature growled.

Storma peered over his shoulder in time to see his other two gang members disappear down the alley.

Storma swung his knife but missed badly, his arm going wide. With its claws, the creature slashed through Storma's forearm. Both the knife and the hand holding it landed with a fleshy thud on the ground. Storma looked at the stump, spewing blood, like it was someone else's.

The nightmarish monster prepared for another attack.

"No!" Storma screamed, but the paw swung around, slicing through his neck. His head rolled away into the gutter as Storma's body fell headless to the pavement.

The Pink Persian was a gentleman's club in only the loosest of terms. Located near the Fortunas starport, its interior was almost universally pink except in places were purple seemed more tasteful. Upon entering, patrons found the bar on their left and booths on the right, with regular tables cluttering the middle. At the end of the bar, a stage was set up along with a metal pole. A female Tikarin, a cat-like humanoid, danced on stage, wrapping her body around the post to the beat of the music. While technically naked, the dancer was covered in tan fur like a lioness.

In an adjacent booth, with a good view of the show, Orkney Fugg watched disapprovingly.

"You call that dancing?" he shouted. "My nana could work the brass better than you!"

The Tikarin paused momentarily to show Fugg her middle claw before going back to her routine.

"Rude!" Fugg replied.

The chief engineer for the *Wanderer*, Fugg was Gordian, a species of stocky, ill-tempered people with the face of a boar, including a pig nose and tusks. On his home planet, he would be drinking fungus beer brewed lovingly in the belly of the mountains. On Fortunas IV, he had to settle for the swill wine they sold domestically. Empty bottles of it littered Fugg's table.

Through the gauzy haze of his stupor and a generally bad mood, Fugg recognized a familiar face. His captain, Rowan Ramus, and their robot were wading through the tables and chairs in his direction.

"You were supposed to be waiting for the client," Ramus said, sliding into the booth.

"You didn't say I couldn't drink while I waited," Fugg replied.

Gen the robot remained standing beside the table. Her eyes were full of fear, as if she had seen a ghost.

"What the hell's wrong with you?" Fugg asked.

Her eyes brightened and her lips contorted into a pained smile.

"Nothing," she said. "Nothing horrible just happened."

"Never mind that," Ramus said, motioning toward the entrance. "Our client just got here..."

A robot waited just inside the front door, its casing painted in a dull orange with areas worn down so the aluminum underneath showed through. Seeing the others in the booth, it walked toward them with a mechanical gait.

For Fugg, this was too much.

"We're taking jobs from robots now?" he protested.

"Ignore him," Ramus said, addressing the machine. "I'm Captain Ramus of the *Wanderer*."

"I'm Bos Kacil," the client said. "We spoke on the comm earlier."

"Good to meet you," the captain replied. "This is my engineer, Orkney Fugg."

"Actually, Mister Fugg," Kacil said, "I'm Parvulian, not a robot. We merely use these mechanized walkers as locomotion."

With a hiss, the chest of the machine cracked and swung open, revealing a cockpit inside. A humanoid, only twenty inches tall with pink skin and large, bulbous eyes, stared out at them.

"Crap on a cracker!" Fugg said.

"As you can see," Kacil continued, his voice higher in pitch than the lower, synthesized speech of the robot, "I ride inside this machine, called a *mech*. Shall we get to business?"

"Right," Ramus agreed.

"I represent the Parvulian Trade Consortium," Kacil said. "Several of our freighters have come under attack recently and our crews have been either killed or captured."

"Are these strictly Parvulian crews?" Ramus asked.

"Only the captains. The rest are humans, Tikarin, and even a few Gordians like your friend here."

Ramus gave his engineer a sideways glance. "Oh, we're not exactly *friends*..."

"Another of our ships, the *Konpira Maru*, has failed to check in," Kacil went on. "We want you to investigate what happened to it."

"My rate's ten thousand per day," Ramus said, "plus another five if we get shot at, not including the robot."

"That's acceptable," Kacil replied. "I'll transmit the last known coordinates of the freighter."

Gen, who had remained silent the whole time, perked up.

"Wait, what about the robot?" she asked.

The next morning, the *Wanderer* jumped to hyperspace en route to the coordinates Bos Kacil had given. On the second day of the journey, Gen was in the engine room, assisting Fugg with routine maintenance. From the robot's experience, *routine* usually meant swearing at the ship's machinery.

After Fugg had kicked a power coupling and started hopping around on one foot, Gen decided to ask a question that had been bothering her.

"Master Fugg," she said, "What kind of Dahl is Captain Ramus?"

"What?" the engineer scowled, holding his ankle while balancing precariously on the other foot.

"I've met several Dahl, but he's not like the rest of his people, is he?"

Fugg snorted loudly, falling over.

"People?" he said, now sitting. "Ramus ain't got people no more."

"I don't understand."

"He's what they call one of the *Forgotten.*"

"What's that?"

"The Dahl have long memories, but when Ramus turned his back on them, they deleted him from their minds. He's not just an exile, Gen, he got *erased!*"

Gen stared at Fugg as if she had more to say.

"What?" Fugg shouted impatiently.

"It's just..." she sputtered, "we were walking in town the other night and a gentleman wanted a word with us. He was very complimentary, but then there seemed to be a misunderstanding and Master Ramus changed. He turned into an animal and killed the man right in front me! It was terrifying!"

"Oh, that's just *Dark Psi,*" Fugg said.

"Dahlvish psionics?"

"Well, not the kind regular Dahl ever learn. Dark Psi is outlawed."

"Is that why they exiled Master Ramus?"

"Naw," Fugg waved his hands. "He learned that after. He fell in with a group called the Psi Lords. They taught him all kinds of crazy shit. Anyway, he doesn't use it much. He's kind of weird about the whole thing."

Gen was silent again. Fugg sighed.

"Yes?" he asked.

"Is Master Ramus a bad person?"

Fugg snorted. "We're all bad people, Gen."

"I always thought I was good."

"That's because you're a stupid robot! Deep down we're all terrible in our own special way. It's part of nature. We act good most of the time, but when push comes to shove, we'll do whatever terrible thing needs doin'."

"Oh..."

"Listen, don't worry about it. It's all good."

"But you just said..."

"Good. Bad. They're all just words, see? They can mean whatever you want."

"I think I have a lot to learn," Gen said.

"Just stick with me, kid," Fugg thumped his chest. "I'll teach you all the ins and outs."

Gen smiled. "Thank you!"

Captain Redgrave and Commander Robert Maycare drank coffee in the captain's office. Each held a porcelain mug emblazoned with the Imperial emblem: a five-pointed star enclosed by a laurel wreath.

The commander took a sip, remembering the skipper's steward never used enough sugar.

Compared to his captain, Maycare was a decade younger with dark hair cut short along the sides and slightly longer on top. While both officers were of noble blood, though not of the Five Families, Maycare was also the nephew of his famous uncle Lord *Devlin* Maycare, renowned throughout the Imperium for his daring feats of sportsmanship and womanizing. Nevertheless, whenever the commander brought up one of his uncle's infamous adventures, Redgrave made a point of telling one of his own.

"We got some good news about my Uncle Devlin," Maycare began, "apparently the paternity test was negative—"

"Did I ever tell you about the time I faced a dozen Talion torpedo boats?" Redgrave asked, interrupting his XO.

Maycare sighed. "Probably…"

"It was just after the third Imperium-Magna war," the captain went on. "I was part of the reprisal fleet, punishing the Talion Republic for siding with the Magna. Anyway, my destroyer got separated from the task force and a squadron of torpedo boats came out of an asteroid belt where they were hiding."

The XO stared into his mug.

"The Tals depend on boats because they can't afford capital ships like us and the Magna. Anyway, they launched a spread of torpedoes, but they didn't count on my ship's maneuverability or how well my ECCM suite could handle their targeting sensors."

"Right."

"Needless to say, I outflanked the boats and finished them off in short order."

"I love that story," Maycare said. "So, my uncle's test—"

The young voice of the chief communications officer crackled over the intercom. "Lord Captain, a courier ship has transmitted an encrypted message for you. It's from Lord Admiral Highcastle."

The captain pressed a button on the comm. "Patch it through, Ensign."

"Aye, Lord Captain."

A monitor recessed into the surface of his desk sprang to life and the face of a man, his face creased with age, appeared. His curly white hair contrasted against his dark, weathered skin.

"Should I leave?" the XO asked.

"No, stay," the captain said. "Computer, decrypt and play message."

"Captain Redgrave," the admiral began, "as you may already know, another Parvulian freighter has suffered an attack. While this is distressing, it has also come to our attention that the Parvulians have hired an independent party to investigate.

"Now, I know you and your crew have been diligent in this matter," the admiral went on, "and I have every confidence that you will find the culprits involved. However, we can't have these xenos acting on their own without the Imperial Navy's involvement. Pretty soon they'll start asking why they need us at all. With that in mind, I'm ordering the *Baron Lancaster* to the freighter's last known coordinates. It's imperative that you find out what's going on, and if you can dissuade this independent party, all the better! Lord Admiral Hightower out!"

The image blinked off.

Commander Maycare got up and headed toward the door leading to the bridge. "I'll have Ensign Clark plot a course, sir."

"Maximum speed," Redgrave grumbled.

CHAPTER SEVEN

On the planet Isylium, in the Talion Republic, Kovel Kerch led his guest to a local farm from where they had parked their gravcar. A Tal, Kerch was dressed in a long tunic and pants, both maroon with an intricate design woven into the fabric. A cape of the same material hung across his back while a round, silver amulet dangled from his neck. Inquisitor Kerch had been sent by the Republic to learn as much as he could about the recent K'thonian attacks on the planet. Today, however, he felt more like a tour guide for his taller, and much greener, companion, a Magna named Judicator Busa-Gul.

Ostensibly allies, the Talion Republic and the Magna Supremacy were hardly equal. The Magna were more powerful and treated the Tals, at least in Kerch's mind, more like a vassal.

Feeling the brunt of the sun on his orange scales, Kerch directed his visitor toward a farmhouse partially hidden by a field of crops.

"Some of the K'thonians landed in that field over there," he said.

The judicator lifted his horns, protruding in a loose spiral, and his fiery red eyes stared off toward the crops.

"How many were killed here?" Gul asked.

"The owner of the farm died before his wife could shoot the attacker."

"What of the corpse?"

"The farmer was buried in accordance with our traditions," Kerch replied.

"No, I meant the *K'thonian*."

"Ah," Kerch nodded, "that was sent to the capital for analysis."

"Pity," Gul said, "I'd like to see one firsthand."

"I'm sure my government will give you full access to the body," Kerch said. "As we always do..."

A grin curled in the corner of the Magna's mouth. "Indeed."

When the two reached the farmyard, a young Tal came running from the house to greet them. When the boy saw the stature of the Magna, he stopped abruptly, not taking his eyes off the visitor.

"Don't be rude!" his mother said, following her son out onto the dirt driveway.

"May we come in?" the inquisitor asked.

"Of course, of course," she replied, ushering them into her home.

The kitchen was much darker than the outside and it took Kerch a moment for his eyes to adjust. Gul was the last to enter, his muscular frame barely fitting through the narrow doorway. Taking a look around the kitchen, he noticed a jar filled with dark liquid sitting on one of the shelves.

"What is that?" the Magna said.

Kerch winced, knowing exactly what it was and that the judicator knew it as well.

"Some of my neighbor's livestock got loose," the mother explained, "and trampled our fields. He couldn't pay money so the local inquisitor awarded us a pint of his blood."

"An example of *Blood Law*, I presume," Gul replied.

"You *presume* correctly," Kerch said with more anger than he intended. "It's our tradition."

"Of course," Gul said. "But why keep it? Why not just pour it out?"

"Oh, we couldn't do that," the mother said. "That would be disrespectful of our neighbor's restitution."

"But it has no value per se..." the Magna went on.

"It's a symbol," Kerch said. "Perhaps you don't understand..."

"I understand," Gul replied. "The humans have an expression: *an eye for an eye*, although I don't think they keep the eye in a jar..."

Kerch's own eyes narrowed. "Indeed."

Lord Andre Santos swirled the wine in his glass while overlooking the gardens of his newly purchased estate. He hadn't set foot in the gardens, but the robots were keeping them well-manicured as far as he could tell. Several bushes were carved into shapes that were not bushes, including a dog and a duck. Santos wasn't clear why a bush couldn't just be a bush, but he had largely given up asking questions at this point.

Probably for the best, he thought.

Drinking wine was becoming a hobby for him. The estate had come with an extensive cellar, stocked with vintages bottled on another planet. Santos imagined robots picking grapes and stomping them under metallic feet in wooden tubs. In Brazil, he had visited a few wineries but never got a taste for wine, preferring coffee. Now he drank it all the time, usually alone. The estate was large enough for a small village, but Santos lived there entirely by himself.

Finishing his glass, the captain of the *Merope* went back inside from the terrace and sat in a cavernous living room on a couch bigger than a school bus.

"Shall I turn on the holoscreen?" a disembodied voice, the estate's AI, asked him.

Without enthusiasm, Santos replied, "*Certo.*"

On one side of the room, between two pillars, an image materialized like a partially translucent curtain. On the screen, an advertisement appeared:

IDEA FURNITURE:
WE BUILD THE PIECES;
YOU DO THE REST!

Suddenly, the ad vanished in a field of static, replaced by images of green jungles and native villages. Stone buildings, some of them destroyed, faded into view and then dissolved again, replaced by pictures of lizard-like people, some of them carrying bladed staffs.

"What is this?" Santos asked, setting aside his empty glass.

"I'm uncertain," the AI said. "The external feed appears to be compromised."

"Compromised? You mean *hacked?*"

"It seems to be a direct transmission, but I cannot determine its origin."

From the speakers built around the couch, a man's voice narrated the scenes.

"These are pictures the Emperor doesn't want you to see," he said. "The Imperium came to Marakata as colonialists, but stayed as occupiers. The Draconian people have suffered ever since."

Reptilian figures crossed the screen running, fire and smoke in the background. The echo of screaming reverberated against the walls of Santos' living room. The din of explosions shook the couch. Santos jumped to his feet.

The scene faded to black, superimposed with the words *Free Marakata* written as if by spray paint across the dark screen.

"The transmission has ended," the AI said. "Would you like to hear some music?"

"No, thank you," Santos said, eyeing the empty glass.

"Would you like some more wine?"

"I've had enough," he replied and then, after a long pause, "I want to know more about Marakata. Tell me everything..."

In Lab 22, in the depths of Warlock Headquarters, Lars Hatcher sat in a medical chair with a tube running from his arm to a bag of green fluid hanging from a rack. Dr. Sprouse, wearing her white lab coat, stood beside him, moving a scanning device over his body.

"What is this?" Lars asked, his chin pointing to the bag.

"My latest cocktail," the doctor replied. "I've made some tweaks to my last formula. This should clear up those headaches you were having."

"Thank you."

Her red lips parted into a smile. "You're welcome."

"What happened to Agent Skarlander's last metamind?"

Dr. Sprouse switched the scanning device off and placed it on a metal tray beside the chair.

"He died," she said.

"Was it Agent Skarlander's fault?"

Her eyebrows drew upward into a peak. She shrugged.

"You realize I can read your mind," Lars said.

"Then why bother asking questions?" she replied.

Lars thought for a moment, his enormous head throbbing slightly. "To be polite, I suppose."

Dr. Sprouse smiled again and patted him on the chest. "Good boy!"

The doctor went to a refrigerated cabinet, took out another bag of green fluid, and returned to the chair to replace the bag that was now almost empty. Pulling the tube from the old bag, she attached it to the new one and made sure the flow was dripping properly.

"He's a clone, isn't he?" Lars asked, again being polite.

"Of course."

"I thought human cloning was illegal in the Imperium."

"You could say the same about genetic manipulation," Dr. Sprouse said. "Not all laws are for all people."

"Warlock Industries is exempt, I take it?"

"It's a powerful corporation. We have many friends in government and the military. It's just the way of things..."

The doctor retrieved the scanner and began waving it over her patient.

"You were *lovers?*" Lars asked suddenly.

Dr. Sprouse paused, the scanner shaking slightly, before starting again.

"I meant with Mr. Skarlander," Lars clarified.

"I see you've *stopped* being polite."

"It was obvious, the way he looked at you... the way he let you speak to him."

"As I said," the doctor replied, "it's the way of things. Besides, it's over now."

"Are you sure?"

"Of course!"

"I wonder if he feels the same way."

Dr. Sprouse shook her head. "I don't think he feels... anything at all."

Lars watched the green cocktail, as she had put it, twist its way down the tube and into his arm. The veins beneath his pale skin were dark and winding like a road through a snowy countryside.

"Clone or not," he said, "he's still human."

"Maybe," she replied.

"And what am I?" Lars asked.

She looked up at him. Her eyes, a lighter shade of green than her new formula, fixed on his, which were simple black orbs.

"Whatever you want to be," she said. "I've made sure of that."

Built to her specifications, Lady Nasri's estate was like an Ottoman palace with arabesque calligraphy featured predominantly along halls lined with marble columns capped with gold leaf. Persian rugs were spread across expansive floors and large, luxurious couches were covered in decorative pillows. The estate's AI, which Nasri had named *Abida* meaning *one who worships*, was dedicated to making her mistress's life as comfortable as possible.

Every morning at precisely 9 AM, Nasri woke to the cries of peacocks played over speakers concealed in her bedroom. After a long bath, she dressed in a silk robe and went to breakfast where a bowl filled with chickpeas mixed with yogurt and garlic waited for her, placed by an unseen robot from the kitchen.

Once finished, she returned to her bedroom where a walk-in closet contained an assortment of clothes. Casual wear hung to the right, while formal wear and gowns took up most of the left. In the center, flanked by cushioned benches, an island of jewelry drawers was filled with the baubles Nasri had purchased with her newfound wealth.

"Abida," Nasri said, "do I have any appointments today?"

"No, My Lady," the AI replied. "However, I've saved a snippet from the news you may be interested in."

"Really?" she asked.

"It involves Lord Santos."

"Shit."

After changing from her robe into a sleeveless, black dress, Nasri positioned herself on a deep couch. Propping cushions against her back, she faced an archway twelve feet across and nearly twice as high, through which a courtyard was visible with a few small trees and a fountain in the center.

"Play it," she said.

The space inside the archway turned solid, displaying Sylvia Flax reading the news.

"A demonstration was held in the capital today," she said, "protesting the occupation of Marakata."

Video of people holding signs and chanting slogans appeared on the screen. Most of the placards were variations of the theme to free Marakata and stop oppressing the Draconian people. Although Nasri had seen other news reports about the topic, she was confident the government knew what they were doing. Whoever these Draconians were, they were no business of hers.

Then a familiar face showed himself, larger than life, in the archway.

Standing on a crude stage, surrounded by demonstrators, Lord Santos thrust his fist into the air, shouting loudly.

"What we're doing on Marakata is wrong!" he yelled to the approving crowd. "I came from poverty and I recognize the repression of the Draconians, because I've lived through it myself! They are our brothers and sisters, and no matter their race or their background, we must stand with them in their struggle. I say this to the Emperor: Stop the occupation *now*!"

Flax reappeared.

"Asked for comment," she said, "the Palace declined to do so at this time."

The screen dissolved away, replaced by the courtyard in the distance.

"That idiot!" Nasri shouted, digging her fists into the couch. She threw one of the pillows across the room where a small robot collected it and scurried away.

"You have a new message, My Lady," Abida said.

"I don't care!"

"It's from Prince Richard."

"What does *he* want?" Nasri asked while exhaling sharply.

"He's requesting your presence at a sporting event tomorrow," the AI went on. "He suggests such a public meeting could be useful under the current circumstances."

Nasri tapped her long nails against her chin.

"Hmm," she murmured. "What kind of sporting event?"

"It appears to be a gravbike race, my lady. *The Regalis Cup*."

"What does one wear to a gravbike race?" Nasri asked.

"As always," the AI replied, "I'm happy to help..."

The grandstands, garnished with red and gold bunting, ran along the shore of the Regalis River. Riders on gravbikes maneuvered through hoops, ten feet in diameter, levitating high above the water. In a pair of boxed seats, Lord Winsor Woodwick and Lord Radford Groen were drinking and watching the race.

Woodwick, a middle-aged man with rounded features and a walrus mustache, brought a gin and tonic to his lips. From English aristocracy, he could tell the difference between top-shelf gin and whatever rubbing alcohol his glass was filled with.

"I say, Radford," Woodwick said, swishing his mustache. "I think that bartenderbot is trying to kill me!"

Reviewing a betting sheet, Radford muttered without looking up, "Wouldn't be the first."

A few years younger than his companion, Groen was losing his hair faster than his money, but didn't seem to notice either. He fumbled for a glass of whiskey on the tray beside him, his eyes fixed on the datapad in his lap.

"Maycare's in the next race," he noted aloud.

"You're not going to bet against him again, are you, old chap?" Woodwick asked, peering over Groen's shoulder.

"His luck can't hold forever."

"I wouldn't bet on it!"

"I already did," Groen replied.

Woodwick rolled his baggy eyes. "Well, you're buggered then. You haven't a chance."

"I always have a *chance.*"

With a shake of his head, Woodwick took another sip from his glass and instantly regretted it. "Awful!"

He set the drink aside but nearly missed the tray as something in the grandstand caught his eye.

"Good lord!" he said, elbowing Groen's arm. "Isn't that Lady Nasri?"

Across the heads and hats of a few dozen onlookers, a woman was making her way up the stairs to the Emperor's box. Prince Richard stood to greet her.

"And the Prince no less," Woodwick went on. "You don't usually see *him* at a sporting event. Not his cup of tea, I'd say."

"So?" Groen replied.

"Try to keep up, Radford! Such a public display? Something's afoot..."

"I don't care."

"It's about Lord Santos, I'd wager," Woodwick said, pulling the tip of his mustache. "Did you see him on the news last night? He's really stepped in it with this whole Marakata business. Quite a kerfuffle if you ask me."

"Nobody's asking you," Groen said bluntly. "I'm sure they know what they're doing."

"Humph!" Woodwick replied, crossing his portly arms. Then, in a low tone, he murmured, "It'll all end in tears..."

Prince Richard waited for Lady Nasri to arrive. She was late, which was not unexpected. When he finally saw her making her way up the grandstand stairs, she was wearing a white dress, contrasting well with her olive skin, and a floppy sun hat. She had adjusted well to her new status, the prince thought. Perhaps a bit too well.

The prince stood and greeted Nasri with a smile and a shake of his hand — Richard was not a hugger — and the two sat in the Emperor's box while the gravbike race proceeded over the Regalis River. A servantbot brought a tray of drinks, each with a spiral of orange peel draped over the side. Richard didn't drink, but he took one anyway just to be polite.

"It's a pleasure to meet you at last," Lady Nasri said, the wide brim of her hat keeping her face in shadow.

"Of course, the pleasure is mine," the prince replied graciously.

Nasri took a taste and smiled, setting the glass down again. Richard raised his glass to her in a salute, then gave it back to the robot who took it away.

"Is this your first gravbike race?" the prince asked.

"I suppose it must be," she replied. "There wasn't a lot of sports on the *Sterope*."

"I can only imagine."

"But this is certainly an interesting spectacle."

"Yes," Richard said, "they hold the Regalis Cup once a year. Everyone who's anyone comes to see and be seen..."

"Is that why you asked me here?" Nasri asked.

"I was planning on it anyway, but I think the timing is fortunate."

Nasri raised an eyebrow, the corner of her lips following suit. "How so?"

"The Emperor has some concerns..."

"Really? What kind of concerns?"

"Your relationship with Lord Tagus, for one," the prince replied, "but perhaps more pressingly, the behavior of Lord Santos."

Nasri shook her head, dipping her hat so her eyes were hidden for a moment.

"As for Lord Tagus," she said, "I have nothing but respect and admiration for him and his family, but that is all. I'm quite aware of his past history with Emperor Augustus—"

"Tagus' son tried to overthrow my father..."

"—but I want no part of that," she went on. "I'm merely finding my way for now and part of that is talking with the other families."

"And so you should," the prince said. "I'd be surprised if you didn't."

A gravbike, twirling through a floating hoop over the river, lost control and fell into the water with a towering splash.

"As for Lord Santos," Nasri said, ignoring the crash, "I'm not sure what my fellow captain is up to these days."

"His behavior of late is troubling," Richard said, leaning closer. "The Emperor is *not* amused."

"Nor should he be..."

"It's important that the Five — sorry, make that Seven — Families remain a united front when it comes to Imperial business, our own petty squabbling notwithstanding."

"I understand," Nasri said. "I hope Lord Santos can be made to see reason."

"So do I," Richard replied. "Perhaps you could help him see the light?"

She thought for a moment.

"Perhaps," she said.

On the planet Lokeren, Philip Veber watched the birds, their colorful wings flashing against the azure sky, while he stood alone on the clifftops. His gray eyes followed the little creatures darting in and out of nests hidden among the rocky crags beneath his feet. Against Philip's bald scalp, the rays from the sun felt harsh, but not uncomfortable. An amulet with an eight-pointed star hung around his neck.

His mother was calling.

"Philip?" she said, walking down the path from the estate to join him. "You shouldn't be out by yourself."

"I'm fine," he replied. "Better than fine."

Her dress billowing in the cool wind coming off the sea, Lady Veber joined her son, taking his hand.

"Until we know you're no longer sick," she said, "I don't want you wandering off unattended."

Philip felt his mother's warm blood pumping through her hand. He knew his own hand felt like ice. He turned toward her, his features sunken and pale.

"I may not look it," he consoled her, "but I'm as well as I've ever been." He saw the concern in her eyes, but felt only irritation. "Really!" he protested.

"Alright, dear," Lady Veber replied. "It's just a miracle I have you back at all."

"You needn't worry, mother. The Necronea have seen to that."

"I wish I knew more about the Necronea..."

"I can't say I understand them myself," Philip admitted. "That holy man, Ghazul, tried explaining them to me. The Necronea tapped into a power — a force of some kind — that transcends death. I'm sure there must be a scientific explanation but I'm not a scientist. All I know is, I was dead and now I'm not anymore."

"What was it like?"

"Being dead?" Philip asked, then shrugged. "Nothing as far as I can remember. There was no passage of time. I heard your voice as I was dying and then I heard Ghazul chanting when I opened my eyes again. It was black... just nothing."

Lady Veber sighed.

"Disappointed?" her son asked.

"No, I suppose not. I just thought—"

"Something about an afterlife?"

"Yes," she admitted, taking a deep breath in the salty air. "It's just as well. Having you back is all I really care about."

She released his hand, which fell to his side.

"Will you be returning to the capital soon?" he asked.

"Yes," she replied. "If you're feeling better, I should visit the palace and pay my respects to the Emperor."

"Does he know I'm alive?"

"I'm sure a little *bird* told him," Lady Veber said. "There's not much he doesn't hear about."

"Safe journeys then," Philip said with a thin smile. "And don't worry about me when you're gone. I've never felt better."

She laughed, turning to go. "Good!"

When his mother had left and Philip was once again alone, he surveyed the view from the top of the cliffs. He held out his hand and one of the tiny birds landed on his outstretched fingers. Swiveling its head, the bird eyed Philip but didn't fly away.

Quickly, Philip captured the bird inside his cupped hands. He felt its soft, delicate feathers brushing up against the skin. Slowly, while his gray eyes stared out over the water, he pressed his hands together until the bird stopped moving. He opened his hands and the lifeless bird fell from his grasp into the crashing surf below.

CHAPTER EIGHT

Like a ripple in a pond of stars, the *Wanderer* emerged from hyperspace above a turquoise planet. A gray freighter floated in high orbit above the world. Except for running lights, the ship was dark.

In the cockpit of the *Wanderer*, Captain Ramus flipped on the intercom.

"I see the *Konpira Maru*," he said.

Fugg's voice came from the speaker.

"How's she look?"

"Not great," Ramus replied. "She's on auxiliary power."

"Are we boarding her or what?"

"Meet me by the airlock."

Ramus brought his ship alongside the freighter, extending a gangway between the airlocks. At 75 yards long, the *Wanderer* was only half the size of the *Maru*.

By the time Ramus reached the airlock, Fugg and Gen were already there. The engineer held a blaster in one hand and Ramus' holster in the other. Ramus took the belt and strapped it around his waist, double checking that his weapon was fully charged.

"Gen," he said, "go to the cockpit and keep an eye on the sensors. Let us know over the comm if anything shows up."

"Neat!" the robot replied.

Ramus took a tiny plug-like comm and placed it into his ear while Fugg did the same. Concealed from the casual observer, the comm would allow them to talk to each other or the ship.

Once Ramus and Fugg reached the relative safety of the other ship's airlock, Ramus checked for a breathable atmosphere.

"It's got oxygen," he said.

"Good," Fugg replied. "We can't burn things without that!"

"We're not burning things."

"Sure, you say that now..."

The airlock opened into a dimly lit hallway of smooth aluminum walls and steel grates, the latter allowing access to the pipes and electronics running beneath the floor. The air smelled heavy and stale.

"It could use some paint," Fugg remarked. "Their decorating is bullshit."

"Shut up," Ramus whispered.

Fugg rolled his brown, beady eyes. "Life support is minimal. This ship's dead as a doornail!"

"Really? Then what's that?"

With the barrel of his blaster, Ramus pointed at a shape farther up the corridor. As they crept closer, the shadow took on a mechanical shape.

"It's a Parvulian mech," the captain said.

The walker, scorched and smoldering, lay on its side against the wall. The hatch in its chest was open and something lay outside it. Something pink.

Ramus rushed to the Parvulian's side. He wore a gray bodysuit like the one worn by Bos Kecil, except burned in places. Bending on one knee, Ramus leaned closer.

"He's breathing," Ramus said.

The Parvulian's eyelids fluttered and opened. Seeing Ramus looming over him, he screamed in terror.

"No! Get away!"

"Take it easy!" Ramus shouted. "Bos Kecil sent us..."

The Parvulian rubbed his eyes and stared at the captain more closely. "I'm sorry. I thought you were one of *them*."

"Who?" Ramus asked.

"I don't know exactly, but they looked a lot like *you*."

"The Dahl attacked your ship?"

"Never trusted them myself..." Fugg muttered.

"No, not exactly," the Parvulian said, coughing. "Their skin was dark violet, and their hair was bright white."

He coughed again. "And their eyes... their terrible eyes..."

"Where's the rest of your crew?" Ramus asked.

"Gone. The female Dahl took them away. They hypnotized the men somehow."

"Then why didn't they take you?" Fugg asked.

"They shot my mech-walker, but they must have thought I was a robot."

"You're safe now," Ramus said, "We'll get you to sickbay."

From down the corridor, a bolt of energy seared the darkness, blowing the tiny Parvulian into pieces. Ramus jumped up and sprinted towards the attacker, firing as he ran. When he reached the source of the fire, he found only a stack of cargo containers.

Fugg caught up moments later, his chest heaving.

"Thanks for waiting for me!" he said.

"Whoever it was is gone..." Ramus replied.

"Well, the Parvulian's toast," Fugg replied. "Also, you've got bits of him in your hair."

"Goddamn it."

Ramus and Fugg searched the ship, hunting for whoever killed the Parvulian. When they reached the crew quarters, Fugg took the cabins on the left while Ramus took the ones on the right. Each stateroom contained double berths, storage lockers, and trunks full of personal effects.

The whole place is a ghost ship, Ramus thought.

Reaching another cabin door, Ramus expected another carbon copy of the half dozen before. The hatch slid open and Ramus stepped inside. This time, he saw a woman lying on the bottom bunk, her arm hanging over the side. Coming closer, he noticed something rusty-brown on her neck. With his weapon drawn and ready, he moved to the center of the cabin, only a few feet from the bed.

"What the hell?" Ramus said.

The woman's head was facing towards the wall, her neck fully exposed. Along her jugular were two puncture marks and dark, dried blood.

Ramus felt someone behind him. He turned in time to see a man with long silver hair in the doorway. His skin was a shade of violet and his eyes were white with black slits.

The man smiled, revealing a pair of protruding fangs.

Despite a strong desire to move, Ramus couldn't. The blood in his veins had turned ice cold.

From the corridor, someone fired a blaster, a bolt of energy striking the stranger in the back and sending him sprawling face first onto the cabin floor.

Ramus glanced from the smoldering corpse to his engineer, Fugg, in the doorway.

"We needed him alive," Ramus said.

Fugg glared at him. "You're *welcome!*"

In his earpiece, Ramus heard Gen's voice over the comm.

"Master Ramus," she said, "things are happening!"

"What kind of things?" Ramus replied.

"A ship just appeared on sensors, next to us," she said. "It just materialized out of nowhere and then jumped to hyperspace. And now a different ship is approaching at high velocity!"

"Okay, Gen," the captain said. "Power up the engines. We're heading back."

Fugg and Ramus returned across the gangway to the *Wanderer*, leaving the body of the strange Dahl behind. The captain headed to the cockpit while Fugg went to the engine room. The hatch to the bridge opened and Gen, still sitting in the command chair, turned.

"I'm so glad you're back!" she said.

"Get out of my chair," Ramus replied.

Settling into his seat, he checked for a visual on the incoming ship. The vessel was at least ten times the size of the *Wanderer*, with a looming superstructure from which masts extended like a crown of spikes.

"Jump capacitors are charged," Ramus said under his breath. "Navcom calculating escape vector..."

The ship's radio crackled.

"Unidentified ship," a stern, official-sounding voice said, "This is the *HIMS Baron Lancaster*. Power down your engines and prepare to be boarded!"

"Are we getting out of here or what?" Fugg said over the intercom.

"It's a Navy ship," Ramus replied. "It looks like they want to talk."

"Oh, well in that case," Fugg growled, "let's invite them over for some goddamn tea and biscuits!"

"Shall I prepare the tea and biscuits, sir?" Gen asked.

Ramus, who hadn't realized Gen was still there, stammered, "What? No! Get out of the cockpit!"

Aboard the *Baron Lancaster*, Ramus sat on a chair behind a metal table while the captain, Lord Redgrave, asked questions in the hot, suffocating interrogation room.

"I already told you," Ramus insisted, "the Parvulians hired us to investigate that ship!"

Leaning forward, his hands spread flat on the table, Redgrave loomed over the much smaller Dahl.

"The Imperial Navy fights pirates," the captain said. "The Parvulians should have contacted us, not some Dahlvish exile..."

"Maybe they got sick of losing their crews."

"We are an empire of laws," Redgrave said. "We'll get to the bottom of this, one way or another."

"Meanwhile," Ramus said, "more people go missing..."

Redgrave took a palm-sized disk from his uniform and placed it on the table. The holo-emitter projected a translucent image of a ship with a black fuselage and wings of thin, purple membranes. Within the wings, bone-like structures ended in sharp barbs.

"As we approached," Redgrave said, "this ship decloaked and jumped into hyperspace. Ever seen a ship like this?"

"Can't say I have."

"I thought Dahls knew everything," Redgrave said.

Ramus shrugged. "Not always. Sometimes we forget."

"I guess you just remember the good stuff..."

"Sadly, no."

"What about the dead woman with the blood drained from her body?"

"I already told you," Ramus said, "she was dead when I found her. Why don't you ask the guy with the vampire teeth?"

"He's not talking..." Redgrave said, tapping the holo-emitter. The image of the ship vanished.

"I've got a missing crew and two dead bodies," Redgrave said. "Give me *one* good reason why I shouldn't throw you into the brig?"

"Because I can help you," Ramus replied.

"How?"

"You've been fishing for these guys for a while without any luck. Did you ever consider you might be using the wrong bait?"

A week later, the *Wanderer* was traveling alone in a nearby star system. In the galley, Fugg sat at the table, drinking from a 24 ounce can of *Genuine Draft Fungus Beer* while Ramus leaned against the counter with his arms folded.

"We're wasting our time," Fugg said.

"Maybe," Ramus replied.

"Explain it to me again..."

"This is the same trade route that was attacked before. If we keep on this heading, there's a chance we'll get hijacked."

"And that's a good thing?"

"If we want to know where those missing crew were taken, yes." Ramus said. "The nanos we swallowed will let the *Lancaster* track us, no matter where we end up."

Fugg pounded his chest, releasing a thunderous belch. "And you think Redgrave is going to just swoop in and save our asses?"

"Maybe."

Gen's voice came over the intercom. "There's a contact on sensors, Master Sirs!"

"On my way," Ramus replied, heading toward the cockpit.

"Send her down to the engine room!" Fugg called after him.

Once the captain was gone, the engineer pressed the beer can against his forehead until the aluminum crumpled. Grinning with satisfaction, he dislodged himself from behind the table and staggered down the corridor toward the rear of the ship.

In the engine room, Fugg punched the call button on the intercom.

"What do you see up there?" he asked.

"It's the ship that Redgrave showed me," Ramus replied.

The *Wanderer* shuddered.

"They're firing," Ramus said over the speaker.

No shit, Fugg thought.

Another hit jolted the ship, followed by two more in rapid succession. A control panel exploded and Fugg threw up his hands to protect himself from the shower of sparks.

"Son of a bitch!" he swore. "She's not built for this…"

Gen stepped through the hatch.

"Thanks for showing up!" Fugg yelled.

"Always happy to help, Master Fugg!" Gen replied cheerfully.

An explosion rocked the *Wanderer* again, sending both Fugg and the robot to the deck.

"The shields appear to have failed," Gen said, lying on her back.

Sprawled on the floor, facing down, Fugg mumbled "You think?"

Struggling to get to her feet, Gen managed to stand upright while the heavy-set engineer took a few seconds longer.

"The engines are offline too," the robot said. "Is this part of Master Ramus' plan?"

"Can't you tell?"

The captain's voice spoke over the intercom.

"They're coming alongside," Ramus said. "Gen, make yourself scarce…"

Gen hesitated, looking perplexed.

"He means *hide*, stupid!" Fugg said.

"Ah, very good," she said. "But where?"

"Try the trash compactor."

"Really?" Gen asked.

"No!"

Ramus met Fugg at a corridor junction just down from the *Wanderer*'s airlock. Both were armed, each with a blaster in their hands.

"Let's make this look good," the captain said.

The hull of the ship reverberated as a vessel docked and secured itself to the airlock. The hatch swung open as Ramus peered cautiously around the corner. The figure who stepped through the doorway appeared similar to the man who attacked Ramus on the Parvulian freighter, but carried himself with a sense of authority, even arrogance. His skin was violet and his hair had a silvery tinge of white.

"My children," he said, "the ship is ours!"

Three more people, all women, boarded. Each wore black and red robes, with heavy collars tight around their necks. The man stayed by the hatch, but the three females came toward Ramus and Fugg who still hid behind the corner. One of the women took the lead while the other two walked slowly behind her.

Ramus nodded at his engineer and both leaped out, firing their blasters. Following the plan, their shots went wide, purposely missing the intruders down the corridor.

The women stopped, but made no attempt to avoid the plasma bolts searing the bulkheads around them. They stared directly ahead, fixing their gaze on Ramus and Fugg. The engineer stopped firing. Ramus looked at Fugg, standing with his mouth open and his weapon hanging loosely at his side. Ramus glanced back at the women. He could hear them in his mind like sirens singing, numbing his senses and clouding his thoughts. The hallway grew darker, like a heavy fog seeping in around the edges. His head wobbling, Ramus saw the light go out and felt his body hit the floor.

Ramus woke with a splitting headache, but at least the pain proved he was still alive.

"Welcome to the larder," a voice said.

Ramus opened his eyes. He was lying on the floor of what looked like a cargo hold, his back against a wall. Fugg was in a fetal position, still unconscious, beside him. People of various races were arranged randomly about the room. Most of them looked sick.

Only one person was standing and he was talking to Ramus.

"Nice to see you awake," he said.

His head cocked to one side, Ramus looked up at the man, a human dressed in dingy workman's overalls.

"Who are you?" the captain asked.

"I'm Marcus," he said, "first mate of the *Konpira Maru*."

"I talked to your captain," Ramus said.

"He's still alive?" Marcus asked.

"No, I'm sorry. One of those *things* killed him."

Marcus nodded. "Their species is called the *Dokk*."

"Why did you say this was a larder?" Ramus asked.

"They keep us here," Marcus said, "to feed on our blood."

Ramus grimaced while Fugg began stirring.

"Where'd those blue bitches go..." Fugg groaned.

"They were purple, you idiot," Ramus said, shaking his engineer awake.

"They're Shadow Maidens," Marcus said.

Fugg opened his eyes, only to scowl at the first mate.

"Yeah? Did they give you that hickey?" he said.

Ramus noticed, for the first time, that Marcus had two puncture wounds on his neck.

"It's not a love bite," Marcus said. "They've fed on me a few times. Luckily, I haven't been here very long, otherwise I wouldn't be able to walk now."

Fugg sat up, his face full of rage.

"That ain't right!" he shouted. "I don't care *how* hot they are!"

Ramus gingerly got to his feet. Unsteady, he kept his balance by leaning against the wall.

"We're getting out of here," he said. "That I can promise you."

Across the room, a large hatch opened with a screech, the mechanism grinding from age. A Dokk male entered holding a blaster pistol.

"Captain Ramus," he said. "Come with me."

The Dokk led Ramus down several poorly lit passageways. Ramus guessed this was a space station, one that had seen better days. From the rust and mildew, it looked to be a hundred years old or more.

At the end of a corridor, a hatch opened into a large room. Through the window ports in the ceiling a bleak, barren planet was visible. In the center of the room, steps led to a raised platform where another male sat on a chair built like a throne. Ramus recognized him as the Dokk who boarded the *Wanderer*. Flanking him were the three women.

When he started speaking, the words sounded like gibberish until Ramus recognized some of them as High Dahlvish, his own native tongue.

The man stopped.

"I apologize," he began again, this time in Imperial Standard, the human language common across the Imperium. "I should have known our languages have diverged too much to be comprehensible. I am Tomil Druril, Blood Prince of this brood."

"You're saying you're Dahl?" Ramus asked.

"Long ago…" Tomil said. "I assume you've never heard of the lost tribes of the Dahl?"

"No."

"Then we are truly one of the Forgotten."

Ramus raised an eyebrow.

"Ah," Tomil said, "so *that* is familiar?"

"Yeah."

"Then, perhaps we are more brothers than you first realized."

"Well, I may be an exile," Ramus admitted, "but what's your story?"

Tomil rested his chin on his hand thoughtfully.

"Centuries ago," he said, "my people dared to practice Dark Psi, forbidden by the elders. As a result, our brood and others like it were banished from the Dahlvish home world into the vacuum of space. The Dahl removed us from their memories as well, as if forgetting could erase us from history. In time, we learned to exist here in the void, but not without… changes."

"So I've noticed," Ramus remarked.

"Forever living on ships, traveling from system to system, we were no longer exposed to sunlight as we once were. We tried producing the needed proteins for our blood, but nothing worked. We grew weaker, almost to the point of extinction. Finally, we did what we needed to do. We drank the blood of those we captured, and we've survived ever since."

"But those people in the cargo hold," Ramus said, "they won't be so lucky."

"Survival has a cost," Tomil said. "Those men are the price we pay to live."

Ramus paused, silently staring out the windows in the ceiling.

"Well," he said finally, "I guess we all have to pay sooner or later. Sometimes, it's just a lot *sooner* than we thought."

Through the windows, the nose of the *HIMS Baron Lancaster* appeared from behind the dead planet. Within seconds the warship fired, strands of orange piercing the darkness and exploding along the surface of the space station.

The room shook violently.

"What have you done?" Tomil shouted.

"That's the Imperial Navy," Ramus replied. "At least *they* haven't forgotten you."

The blood prince motioned toward the door.

"Take the prisoner back to his cell," Tomil said, "He can die with the rest of them!"

The impact from a plasma cannon rocked the cargo hold, sending Marcus to the deck.

"Sounds like the *Lancaster* is here," Fugg said, still sitting. "Humans love being punctual if it means killing people..."

Flat on his back, Marcus sat up on his elbows.

"Aren't they going to help us escape?" he asked.

"Only if it's in a body bag!" Fugg replied, pressing a finger against his ear. "Can you hear me, robot?"

"Loud and clear, Master Fugg, sir!" Gen's voice came over his earpiece. "I've docked at the starboard airlock, but you may want to hurry. The station's breaking apart!"

The hatch to the cargo hold rattled open, followed by a scream and a severed arm holding a blaster. Standing over the Dokk guard lying dead in the outer corridor, Ramus was engulfed in blue light as his body changed back from wolf to Dahl form.

"It's about goddamned time!" Fugg remarked.

"Did you hear from Gen?" Ramus asked.

"She's at the airlock," Fugg replied.

"Then get everybody to the ship," Ramus said, "I'm going after the leader."

"You haven't killed him yet?"

Ramus bent on one knee, prying the blaster out of the dead Dokk's hand. "I'm working on it..."

Turning down a hallway, Ramus spied a sign pointing to the hangar. He took off running, wary of the floor buckling under the stresses of the *Lancaster's* bombardment. He fought to keep his balance, reaching the hatch he was looking for. As the door opened, he saw the Dokk ship on the far side of the hangar. Black and dark purple, the vessel perched on the deck like a bat with wings extended. Tomil and the rest of his brood were climbing a loading ramp extended underneath.

Ramus pointed his blaster, but hesitated.

As an exile himself, Ramus understood the hardships and the hard choices one had to make. Survival sometimes meant doing terrible things, things that changed you forever. Was he all that much different from these people who traced their blood line back to a race that no longer even acknowledged their existence?

Ramus watched the ship taking off.

"Screw it," he said and fired.

A bolt of hot plasma struck the ship in the tail section. Bits of hull near the thruster exhaust smoldered orange for a moment, but quickly fizzled out. The craft hovered while its landing gear retracted and disappeared through the open hangar door into space.

Silently, Ramus watched it go.

Aboard the *Baron Lancaster*, Redgrave balanced on the edge of his command chair, his hands balled together in a knot. Computer consoles, each manned by bridge officers, fanned out in a semi-circle, everyone watching a panoramic screen at the front of the bridge. On the screen, the space station was breaking into pieces as heavy plasma cannons pummeled it mercilessly.

"Report," Redgrave said.

The chief tactical officer turned, her blond hair pinned tight against her head.

"An unknown vessel is emerging from the station hangar, Lord Captain," she replied.

"On screen!"

A ship like a winged demon appeared.

"Lock onto target!" the captain shouted.

Like an ephemeral spirit, the Dokk ship faded while the captain watched helplessly as it disappeared.

"The vessel has cloaked," the tactical officer said. "We've lost sensor contact."

"Goddamnit!" Redgrave shouted.

"Wait," she replied. "I'm detecting a particle trail. It must be damaged."

"Can you get a lock?"

"Yes, sir!"

"Well, what are you waiting for, Lieutenant? Fire at will!"

Along the hull of the *Baron Lancaster*, a cannon turret swung around, a shaft of plasma erupting from its barrel. Like a lance of fire, the bolt hurled toward a patch of space, empty except for a nearly indiscernible trail of green vapor leading back to the station. The plasma struck the cloaked vessel, its structure outlined by the explosion. Now exposed, the Dokk ship became an easy target, suffering another hit before disintegrating into fragments.

The tactical officer pumped her fist in the air. "Got it!"

Standing beside his captain, Commander Maycare crossed his arms.

"What about the *Wanderer*?" Maycare asked.

"She's also pulling away from the station," she replied.

Maycare glanced questioningly at the captain.

"Let her go," Redgrave said. "A deal is a deal..."

"Sir?" Maycare asked.

The captain trained his eyes on the XO.

"I have a hunch we'll be needing them someday," Redgrave said quietly. "Besides, it never hurts to keep a card up your sleeve..."

On the main screen, a tiny vessel of yellow and gray accelerated off into the distance before jumping into hyperspace with a flash. Left behind, the abandoned space station broke apart, its forgotten pieces falling across the surface of the dead planet below.

CHAPTER NINE

The trophy for the Regalis Cup was a tall, extravagant affair plated in silver with ornate handles on either side. Along the basin, the names of previous winners were engraved, including the name *Lord Devlin Maycare* three times.

Straddling his gravbike, Maycare felt confident a fourth was in the offing.

Blue and silver with the number *nine* on the back, Maycare's gravbike was six feet of sleek aerodynamic chassis and not much else. Maycare leaned out over the handlebars, just behind a narrow windscreen. His racing suit was fire-resistant, which he considered more of an open challenge than a safety precaution. He also wore a helmet, mostly to keep his hair in place and so he could hear Bentley, his robot butler, in the earpiece.

"I'm afraid Lord Grayson remains ahead of you, sir," the robot said.

"Again?" Maycare replied.

The race route followed the Regalis River from the old 72nd Street Bridge in the north to the Bannister Bridge in the south for five laps. In between, ring-like gates hung above the water at different intervals and heights, which racers had to pass through, sometimes upside down.

Before the race, Maycare always ate a light lunch.

Sweeping along the shore, he could barely make out the white grandstands as they wiped by. Maycare knew many in the crowd were rooting for him, and even more rooting against, but he pushed that to the back of his mind. Even so, he couldn't help but wonder if a certain mousy academic named Professor Jessica Doric was watching from his private box. If she was, Jess probably wouldn't appreciate the skill with which Maycare threw his gravbike into a steep climb to clear one of the vertical gates and then rolled inverted so he could dive to the next ring two hundred feet below. She probably wasn't watching at all, her eyes glued to some ancient annals of Dahlvish history or some such. So irritating!

"Grayson's pulling away," Bentley spoke in his ear.

"The hell he is!" Maycare shouted.

The *Number 9* skirted the waves of the river, the gravbike's propulsion unit sending up tall shafts of water in its wake. The back of the leader's bike was just visible ahead. His hand on the throttle, Maycare twisted the handle until the bike reached maximum thrust. He felt himself pressed increasingly against the seat, but dug his boots into their slots, keeping him at the front of the controls.

Grayson was too cautious, Maycare realized. Perhaps taking his lead for granted, he was flying too slow. Maycare pulled alongside him, the two bikes nearly touching, and Maycare gave him a two-fingered salute before peeling away through another gate. Passing just behind, Grayson lost control and went spiraling downward until careening into the river with a towering splash.

Nothing else stood between Maycare and the finish line.

Professor Jessica Doric, with dishwater blond hair and dull brown eyes, was sitting in Maycare's private box. On her lap, a datapad displayed one of the chronicles of Dahlvish history she was especially fond of. Beside her, Bentley the butlerbot gave her a nudge just before Maycare won, but the robot needn't have bothered. The crowd's wild cheers would have probably roused Doric from her book.

"Oh, good!" she said, standing along with the rest of the people in the neighboring boxes. Unlike the other women around her, Doric was not wearing a decorative hat and had to shade her eyes from the sun.

"We should meet him at the victory circle," Bentley suggested.

"Is that allowed?" Doric asked.

"Of course," the robot replied.

Not fully believing the butlerbot, Doric followed him down the grandstand steps to an area cordoned off from the rest of the onlookers. Maycare had already removed his helmet, his dark hair remaining mysteriously coiffed, and was leaning against his gravbike. The race organizers, a collection of officials and dignitaries, had surrounded both the racer and his bike so that Doric had trouble finding a path until Bentley made one in a polite but forceful way.

"There you are!" Maycare shouted. "Come look at my new trophy!"

The Regalis Cup, its sides glinting in the afternoon light, sat on a flower-covered table, along with several bottles of champagne. Maycare poured a bottle into the silver cup.

"That seems like a waste of champagne..." Doric chided him.

"Not at all!" Maycare laughed and dumped the foaming contents over Doric's head. She screamed, feeling the cold bubbles run down her back.

"Devlin!" she protested. "What are you doing?"

"Sorry, Jess," he said, grinning.

Looking like a drowned rat, Doric shook her arms and hands dry.

"I'd prefer you call me *Jessica*," she said.

Mugging for the cameras, Maycare swung the trophy around, spilling more champagne, a few splashes managing to hit Doric yet again. Behind a velvet rope, reporters with cameras recorded the scene, broadcasting the images across the planet and, eventually, throughout the Imperium.

Her hair dripping, Doric glared through stinging eyes. She wanted to cry, but bit her lip, refusing to embarrass herself. Maycare had taken care of that already.

Henry Riff's one-bedroom apartment smelled like burnt noodles and old socks. In the corner, the water in his fish bowl was dangerously low which had not gone unnoticed by his goldfish who stared at Henry, sitting in the middle of the room, with great concern.

Henry scratched his disheveled hair. On the floor, facing up, his datapad projected a life-sized hologram of an IDEA Furniture shelving unit standing upright with shelves perfectly aligned. Past the floating image, the actual unit Henry had assembled leaned to one side before slowly falling over completely.

The goldfish turned away, swimming to the other side of the bowl.

Henry sighed and went to pick up the pieces of his new shelf when a buzzing caught his ear. His phone was ringing but he wasn't sure where. Papers and other loose objects became airborne as he searched frantically for the phone. Eventually, digging with his hands between the couch cushions, he pulled it out triumphantly and answered. Professor Doric's face greeted him on the screen.

"Are you alright, Henry?" she asked.

"Sure thing," he replied, breathing heavily. "Sorry about that..."

"Have you done that research I asked for?" she said curtly.

"Not yet."

"Henry!"

"Sorry, Professor—"

Doric's stern expression softened. "I'm sorry, Henry. I'm not mad at *you*."

"What's the matter?" Henry asked.

"Lord Maycare embarrassed me again," she replied, glancing away from the camera.

"Oh, right, I saw on the news. He got you good!"

Doric glared back. "I'm aware of that."

"I'm sure he didn't *mean* it."

"Of course," she replied. "He never *intends* any harm but that doesn't make it any less infuriating!"

"Sorry, Professor."

"Sometimes I wonder if he respects me or the work I do for him."

Henry didn't reply immediately, thinking about his own work for Doric.

"Maybe you should quit," he said finally.

"Quit?"

"Well, if you're not happy..."

"What about my research?"

"I'll always be there to help."

Doric smiled. "I know you will, Henry. Unfortunately, neither of us are independently wealthy."

"Is money so important?" Henry asked.

"Realistically? Yes, I'm afraid so. It's nice that Lord Maycare has his own starship and unlimited funds. It makes things a lot easier."

Henry's eyes drifted from the phone to the pile of shelving on the floor. He shrugged. "I guess."

"Well," she went on, "enjoy the rest of your weekend. Don't worry about that research. I didn't mean to be cross…"

Henry grinned and swiped away a loose clump of hair hanging across his forehead.

"Thanks, Jess!" he said.

"Please, Henry," she replied. "Call me Professor Doric."

Henry's shoulders slumped. "Sorry."

"Goodnight," she said, and her face vanished from the screen.

Staring at his phone, Henry took a deep breath and exhaled. "Bye."

By design, Bentley was a butlerbot. With blue and silver trim, he was by all accounts an outdated model with slower processors than newer butlerbots. Most of the designs currently rolling off the dy cybernetics assembly lines had gravitronic brains with the ability to learn organically like a human brain does. Bentley's AI had a fraction of the computing power of the current models, but Lord Maycare, who could buy as many as he wanted, chose to keep him instead. Sometimes Bentley wondered why, but he never asked his master. Maybe old and familiar was more comforting than new and shiny.

Having poured a martini with an olive on a toothpick, Bentley took it out to Maycare lounging in his swim trunks beside the pool of his West End estate. The robot set the drink beside his master, but remained instead of returning inside. To further make his point, Bentley stood opposite the sun, casting a shadow over Maycare's otherwise tanned body.

Maycare lowered his sunglasses, his brown eyes peering over the rims. "What is it, Bentley?"

"I think you should apologize to Miss Doric," the robot replied.

"Whatever for?"

"You publicly embarrassed her at the Regalis Cup."

Pushing his shades back, Maycare took on a thoughtful expression. "How long have you known me?"

"Since you were a boy."

"And in all that time, how often have I embarrassed someone?"

"Including myself?" Bentley asked. "More times than I can count."

"Exactly! If I apologized every time I upset someone, I'd be constantly saying *I'm sorry.*"

"This instance goes beyond hurt feelings," the robot replied. "Your lack of respect for Miss Doric was abominable, even by your usual standards."

Maycare sat upright, or as much as was possible in a lounge chair.

"That's not fair, Bentley! Jess is the best employee I've ever had — I mean, without actually *having*..." Maycare stopped. "Are you rolling your eyes at me?"

"As the head of the Maycare Institute of Xeno Studies," the robot went on, "Miss Doric is highly qualified and professional. She's not one of the women you usually entertain."

"Yes, yes, I know. I mean, she's not really my type, is she?"

"I think my point has eluded you, sir."

"Really? No, I don't think so," Maycare said. "Besides, I'm not *her* type either. The boy seems more her style anyway."

"Henry Riff?" Bentley asked.

"He's a good kid, that Henry. A bit twitchy, but nice."

The robot, sensing he was losing his master's train of thought, stomped his metallic foot against the pavement. The resulting *clang* gave Lord Maycare a jolt.

"Are you malfunctioning?" Maycare asked with concern.

"No," the robot said. "However, I must strongly advise you to rethink apologizing to Miss Doric."

"Apologize? I thought we already covered that? Anyway, I'm sure something will come up and she'll forget all about it. That way, I don't have to say I'm sorry and she'll move on. A win-win!"

"I really don't think—"

"A win-win, Bentley," Maycare said. "A win-win!"

After arriving on Aldorus and spending much of the day in meetings in and around Regalis, Lady Veber was relieved to be done with them so she could attend to the real reason she came to the capital.

The back seat of Lady Veber's oversized gravcar was more like a crescent-shaped couch, the upholstery a supple leather with silk stitching. Her legs crossed, Lady Veber drank from a champagne flute while the buildings of the West End slid by through the tinted windows. Besides the official structures of the Imperial government, the vaulted estates of most of the nobility were also located on this side of the Regalis River. Her family kept a mansion here as well, but the gravcar flew past it, traveling on to the destination Lady Veber had given the AI pilot. Once there, the gravcar hovered for a moment before descending into the courtyard of the Maycare estate.

A blue and silver robot waited patiently on the ground.

"Welcome, My Lady," Bentley said as the door to the gravcar swept open.

"Thank you," she replied, offering her hand to the robot so he could help her exit the vehicle.

Safely standing on the gravel driveway, Lady Veber took a second to admire the battlements of the Maycare manor. Built like a castle, the home had a solid, masculine quality. Lady Veber kept a wry smile in check, wondering if the Maycares were compensating for something.

"This way, please," the butlerbot said.

Lady Veber followed the robot into the main hall, crowded with a collection of artifacts from throughout the Imperium. Some were books or jewelry, all easily recognizable, while others, strangely shaped items with indiscernible engravings, were completely alien to her. Most of these were in display cases, presumably wired to alarms, and several glowed of their own accord. Lady Veber couldn't begin to guess where Devlin Maycare had gotten them all.

Bentley led her to a study were Lord Maycare greeted her with a kiss on the cheek.

"It's good to see you, Becca," he said with his usual familiarity that she found so irritating.

"Hello, Devlin," she replied.

"I haven't seen you in ages," Maycare went on. "How have you been?"

The robot, who lacked a trachea, made a noise that sounded vaguely like he was clearing his throat.

"Oh, right!" Maycare said, snapping his fingers. "Your boy's been sick. How's he doing?"

"Thank you for asking," Lady Veber replied with a nod. "He was very ill, but he seems to be better now."

"Well, that's certainly good news!"

Emotions that she had kept hidden welled up in Lady Veber's chest and made her skip a breath.

"Are you alright?" Maycare asked.

"Perhaps My Lady would care to sit?" Bentley suggested, offering one of the armchairs nearby.

Comfortably seated, with Maycare sitting beside her, Lady Veber exhaled and tried to maintain an air of dignity. A woman in her position did not cry. That would be unacceptable.

"I need your help, Devlin," she said.

Unlike Henry Riff's apartment, Jessica Doric's flat was carefully vacuumed, dusted, and the pillows matched the sofa. Also, instead of a pile on the floor, Doric's books were arranged in mahogany bookcases that didn't fall over.

In an armchair beside a reading lamp, she held a book in her lap. A cup of tea, whiffs of steam curling upward, rested on the table next to the chair. It was late, but Doric made a point of some light reading before going to bed. The title of the book was *Quantum Entanglement & the Modern Woman*.

Across the room, her phone chimed.

Extracting herself from the chair, Doric nearly tripped over her flannel nightgown as she snatched the phone off the coffee table and looked at who was calling. With a sigh, she answered.

"Lord Maycare," she said.

"Jess!" his voice erupted through the speaker. "I can't see you."

"Just a sec..."

Doric held the phone at arm's length and flicked on the camera.

"There you are!" Maycare said, his square jaw taking up most of the screen. "What the devil are you wearing?"

Pulling the collar together with her free hand, Doric tried to avoid showing any more of her nightgown than necessary. "What can I do for you, sir?"

"Can't the old man call you once in a while? You know, just to see how things are going?"

Despite herself, Doric grinned. "No, of course you can."

"Well good!" he said. "But actually, I'm calling about *work*..."

She felt her eyes glaze over, her smile dissolving away. "Yes, sir."

"Lady Veber, of all people, just dropped by," Maycare explained. "Something incredible has happened to her son."

"Oh? I heard he was sick..."

"More than sick. The poor boy actually died!"

"Good lord!"

"But then he got better..."

"I don't understand."

"Apparently, Lady Veber got mixed up with some cult leader named *Ghazul*. Ever heard of a race called the *Necronea*?"

Doric's eyes widened. "Actually, yes."

Maycare laughed. "I knew it! That's why I called you."

"What does this have to do with Philip Veber?"

"Well, this Ghazul fellow raised Philip from the dead."

"How is that possible?" Doric asked.

"Hell if I know, Jess, but that's what Lady Veber wants us to find out!"

"Okay," Doric replied. "I'll start investigating in the morning. I should call Henry, too."

Maycare was smiling, but Doric thought he was looking unusually smug, even for him.

"You know, Jess," he said. "Bentley was just suggesting that I apologize to you."

Doric felt her chest tighten. "Why?"

"For dumping that champagne on your head," he replied. "I knew you would've forgotten about it by now."

"I didn't forget."

"Well, Bentley said I was disrespectful, but I think his programming is off."

Doric nodded slowly, her fingers stiffening around the flannel in her hand.

"It was all in good fun," Maycare continued. "Can't I have a little fun with you?"

"Uh-huh."

"Wait, I think you *are* mad..."

"Uh-huh."

"Well, don't be! I mean, that's just silly!"

"Oh, really?"

"Sure! I mean, there's no reason to be sore about it, is there?"

Doric didn't reply.

"Now, listen," Maycare floundered. "I'm your boss so there's no sense holding this over me so just get over it, for Pete's sake!"

"It's really late," Doric said, not looking at the screen anymore.

"Hold on! You're making this awkward... If anything, you should apologize to *me*!"

"I'm going to bed."

"Alright," Maycare replied, his dark eyebrows furrowed, "but I'll expect you at the estate bright and early..."

"No," she replied.

"What? Why not?"

"I quit," she said, stabbing at the *END* button.

Since communications could not move faster than the speed of light, courier drones packed with data moved between the star systems of the Imperium, disseminating news, electronic correspondence, and anything else that needed knowing. A drone jumped into a system, dumped its data to a remote satellite, and then jumped away again, leaving the satellite to transmit the data to the local nodesphere. All information was heavily encrypted so only the intended recipients, in theory, would receive their messages.

Orbiting a nondescript planet circling an unremarkable sun, Magnus Black's spaceship, the *Starling*, passed silently through the darkness while its comm array pinged the local satellite, looking for messages.

Magnus sat alone in the confined spaces of the galley, eating a packaged meal dispensed from a machine. The food, roast beef and mashed potatoes, was filled with nutrients and the faintest taste of rusted metal. Magnus stared into nothingness until a chime told him he had mail. He dumped the remainder of his feast into the matter reclaimer and climbed a ladder up to the cockpit where a green light was blinking on the controls.

As a hired killer, Magnus received contracts from a variety of sources. Open contracts, broadcast in code across the Imperium, were available to anyone, but jobs directed specifically to him usually arose from word of mouth. His reputation among criminal syndicates and governments alike was well known.

When Magnus began reading the new message, he quickly realized the scope of what was being asked. This was a high-value target but, on the other hand, the payout was impressive. Half of the money was already sitting in a numbered bank account with an access code attached to the contract. The rest would be available after the job was done.

Still, something was off.

Magnus, snug in the pilot's chair, steepled his fingers and contemplated the text. There was no sender's name, but that wasn't unusual. All he really needed was the name of the mark, and the message was kind enough to include where the target would be and when. However, this hit would send ripples across the Imperium. Magnus wasn't sure he wanted to get swept up in the repercussions.

Magnus considered for a long time before coming to a decision. When he did, he tapped in a reply and sent it off into the void where it would head invariably back to the anonymous sender:

CONTRACT ACCEPTED.
MAGNUS BLACK.

CHAPTER TEN

Silandra Oakhollow gathered herbs in the forest near her village. Her brilliant green eyes shined above angular cheek bones and a light brown complexion like freshly cut timber. As she knelt among the wild flowers and tall grasses, her long, hazel-colored hair peeked from beneath the hood of her cloak. Straightening, she pulled the hood back, revealing pointed ears.

A Sylvan, Silandra's people were related to the Dahl but, while her distant cousins were interested in collecting all forms of knowledge, the Sylva focused their studies on nature and the wild things inhabiting it. Even their psionics centered on woodland animals, communicating with the creatures who knew the forest best.

Silandra packed a handful of herbs into a pouch hanging from her belt. The woods, dim even when the sun was high, were growing darker now that dusk had arrived. Silandra turned to head home when the noise of fighting and a tumbling crash caught her ears. Remaining unseen, she crept toward the sounds.

In a clearing flanked by a rocky hillside, Katak warriors had cornered a man swinging a sword. The Katak were froglings, primitive by nature, with slimy blue skin and wielding wooden spears with flint tips. The man wore some sort of modern armor, heavily engraved, with a helmet covering his face. Silandra realized he was protecting something partially buried from a rock fall. As she drew closer, she saw it was a robot, lying face down, with stones covering much of his body.

The knight slashed at the Katak who were nearly a foot smaller, but outnumbered him five to one. They seemed content to surround him, waiting for an opportunity to strike.

Concentrating, Silandra reached out with her mind into the thoughts of the froglings, casting images of giant snakes slithering out of the shadows. The Katak made loud, chirping noises, glancing at each other until one of them threw down his spear and ran deeper into the woods. The others quickly followed, leaving the man with his sword hanging by his side.

Silandra stepped into the clearing.

"Hello," she said.

Seeing her, the man in armor sheathed his weapon and removed his helmet. Expecting a human, Silandra was surprised that he was something else entirely. His skin was a dark, olive green with bony protrusions running along the line of his chin. She had no idea what he was, but he bowed lavishly in her direction.

"Greetings," he said. "May I assume you are somehow responsible for these creatures' hasty retreat?"

Silandra laughed at his formal speech.

"Why, yes you may!" she said, grinning.

"I am Sir Golan of the Cruxians," he said. "Who might you be?"

"Silandra Oakhollow of the... uh, town of Gowyn I guess..."

"Well met! May I inquire if this town of Gowyn is nearby?"

"It's about a half hour walk."

"Good," Sir Golan said. "I'm afraid my squire is damaged and in need of repair."

He motioned toward the robot still buried beneath the loose rocks.

"Never mind me," the robot said, his voice muffled by the dirt.

Silandra and Golan spent a few minutes freeing the robot. His right arm was mangled and parts of his chest were dented in several places.

"Thank you so much!" the robot said, trying to dust himself off with his good arm.

"Do you have a name?" Silandra asked.

"Squire," he said. "My name and function, you might say..."

"Well, let's get you to Gowyn," she said. "As luck would have it, I believe there's a tinker in town."

Gowyn was a village in the trees, fifty feet up in the forest canopy. Circular platforms were centered around thick tree trunks with rope bridges spanning the gaps between them. On one of the platforms, hanging above the door of a rustic building, a wooden sign read *Bragor's Tavern*. Inside, the lights flickered, the patrons yelling each time they did. With each shout, a single but higher pitched voice, no less emphatic, demanded they all "shut up!" That voice belonged to a Gnomi named *Mel Freck*.

In the backroom of Bragor's Tavern, just past the kitchen, Mel was working on the power generator. Only three feet tall, with pointed ears and light pink hair, she could fix all things electronic or mechanical. Focusing her sonic spanner on the generator controls, she heard another chorus of shouts as the light bulb above her turned on and off again.

"Stop your bitching!" Mel yelled over her shoulder, then, in a quieter voice directed at the control panel, "Crap on a cracker..."

Bragor, a Sylvan with raven hair and sharp, pointed features, stuck his head into the room.

"How's it going in here, eh?" he said.

"Fine," Mel said flatly.

"The folks at the bar are trying to watch the gravbike races but the power keeps turning off the TV..."

"This generator's a mess," Mel went on. "You're lucky to have any power at all!"

"Well, can't you wait until the races are over?"

"I didn't come all the way from Technotown to sit around."

"I'll pay for your drinks," Bragor offered.

"Well, why didn't you say so?" she replied, slamming her spanner on top of the control panel.

The two returned to the main room where a teak bar was crowded with Sylans watching a video monitor hanging from the ceiling. Mel noted the brightly colored gravbikes streaking across the screen.

She climbed aboard one of the stools and Bragor brought her a sudsy mug of beer as an advertisement filled the monitor:

DRINK GENUINE GORDIAN FUNGUS BEER!
NOW WITH MORE SMOOTH FUNGUS FLAVOR!

Sisa Oakhollow sat in her room carving a figure out of yew wood. She hadn't decided what the figure would look like, but in her mind, it was a young Sylvan girl like herself. Like her mother, Sisa had bright, green eyes and high, sharp cheek bones, but both her hair and complexion were darker like dull copper.

Sisa heard a noise from the front of the house. Setting her carving aside, she rose and ran to the door, expecting to see just her mother coming home. Instead, she found her in the front room with two strangers, one of them a robot.

"Don't just stand there, Sisa," her mother said. "Help me with Mr. Squire."

"Oh, just *Squire* is sufficient," the robot said.

Sisa grabbed one of his arms, putting some of the weight onto her shoulders. The other stranger carried the other arm, burdened as he was with his helmet and armor. She noticed he also had a sword slung on his belt.

The two of them lugged Squire to a chair made from gnarled beech and leather.

"I'm most grateful to you," the stranger said in a formal tone.

Sisa snickered, not sure why he was talking that way.

"No problem," she said, smiling.

"This is Sir Golan," Silandra said. "He's some kind of knight, apparently."

"Really?" Sisa asked.

"At your service," Golan replied with a low bow.

Sisa gave a sideways glance to her mother who simply shrugged.

"Perhaps Sir Golan is thirsty," Silandra suggested.

Sisa nodded and ran to the kitchen to pour some water into a clay mug. When she returned, Golan had also taken a seat, his helmet and sword placed close by his side. Sisa noticed his armor was carved in the same intricate design as the robot's chest and head.

"What happened?" she asked.

"Katak," Silandra said.

"These frogmen," Golan began, "do they cause trouble often?"

"No!" Silandra said. "Not usually, but lately they've been acting strangely."

"How so?"

"Something has them riled up," Sisa's mother replied. "I've no idea why."

Squire raised the finger of his good hand. "Might I inquire about my repairs?"

"Of course!" Silanda said, slapping her forehead. "Sisa, go to your father's and see if that Gnomi tinker is still there."

"It's getting late..." Sisa replied doubtfully.

"Just go!"

The young Sylvan rolled her eyes and, grabbing a wool cloak, hurried out the door.

Mel was downing her third beer when a young Sylvan came charging through the door into Bragor's Tavern. While smaller than the adults, she was still a few inches taller than Mel herself. This might have bothered her after the first beer, but now Mel's view of the universe had grown more agreeable. She was even enjoying the gravbike races, although only for the crashes.

The girl ran to Bragor behind the bar and pointed in Mel's direction. After a short conversation, the two of them approached the tinker.

"Excuse me," Bragor said, "my daughter Sisa was wondering if you could fix a robot at her mother's house."

"But I haven't finished fixing your generator..." Mel started.

"It can wait until morning," he replied.

"What kind of robot?" she asked. "It's not gravitronic, is it?"

"I don't know what that is," Sisa said.

"Nothing but trouble..." Mel replied.

Sisa took Mel's arm and helped her off the stool. Unsteady at first, the Gnomi found her legs and even took a step without the girl.

"Maybe this isn't a good idea," Bragor said.

"I'm fine!" Mel said and fell face first on the floor.

When Mel regained her senses, she was laying on a couch made from beech wood and straps of leather. His back to her, a robot sat in a nearby chair while a woman appeared from the kitchen carrying a tray full of coffee mugs.

"Where's the little girl?" Mel asked.

"I sent her to bed," the woman replied. "I'm Silandra, by the way."

"You're Bragor's wife?"

"Oh, we're not married."

Feeling suddenly awkward, Mel pointed a thumb at the robot. "Is this the patient?"

The robot rotated his head completely around until it faced her.

"A pleasure to meet you," he said.

"Don't do that!" Mel shouted.

"Fair enough!" the robot said cheerfully, turning his head back to the front.

"His name is Squire," Silandra said. "He's pretty beaten up."

"Did Sisa bring my tools?"

"Yes, by the door."

Mel hopped off the couch and, a little wobbly, retrieved the satchel beside the front door. She dropped it again at the robot's chair and pulled her sonic spanner from the bag.

"This is going to hurt," she said.

"Really?" Squire asked.

"No, you're a robot."

"Oh, yes. Quite right."

"Definitely not gravitronic," Mel muttered quietly under her breath.

Into the night, Mel tinkered with Squire's frame, repairing the damage and tuning his systems. She quickly realized that his software was woefully outdated.

After a few hours, she straightened her aching back and took a long stretch, her arms reaching for the ceiling. While a software update was downloading from the local nodesphere into Squire's brain, Mel decided to stretch her legs by taking a quick tour of the house.

Before going to bed, Silandra had dimmed the lights in most of the rooms, but Mel was able to find her way. The Gnomi had excellent night vision, their ancestors having lived mostly underground.

Down the hall from the living room and kitchen, Mel softly cracked open the door to Silandra's bedroom. She was sleeping soundly in a single bed.

Bragor must spend his nights somewhere else, Mel thought.

Sisa's room, next door to her mother's, was smaller but decorated more extravagantly with paintings and carvings. Mel wondered if the girl had made them all herself.

When Mel reached the final door in the hallway, she noticed a light coming from underneath. Hearing nothing, she tried the doorknob and walked in on a strange man with dark green skin. Bare from the waist up, he sat with his legs crossed and holding a sword in his outstretched hands. Before him, a pair of burning incense sticks were displayed on a small, wooden altar. Mel was about to apologize when she realized the man was ignoring her, unaware she was there. She closed the door again and returned to the living room.

Mel checked that the download was complete and reinitialized the robot's operating system. When Squire came back online, Mel was eager to ask him a few questions.

"Who the hell is that green guy?" she said.

"Sir Golan?" the robot replied.

"I guess."

"He's my master."

"I just saw him," Mel went on. "It's like he was in a trance."

Taking a moment to process, Squire replied, "Oh, I suspect he was meditating. Sir Golan is quite dedicated to thinking deeply about things."

"What kind of things?"

"Well, he's Cruxian, you know. They live a life of introspection, reflecting on their actions, both past and present."

"I've never heard of them," Mel confessed.

"Few have, actually," Squire said. "I suppose because they're nearly extinct."

"Are they dying out or something?"

"By their own hand, I'm afraid."

"What's that supposed to mean?"

"Many centuries ago," the robot explained, "the Cruxians were a wealthy, enterprising race. As Sir Golan would tell you himself, they wanted everything and believed they could achieve anything they set their minds to. However, due to their greed and hubris, there was a great war and most of their race, nearly all life on their planet really, was destroyed. Those who survived dedicated their lives to redeeming themselves and, metaphorically, their species. They scattered to the four winds, looking for ways to reclaim their honor."

"Like how?" Mel asked.

"Wandering from place to place, mostly," Squire replied, "helping people when they could..."

Mel closed the lid on Squire's chest which was filled with the repairs she had spent the last several hours completing.

"How's that working out for you?" she said.

When Golan was a boy, he remembered training with his master in a temple overlooking the Cruxian capital. When the sun set, the glow of the horizon would mix with the lights of the city, the colors like paint spilled across a canvas. When the bombs began falling, the only color Golan remembered was the orange of fire and the blackness as the lights went out.

Deep in meditation, he almost didn't hear the crash as Katak warriors broke through the window and spilled into the bedroom. Once aware of what was happening, the Cruxian knight was instantly on his feet, his sword at the ready. Two of the froglings held spears while the other two carried spiked clubs. The room was small, giving Golan the advantage by preventing the Katak from attacking all at once.

Golan remembered the day his master gave him his sword. It was a single-edge blade with writing down the side, a prayer of forgiveness and fortitude. As a young man, he didn't fully understand why a weapon of death would be engraved with a prayer. His master called the sword *Rippana*.

Golan sliced through the spear, breaking it in half, before whirling around to cut the Katak warrior across the chest. The second frogling died when Rippana carved him down the center of his head, between two bulging eyes. The third warrior raised a spiked club high above until both his arms were separated from his body. The final opponent met his end exiting through the window, his last view of the world a glistening blade of steel protruding from his chest, the letters of an unknown language etched across the metal.

Before the bombs fell on the Cruxian capital, Golan's master finally explained the reason for the prayer on the young knight's sword. During battle, an honorable knight must remain strong, but never feel hate or malice toward those he fights. Most of all, he must absolve them of their sin so that they can travel to the next life cleansed of whatever led them to leave this one.

In the hallway, Golan rushed toward the sound of fighting. Squire and a tiny woman were struggling with a pair of Katak. The female was kicking a frogling in the leg while Squire was using a chair to hold off the other. Golan made quick work of both enemies, cutting them down with quick motions, severing their spines. Golan, Squire, and the small woman stared blankly at each other until a scream drove them back down the hallway. Silandra stood at the door to her daughter's room. The knight thrust himself past her, but the room was empty except for broken furniture and a shattered window.

"They've taken Sisa!" Silandra shouted.

CHAPTER ELEVEN

The *Jewel of Amann* cruised slowly across a backdrop of stars. A starliner that had seen better days, the *Jewel* was small compared to the interstellar liners monopolizing most of the leisure travel industry. Her route never left the same system, flying from one planet to another just below the speed of light. Mostly, her bookings were people on pensions who couldn't afford the more expensive cruises between systems. In that respect, the *Jewel* wasn't a starliner at all, but the brochures didn't mention that.

In what barely passed as a first-class cabin, Sylvia Flax lay on the bed reviewing notes on her datapad. The bedsheets were still made, but she had pulled the pillow out and propped it behind her back against the headboard. The cabin displayed a rustic charm that the newer liners ignored for the sake of expediency. The furniture was mostly real wood with a desk in one corner and a bureau with a mirror in the other. The bathroom wasn't much to brag about, but Flax had seen worse in her time as a field reporter. Those days, like the *Jewel*'s heyday, were long gone, but it felt nice to be out on assignment again.

Flax should have known something was up when the editor-in-chief had called her into his office and closed the door. A bald man with a bad stomach, the Chief began speaking before Flax could even sit down.

"What do you know about IDEA Furniture?" he growled, holding the center of his chest.

"You should do something about that heartburn," Flax said. "They have pills now. It's called medical science…"

"Whatever!" he replied. "I've got a guy who says IDEA is putting grunka meat in their meatballs."

"Is that bad?"

"I don't know, do you *want* grunka meat in your meatballs?"

"That depends," Flax said, "I don't know what a grunka is..."

"Well, it ain't good, I can tell you that. It causes intestinal upset and ballistic diarrhea."

"Ballistic diarrhea? That's not real."

"It's a thing. I'm telling you!"

"Okay, so this guy has proof?" Flax asked.

"Yeah, and he wants the famous Sylvia Flax to get the scoop."

"So, what's the problem? I'll interview him down here at the station."

"The problem," the Chief said, "is that he thinks IDEA is trying to kill him and he won't do an interview unless you meet him."

"Where?"

"On a ship."

"Which one?"

"The *Jewel of Amann*."

"Never heard of it."

"I got you a ticket," the Chief said. "It's probably on your datapad already."

"I'm going by myself?" Flax asked.

"He's a harmless little guy. You shouldn't have any trouble."

"What's his name?"

"Walter Ruggles."

Walter Ruggles' stateroom was a box, ten feet by ten feet, with a communal bathroom down the hall. While luxurious compared to third-class standards, this second-class cabin was only slightly larger than a typical prison cell.

At least I have a window, he thought.

Ruggles was in his late fifties, bald on top with dark hair around the sides and just a hint of a mustache. His suit, which had been fashionable around the same time the *Jewel of Amann* was newly christened, was now threadbare in places and stained in others. He also wore a checkered bow tie and a pair of glasses with dark, round frames.

Although he knew Sylvia Flax was coming to his cabin, Ruggles still jumped when she knocked. Having only seen her on holovids, he was equally unprepared for her beauty in person. The sconce in the corridor lit her hair like an eruption of brilliant blue as her eyes glared back at him with irritation.

"Are you Ruggles?" she asked.

"Shush!" he replied, grabbing Flax by the wrist and pulling her into his room. He stuck his head into the hallway, peering both left and right.

When the cabin door slid shut, the reporter was standing with hands on her hips, her head cocked to one side.

"I'm sorry," Ruggles said. "I can't be too careful."

"Why?"

"IDEA agents are everywhere..."

"The furniture store?" she replied doubtfully.

Ruggles smiled, realizing he knew far more about the topic than she did.

"Furniture is just the tip of the iceberg," he explained. "They sell textiles, rugs, even small appliances."

"I've seen the commercials—"

"But it's the food," Ruggles interrupted. "That's the real scandal."

Flax sighed and glanced around the room. She took the only chair and sat in it, crossing her legs as she pulled a datapad from her bag.

"Yeah, my editor seems to think this could be big," she said.

"Oh, it is!" Ruggles replied. "It could ruin the company. That's why they'd do anything to keep me quiet."

"Uh huh."

Pulling a briefcase out from under his single bunk, Ruggles opened it and removed a stack of disheveled printouts. He scanned the pages for a moment before holding them out like playing cards during a magic trick.

"You don't have soft copies?" Flax wondered.

"No, those could be hacked."

"Right," she said. "So, maybe you could just *tell* me what's going on?"

"It's the meat," Ruggles said. "They're putting strange meats in their meatballs."

"It's a big galaxy, Mr. Ruggles," Flax said. "There's lots of strange meats out there. That doesn't make it a crime to put it in food."

"You don't understand! IDEA prides itself on their meatballs. It's the flagship of their restaurant. They sell billions of pounds of them but nobody knows what's actually in it!"

"So, basically you're saying it's a public health issue?"

"Well... yes!"

"Okay, fine," Flax said. "I can work with that..."

The captain of the *Jewel of Amann* was an older man, in his sixties and close to retirement. In the twilight of his career, he took command of the *Jewel* as a relaxing way to live out his final years before calling it quits. Sitting in the captain's chair and puffing on a pipe, he watched the view screen at the front of the bridge with mild interest, his thoughts drifting in and out of memories until his first mate chirped about something on the sensors.

"Several contacts on an intercept course, Skipper," the second-in-command said.

The captain inhaled abruptly, coughing on the smoke.

"What?" he wheezed.

"Sir, there's multiple ships inbound," the first mate replied.

"What for?"

"Uh... I don't know, sir."

"Well, scan the blasted things!"

The captain chewed on the stem of his pipe, unsure why anyone would bother with an old tub like the *Jewel*.

"Their transponders are off," the first mate said after completing his scan, "but the craft appear to be Celadon."

The Celadon Corsairs were rivals of the Pirate Clans, and even more feared. They were the beginning of a supply chain of slaves leading all the way back to the Magna home world across the border. Celadons kept whatever cargo they could plunder, but any captives were sold like chattel in the infamous slave pens of Oras Dracilor.

The captain shuddered at the thought of it.

"Broadcast a distress call," he said, "and prepare to repel boarders..."

Like most Celadons, Golub was four feet tall with a disproportionately large head. Both his ears and nose were long and pointed and his skin, even in the murky light of the assault ship, was a pale green. Strapped securely into his seat, he watched as the rest of the corsair vessels descended on the *Jewel of Amann* like a pack of wolves on a lumbering beast.

Golub loved being a pirate. He especially enjoyed meeting new people and hearing them scream. Of course, he didn't know what they were saying since he mostly just understood Celadonese. They didn't teach the human language in schools on Celadon. Golub knew Ougluk and enough Magna to get by and even a few words of Sarkan, but tried to avoid them as best he could. He didn't trust the Sarkan, although honestly, they weren't as bad as humans. That's probably why Golub liked hearing humans scream.

The humans, who had no respect for anyone except themselves, called Golub and his people *goblins* because the Celadons looked like creatures from their folklore. Truth be told, the Celadons didn't respect other races, especially those taller than themselves. Golub's people didn't like smaller races either, except to bully them whenever possible.

The assault ships disabled the engines of the *Jewel* and came alongside in preparation to board. Golub felt a shudder as explosives blew the airlock open. He and the other corsairs readied their laser rifles before storming into the corridors of the *Jewel*.

The rest was the usual routine. Teams split up and neutralized any feeble resistance the ship could muster. This was another aspect Golub enjoyed. As a rule, they wanted to keep as many passengers alive as possible so they could be sold later on, but anyone who actively opposed them could be cut down as brutally as necessary.

Outside the bridge, Golub stopped to examine a human body, one of the crew apparently. He was older than the others and heavy around the middle. He wore an officer's uniform, now torn and partially charred. Beside him, next to his outstretched hand, a pipe lay on the floor. Golub bent and took the pipe, inspecting it a moment before tucking it inside a pocket. Most loot was shared among the pirates, but not everything. Golub liked taking a few trinkets just for himself.

A few decks down, among the passenger cabins, he and his team began searching the rooms. Expensive items were thrown into the hall to be collected later. When encountered, travelers were especially fun. They yelled incomprehensibly at Golub, which he took as an excuse to strike them with the stock of his rifle.

Opening another cabin door, he saw a man in the room with glasses and a ridiculous mustache. Golub hesitated, remembering his orders, which gave a blue-haired woman, also in the cabin, the opportunity to punch him across the nose, knocking the Celadon flat on his back.

Golub didn't always love being a pirate.

In the officers' lounge of the *HIMS Baron Lancaster*, Commander Robert Maycare sat comfortably while reading the recent gravbike racing scores on his datapad. His uncle, Lord Devlin Maycare, had won recently on Regalis. The article showed an image of him pouring champagne over a woman's head with mousy brown hair. She did not look amused.

Always the ladies' man, the commander thought.

Someone cleared her throat and Maycare looked up to see the Chief Operations Officer, Lieutenant Kinnari, standing over him. She was the only Dahl on board, with pointed ears mostly hidden beneath jet-black hair.

"Hello, Lieutenant," Maycare said.

"Reading anything interesting, sir?" she asked, taking the other chair at the table.

"Not really," he replied. "Just some of my uncle's exploits..."

"He's quite a sportsman, I'm told."

"The Maycares come from a long line of adrenaline junkies. I guess we just find different ways to get our fix."

Kinnari smiled, soaking in what Maycare was saying. The commander always got the feeling Dahls lived vicariously through human antics, as if they could never have any of their own.

"Have you seen the captain?" she asked.

"The old man had an appointment with Doc Baines," Maycare said. "If you can call it that."

"Sir?"

"You know the rumors about him and Samantha…"

"I try not to engage in petty gossip."

Maycare chuckled. "Really? I thought Dahls *loved* collecting information."

"Only if it's factual," Kinnari said. "Unsubstantiated rumors are nothing but hearsay."

"True, but imagination is usually a lot more fun," Maycare replied.

"I'm sure neither the captain nor Doctor Baines would appreciate people talking behind their backs."

The commander sighed. "No, I suppose not."

"On the other hand," she went on, "Samantha and I are good friends, so if there was a relationship between them I'd certainly know."

Maycare looked at the lieutenant sideways.

"So, what are you saying?" he asked.

"Nothing."

"You know something, don't you?"

"Not at all."

"Sure?"

Kinnari, who actually had a lovely smile the commander just realized, grinned while looking away.

"Well, he's too old for her anyway," Maycare said, provokingly.

"Oh?" she replied. "It's been my experience that human males often seek a younger mate."

Maycare folded his arms. "You're quite the romantic…"

"I mean clinically speaking."

"*Very* romantic!"

Kinnari's pale skin turned a shade of red.

"I'm just saying…" she sputtered, "that age is often not an issue for humans, especially if the woman is of child-bearing age."

Maycare stared at the lieutenant blankly.

"Perhaps this isn't an appropriate topic…" Kinnari said, her face now a deep crimson.

"Not with *you*, apparently."

A black band around the commander's wrist vibrated. Maycare quickly tapped the band and it began speaking.

"Lord Commander," the voice of a young ensign from the bridge said, "we've just received a distress call, sir."

"Understood," Maycare replied, standing. "Notify the captain!"

When the *Baron Lancaster* arrived, the *Jewel of Amann* was floating listlessly on backup power with nothing but life support, gravity, and emergency lighting still functioning. Commander Maycare, along with a detachment of marines wearing combat armor, used the transmat to materialize directly onto the liner's bridge.

"How does it look?" Captain Redgrave said in Maycare's earpiece.

The commander glanced around at the destroyed consoles and bodies littering the floor.

"A mess," Maycare replied. "It looks like they killed everyone on the bridge and pulled out the electronics."

"Any hostiles?"

"Not yet."

Unlike this uncle, Commander Maycare was more used to military ships than luxury starliners, although in its current condition, he wasn't sure whether this ship had ever been truly luxurious.

Passing cautiously down hallways of scorched wallpaper and broken sconces, the commander and his marine escorts checked each room, hoping to find survivors. Mostly, they found ransacked cabins empty of people and precious belongings. Maycare became increasingly convinced this was the work of pirates, although the lack of people, except for a few dead crew members, left him concerned.

"Sir," one of the marines said.

"What is it?" Maycare replied.

The marine pointed her blaster rifle toward the open door of a stateroom.

"I heard something," she said.

His own blaster pistol at the ready, the commander nodded and stepped past her through the doorway. Inside, the cabin was surprisingly undisturbed. Luggage remained unopened and the drawers were still in the dresser. It was a small room, probably second-class by the look of it, Maycare thought. The only other door was a closet, but someone had wedged it closed with wood from the bed frame.

A noise, like a soft thumping, came from inside.

With the marine giving him cover, Maycare removed the wedge and tapped the controls. The door opened and a small green man, his hands and feet tied, fell out. His mouth was covered with a piece of cloth.

The commander immediately recognized him as Celadon by the goblin's big head and pointed ears. Lying on his side, the Celadon glared at Maycare with eyes full of hatred and a touch of fear.

Maycare leaned down and removed the gag from his mouth.

"You got something to say?" the commander asked.

The Celadon spewed a series of screeches and low growls. Maycare noticed a few drops of spittle landing on his boots.

"Any idea what he's saying, sir?" the marine asked.

Maycare rubbed his boot against the back of his pant leg.

"No idea," he replied, "but I have a feeling the Captain will..."

A babelbot was not actually a robot at all. It was a program run by the ship's AI aboard the *Baron Lancaster*. By wearing an earpiece, a person could hear an automatic translation of whatever someone said. Captain Redgrave, sitting in a chair in an interrogation room, wore such an earpiece so he could understand the Celadon sitting across a metal table. To make sure the pirate kept wearing his own device, his hands were shackled to the table. After hours of questioning, Redgrave knew the creature's name was *Golub*, but not much else.

"I'm this close to flushing you out an airlock, Golub," the captain said.

"How human of you."

"Goblins aren't known for intelligence, but you've really screwed the pooch on this one."

"Was your mother on board? I didn't recognize her..."

"Sylvia Flax was on the passenger list," Redgrave said. "Was she the target of the attack?"

"Who?"

The captain showed Golub her picture on the screen of a datapad.

"Ah, that's the one who punched me in the nose!" the Celadon said. "Such a mean lady!"

"So, you knew she worked for VOX News?"

"What? No! We don't watch that human propaganda."

"You never saw her before?"

"Not until she attacked me," Golub said. "I hope they put her in the pit."

"Pit?" Redgrave asked.

"Nothing."

"You've got nothing to lose but your life. What pit are you talking about?"

"There's a pit where the bigger Ougluks fight," the Celadon said. "Sometimes they put a human down there just to make things interesting."

"Barbaric."

"It's not so bad. The human doesn't last long."

"Sylvia Flax is a well-known celebrity. If anything happens to her, you'll regret it."

"I don't care what happens to a human," Golub said. "Your people destroy everything you touch."

"You're a slave trader," the captain replied. "You're not exactly standing on high moral ground."

"Celadons are pirates, not slave traders! Sure, if a Celadon comes across a screaming human that doesn't get killed, he might pass the human along to the Ougluks. *Those* are the slavers."

"So, you're saying the Ougluks have Flax now?"

"Probably."

"Where can I find them?"

"Bend over and check your ass."

The captain took a long breath, exhaling slowly.

"Computer," he said. "Unlock the shackles."

The metal bracelets holding Golub's wrists to the table snapped open, freeing him. Captain Redgrave, dropping the datapad to the floor, reached across the table and grabbed the goblin firmly by his long, crooked nose.

"Ow!" he protested, but the captain was already pulling him across the table.

When the door outside the interrogation room opened, the captain emerged, nose in hand, as he dragged his stumbling captive along the polished deck.

"Let go!" Golub shouted, but the captain only clenched tighter, picking up his pace down the hallway.

After passing a few bewildered crewmen, Redgrave reached an open hatch and tossed the pirate in. Landing with a thud, Golub got to his feet in time to see the hatch closing. Redgrave stared back at him through a small porthole in the door.

"Look around," the captain said.

Delicately cradling his nose between his hands, the pirate's eyes glanced around the tiny room. Turning, he saw behind him a near identical hatch, but through the porthole, there was only empty space.

"You have until the airlock depressurizes to tell me what I want to know," Redgrave said. "Then I push this red button and you become one with the universe."

"You call *us* barbarians?" Golub shouted through the door. "*You're* the monsters!"

On the wall beside the captain, the reading on a pressure gauge slowly dropped. Golub began holding his ears.

"Can you feel them popping?" the captain asked.

"I'm not telling you anything!" came the muffled response through the hatch.

"How good are you at holding your breath?"

On the other side of the porthole, the Celadon pressed a hand against his bulbous head.

"Better hurry," the captain said, watching the pressure gauge continue to drop steadily. "Not much longer."

Golub's posture wavered, his legs buckling until he fell to one knee.

"Wait..." he muttered.

"What's that?" Redgrave said, putting his hand to his ear.

"Wait!"

The captain slammed his fist against a button beside the hatch. The gauge level abruptly stopped.

"The next button I push will either open this door or the hatch on the other side," Redgrave said. "Which one is up to you..."

"The Ougluks have a base on an asteroid," Golub wheezed. "I know where it is."

CHAPTER TWELVE

The *Sorcerer* approached a space platform orbiting a gas giant swirling with clouds of orange and red. Owned by Warlock Industries, the station was a framework of metal to which a single habitation module was attached. Except for a few navigation lights, the platform was dark, perpetually orbiting in the shadow of the gas giant.

The *Sorcerer* sidled up to the platform as a gantry extended to meet it. When the atmospheres equalized and the airlock opened, Oscar Skarlander emerged, stepping onto the station with Lars Hatcher just behind him. A young technician with a waxy complexion and a gray lab coat greeted the Warlock agent.

"Welcome aboard," the tech said.

Skarlander waved the greeting aside. "Where is it?"

"This way, sir," the tech replied.

The tech led the two new arrivals through a corridor smelling of ozone and perspiration and into a laboratory. A mass spectrometer and an assortment of other instruments cluttered work benches along the walls, and a table, basking in harsh light, took up the center of the room. An open book lay on the table.

Skarlander bent over the book, appraising it like a collector.

The pages, especially the edges, were burned and brittle. Even the gentle brushing of the air from Skarlander's movement caused tiny fragments to tear off and drift away. Whatever pages were intact were covered with archaic lettering, an ancient script the agent didn't recognize.

"This is all that's left?" he asked.

"The special ops team said the Null Cult they got it from was immolated," the tech replied.

"Immolated? As in burned alive? By whom?"

"I suspect the special ops team," the tech said, "but they insisted the cultists were dead when they got there."

"Well, this relic is worthless," Skarlander remarked.

Lars, his bulbous head pulsing, spoke up. "Not exactly."

Skarlander raised an eyebrow. "Really?"

"I'm sensing a strong energy coming from it," the metamind replied.

The agent stepped back. "Radiation?"

"Psionics," Lars said. "Something very old and very powerful."

"Can we use it?" Skarlander asked.

Lars shook his head.

"What a waste of my time," Skarlander sighed.

"I think there's more like this one," Lars replied, staring at the book. "This one seems connected to others."

"Can you find them?"

"Maybe," Lars said. "Are you sure you want to?"

"Why the hell not?"

"Finding them and controlling them are two different things. Just ask those Null Cultists..."

Skarlander glared at the metamind.

"Just find them," the agent said. "Leave the rest to me."

Like most days on Lokeren, the weather was warm but not oppressive, and the humidity was low. From her balcony, Lady Rebecca Veber watched her two guests materialize on the transmat pad before her staff led them inside the estate. Each arrived separately and alone. This was meant to be a place of safety, neutral ground on which disputes could be reconciled in a civilized fashion. Bodyguards were not needed.

Of all the rooms of the Veber estate, the former dining hall was the one most used. Where a long, rectangular table once stood, now a round one sat in the center surrounded by seven tall-backed chairs like something from Arthurian legend Lady Veber read about when she was still a child. Now, as an adult, she understood the significance. No one at the circular table was above anyone else, although the Veber matriarch could argue some sat taller than others.

Lady Sheba Nasri entered the hall first. Her gown was crimson with stripes of white, trailing behind her across the tiled floor.

"Thank you for coming," Veber said, offering her hand. "Your dress is divine."

Nasri smiled and gripped Veber's hand a little too tight.

"You're too kind," she said. "I've chosen these colors for my royal house. Do you like them?"

"Of course! They certainly make a statement..."

"Well, it's important to make a good first impression," Nasri replied. "Am I really the first to arrive?"

"Fashionably early, let's say."

"Good."

A robot directed Lady Nasri to her seat. As she sat down, a figure appeared in the doorway. Dressed in a tunic of dark red with black pants, Lord Andre Santos paused before crossing the threshold.

Veber laughed, spreading her arms apart. "Come in! Come in! There's nothing to be afraid of."

The ship captain approached and kissed the back of Veber's hand.

"That remains to be seen," he replied with a narrow smirk.

"This room is perfectly safe," she assured him. "The Five Families have had many a summit here and managed not to kill each other."

"Did you add the extra two chairs for our arrival?" Santos asked, motioning toward the table.

"Every chair represents a house," Veber replied, "but the table still has enough room."

Lady Veber and her guest walked to the table. A robot had already brought Lady Nasri a wine glass. Santos nodded to her.

"Captain," he said.

"I prefer *Lady Nasri*, if you don't mind," she replied.

"It looks like you've traded a flight suit for dresses now," Santos remarked.

"And *you've* finally picked your family colors I see," Nasri said.

"Black and red seemed fitting somehow," Santos replied.

She scoffed. "Only for a revolutionary..."

Lady Veber cleared her throat.

"We'll have time to discuss the finer details of symbolism," she said, "but first let's sit down and eat dinner. I'm starving and nothing good ever comes from an empty stomach."

The others agreed and everyone took a seat while a small cadre of robots brought in trays of food and drink, all of it looking delicious and expensive.

When Annis the handmaiden entered Philip Veber's private quarters, she found the main room dark and musty and the window shutters closed. An older woman with a round face, Annis put down the tray containing Philip's dinner and grasped the octagram amulet around her neck.

From the bedroom, shimmers of light shone through a crack in the doorway. The handmaiden passed through the main room and slowly pushed the door open. Inside, Philip's bedroom, which had been quite open and large, was now crowded with cages containing a menagerie of different animals. Instead of making noise, they each seemed eerily quiet.

On the far side of the room, where the bed formerly sat, Philip Veber stooped over a wooden table, his back to the handmaiden.

"Lord Philip?" Annis asked.

Philip straightened and turned. On the table, a small mammal the size of a cat lay immobile. Annis noted that the animal was completely shaved and archaic lettering was tattooed across its body. Also, the same octagram design as the handmaiden's amulet was carved crudely into the table top.

"What is it, Annis?" Philip replied, somewhat irritated.

"I brought your meal," she said.

"Thank you."

Curiosity overtaking her, the handmaiden stared at the creature on the table. "What are you doing?"

Philip's eyes brightened, as if happy to share his work.

"Come," he said. "I'll show you."

Annis approached the table. For the first time, she noticed a soldering iron beside the animal. She also smelled the faint odor of burnt flesh.

"I should really thank you," Philip went on, putting his hand on the handmaiden's shoulder. "All of this is because of you."

"Really, sir?"

"Oh, yes. If it wasn't for you, my mother would have never known of the Necronea and the gifts they offer us."

"They give hope," Annis said.

"More than that!" Philip said excitedly. "Death is no longer to be feared! We can now harness death and make it do our bidding..."

The handmaiden's eyes settled again on the motionless animal on the table. "Is that what this is?"

"Absolutely! Since re-awakening, fresh knowledge has been flooding into my mind as if the Grand Master was talking to me..."

"The Grand Master? Do you mean Ghazul?"

"Yes, of course! His mind talks to mine and each day my abilities grow stronger!"

"To do what?"

"To reanimate the *dead*!"

The handmaiden's heart was beating rapidly. She found it hard to catch her breath.

"Lord Philip," she said. "I didn't know this would happen..."

The young Veber smiled. "It's no matter. I still have you to thank."

Annis bowed her head. "I do my best to serve you."

"Indeed," Philip replied. "I appreciate all that you've done."

"Thank you."

"But," he went on, "there's one more thing I need to ask of you. Only then will my powers be complete..."

Much to Sheba Nasri's surprise, the meal Lady Veber served was no better than what her own robots fed her back home. Nasri sat at the round table with Lady Veber between her and Lord Santos in his ridiculous red tunic. The rest of the chairs were vacant but with place settings nonetheless, as if the other royal families might show up at any moment.

"Such a delicious meal," Nasri lied, putting down her fork.

"Thank you, my dear," Veber said, casting a glance at Santos, hidden behind his napkin.

"Yeah," he said, wiping his mouth. "I'm going to get fat if I keep eating like this!"

"Actually," Veber said, "there's pills for that. Little nanos will burn the extra calories for you."

"Of course there is..." he murmured.

"Let me guess," Nasri remarked, "you're against pills that keep you from getting fat?"

"It's no coincidence that the rich are fat cats," Santos said. "But at least you can tell who the enemy is..."

Nasri rolled her eyes. "Nobody's your enemy here, Andre."

"Said the spider to the fly..."

Robots brought cups of coffee and tea from the kitchens. Both Nasri and Santos chose coffee while Veber preferred tea. Nasri poured sugar and cream into her cup while Santos kept his coffee black.

"I must agree with Lady Nasri," Veber said finally. "I hope you don't view any of us as your enemy, Lord Santos."

"As I see it," Santos replied, "I'm a fly in the ointment that you rich folks have been bathing in for centuries."

Nasri scoffed loudly, showing her scorn.

"There are no crowds here to rabble-rouse," she said. "You can stop with the rhetoric."

"It's the truth!"

"Alright," Veber said calmly, holding her hand above her tea cup. "We're not here to insult each other."

"Why *are* we here?" Nasri asked.

"My family has always enjoyed the position of mediator," Veber replied. "As a largely neutral party, we've resolved many of the royal squabbles that have flared up over the years."

"That was with *five* families," Nasri went on. "Now with seven, does your family really have the same clout?"

Lady Veber smiled but Nasri thought she heard teeth grinding behind those lips.

"Anyway," Nasri said, "I've shown my willingness to live within the rules of royalty. I fully intend to be a productive voice in our dealings. I don't see any value in rocking the boat."

Now it was Santos' turn to scoff. "That's pretty obvious!"

Nasri pointed a slender finger at the captain. "Do you really think you can change a system that's been around for seven hundred years?"

"I can certainly try!" Santos said.

"As one of the original Five Families," Veber said, nodding to Lord Santos, "I want to assure you that your voice is being heard. If there are changes you feel should be made, we are willing to listen."

Santos, perhaps not expecting that response, raised an eyebrow and then his shoulders in a shrug.

"If that's true," he said, "then maybe things will work out."

"Good," Veber replied.

"But words are cheap," he continued. "I want to see real action before I'm convinced."

"Of course," Veber said gently. "Now, I'm sure the two of you are tired after your trip from the capital. My staff has prepared suites for both of you to rest. I hope they'll be to your satisfaction."

Skirting the edge of the Lokeren atmosphere, Magnus Black opened the airlock of the *Starling* to the outside. He took a moment to peer through the visor of his vacuum suit at the turquoise oceans and an island chain, like a string of pearls, more than twenty miles below. Magnus then took a step through the hatch and began falling.

Plummeting past the speed of sound, Magnus checked the altimeter several times before deploying his chute. A black paraglider, coated in sensor-absorbing material, unfurled, slowing his descent to a manageable speed. Once Magnus reached an altitude with sufficient oxygen, he removed his helmet and let it fall away. The wind rushed across his closely shaved scalp. Still high above the water, he could already smell the salt in the air.

Magnus timed his drop to coincide with the setting of Lokeren's sun. The orange light was receding along the distant horizon as Magnus rode the paraglider several miles toward his target. When the Veber estate became visible, it was a small incandescent spot growing larger and brighter with each passing minute. From his research of the mansion's security, Magnus knew they were only scanning for vehicles at least the size of a gravcar. They could also detect a transmat signature, but since the *Starling* lacked a transmat, the point was moot.

While still in orbit, Magnus received an encrypted transmission, giving him more details about who he came to kill. He now knew the room and when the target would be there. Tracing the message back, Magnus was surprised by its source.

Now in darkness, the estate was cast in deep shadow except for the walkways lit with small lamps. Magnus knew there were spotlights too, but he hoped to avoid seeing those turned on until he was already gone.

Magnus landed softly on the roof, the white gravel barely making a sound. Bundling the paraglider into a ball, Magnus hid it beside an AC unit, along with the rest of his vacuum suit and rigging. He took stock of his position, orienting himself with the map of the compound he had memorized. Moving quietly to the edge of the roof, he took a quick look over the side and was pleased to see the balcony he expected.

With a rope, Magnus lowered himself down. Light, filtered through sheer curtains, came from within a suite beyond a pair of French doors. Magnus was prepared to pick the lock, but trying the handle, he found the doors were unlocked. Through the glass, he could see someone moving.

Magnus waited until the person disappeared into a side room before he cracked the doors open and crept inside. The air, especially compared to the cool breeze outside on the balcony, was muggy and warm. The furniture was mostly teak and rattan, the dark browns contrasting with the white linens covering cushions and pillows around the main room.

Magnus removed a wand-like tube from his belt, pointing the device at the doorway where the target had gone. When the man reappeared, he was wearing a pair of black pants and a red tunic, opened down the side to reveal a plain undershirt.

"Good evening," Lord Santos said calmly.

Magnus pointed the tube at him.

"Is that a gun?" the captain asked.

"Something like that," Magnus replied.

"So, you've come to kill me?"

"Something like that."

"Shouldn't you get on with it then?"

Magnus lowered the weapon a few inches, but still pointed it in Santos' direction.

"I received final details about your location while I was still on my ship," Magnus said. "It was encrypted but I managed to trace its origin."

"Oh, really?" Santos replied, his eyebrow arched.

"It came from this room."

A sly grin rose in the corner of Santos' mouth. After a pause, he shrugged and smiled broadly. "So it did."

Magnus shook his head. "Why put a hit out on yourself? Do you have a death wish?"

"One dead martyr is worth a thousand screaming revolutionaries," Santos replied.

"That's nuts."

"Is it?" Santos asked. "I want to bring down this empire, but I've seen enough revolutions to know one voice, even a well-placed one, is easily drowned out by others. Change, I mean *real* change, comes from extraordinary circumstances. A shocking assassination for example..."

Magnus nodded. "Batshit crazy."

"Well, let's agree to disagree," Santos went on. "But I paid you to do a job and I expect you to finish it."

"How will I get paid the rest if you're dead?"

"It's all arranged, Mr. Black. I promise you'll get what's owed."

"Fine," Magnus replied and raised the wand.

"What is that, by the way?" Santos asked.

"It's a sonic weapon," Magnus said. "Silent but effective."

Santos chuckled, but his laugh died quickly as an invisible wave ruptured the blood vessels in his lungs. He coughed and blood poured from the sides of his mouth. He fell to his knees before collapsing onto his side. His eyes, still open, were red where they were once white.

Magnus prepared to leave, but the door to the suite burst open and several robots, each armed with blasters, came charging into the room. Magnus fired the sonic wand, but the weapon had no effect on the robots.

"Drop it!" one of them shouted.

Seeing no other alternative, Magnus let the tube fall to the carpet. From behind the robots, a woman came forward. Magnus recognized her immediately.

"Who are you?" Lady Veber asked.

Magnus didn't bother answering.

"No matter," she said. "It won't be hard to find out."

"How did you know I was here?" Magnus asked.

Veber smiled. "There are hidden cameras in all the suites."

Magnus closed his eyes. "That's disappointing."

"I'm sure," Veber replied and motioned to the robots. "Take him away."

Bentley the butlerbot found his master, Lord Devlin Maycare, hidden behind a stack of books in the Maycare estate library.

"Catching up on your reading?" the robot quipped.

Maycare's head popped up, his usually robust and carefully manicured hair tangled and flattened.

"Don't be an ass," he said.

"My apologies, sir."

"Where did we get *all* these books?" Maycare asked.

"Well," the robot replied, "most have been in your family's possession for generations. However, since you hired Miss Doric, she has acquired a good deal more."

"Why so many? Shouldn't they be scanned in somewhere?"

"I suspect a good many are," Bentley said, "but it's good to have the originals on hand safe and sound, so to speak."

"It's just as well," Maycare sighed. "I'm not much of a reader. I don't suppose some of these have been made into holofilms?"

"Doubtful, sir."

Maycare sat back heavily in his chair. Some of the books toppled over, sliding down the pile onto the table and then onto the floor with a *thump*.

"Damn it," he said.

"No luck helping Lady Veber, I take it?" Bentley asked.

"Of course not!"

"You *could* just apologize to Miss Doric."

"No!"

"Pride can be a painful thing," the robot said. "It often gets in the way of what we want."

Maycare glowered at the stack in front of him. "If only I was smarter."

"Yes, that *would* be helpful, sir."

His master glared at the robot instead of the books.

"You can be replaced, Bentley."

The robot shrugged his mechanical shoulders.

"Are you familiar with *King Lear*, sir?" he asked.

"No, I've never heard of the Lear family," Maycare replied.

"Actually," Bentley said, "it's a play from an ancient Englishman named William Shakespeare."

"Is it a holofilm?"

"Yes."

"Well, I still haven't seen it."

"Anyway," Bentley went on, a pained look in his eyes, "it's about a king who's surrounded by people who only tell him what he wants to hear. In fact, he exiles one of his own daughters, the only person brave enough to tell the truth."

"I can see why I didn't see the film..."

"The only other person who tells the king what he actually needs to hear is the king's fool."

"So?"

"The point I'm making, sir," Bentley replied, "is that every king must have a fool or risk becoming a fool himself."

Maycare stared blankly at his butlerbot.

"Nevermind, sir," the robot said. "I'll bring in your dinner."

CHAPTER THIRTEEN

The forest grew brighter as a heavy morning mist hung among the low branches. Sisa Oakhollow, her hands tightly bound, followed the Katak warrior in front of her while several others trailed behind. The leading frogling trudged ahead, his webbed feet making hardly any sound among the leaves and twigs. His back, moist and shiny, reflected dapples of dawn piercing the canopy from above.

"Where are you taking me?" the girl asked, but the front warrior said nothing. None of them had spoken a word since dragging her out of bed and into the night. She could sense the froglings were agitated. They had lost many fighters in the attack.

Sisa reached out with her mind.

Why are you doing this? she thought.

The lead Katak stopped. Turning to face her, his throat swelled and he made a loud croaking noise. In her head, Sisa heard him think, *Be quiet!*

They started walking again, but after an hour or two, they stopped. The warriors formed a perimeter in a semi-circle between the girl and a stand of birch trees.

Sisa heard movement from the trees. Several small humanoids emerged. Each looked like a toadstool, tiny eyes peering out from under a cap of red with white spots. Their arms and legs were short, sprouting from their squat bodies. Like the Katak, they carried spears.

Sporemen, Sisa thought.

The froglings chirped excitedly, thrusting their weapons in the air. The sporemen did the same.

"Alright," Sisa said. "Everybody calm down."

The lead Katak shook his spear at her, then pointed back at the fungus people.

Sisa formed words in her mind. *What do you want from me?*

Translate, he thought back. *What do they want?*

Concentrating, Sisa focused on one of the sporemen. As a fungus, his thoughts were difficult to understand at first, but after a few minutes, Sisa began comprehending the situation.

You're trespassing, she told the frogling telepathically. *They want you to leave.*

No, the leader replied. *We must go this way.*

Well, I don't think they're going to let you, she thought.

So be it!

With one of the froglings guarding Sisa, the others rushed into the trees and attacked the sporemen. The two sides squared off, each lunging with spears. Sisa could feel their fury and fear, mixed with her own. She didn't understand why any of this was happening, why they kidnapped her, or why this was so important that someone had to die because it. Mostly, Sisa just wanted to be home in bed, the smell of her mother's hotcakes wafting down the hall from the kitchen.

The Katak shouted when they died, croaking their last breath, but the fungus people, gentle in their own way, made no sounds at all. They fell quietly, like the morning fog burning off in the sunshine.

The treetop village was in uproar, the Gowyn townspeople running from one platform to another, looking for their missing Sylvan. From what anyone could tell, only Sisa had been taken. To Silandra, her mother, this made it all the worse.

"Why would they take my daughter?" she asked the others, but their concerned stares held no answers.

Bragor arrived with a few of his usual patrons, all armed with blasters.

"We've searched the whole village," Bragor said. "There's no sign of her."

A foot taller than the others, Sir Golan stood at the back of the crowd. Squire was beside him.

"I will find her," the knight announced.

Everyone turned, their eyes fixed on this stranger that some of them were seeing for the first time. A crescendo of their murmuring voices escalated until Sir Golan spoke again.

"By my sword," he said grandly, "I shall return her safely."

Bragor's mouth was forming a question when Silandra interrupted.

"I'll go with you," she said.

"No," Bragor said. "I should go."

"I can sense her," Silandra said, shaking her head. "You can't."

Bragor looked at his feet but said nothing.

Sir Golan and the robot waded through the crowd until they reached the mother. Silandra caught a glimpse of Mel at their heels, her body hidden behind the taller Sylvans.

"Do you have any idea where they might've taken her?" the knight asked.

"I don't know," Silandra replied. "They've never attacked us before. Usually, we have good relations with them."

"They must have towns somewhere..." Mel said.

"They have settlements in the swamp to the West," Bragor said.

"Alright then," Sir Golan said. "That's where we'll start."

"Shouldn't we send a larger group?" Bragor asked. "Everyone wants to help."

"If Sisa is a captive," Squire replied. "It would be better if we didn't appear hostile."

"Well, I'm going..." Mel said.

"Why?" Sir Golan asked.

"Ah, because your robot might need more repairs," Mel replied. "I'm very serious about my service plan."

"Service plan?" Squire said.

"Your money back, guaranteed!" Mel said. "Also, I threw in a few things and I want to make sure they work okay."

"What kind of things?" the robot asked.

Mel looked off to the side.

"You know," she said, "upgrades..."

They followed the Katak tracks into the thickening woods. Sir Golan, in full armor, led the search party with Squire behind him.

Mel and Silandra walked together. The noises from the town faded into the background.

"Why did you say only *you* could sense Sisa?" Mel asked.

"Only Sylvan women are psi sensitive," Silandra replied. "Mothers and their daughters are especially linked."

"Can you feel her now?"

"Only weakly."

"But at least that means she's alive..." Mel said.

"Oh, yes," Silandra smiled. "If I didn't sense her at all, I don't know what I'd do right now."

"You two must be pretty close," Mel said.

"Sisa was always independent," Silandra said. "She doesn't like how aware I am of her feelings. She calls it *spying*."

"I never knew my mom."

"No?"

"I was an orphan," Mel went on. "I never knew either of my parents."

"I'm sorry."

"But Sisa's father is still around..."

"Bragor is a good father," Silandra said. "He loves Sisa very much."

"It must drive him crazy knowing he can't understand her the way you can."

Silandra laughed softly until it became a sigh.

"It's not always a blessing," she said. "When she's happy, I'm happy, but when she's sad, I can't help but feel sad too."

The search party wound their way between the larger trees, cutting through brush with Sir Golan's sword. The trail cut by the Katak before them made the going easier and, Mel hoped, faster. The tracks themselves, four-toed feet, slightly webbed, were easy to distinguish from Sisa's own tiny soles.

"How far are we from Gowyn?" Mel asked the robot.

"My GPS says approximately three miles," Squire replied.

"Good to hear your satellite tracking is still working."

"I must admit that Sir Golan is not well-versed in technology," Squire said. "My capabilities have often proved useful to him."

"Are you saying he can't use a computer?"

"It's not that he can't. He simply chooses not to."

"Why?" Mel asked.

"He prefers the simplicity of less modern things."

"But he has you, doesn't he?"

"He's not a Luddite, Miss Freck."

"Sorry," Mel replied. "I'm sure it's nice to have you around."

"One would hope," Squire said, "but I faithfully endeavor to be useful whenever I can..."

Sir Golan stopped suddenly.

"What's wrong?" Mel asked.

"There's been a battle," he replied, pointing Rippana, his sword, at several mounds sticking out of the leaves and grass. Drawing closer, Mel recognized some of the shapes as Katak corpses.

"Sisa!" Silandra started but stopped herself. "No, she's not here. I can still sense her elsewhere."

Among a stand of birch trees, froglings and fungus creatures lay motionless, spears stuck into the ground like poles marking a burial place.

"These are sporemen," Silandra said. "This is their territory."

"Perhaps they didn't approve of trespassers," the knight said grimly.

Something moved, snapping a fallen branch. Sir Golan was instantly on guard.

In the midday shadows, a large mound with four trunk-like legs moved toward them. At the end of a long neck, a face like a thick flower with four petals turned in their direction. The petals peeled open, revealing a structure like a starfish full of teeth.

"Get back!" Silandra shouted. "It's a Kamal Maut!"

Sir Golan took a step backwards while Mel hid behind a tree.

"According to my translation," Squire said, "that means *Death Lotus*."

"Thanks," Mel said. "Very helpful."

As if ready to roar, the Death Lotus opened its maw wider, but instead of sound, a cloud came pouring out.

"Spores," Silandra said. "They're poisonous if you breathe them in..."

"I can't get close without passing through the cloud," the knight said.

"Maybe you should've brought a gun!" Mel shouted, still behind the tree.

"Didn't you mention upgrades to my system?" Squire asked.

"Of course!" she replied. "Use the displacement field."

"I fail to see how that would—" Squire began.

"Just do it!"

A dome of blue energy, with Squire at the center, burst into existence, enveloping the party beneath it.

"Now, walk toward that thing," Mel said.

The robot started toward the Death Lotus, while Sir Golan remained in between. As Squire got closer, the toxic spores collected against the outside surface of the dome.

"Keep going!" Mel urged. "Just don't let its mouth puncture the dome..."

The displacement field pushed against the creature, bending inward like a hand pushing against a balloon.

"You can attack it," Mel told the knight. "The field is one-way."

Sir Golan took a swipe at the Death Lotus, cutting into its mossy hide. Spurts of blood sprayed against the outside of the dome.

"Now I have you!" the knight shouted, sending his sword through the barrier and into the creature.

The Death Lotus staggered as its front legs gave out, falling clumsily on its side.

"Splendid!" Squire said.

Mel came out, brushing herself off.

"Yeah, well," she said, "it works against solid objects as long as their mass isn't too big. I figured it would work in this case..."

"But you weren't sure?" Sir Golan asked, his eyebrow raised.

"Consider this a field test," Mel replied.

Sisa felt sick.

The froglings had waded into the sporemen, killing them all while losing several of their own. Sisa wanted to throw up, but the head Katak who had survived kept tugging at her bindings, pulling her along.

The forest floor beneath her feet became damp as the land turned swampy. Also, the daylight began to fade and Sisa found herself tripping over roots lurking in the gloom around her feet, now soaking wet. The noises changed, too, as insects and lesser amphibians filled the air with a cacophony of different cries.

When Sisa saw the first skull, she didn't recognize it at first. A series of long stakes, each crowned with a skull, led the way into the Katak village where campfires drew the froglings home like moths. Huts, made from driftwood and held together with mud, were nestled on bits of land surrounded by pools of water.

The townspeople came out to greet the arriving band of raiders. They gathered around Sisa, peering with wide eyes at her strange appearance. They took her to the center of the village where a large bonfire was burning. On the other side of the flames, from an earthen lodge larger than the surrounding huts, a Katak with black and yellow skin came tottering out. A vest made from dried reeds hung on his chest and he carried a staff with yet another skull on the end. Sisa wondered where they were getting them all.

He swayed back and forth from one webbed foot to the other until he was next to the girl. He looked her up and down, only then giving a loud, approving croak. His breath smelled so rancid, Sisa nearly choked.

What do you want from me? she asked, reaching into the old frogling's mind. Distorted images flooded back to her.

Sisa screamed.

"Something's wrong," Silandra said.

"What is it?" Mel asked.

"I felt Sisa crying out," Silandra replied. "Her thoughts were of something horrible, grotesque..."

Sir Golan stopped, both he and Squire looking back.

"Ladies?" the knight inquired.

"I think we should hurry," Mel said.

"Without question," Sir Golan replied, "but we've lost the trail in this swamp..."

The forest, and the solid ground from which it grew, had turned to doughy mosses and muddy ponds filled with intractable reeds. The webbed footprints ended at the water's edge.

Silandra focused her mind, her brows furrowed as she stared into the deepening twilight. She pointed.

"That way," she said.

The knight started off again with Mel and Silandra following, but Squire remained where he stood.

"What is it?" Sir Golan asked, stopping.

"Terribly sorry," the robot replied. "I appear to be stuck."

The robot was in the process of sinking, the mud coming up to his shins and rising.

"This is quite embarrassing," Squire said.

Mel shook her head at him. "The ground's too soft."

"We need to hurry," Silandra said.

"Well, we can't just leave him like this!" Mel replied.

"Go on without me," Squire pleaded. "I'm sure I'll be perfectly fine here... alone in the dark."

Sheathing his sword, the knight picked up a fallen branch and wedged it into the muck around the robot's leg.

"While I press down," he said, addressing Mel and Silandra, "you two push until we break the suction of the mud."

The two women glanced at each other and then, together, began pushing on Squire as the knight laid his weight on the log. After a few attempts, the wet ground made an unappetizing sound and the robot came free.

On his back, Squire was emphatically appreciative.

"Thank you *so much*!" he said. "I was sure this would be my grave, neck deep in a bog."

"Forget it," Sir Golan said.

"As you wish. Deleting data file..."

In the mind of the Katak chief, Sisa saw a face, although it was more skull than alive. The eyes, suspended in the otherwise empty sockets, blazed fiery orange. With no lips, his teeth were bare, grinning a horrific smile. What skin remained was wrapped tightly like paper dried over centuries.

She heard her screams before realizing she was the one screaming. The chief poked her with his staff and she stopped.

The chief spoke to his tribe and the Kataks squawked in apparent approval. Sisa wasn't sure what he said, but she thought it meant something like *tribute* or maybe *gift*. Or was it *sacrifice*? She wasn't sure she wanted to know.

The frogling leader who had dragged Sisa halfway from her home to the Katak village became agitated. He grunted and pointed his spear at the girl and then back the way they had come. Sisa got the feeling he wasn't happy with whatever arrangement had been made. Perhaps the cost of the warriors that died was too high a price to pay, but the chief was having none of it. With his staff, he gestured at Sisa and pointed in the other direction, deeper into the swamp. Eventually, the warrior relented, pulling on her bindings again. Along with two other Katak, he led Sisa away.

They walked down another trail away from the village. The natural light gone, one of the froglings lit a torch. Hemmed in by darkness and vegetation, Sisa couldn't see much beyond the bobbing light. She became aware of shapes looming on either side of the trail. Most were about three feet tall but with smooth curves, making them unnatural in a jungle of jagged edges. They also leaned at odd angles as if a disturbance had pushed them up out of the ground. It was only until the frogling with the torch came closer to one that Sisa saw them for what they truly were. Like stone ghosts, they were gravestones that had sunk into the marshy ground. An immense cemetery, countless ages old, that time had flooded and forgotten.

Behind her, coming from the village, an explosion pierced the darkness.

Silandra said the Katak were normally peaceful, but Squire was finding that hard to believe as spears came flying out of the darkness. Up ahead, the bonfires of a village were visible.

"Should I use the displacement field?" Squire asked Mel.

"No!" she said. "It's too weak. Use your energy shield..."

"My what now?"

"The thing in your arm!"

Surprised, like finding he had an extra elbow, Squire noticed a button on his left arm. He pushed it and a field of translucent energy, three feet tall and two feet wide, materialized. He lifted the shield, deflecting a spear harmlessly into the underbrush.

"Get behind me," he said and both Mel and Silandra took cover at his back. Meanwhile, Sir Golan remained at the front, diverting incoming spears with his sword.

Mel reached into her satchel and removed a spherical object, slightly larger than her tiny hand.

"What's that?" Silandra asked.

"A stun grenade," she replied. "It creates a blast but it shouldn't hurt anyone."

Mel chucked the grenade toward the village. A moment later, one of the bonfires exploded in a shower of burning logs. Several froglings fled in a panic, their bodies covered in flames.

"Oops..." Mel said, her eyes widening.

"Let's go!" Sir Golan shouted, rushing forward.

By the time Squire and the others reached the knight, Sir Golan had dispatched the defenders and had their chief on the ground, the tip of Rippana at his throat.

"Don't kill him!" Silandra cried, gripping the knight's shoulder.

Sisa's mother knelt beside the elder Katak. The chief murmured a low croak, his eyes glazed by age. Silandra remained still, focusing on the frogling.

"What's she doing?" Squire asked Mel.

"Talking with him," she replied.

"Telepathy?"

"I guess so."

"Can you upgrade me with that?" Squire wondered.

"I don't think robots can use psionics," Mel said.

"It would be nice to know what people are thinking."

"Maybe..."

Silandra stood, but the old chief was no longer breathing, his eyes still open but lifeless.

"What did he say?" Sir Golan asked.

"There's an ancient cemetery farther to the West," Silandra replied. "They've taken Sisa there."

"Did he say why they kidnapped her in the first place?" Mel asked.

"I'm not sure," the Sylvan went on. "Some kind of offering..."

"To whom?" Mel asked.

"He said a strange, decaying man came to the village one day promising everlasting life if the chief gave him a sacrifice. The chief was old and dying, so he agreed."

"A lot of good that did him," Mel said, giving the dead chief a light kick.

"Please, let's hurry," Silandra urged. "I sense her fear."

"Onward!" Sir Golan shouted.

With the warrior in front, Sisa in the middle, and the two other froglings in the back, the group followed a meandering path through the cemetery. Sisa, pulled along by the Katak warrior, kept a telepathic link with him so she could understand what he was thinking.

Keep moving, he said in her thoughts.

What is this place? she asked.

The garden of the dead, he replied.

After a few minutes, they reached a crypt of white marble, tilted slightly, with a pair of torches burning on either side of the entrance. From the interior, multiple creatures appeared through the doorway. Each was humanoid, hunched over, and at times using their hands to steady themselves as they moved. Their skin, where not covered by filthy rags, looked diseased and partially rotted.

Ghuls, the warrior said.

What do they want? Sisa replied.

You.

Sisa shrank away but the warrior yanked her back.

"No!" she said aloud.

In the distance, in the direction of the village, her mother's voice cut through the night.

"Sisa!"

The girl struggled against the Katak warrior, but the other two froglings pushed her from behind.

"No!" Sisa screamed.

The Ghuls, three in all, met them just outside the crypt. The warrior chirped something from deep in his throat, handing the girl to the nearest of the creatures.

Sisa screamed again and, in the distance, her mother's voice began shouting her name. The girl could see a light approaching, but still far off. She kicked at the Ghul, but he was surprisingly strong. He dragged her toward the crypt entrance.

"Sisa!" shouted Silandra's voice.

"Help! Help me!"

Past the threshold, the stench inside the tomb filled Sisa's nostrils. She made another lunge toward the entrance, but the Ghul gripped her arm tightly as the other two tugged at the heavy metal door.

Seeing the warrior still outside, Sisa thrust her thoughts into his.

Don't do this! she yelled.

It's already done, he replied.

She heard her mother still calling her name as the door shut. Then there was only silence and the entombing dark.

CHAPTER FOURTEEN

Sylvia Flax could smell Walter Ruggles' aftershave. Hunkered down in the chilly, unlit hold of a Celadon starship, she recognized it instantly and knew he was somewhere among the other passengers, all held captive in the darkened room. Apparently, he had survived the pirate attack after all.

When Flax first got a whiff of Ruggles' cologne, she was sitting in his cabin on the *Jewel of Amann*. It was one of several things about him that annoyed her.

"Why do you wear those glasses?" she had asked, sitting in his room.

"To see," Ruggles replied matter-of-factly.

"Obviously," she said, looking up from her datapad, "but why not get your eyes corrected?"

"I have astigmatism."

"What about implants?"

"Not on *my* salary..."

Flax sighed, tilting her head.

"You're quite a catch, Mr. Ruggles," she said.

At that moment, the ship rocked sharply, and an alarm went off in the corridor. The jolt knocked the datapad from Flax's hand. It slid across the floor and under the bed.

"Well, shit!" Flax said.

"It's the IDEA people!" Ruggles shouted in a panic. "They found me!"

"Don't be ridiculous," Flax replied.

The lights flickered and Flax felt the artificial gravity fluctuate. Her stomach turned.

Ruggles was heading toward the closet.

"Where are you going?" Flax asked.

He tapped the control, opening the closet door.

"What do you think?" he said.

"If IDEA can track you in the middle of nowhere, I'm sure they'll find you in a closet."

Sounds of explosions and blaster fire filtered through the walls and floor. Flax considered leaving, perhaps to find someone from the crew, but Ruggles objected.

"Stay with me!" he pleaded.

"That's sweet, Walter, but I don't plan on spending my last moments with you."

The door to the corridor slid open and a small, green-skinned man stood in the threshold. His head was too big for his body and his nose and ears were too big for his head. Everyone stared at each other until Flax jumped up from her chair, crossing the tiny cabin in a single step. She lunged at the man, punching him on the nose and knocking him down.

The little green man cupped his nose as blood poured from between his fingers. He was also screaming.

Flax touched the controls, closing the door.

"What is that?" Ruggles asked.

"Celadon I think," Flax replied. "Nasty little bastards..."

Finding some electrical cord, Flax tied the Celadon's hands and feet. Mostly to stop the noise he was making, she also tied a piece of cloth torn from the bed sheet around his mouth. The blood was already starting to dry around his nose.

"Now what?" Ruggles asked.

"Help me stick him in the closet."

"But *I* was going to hide in there..."

"Sorry, hero," she replied snidely. "We're going to take his gun and find a lifeboat or something. We don't want to get caught by these guys."

"Do you think they work for IDEA?"

"No!"

Although they left the cabin together, Flax and Ruggles quickly became separated amid the confusion of Celadon pirates and panicking passengers. In the end, Flax was captured, disarmed, and hauled aboard a corsair starship. Now, crouched in the hold, she felt both relieved that Ruggles managed not to die, and irritated that she had not done better than him. With a sarcastic smile, she realized they were literally in the same boat.

With the first name of *Bortok* and the last name *The Enslaver*, the leader of the Ougluks had a reputation for brutality that served him well. Six feet six inches tall, with wide, muscular shoulders, he intimidated nearly everyone he met. Even so, in his private quarters inside the Ougluk base on an abandoned asteroid, Bortok considered himself more of an art lover.

On the wall, a large computer monitor hung in a gilded frame like an expensive painting. Images of famous artworks cycled across the screen as Bortok reclined in a comfortable armchair.

The first picture, *Inevitable Conclusion* by the Magna artist Zhug-Doja, showed a city burning against a blackened sky. The next few paintings were Gordian still lifes featuring, for the most part, casks of beer surrounded by sausages. While Bortok appreciated the subject matter, he found it visually uninteresting. However, these were still a far cry better than anything the Dahl had produced. With their idyllic landscapes of pink blossoms and wispy waterfalls, they made the Enslaver want to choke himself.

The next piece was by a human painter named Goya, titled *Saturn Devouring His Son*.

Say what you will about humans, Bortok thought, *they know how to make great art.*

Hearing a chime, he watched the painting on the screen dissolve into the face of a man who looked similar to a Dahl except for his bright, vermilion skin and dark red hair.

"What do you want, Cirion?" Bortok asked.

The Sarkan, or Red Dahl as they were also called, stared from the screen with a sour expression.

"The Celadons have arrived with their latest shipment," Cirion replied.

"Get them ready for me. I'll be there in a bit..."

Before the connection blinked out, Bortok caught a glimpse of Cirion rolling his eyes.

The Red Dahl may love their psionics, Bortok thought, *but it's hard to cast a spell with a broken neck...*

After getting dressed, the Enslaver left his quarters and made his way through the tunnels carved from the surrounding asteroid. It had been a mining colony long ago before he had found it abandoned. Nobody knew where it was, except him and his men. Hidden among the other floating rocks in the otherwise uninhabited star system, it was the perfect hideout from the Imperial Navy.

Bortok walked into an open chamber with a high ceiling and a deep hole dug in the center. Two bare-chested Ougluks brawled in the pit, with only their fists as weapons. The Enslaver liked a little blood sport before seeing the newest meat the Celadons brought him. He hated those sniveling little pirates, but they did the dirty work for him. It was a good system.

Passing the pit and down another corridor, Bortok arrived at the hangar where a cargo ship was sitting on heavy struts. The bay door was already open and the captives were lined up in orderly rows.

Bortok didn't like what he saw.

Sylvia Flax stood in a line with other passengers from the *Jewel of Amann*. In the row behind her, she heard Walter Ruggles mumble about IDEA agents. She wasn't sure if he was certifiably insane or merely an imbecile. All she knew was, of her worst assignments, this was in the top five.

Besides the Celadons, Flax recognized the other brutes as Ougluks and remembered their reputation as slave peddlers. She had no idea where they had taken her, but when one of the Ougluks trudged in her direction, she knew she was in trouble.

He shouted at the Celadon corsairs in another language, motioning angrily at the humans. The main Celadon shrugged, which Flax took to mean "you get what you get." The big Ougluk boxed the ears of the Celadon, who fell moaning to the ground. The other Celadons jumped and chattered amongst themselves. The Ougluk shouted a few more words, curses most likely, before turning to the captives.

"I'm Bortok the Enslaver!" he shouted in standard Imperial. "Welcome to the rest of your life!"

He chuckled at his own joke.

That's never a good sign, Flax thought.

"Of course, I can't say how long that's going to be..." he went on.

Called it.

"Normally my Celadon brothers bring us people I can use," Bortok said. "Slaves need to be young, able folk. People I can sell to the highest bidder! I don't know what hole they dragged this miserable lot from, but you wouldn't fetch a pittance. You're a waste of my time, that's what you are!"

"See here!" someone said behind her.

Ah, crap, Flax thought.

The Ougluk's face, which was previously contorted into a scowl, flattened into a curious expression of interest.

"What's your name, sir?" he said with surprising respect.

"Walter Ruggles of IDEA Furniture."

"IDEA, huh?" Bortok said, looking worried. "I certainly don't want trouble with *them*."

"Well, I should hope not!" Ruggles replied, stepping forward. "We're nobody to trifle with, I assure you!"

The previously towering slave trader slouched as Ruggles approached.

"This has all been a terrible misunderstanding..." Ougluk said meekly.

"Really?" Ruggles replied.

Rising to his full height, Bortok straightened and slapped Ruggles' face, knocking the frail man to the ground and sending his glasses through the air, landing at Flax's feet.

"...that I give a shit who you work for!" he finished.

Curled in a fetal position, Ruggles whimpered quietly in a heap.

Flax wanted to do something. Her right foot edged forward just an inch, but she stopped herself before anyone could notice. There was no point sticking her neck out if they'd just end up dead.

Bortok leaned over and grabbed Ruggles by the collar and began dragging him the way the Ougluk had originally entered. Over his shoulder, he shouted at the Celadons.

"Bring the rest!"

On the monitor, the image of Bortok blinked off. Cirion groaned and turned away from the screen. Sometimes, dealing with these barbarians was just too much.

On this isolated rock in space, Cirion's office was his only sanctuary. His quarters were shared with Bortok's brutish subordinates, but here at least he had privacy. With the door shut, he could almost imagine being back home, far from these low-bred creatures, surrounded by his own kind. The Red Dahl were mental titans compared to the Ougluks and their stunted half-cousins, the Celadons. Laying back in a chair, Cirion stretched out his arm and, focusing his mind, manifested a twirling sphere of energy in the palm of his hand.

This is power, he thought. *The power to make something from nothing.*

He sneered, thinking about his own cousins, the Dahl. They once had everything, their fingers reaching throughout the galaxy. Then they threw it all away, turning inward and leaving their far-flung holdings to rot. The farthest outposts, isolated and forgotten, had to fend for themselves. It was there that the Sarkan evolved into a new people with their own beliefs and skin color.

Now look at the original Dahl, Cirion thought. *They grovel at the feet of the humans, complacent in the spread of the human plague across the stars. Only the Sarkan see the true path...*

The communicator in his ear chimed.

"Yes, sir?" he said.

A deep voice replied, "Come here at once."

"Understood."

Cirion collected his datapad and left his office, making sure the door was securely locked behind him. Through a passageway cut unevenly through the asteroid, he wound his way to a large chamber used as an assembly hall. Long tables ran the length of the room, leading, on the other end, to a raised platform. Standing on the stage, a Magna watched him with eyes blazing red.

Cirion's chest tightened.

"Ipak-Bog," the Sarkan said. "What can I do for you?"

The Magna was two feet taller than Cirion, wearing a kilt-like garment stretching to the floor. From the belt up, he was bare-skinned, revealing a massive, muscular body along with gray, ram-like horns. His voice rolled over the Red Dahl like thunder across a plain.

"What is your report?" Bog asked, but not as a question.

Shaking slightly, Cirion glanced at his datapad.

"A new shipment has arrived, sir," he said, almost whispering.

"And?"

"The quality seems... substandard."

Bog's eyes simmered, focusing directly on the slender-framed Sarkan.

"Disappointing," he said after a pause.

"But..." Cirion went on hurriedly, "there *is* something you might like."

"Go on."

"The Celadons downloaded the ship's passenger list and there appears to be a VIP aboard, a human named *Sylvia Flax.*"

Gradually, like a glacier working its way across a continent, Bog's mouth curled into a smile, or at least as close to one as Cirion had ever seen on the Magna's face.

The Celadons gathered the captives together and herded them through an arched tunnel into a main room where several Ougluks were assembled around a hole in the ground. They made room for the prisoners to get a view into the pit. Peering over the edge, Flax saw one of her burly captors, barely clothed and covered in horrific scars, standing below. The Ougluk was dirty and smeared with blood, but probably not his own.

Bortok lugged Ruggles to the lip of the pit, yanking him to his feet.

"I can't see what's happening..." Ruggles sputtered.

"Allow me to explain," Bortok replied, releasing his grip. "Down there, which I imagine is a fuzzy blob to you, is one of our less genteel enslavers. Frankly, he doesn't have the temperament to be a slave trader. He prefers smashing things."

"He sounds horrible," Ruggles said.

"Indeed he is!" Borok admitted. "Why don't you say hello?"

Bortok shoved Ruggles in the back, sending him like a rag doll into the pit. His arms and legs flailing in midair, the furniture salesman landed in a lump of poorly tailored clothes at the bottom.

Flax heard a muffled groan.

"Get up, human!" Bortok shouted. "There's no sport in just lying there!"

"Stay down!" Flax said without thinking.

"Shut up!" Bortok ordered, swiping the empty air in her direction. "No interference from anyone!"

Ruggles pulled himself to his knees and elbows, his head still resting on the dirt. He coughed, making a cloud of dust appear around him. With more effort, he got to his feet on wobbly legs.

"I'm blind without my glasses," he said.

"Look for the blurry mass of green in front of you," Bortok replied. "When he gets close enough to see, he's probably too close..."

"What?"

The Ougluk in the pit charged at Ruggles, who looked like an animal caught in the headlights of a truck. The brawler wrapped his thick arms around him as Ruggles gasped while the air in his lungs was squeezed out. His legs dangling, he managed to kick the Ougluk in the crotch. The brute dropped him, allowing Ruggles to scurry away to the far side of the hole.

"Low blows are against the rules, Mr. Ruggles," Bortok said. "Just kidding. There are no rules!"

In the pit, the Ougluk roared in anger and pain. Pounding his chest, he recovered quickly and charged toward Ruggles on the other end. The human didn't immediately react, perhaps not seeing the green behemoth rushing toward him. At the last second, his eyes suddenly wide, Ruggles darted out of the way with a loud, throaty shriek. He took refuge back where he had started, just below where Flax was standing.

"Isn't this fun?" Bortok asked with a wide grin. "Wait till he gets an arm torn off. That's always entertaining!"

His hair soaked in sweat, Ruggles squinted in the dark pit. On the other side, the Ougluk took his time, clearly recognizing his advantage. Flax watched them, knowing how this was going to end. It made her sick.

"Son of a bitch," she said and jumped into the hole.

Landing next to Ruggles, she shoved the glasses into his hands.

"Put these on, you idiot," she said.

"Who? What?" Ruggles stammered.

"Put 'em on!"

Obeying, he winced once he got a good look at the Ougluk sharing the pit with him.

"Good god!" he said.

"I distinctly said no interference!" Bortok raged, shaking his fist. "Was I talking to *myself?*"

Flax looked up.

"If you kill him," she said, "you'll have to kill me too!"

Bortok took a breath, calming himself.

"I see," he said. "As you humans say, that would be like throwing the baby out with the bathwater. Even an Ougluk wouldn't do that."

Flax nodded and smiled, surprised that it actually worked.

"That was sarcasm!" Bortok said. "Kill them both!"

"Stop!" someone ordered.

Bortok, Flax, and everyone else turned their heads. Next to the pit, a Magna stood beside a Red Dahl, tiny in comparison.

"What is this nonsense, Bortok?" the Magna said.

"Ipak-Bog," the Ougluk replied, staring at the ground. "We were just trying to have a good time..."

"By wasting livestock?" Bog asked. "I was unaware the needs of my home world meant so little to you."

"No! It was just a little fun."

"Get them out of there!"

CHAPTER FIFTEEN

Judicator Busa-Gul arrived at the Ministry of External Security with the information he had gathered while visiting the Talion Republic. The offices of the ministry were located on the Magna home world Diavol, in the Consilium, a dark pyramid overlooking the city of Oras Dracilor. The Consilium was, for all practical matters, the center of the Magna Supremacy government. Those who worked in the building also lived there and, for the remainder of their lives, never left.

Gul, in his golden kilt and spiraling horns, waited in the lobby, a room devoid of furnishings except for a slab of basalt serving as a bench. The walls and floor were black as slate, fixtures in the corners providing the barest minimum of light.

After many minutes, a pair of heavy doors opened and Gul rose from the bench and walked inside. Once the doors shut behind him, Gul became aware of a desk on the far side of another largely empty room. Like the lobby, the walls and floor were dark stone. Above the desk, the Magna emblem was carved into the rock. It was a crescent lying on its side with the points sticking up. Cradled between the points was a circle and, below the crescent to the left and right, two more circles. The whole of the emblem was encrusted with rubies, the red contrasting against the black of the walls.

"Come forward and report," a voice said from behind the desk. In a high-backed leather chair, a Magna sat with horns weathered by age. Around his neck, he wore a gold crescent hanging by a chain.

Gul crossed the long chamber until he was a few feet from the desk which he realized was cut from basalt like the bench outside.

"Minister," he said. "I have the information as requested."

"What did you find?" the minister replied.

"The K'thonian raiders have continued to plague the Tals, especially along the outskirts of their republic."

"That's not unusual."

"Correct, but the frequency and nature of the raids have changed," Gul said.

"Nature? What do you mean?"

"In the past, the K'thonian attacks seemed random, even malicious. The raiders appeared without warning and killed and destroyed whatever they could find. Recently, the raids have increased markedly and the Tals have noticed something peculiar. Instead of merely razing settlements, the K'thonians seem to be looking for something specific."

"Such as?"

"Books, Minister."

Gul heard a deep chuckle come from the other side of the desk.

"You must be joking," the minister said. "Those mindless savages aren't the reading type!"

"No, indeed," Gul replied. "In fact, I had an opportunity to study a K'thonian specimen — dead of course — and found the corpse surprisingly primitive. However, upon closer examination, I discovered the body contained several unused organs, remnants of an earlier time evolutionarily speaking. Also, the fact that the K'thonians use psionics suggests they were not always so backward."

The minister pulled at his chin, thinking deeply. After a long pause, he said, "Someone or something is pulling their strings."

"Indeed," Gul replied eagerly. "The K'thonians appear to be thralls of some sort, under the influence of some greater power."

"Obviously, the most important question is whether this poses a threat to our interests..."

"It's still too soon to tell, Minister."

After another pause, "Fine work, Judicator," the minister said. "You have impressed us yet again. I assure you, the Supremacy has not overlooked your achievements."

Gul bowed slightly. "Thank you."

"You may go," the minister said, waving toward the doors that were opening as he spoke.

The yacht of the Veber family reflected much of Lady Veber's own aesthetics. Unlike most starships, which featured metal walls and technology on constant display, the yacht's interior was more like the estate on Lokeren. The walls were painted in shades of white and pale blues. Ceramic tiles, decorated with the family's scallop motif, lined doorways and corridors. In Lady Veber's stateroom, where her style was most apparent, bare bulkheads were covered with paintings and lavish tapestries.

Resting comfortably on a chaise lounge, Lady Veber was deep in thought. With a start, she roused herself, blinking several times.

"Computer," she said, "call Lord Maycare's estate on Aldorus."

"Yes, My Lady," the computer responded.

One of the walls of the stateroom flickered and the larger-than-life face of Maycare's butlerbot appeared. Lady Veber wondered why he kept such an old model.

"My Lady," Bentley said. "Good to see you again."

"I want to talk to Devlin," Veber replied. "Is he available or has he gone gallivanting off somewhere?"

"No, he's here at present. Let me get him for you."

After several minutes, Lord Maycare appeared on the screen. His hair looked as if someone had tried, unsuccessfully, to comb a rat's nest with a rake. Also, an unkempt beard covered much of his face. The gray strands in the beard made him look older than Lady Veber had ever seen him.

"Good god, man!" she cried. "Have you been kidnapped?"

Maycare, clearing his throat, tried to mat down his unruly hair. "No."

"Are you ill?" Veber asked more calmly.

"Actually, I've been hard at work researching your son's condition."

"Researching? Don't you have people for that?"

"Well," Maycare replied, his eyes lowering, "there's been some employee turnover..."

Lady Veber huffed in exasperation.

"Listen, Devlin," she said, "Philip is getting worse by the day. I need you to find something — *anything* — that could help."

"I understand."

"I'm heading to Aldorus now—"

"Really?"

"Yes," she replied, "I have some unfinished business in Regalis, but I'll only be there a short time before returning home. It's important that you've made some progress before I do."

"Yes, Becca."

"I'm counting on you, Devlin!"

Maycare nodded. "Understood."

The screen went blank, returning the stateroom wall to its original appearance. Lady Veber pulled herself off the chaise lounge and left her quarters with a sense of determination in her stride. Taking a lift to a different deck, one less fancy than the one she had left, Veber stopped at a metal door and placed her hand against a palm sensor. The door slid open. Inside, Magnus Black sat on a bed, looking out the window.

"It's a better view than a prison cell," Veber said.

Lady Nasri found herself eating cookies and drinking tea with Lord Tagus II in his West End estate. The room, with its Victorian style and blazing fireplace, was the same as last time, but the circumstances were vastly different. The old man took a sip and placed his cup on the coffee table in front of the large couch they both shared.

"This was not exactly what I had in mind," he said.

"In what way?" she replied.

"One doesn't usually kill the head of a royal household."

"I told you," Nasri insisted, "I had nothing to do with it!"

One of his bony shoulders, beneath his well-worn, black and yellow tunic, rose in a feeble shrug.

"You must admit," he continued, "the timing of his death was not ideal. It has raised a good many questions, most of them shouted rather *loudly*."

"The hysteria of the general public means nothing. The truth remains that I am innocent!"

"I hope that's true, Lady Nasri. The consequences otherwise..."

Sitting in silence, Tagus took another cookie and, taking a bite, chewed laboriously. Hearing the slow, crunching sounds coming from the old man made Nasri cringe. She focused on the flames in the fireplace.

"On the other hand," Tagus said finally, "without an heir, the House of Santos is no more and we're left with six families instead of seven."

"Is that a good thing?" Nasri asked.

"Well," he replied, "there's no one to break a tie if the families find themselves evenly split."

"I suppose a stalemate is better than losing."

"Rightly so."

A butlerbot came to the room, apologizing for the intrusion.

"What is it?" Tagus asked.

"Lady Veber is here to see you," the robot said.

Nasri felt herself turning red, but hoped the dimly lit room would keep her secret.

"Well, send her in obviously," Tagus replied.

Lady Veber swept through the doorway in a well-tailored gown. *A bit overdressed*, Nasri thought.

"What a pleasure to see you," Tagus said, standing momentarily until Veber took a seat in the chair across from the couch. "Would you like some tea?"

"No, thank you," Veber replied, her mouth in a tight smile.

"What brings you here?" the old man asked.

"I wanted to talk to you about the death of Lord Santos," she replied, glancing at Nasri beside him on the sofa.

"As I explained to Lord Tagus," Nasri spoke up, "I don't know who killed Andre and I'm just as upset as anyone about what happened."

"There's a great many people upset, actually," Veber said. "VOX News won't stop talking about it."

"It's troubling," Tagus agreed, "but what can be done? Do you have any leads as to who might have been involved?"

"As a matter of fact," Veber said, leaning in, "I do."

From a shadow in the corner of the room, a figure appeared. He was dressed in black with hair shaved close to the scalp. The light from the fire danced along the features of his face.

Lady Nasri gasped while Lord Tagus merely surveyed him with detached interest.

"A friend of yours?" Tagus asked, turning to Lady Veber.

"Not exactly," Veber replied. "His name is Magnus Black."

"He must be very skilled to get past my security undetected," Tagus remarked.

Nasri took a deep breath, trying to regain her composure. "What's this about?"

"It's partially about *you*, my dear," Veber replied.

"How? I've never seen him before in my life."

"Actually, he's the man who killed Lord Santos," Veber said.

"Then arrest him!" Nasri shouted.

"I was going to," Veber went on, "but it occurred to me that I might have a different use for him."

"I don't like the sound of that..." Tagus said.

"You see, with Lord Santos gone," Veber went on, "the families are evenly divided. As you pointed out, Lady Nasri, with the seven families my own house's influence was weaker and now with six, that's even more true."

"I'm calling the police," Nasri said, but as she tried to stand, her legs no longer responded. "What have you done?"

"If something happened to you, my dear," Veber said calmly, "My family's place would return to its former importance."

"My hands," Nasri said. "I can't feel them."

"Mr. Black has been kind enough to poison you," Veber said.

"How?" Tagus asked.

"In the food," Veber replied.

"Highly unlikely," Tagus remarked skeptically. "Everything I eat is carefully scanned."

"I used a binary poison in the cookies and the tea," Magnus spoke for the first time. "Separately they're completely inert, but combined together they become quite toxic."

"Why in heaven's name would you poison me too?" Tagus asked angrily.

"I felt that poison would be appropriate," Veber replied, "since that's what you gave my *son*."

Lord Tagus coughed, the spittle on his hands a dark red. "Don't be ridiculous!"

"On the contrary," Veber said coldly, glaring at the Tagus patriarch. "It made perfect sense once I realized it. You resented that I broke the tie that made Hector Augustus the new emperor instead of you. Of course, you weren't foolish enough to attack me directly. Killing the head of a royal household would be too dangerous, so instead you went after my son."

"This is madness," Tagus said. "There must be an antidote..."

"I'm afraid not," Magnus replied.

Turning to Lady Veber, Tagus struggled to raise his hand toward her. "I'll give you whatever you want, I swear!"

"Dying will suffice," Veber replied.

The old man fell off the couch while Lady Nasri slumped against the cushions. Barely able to keep her head upright, she stared at Lady Veber through a darkening haze. Veber stood, joined by Magnus Black beside her. As she died, Nasri watched them walk away, fading into a blanket of flickering gauze.

Jessica Doric read the rejection notice on her datapad. Since quitting her job with the Maycare Institute of Xeno Studies, Doric had applied to a number of other institutions, from colleges to private research organizations. She even tried getting her old job back as a professor at the University of Regalis, but the dean felt Doric's time with Devlin Maycare had tainted her academic credentials. In the back of her mind, she considered the idea of working for Warlock Industries, but quickly discarded the possibility, in part because they had tried to kill her at least twice.

Just off the hallway to Doric's bedroom, a pile of dirty clothes was slowly ripening. Unwashed dishes filled the sink while a few others lay about the apartment in strategic locations. Books were also scattered across the living room floor. Doric felt compelled to research the Necronea, her professional and personal curiosity gnawing at her mind at all hours of the night. Sleeping had become a luxury, as well as bathing and most other forms of hygiene. None of the sources available to her, including articles on the nodesphere, could give Doric the detailed answers she was looking for. With bitter irony, she realized the truly useful bits of information were stored in Maycare's own private library. She could think of at least a dozen books that currently lay out of reach.

Sitting on the couch, she felt a vibration beneath her. Leaning to one side, she pulled her phone from under her leg and saw Lord Maycare's picture, framed in dramatic profile, on the screen.

Shit, she thought.

Knowing she hadn't washed her hair in nearly a week, she answered with voice only. "Hello?"

"Jess!" Maycare shouted, as if not seeing her meant he had to talk louder. "Are you there?"

"Yes," Doric replied in a normal tone. "Stop shouting."

"Sorry," he said. "Why aren't you on vidcam?"

"I don't feel like seeing you right now."

"Ah, don't be like that, Jess! I wanted to show you something."

"Where are you?" she asked.

"I'm downstairs," he replied, "in front of your building."

"I'm pretty busy..."

"Come on!" Maycare pleaded. "Give me a chance..."

Doric sighed, running her fingers through her hard, brittle hair.

"Okay," she said. "Give me a minute."

Half an hour later, Doric appeared at the entrance to her apartment building. She was dressed and showered and wore something from the back of her closet, a gray dress with brown street shoes. Outside the main doors, Maycare was standing beside a shiny blue gravcar. Shaved and dapper as usual, he was dressed in a nice suit and tie. She joined him outside.

"Jess!" he said and waved his hand over the hood of the car. "How do you like it?"

Doric scrutinized the vehicle doubtfully and then did the same to Maycare. "It's okay."

"It's brand new!" he went on excitedly.

"So, you bought another car? Is that what you wanted me to see?"

"No, Jess," he shook his head. "I bought *you* a new car!"

"What?"

"I wanted to apologize about how terrible I've been acting and beg for your forgiveness."

"So, you bought me a car?"

"Well," Maycare said, "I wanted to buy you flowers—"

"I like flowers..."

"—but Bentley said that would be inappropriate."

"Remind me to thank him."

"I thought a car would be better anyway. I mean, you could use it for work..."

"Hold on," Doric said. "Who said I wanted to go back to working for you?"

Maycare's chin, normally square and facing skyward, sank abruptly. Doric's eyebrows rose.

"Don't you like the color?" he asked.

Blue was her favorite color actually, but she wasn't about to mention that.

"I don't need a car," she said. "What I *want* is your respect."

"I do respect you!" he said.

"I don't believe it."

Maycare came out from behind the gravcar and grabbed Doric by the shoulders. She shrunk back, or attempted to, but Maycare's hold was tight and unrelenting.

"Of course I respect you," he said. "I'm lost without you, Jess. I'm just too pigheaded to realize it sometimes!"

"This is also inappropriate by the way," she muttered.

Maycare released her immediately and took a step back. "Sorry."

"Alright, Lord Maycare," she said. "I'll go back to work for you."

"Really? That's wonderful!" he replied. "What about the gravcar? Should I take it back?"

"Oh, no," she said firmly. "I'm *keeping* the car."

Dr. Sprouse followed a corridor through the bowels of Warlock headquarters. She stopped at an unmarked door and knocked. From within, a man's voice spoke. "Come in!"

The doctor closed the door behind her once inside a long, narrow room with no windows. At the other end, a man with a hairless, throbbing head leaned over a workbench.

"Good evening, Dr. Sprouse," Lars Hatcher said without looking up.

"It's morning, actually," she replied, stopping just behind his chair. On the bench, an ancient book with burned pages lay beside several instruments. "How's it going?"

Lars sat up, as if studying the question in his mind. Dr. Sprouse wondered if he was, in fact, studying her mind instead.

"No," Lars said. "I'm not reading your mind."

"Clearly."

"I meant," Lars admitted, "not at first."

The doctor put her hand on the metamind's shoulder as she leaned past him to get a better view of the tome. "The craftsmanship is amazing. The cover material looks odd though…"

"It's someone's skin."

"Anyone I know?"

"Not unless you knew someone from a hundred thousand years ago."

"Hmm," she murmured. "You're sure it's that old?"

Lars pointed at some of the pages, the edges singed to a crisp.

"Carbon dating shows the latter pages are slightly more recent, but overall," he said, "it's a very old book."

"Any idea where it came from?" Dr. Sprouse asked.

"Outside the Imperium. Perhaps beyond the Talion Republic."

"How did it get here then?"

A thick blood vessel in Lars' head pulsated. The doctor instinctively pulled her hand off his shoulder.

"Difficult to say," Lars replied. "Many parts of the Talion Republic were looted by Imperial forces after the end of the last war with the Magna Supremacy. We wanted to punish the Tals for supporting the Magna and apparently, taking their art treasures was part of that. On the other hand, it could have been smugglers."

Dr. Sprouse crossed her arms. "Skarlander will want facts, not speculation."

Lars, for the first time, turned his eyes to look at her. "I know."

As if by magic, a book lifted off a neighboring shelf and floated across the room until landing on the table. Cracking it open, Lars flipped through several pages until finding the spot he was searching for.

"This is a book in High Dahlvish," Lars said, pointing to a paragraph of intricate script. "It talks about a psionic ability the Dahl use to travel great distances with only their minds."

"Like a transmat?"

"Not exactly," Lars said. "They don't actually travel physically. They project an ethereal image of themselves instead."

"Does the other book talk about the same thing?" Dr. Sprouse asked.

"I'm not sure," Lars replied. "After piecing together the burnt page fragments, I'm beginning to think the book allows the user to travel, but it's unclear how. Perhaps using a portal of some sort."

"If we could understand the method," Dr. Sprouse said, "it could revolutionize how we travel between planets..."

Lars nodded.

"I'll need more of these books before that can happen," he said.

"Then let's get you more books," the doctor replied.

The Veber family yacht settled into orbit above Lokeren. Standing on the transmat pad aboard her ship, Lady Veber was thankful to be home again. No longer needed, Magnus Black had already left, returning to the *Starling*.

She wondered if she would ever see him again but, re-materializing on the surface, Lady Veber's only ambition was to see her son. The consequences of her actions might mean a death sentence, but knowing she had avenged her boy's illness gave her a sense of relief. The rest would take care of itself.

From the transmat pad near the cliffs overlooking the ocean, Lady Veber walked purposefully up the trail to the estate. A few staff members and one or two robots met her at the entrance. She heard them talking about the state of her affairs— budgets and personnel issues— but their words were clutter to her ears. She drowned them out with thoughts of Philip and how he might have been faring since she was away.

In the wing of the estate where their private quarters were located, Lady Veber passed her own door on her way to Philip's. Although she was tempted to enter unannounced to surprise him, she paused to knock. She waited, but hearing no response, she tried the handle and went in. The lights were off, except for a few candles burned down to stumps. Concerned, she crossed through to the bedroom.

Before Lady Veber had left for Aldorus and the capital city, she had been aware that her son had started collecting animals so she was not surprised to see the cages, even if their silence was unnerving. Her attention, however, was immediately drawn to a figure standing with its back to her in the dull candlelight.

"Philip?" she asked.

The person turned. Now in less shadow, it was clearly a woman and completely naked. She was also without hair and her skin was tattooed with strange lettering across her entire body. It took Lady Veber a moment to recognize her as Annis, the handmaiden.

"Annis—?" Lady Veber began but stopped.

The handmaiden's eyes, cloudy white without pupils, showed signs of recognition, but didn't reply. Behind her, beside a wooden table, the rough outline of a door was scrawled onto the wall with white chalk. Lettering like that written on Annis' flesh was inscribed around the edges of the fake door.

"Where's my son?" Lady Veber pleaded.

Annis, or whoever she was now, began moving toward her with plodding steps. With a scream, Lady Veber ran out of the room, slamming the door behind her.

CHAPTER SIXTEEN

When the stranger first arrived at the Katak village, one of the younger froglings went to the chief's hut and told him the news. Lying in a cot covered with moss to comfort his tired bones, the chief struggled out of bed, standing with the help of his wooden staff.

"There's some people here," the young Katak croaked.

"Alright," the old frogling said. "I'll be there in a moment."

When the chief emerged, most of the villagers had assembled around the main bonfire still smoldering from the night before. On the far side, the stranger waited. He was taller than the Katak or even the Sylvan. He wore brown vestments and carried a tall staff of curved wood, topped with a skull. His skin was gray and chalky like bleached bones, and his eyes blazed like fires from otherwise empty sockets.

The stranger was not alone. Accompanying him were creatures the chief learned later were called *Ghuls*. Like their master, they were somewhere between alive and dead, with rotting skin hanging off their bodies in various stages of decay.

As the chief approached, the stranger reached into his mind.

Greetings, the stranger said telepathically.

Who are you? the chief thought.

I am Ghazul of the Necronea.

Necronea?

My people live below the ancient cemetery west of here, Ghazul said.

What do you want?

The chief could feel the stranger's eyes staring through him, examining every fiber of his being.

You've served your village a long time, Ghazul said, *but now you see the end is coming and you're afraid.*

All things die, the chief replied.

But do they have to?

What are you suggesting?

Life everlasting, the stranger said. *I'm offering you and your people life without end, and in return, I ask only that you provide us with what we need.*

Which is what?

His mouth, without lips, turned up at the corners, baring his teeth in a gruesome smile.

Sacrifice.

When Sir Golan and the rest of the group arrived at the crypt, the three froglings outside were heading back toward the village. Unlike the rest of the Katak, these warriors showed no interest in fighting.

"Tell them their chief is dead," the knight said, turning to Silandra.

Silandra focused on the Katak, singling out the apparent leader.

"He says *good,*" she replied after a pause. "He says their chief made a deal with the man who lives below the graves. He says they were promised endless life but given only death."

"What about Sisa?" Mel asked.

"She's inside the crypt," Silandra replied.

Sir Golan approached the marble building, giving the door a firm shove.

"It appears to be locked from the inside," he said, tapping the metal with the tip of his sword. "The door is thick, too. I doubt even Rippana could do more than scratch it."

Mel reached into her satchel, removing a tool shaped like a small wand.

"What's that?" the knight asked.

"A plasma torch," Mel said.

"How novel..."

Mel stared at him, her eyebrows raised.

"It's... really not."

"Fair enough," Sir Golan replied, sheathing his sword and crossing his arms.

Sizing up the door, Mel set the torch against it, a brilliant blue light erupting from the tip, and began cutting a long, narrow swath across the metal surface. In less than a minute, a slab fell inward with a loud, echoing crash.

Sir Golan stepped inside first, calling in the rest soon after. The crypt was a single room with a limestone sarcophagus filling most of it. Figures were carved along the sides of the coffin and the lid, but the knight did not recognize the creatures depicted.

"What are they?" he asked.

"I have no idea," Silandra replied.

"They're running from that fellow there," Squire remarked, pointing at a biped figure with tentacles coming from its face.

"It's the same person portrayed on top," Sir Golan said, motioning to the lid.

Sculpted in relief, the humanoid lay facing the ceiling, his arms crossed. A pair of angry eyes glared from beneath heavy, curled brows at the center of a domed head. Instead of a mouth, four tentacles protruded from his lower jaw. Each feeler coiled around itself, reaching out as if to touch Sir Golan and the others.

"Who cares?" Mel shouted, throwing her arms in the air. "Has anyone noticed there's no other exits in this room? Where did Sisa go?"

Sir Golan, realizing she was right, took another look at the coffin lid.

"Help me with this, Squire," he said.

The Cruxian and the robot pushed against the top of the sarcophagus. At first, the lid remained stubbornly motionless, but after a few more attempts, the limestone gave way, sliding a few feet to the side.

Sir Golan peered over the side.

"It's empty," he said.

"How can that be?" Mel asked.

"Except for a staircase," the knight went on.

Mel clenched both fists and shook them. "Gah!"

"You're very excitable," the knight observed.

When Silandra reached the bottom of the staircase, the others had fanned out into a circular chamber lined with blazing torches.

Thick roots twisted along the walls and hung from the ceiling. The air smelled dank and rotten.

"There's tunnels going in every direction," Mel said, shining a flashlight down one of the passages.

"The floor is covered in tracks," Sir Golan noted. "Difficult to tell which ones are fresh."

"Can you sense your daughter?" Squire asked.

In her mind, Silandra focused her thoughts on Sisa like squinting at a fuzzy object in the distance.

"I think..." she began, "I think she's in that direction."

Silandra nodded toward a tunnel no different than the rest.

His sword drawn, Sir Golan cautiously plodded inside with Mel behind him providing light. Silandra followed and Squire, with his energy shield active, protected the rear. The path was narrow and serpentine, everyone except Mel having to crouch at times to avoid hitting their heads.

Scraping the top of his helmet against the tunnel roof, Sir Golan sent a scattering of loose dirt into Mel's face.

"Watch what you're doing!" she protested.

"I beg your forgiveness," the knight replied ceremoniously.

"Why do you talk like that anyway?" she asked.

"Like what?"

"Never mind..."

Sir Golan stopped.

"What is it?" Mel asked.

"If you wouldn't mind," he said, "shine your light over there."

The beam of the flashlight landed on an object protruding from the ceiling at an angle. The knight tapped his sword against it, producing a wooden sound.

"I believe it's a coffin," Sir Golan said.

Silandra came closer and noticed the end of the coffin was torn open, the edges splintered.

"It's empty," she said.

As they continued, they came across more caskets poking from the dirt, each one broken and empty. A few were scratched along the sides as if by claws. Silandra became aware of another pattern.

"The tunnel keeps changing direction every time it hits a coffin," she said.

"Oh, lord," Mel said. "They're using the tunnel to access the bodies. I bet all the tunnels are used for that. There must be hundreds of graves in that cemetery."

"To what end?" Squire asked.

"Hell if I know!" Mel replied.

Squire emerged from the narrow tunnel into a spacious chamber, the others having come out before him. The walls of the domed room were red clay with rocks jutting from between tree roots. Entrances to several more tunnels were visible in the dim light and the roar of flowing water was coming from the far side.

"Sisa's footprints are going that way," Sir Golan said, motioning toward the thundering noise.

Mel trained her flashlight in that direction, the beam catching watery mist floating through the air.

"She's close," Silandra said anxiously.

"Make haste!" Sir Golan shouted, starting to run.

Following his master, Squire and the others quickly caught up with the knight at a wooden bridge on the edge of a cliff. An underground river cascaded below, disappearing into the dark. The other end of the bridge was lost in the gloom.

"Looks kinda rickety," Mel remarked, scanning the planks with her light.

From somewhere up ahead, a girl's voice cried out, echoing off the rocks. "Let me go!"

"Sisa!" Silandra shouted.

"Mom?"

Silandra sprinted down the bridge with Sir Golan close behind. Mel looked at Squire for a moment before running after them. The robot followed, his heavy feet clomping against the soft, soggy wood. When he caught up, his master was slashing the arm off a humanoid creature with sickly skin and glazed eyes. Silandra and Sisa, illuminated by Mel's flashlight, were sharing an embrace. With a stroke of Rippana, Sir Golan sent the creature's head flying into the water rushing below. The rest of its corpse collapsed against the railing.

"What is that thing?" Mel asked.

"A Ghul," Sisa replied, buried in her mother's arms.

"Foul monsters," Sir Golan muttered.

Watching Silandra and her daughter together, Squire regretted his lack of emotional depth. He wondered if Mel could give him an upgrade.

From the darkness, farther down the bridge, sounds started coming closer.

"We should go," Mel said, turning back the way they had come.

"You go," Sir Golan relied. "I'll hold them off while you make your escape."

"Should I stay too?" Squire asked.

"No need," the knight said. "Now be off!"

Reluctantly, Squire obeyed his master and followed Mel and the two Sylvans. Before they reached the end of the bridge, Mel stopped.

"What is it?" the robot asked.

"Look!" Mel replied.

The hulking shape of a man blocked their way. Eight feet tall, the creature was covered in patches of skin, each different but all sewn together in a jigsaw puzzle of flesh. On each patch, an archaic letter was tattooed and glowed with a bluish hue.

"It's a golem," Silandra said, "held together with Dark Psi."

"Dark psionics?" Mel asked. "I knew someone who used that..."

"It's an abomination," Silandra replied.

"He wasn't so bad..."

The flesh golem planted one of his heavy feet on the bridge. Squire felt the planks shake.

"Without Sir Golan," the robot said, "I don't know how to stop this monster."

"The power comes from the ancient writing on his skin," Silandra said. "We must destroy that to destroy the golem."

The creature's other foot came down hard on the bridge. His eyes were nothing but specks of black like shards of coal.

"Mel," Squire said, "you didn't happen to upgrade me with a flamethrower by chance?"

"There wasn't enough time," Mel replied.

"That's a pity."

"Wait," Mel said, reaching into her bag. "This'll do the trick."

She pulled out a metallic cylinder and, removing a round pin on the top, tossed it at the golem's feet.

"Stop!" Silandra shouted but the device exploded, engulfing the creature in a fireball.

Covered in sticky, burning napalm, the golem waved his arms and stomped his feet. The bridge swayed and buckled beneath the shifting weight.

"Uh oh," Mel whispered.

Flames climbed up the golem's body, consuming patches of flesh as they rose. The strange, mystical lettering turned from blue to orange, and then to nothing as the skin burned to ash.

"Run!" Silandra screamed, grabbing her daughter as they stumbled back down the bridge.

The golem's massive shape, now almost completely black, teetered like a thick tree about to fall, and then it did. With a deafening sound as loud as the rushing waters below, the creature landed face first, snapping the wood planks like kindling. The supports under the bridge splintered, sending the whole structure sideways.

Squire felt himself floating in midair, the cavern swirling around him until air became liquid and he was submerged.

When Mel woke, the first thing she noticed was the water pouring out her mouth as she lay on her side. The second thing, as her lungs emptied, was a bluish tinge coloring her hands and the mud around her. She thought in horror that the flesh golem had returned, but rolling over and looking up, she saw only Squire standing beside her and the dome of his displacement field protecting them both.

"Where are we?" she asked, coughing out the last drops of water.

"I'm not exactly sure," Squire replied, "but I should think we're somewhere under the bridge."

Mel sat up. The ground was spongy and covered in shallow puddles. Although her satchel was missing, she still held the flashlight firmly in her tiny hands. She shined the beam on the wall of the displacement field but saw only darkness beyond it.

"Are we underwater?" she asked.

"Did I not mention that?" the robot said.

"No!"

"We fell into the water after the bridge collapsed," Squire explained. "I switched on the displacement field, letting the liquid run out through the one-way membrane."

"Huh," Mel said. "That was genius!"

"Oh, thank you so much," the robot said as if embarrassed by the compliment.

"What about Silandra and Sisa?"

"I'm afraid you were the only one near me. I don't know where the others are at the moment."

Mel got to her feet.

"The air in here won't last long," she said. "We should find the shore."

Mel and Squire started walking, the dome moving along with the robot. Mel nearly tripped over the bones of a ribcage sticking out of the river bottom. She wasn't exactly sure if this was a river at all, but she could vaguely see water running across the surface of the displacement field. Whatever was covering the dome, it had a fast current. In time, the ground started slanting upward which she took as a good sign. When the top of the dome broke the surface of the water, Mel was no longer sure.

The halo of torchlights shined on the other side of the field. Shapes moved back and forth. Many shapes.

No longer underwater, Squire switched off the dome. Mel, her pink hair dangling damply around her shoulders, looked with wild eyes at the people she saw. Like Ghuls, their skin was discolored and even absent in some places, but they also wore armor fashioned from bones and carried hooked swords like the blades of a scythe. One was in brown vestments like a priest and held a curved staff with a skull on the end. Beside him, next to an altar-like stone table, Silandra was visible. Only then did Mel notice someone else, a girl lying on the table.

She wasn't moving.

Death was not the end, Grand Necromancer Ghazul believed. For those with the power and knowledge, death was only the beginning of everlasting life. His people, the Necronea, were the embodiment of reanimation. As the Spring knows the Winter, they knew death as the dark before the light.

Ghazul watched the Sylvan woman emerge from the subterranean river, both her and the daughter in her arms soaked to the bone. He reached into her mind and learned the woman's name, *Silandra*, and felt the deep sorrow flowing from her heart. She did not understand what Ghazul already knew and he pitied her for that. She saw only death in her daughter's face where the Grand Necromancer saw hope.

Surrounded by the Necronea, she also felt fear, but Ghazul assured Silandra there was no danger, directing her to lay Sisa's body onto the stone table. After doing so, she turned to him.

"Why did you steal my daughter?" she asked aloud. "What possible good could come from this?"

Although the blazing eyes in his head could convey no emotion, Ghazul sympathized with the mother's anger, knowing that she was ignorant of the great honor for which her daughter was intended. He did his best to explain.

"I know this must be strange," Ghazul said. "For you, life is a precious, finite thing, with a beginning and an end. Or perhaps you believe there's life after death, but a place from which we cannot return."

"Yes," Silandra replied, slowly nodding.

"My people believe something quite different," the necromancer went on. "From the teachings of the Old Ones, we learned that we can, indeed, return. That death is merely a state of matter that, like ice to water, can change if need be."

"Who are the Old Ones?"

"They were the first to exist before existence began, even before the stars started burning. They lived in the infinite blackness where light was still just a dream."

"Get to the point!" Silandra shouted. "I don't care about your religion!"

"You must understand," Ghazul replied calmly, "for everything there is a price. To keep the Old Ones sated, we must offer a sacrifice of purity. Your daughter Sisa was to be that sacrifice."

"She's dead!"

"It's true that she's no longer suitable as an offering, but I can assure you she isn't lost. I am fully capable of restoring Sisa to you."

In the river, the dark water began changing color, brightening with a bluish glow. An orb of energy broke the river's surface, slowly rising out of the water. When it was entirely on the shore, the ball of blue disappeared, leaving a small girl and a robot in its place.

Although pleased to be on dry land, Squire was acutely aware that he and Mel had walked into a formidable situation. Even with upgrades to his systems, the robot knew that without Sir Golan, he was outmatched by the sheer number of armed Necronea present. Squire had no idea where his master was at the moment, but hoped he was not injured or worse. The thought of Sir Golan drowning or even being killed upset the robot's programming.

"Do you have any weapons?" he asked Mel.

"No," she replied. "I lost my bag in the river..."

The Necronea quickly surrounded them, forcing both the Gnomi and the robot to join Silandra beside the stone altar. Sisa, her skin a pale blue, lay resting on the table. To Squire, she looked tiny, but her face appeared strangely calm, even beautiful.

"What's going on?" Mel asked.

"This is Ghazul, a necromancer," Silandra said. "He promises to bring Sisa back from the dead."

"How is that even possible?" Mel wondered.

"By using Dark Psi..." Silandra replied.

"She'll be like we are," Ghazul said proudly. "As Necronea, she will live forever and never know death again."

Mel frowned, her eyes turning serious.

"I knew someone once," she said. "He died, but they said they could bring him back by downloading his personality into a robot."

"Fascinating!" Squire said.

"I loved him and I would've given anything to get him back, but whoever was inside that robot wasn't the Randall that I knew anymore."

Silandra was silent, her brows furrowed in thought. After a few moments, she turned to the Grand Necromancer.

"Sisa was my only daughter," she told him. "When you took her away, you stole the most precious thing in my life. As Mel said, I would do anything to bring her back, but that's not what you're offering."

"No?" Ghazul said.

"You were right about her purity," she went on. "I can't say I understand how Dark Psi works, but I know I don't want you defiling her with it."

Now it was the necromancer's turn to be silent.

"As you wish," he sighed. "You may take her in peace. We will not prevent you."

"Really?" Mel asked. "You'd just let us walk out of here?"

"No," he said. "Not *you.*"

"What?"

"We still require someone pure to sacrifice or the Old Ones will become angry."

"Why are you looking at me?" Mel asked, pointing at herself.

"You are a virgin, correct?"

Mel laughed uncomfortably.

"Don't be stupid," she said. "I've been with lots of guys..."

"You're obviously lying," the necromancer replied.

Squire leaned closer to the Gnomi, whispering in her ear. "It *is* pretty obvious."

"You're not helping!" Mel shouted.

"The others may leave," Ghazul told Mel, "but you must pass through the doorway."

"What doorway?" Mel asked.

The Grand Necromancer waved his staff at the ornate drawing of a doorway carved into the side of a stone wall. Along the outside of the drawing was lettering similar to those on the flesh golem. These letters also began glowing. At the same time, the center of the doorway faded away, its edges falling inward like a waterfall from above.

One of the Necronea grabbed Mel by the arm and forced her toward the portal. She punched and kicked him, but Mel's small size kept her from landing a solid blow.

"Stop!" a voice shouted.

Much to Squire's relief, Sir Golan appeared and immediately sent Rippana through the nearest Necronea. The sword pierced the bone armor, sticking out the other side. Unfazed with the blade dangling from his chest, the undead fighter struck the knight squarely across the face, launching him backward several feet.

"Knight in shining armor, my butt," Mel remarked.

"Stop this nonsense!" Ghazul shouted. "You cannot harm us and we cannot die! The girl must go through the portal or the Old Ones will enact their vengeance on all living things. What we do here is for your benefit, not ours! We protect you from the terrible power of the Void!"

"You're saying if I don't go through, terrible things will happen?" Mel asked doubtfully.

"The end of all things," Ghazul said. "You must do this. It is the only way."

Mel stared into the doorway.

"Don't do it!" Silandra yelled.

"It's okay," she replied. "Since Randall died, things haven't been exactly great."

"That doesn't mean—" Silandra started.

"People have been making sacrifices right and left," Mel stopped her. "Maybe it's finally my turn."

The Necronea holding Mel released his grip. Standing on her own, she took one last look at the others and smiled.

Then she disappeared through the doorway.

CHAPTER SEVENTEEN

The *Baron Lancaster* dropped out of hyperspace. On the bridge, Captain Redgrave studied the expanse of nothingness on the main monitor. The star charts listed this system as uninhabited, without planets or other redeeming qualities that would attract a permanent settlement. Decades ago, mining companies had arrived and promptly stripped the larger asteroids of precious metals and anything else of value. When there was nothing left, the companies moved on. According to Golub, the Celadon the captain had interrogated, the Ougluks found one of the abandoned mines intact, a hollowed-out asteroid they turned into their base.

"Set a course for the mining colony," the captain said.

"Aye, Captain," the helmsman replied.

The asteroid was hidden amid a belt of loose rocks and small planetoids like specks of dust collecting in the corners of a room. Far from the inner star, the Ougluk base appeared cold and forgotten.

"No energy signatures or residual heat," the science officer said.

"Do a deep scan," Redgrave replied.

After a long pause, the officer said, "It appears to be shielded, but there's definitely life signs."

So, Golub was telling the truth after all, the captain thought.

"Target the surface and fire a salvo," he ordered.

Like outstretched fingers, streams of plasma lanced from the *Baron Lancaster*, erupting in plumes of gray powder and molten rock on the asteroid. With their position obviously compromised, the Ougluks energized a force field around the base, covering the rock in a hazy, blue cocoon.

"Missiles inbound!" another bridge officer shouted.

"Activate shields and bring point-defenses online," Redgrave said calmly.

Rapid-fire lasers traced in the direction of the incoming missiles until three explosions, each an intercepted missile, flashed on the main view screen.

"Another salvo," the captain said.

Blaster cannons, each larger than a house, spewed another barrage at the slaver base.

"Keep firing!" Redgrave barked. "They can't withstand that much damage for long."

The captain touched the device in his ear.

"Be ready, commander," he said. "Their shields will be down momentarily."

"Yes, sir," Commander Maycare's voice came through the earpiece.

In his quarters, Bortok balanced a palette on his thumb while standing in front of a partially completed canvas. On the other side of the easel, another Ougluk rested his hand on the sculpture of a man's head, bearded with a receding hairline, sitting on a table. The Ougluk wore a loose robe with a heavy gold chain across his chest. He stared contemplatively at the bust.

Bortok grunted.

"No, no," he complained. "You don't look philosophical enough..."

The other Ougluk snarled.

"Oh, never mind," the Enslaver sighed, dabbing his brush at some paint on the palette.

Holding the brush up to the canvas, his hand lurched as the floor suddenly shook. Dust from the ceiling rained down, filling the room with a cloud of fine powder. Bortok dropped the brush, seeing the long, haphazard line he had just made across the painting.

"Goddammit!"

"Did we hit something?" the artist's model asked.

"How the hell should I know?"

Dropping his brush and palette, Bortok ran into the hallway just as another quake rattled the asteroid. Over an intercom speaker, Cirion's voice crackled.

"Bortok, come to the command center immediately!" he said.

Bortok made this way through the base, narrowly avoiding a cave-in after another blast. Covered in chalky residue, he burst into the command center yelling, "Don't you people care about *art*?"

Cirion, standing beside a computer console, gazed incredulously at the Enslaver and pointed to the main video monitor. A heavy cruiser filled the screen.

"It's the Imperial Navy," the Red Dahl said.

"How did they find us?" Bortok replied. "I bet it was one of those Celadon pirates. Those sniveling twerps!"

"Most likely," Cirion replied. "However, the fact remains there's an Imperial warship firing on us."

"Well, put up the shields!"

"I already did. We're also returning fire for all the good that'll do."

"Is it just the one ship?" Bortok asked.

"Yes, but we're no match against a heavy cruiser. Our force field will fail before long..."

"That's a defeatist attitude!"

"It's science," Cirion replied.

Bortok made a fist. "This is the only science I believe in!"

Being tied to an anthill. Spiders crawling all over you. People described the sensation of being transmatted in different ways, but Commander Maycare never minded it much.

What he *really* didn't like were the people shooting at him when he arrived.

Materializing on the asteroid, Maycare hit the ground, his combat armor absorbing the impact of a blaster bolt. Rays of energy laced the air where he had just been standing. The marines accompanying him returned fire.

The commander gathered himself and tried to assess the situation.

Ougluk slavers were shooting from down the corridor twenty yards from where Maycare and his marines had appeared. The deep penetration scans had shown this was the main artery leading from the hangar deck. Captain Redgrave had wanted them to cut the Ougluks off from their ships, preventing them from escaping, especially with any captives.

From the view inside his helmet, Maycare could see three infrared signatures ahead. He snapped off a few shots from his blaster rifle, mostly to keep the slavers' heads down while his marines took up better positions.

"Flash grenades," he said into his helmet microphone.

Two marines loaded canisters into tubes slung beneath their rifles and, with a popping sound, launched them down the corridor. Two loud bangs, accompanied by blinding flashes, lit up the end of the hallway. Before the glare had died down, Maycare was already on his feet and running. When he got to the three Ougluks, they were holding their hands over their eyes and ears. The commander killed two of them point-blank while a marine finished off the other one.

"Spread out," Maycare said, pointing around the large room.

"What's that?" one of the marines asked.

In the center of the room was a large hole.

Before he could answer, Maycare felt something crash into him, sending them both into the pit. The commander rolled as he landed, but when he stood, he was struck under the chin, sending his helmet flying off. Blinking, Maycare saw a heavily scarred Ougluk rushing toward him.

"Whoa there, fella!" the commander said, but the Ougluk wrapped two giant arms around him, lifting Maycare's feet off the ground.

"Could somebody shoot this guy?" the commander grunted.

"Can't get a clear shot, sir!" he heard one of the marines say.

The Ougluk roared, the stench of poor dental hygiene blowing in Maycare's face.

Enough of this, the commander thought and drove his forehead into the Ougluk's nose.

With a howl, the brawler let go, dropping the commander to the ground. Maycare looked up in time to see the Ougluk's skull disappear in a crimson cloud of blaster fire. The pit fighter, minus everything above the neck, landed on his back in the dirt.

Maycare stood and went looking for his helmet.

Walter Ruggles remembered the first piece of IDEA furniture his family brought home when he was a little boy, a Gilly bookcase. Like all IDEA furniture, it came unassembled and Ruggles' father, swearing the entire time, had to put the bookcase together himself. His parents bought most of their furniture from IDEA, exposing the young Ruggles to a life of wood veneer and strangely shaped wrenches.

Across from his cell on the slaver asteroid, Ruggles easily recognized the IDEA stool the guard was sitting on. It had a round seat with a birch veneer and was entirely too small for the oversized Ougluk. The guard kept adjusting himself, never fully getting comfortable. Ruggles almost felt sorry for him, but only just.

They were in a room, although he couldn't tell how big, with rows of cells like his own. Orange light strips ran along the pens, only giving enough illumination to see a dozen feet in any direction. The only bright spot was a heavy door at one end of the room.

"Excuse me," Ruggles asked the guard, "could I use the bucket again?"

The guard grunted. "Go in the corner."

"I'd rather not—"

An explosion interrupted him as a large portion of the heavy door disintegrated, hurling pieces of burning metal into the room. Instinctively, Ruggles curled into a fetal position, covering his head as best as he could. The sound of blaster fire filled the air for several seconds before everything went quiet except for some quiet whimpering. Ruggles realized the whimpering was coming from him.

He peered out from behind his hands. The guard was lying on the ground with a smoking hole in his chest, but the IDEA stool seemed unharmed.

"Is everyone alright?" someone in military armor was asking. He was moving from cell to cell, freeing the captives as he went.

"Thank goodness!" Ruggles said, anxious for the soldier to free him as well.

"Is Sylvia Flax here?" the soldier asked. "I'm looking for Sylvia Flax..."

"I know her!" Ruggles replied, standing up.

The armored soldier came to the cell. "You do?"

"Yes."

"Where is she?"

"There was a Magna named Bog or something. He took her away."

"We haven't found a Magna yet," the soldier said, opening the cell door.

"Well, there was also a Red Dahl with him — I didn't catch his name. If you find him, I'm sure he'll know where they went."

The soldier nodded and saluted with two fingers against the side of his helmet. Ruggles noticed the helmet was dented.

"Wait," Ruggles said, seeing the soldier start to walk away.

The man in the armor stopped. "Yes?"

"What about me?"

"Go out the door," he replied. "If you hear shooting, walk the other way."

Not waiting for a response, the soldier turned on his heel and headed out through the smoldering hole in the door.

"Thank you?" Ruggles said weakly.

Looking anxiously around, he noticed the IDEA stool beside the dead guard. Without another word, Ruggles snatched it under his arm and shuffled off, along with the other passengers, as they made their way toward freedom.

In the command center, Cirion watched the feed from a security camera showing a soldier in combat armor leaving the slave pens. The Sarkan pressed his fingers against the screen, zooming in. On the collar piece of the soldier's armor, he noticed a silver oakleaf insignia.

A naval commander, he thought. *What I wouldn't give to kill one of those...*

Bortok stuck his large, green head through the doorway.

"Unless you've got something better to do," he snapped, "get your ass out here!"

Cirion sighed through his nostrils. "Yes, sir!"

The corridor outside the command center was filled with containers acting as a barricade. Ougluks, including Bortok himself, were firing over the barricade at Imperial marines farther down the hallway. Portions of the metal containers had melted from blaster hits while bits of the walls and ceiling were missing chunks of rock and darkened with burn marks.

A shaft of energy struck one of the Ougluks, a burst of flame erupting from his chest. Taking a step back, he collapsed into a ball, dead and still smoking.

Bortok stopped firing his rifle long enough to lament his fallen comrade.

"No!" he roared. "He was my best model!"

"I think we're past that," Cirion said.

"You know nothing about art!" Bortok replied bitterly.

More blaster volleys streaked down the hallway, passing just over their heads. The air smelled heavily of ozone.

"Those idiots!" Bortok scoffed. "They got the slaves already. Why don't they just pulverize us from space?"

"They're obviously still looking for something," Cirion said.

"Yeah, like what?"

Amongst the din, Cirion heard an electrical crackling behind him. Turning, he noticed a cylinder on the ground. A foot long and several inches wide, it was nondescript except for Imperial markings along the side. The Sarkan only took a moment to realize what it was.

"Bomb!" he shouted.

Cirion lifted his hands, crossing his arms together at the wrists. While Bortok was still looking around, a blue translucent shell covered Cirion's forearms, creating a psionic shield between him and the device. When the bomb exploded a half second later, the Red Dahl was thrown backwards through the doorway into the command center before everything went black.

When Cirion regained consciousness, he was lying on his back with a human standing over him. It was the same soldier with the silver oakleaf.

"Where is she?" the human was saying, his voice muffled as if far away. Cirion realized his eardrums had probably burst.

"Who?" he replied.

"Sylvia Flax."

Cirion coughed, his lungs filled with dust from the explosion. Looking past the commander's legs, he could make out the remains of Bortok's corpse scattered around the room and the corridor beyond.

The commander nudged the Sarkan with the barrel of his blaster rifle.

"Talk to me," the human said.

"You're too late," Cirion said. "The slave trader took her away."

"Is his name Bog?"

Cirion nodded weakly, his body aching all over. "Ipak-Bog."

"Where did he take her?"

"The Magna home world, of course."

"How long ago?"

"They're probably to the border by now. I told you it was too late."

The commander pointed his rifle between Cirion's eyes.

"You better hope not," he said.

An enormous hand the color of emerald reached into the pit where Ruggles and the Ougluk brawler had been fighting. Sylvia Flax took it and felt herself hoisted up, landing on her feet next to the towering Magna.

"Thanks," she said as someone began pulling Walter Ruggles out as well. He crawled over the lip of the hole on all fours before struggling to his feet.

"Yes, thank you very much," Ruggles said weakly.

Ipak-Bog was silent, but his Sarkan associate smiled, his teeth white against his bright red skin.

"We're so glad you weren't injured," he said, speaking to Flax while ignoring Ruggles entirely.

Flax's eyes went from the Red Dahl upward to the Magna standing beside him. Bog met her gaze, his head bent downward.

"Who are you?" she asked.

"I'm Cirion and this is Ipak-Bog of the Magna Supremacy."

"Delighted, I'm sure," she replied.

"The pleasure is all ours," Cirion said. "Of course, we recognized you immediately. It's a shame Bortok doesn't watch the news."

The Ougluk, only a few feet away, scowled and left, grumbling something Flax couldn't make out.

"It's nice to be recognized," Flax said.

"Fortunately," Cirion went on, "our host's short-sightedness didn't lead to anyone getting hurt."

"I'm a little roughed up," Ruggles said, raising his finger.

"It's time for us to go," Bog spoke finally, his voice sounding like a mountain crumbling.

Cirion nodded rapidly, ushering Flax to follow them. When Ruggles took a step in their direction, the Red Dahl gave him a glare, stopping him in his tracks.

Flax accompanied Cirion and the Magna to the hangar where a small starship was berthed. On the outside, the ship appeared no different than a hundred different vessels Flax had seen, but once inside, she was surprised by the lavishness of the decor. Instead of the usual metal and plastic, the interior cabin was adorned with woodwork and furniture covered in luxurious fabrics. Everything was trimmed with intricate metal inlays of gold and platinum.

Flax almost didn't notice that she was now alone with the Magna.

"Ah, what happened to the Sarkan?" she asked.

Taking the pilot's seat at the front of the cabin, Bog closed the hatch to the outside with a flip of a switch.

"Cirion won't be joining us," he said.

"Hmmm," Flax mumbled.

"Please be seated," Bog said. "We'll be leaving shortly."

A flutter in her chest, Flax took one of five chairs, each molded from cherry wood, facing the front where Bog was sitting. The Magna didn't turn or otherwise acknowledge her as he completed his pre-flight checks. Flax took the time to run her fingers along the plush material beneath her. She wondered if she could get this for her apartment back on Regalis before realizing she might never see her apartment again.

The ship rose from the hangar deck, skimming along until the gray, rocky walls of the asteroid fell away, replaced by the empty blackness of open space. The unpleasant feeling in Flax's belly intensified.

"Where are you taking me?" she asked, keeping her voice as calm as possible.

"To my home world," Bog replied.

Her heart sank. "Diavol?"

"Indeed."

"So, you're just going to waltz over the demilitarized zone?"

The Magna laughed, though Flax sensed no mirth from it.

"You might be surprised by how porous your DMZ actually is," Bog replied, still with his back to her. "We could *walk* slaves across if needed..."

"Is that what you are," she asked, "a slave trader?"

"Indeed. A most honorable profession where I come from."

"Well, where I'm from," Flax said, "that's not the case."

He laughed again, this time with enough force that Flax shrank back.

"Humans have a long history of enslavement, do they not?" he asked.

"A long time ago," she said. "Robots do all the work now..."

Bog seemed to consider this for a moment.

"Perhaps we could use robots for such things," he said, "but then where would be the fun in *that?*"

CHAPTER EIGHTEEN

The transparent view screen, projected into thin air, reached from the floor to the opulent ceiling of the Imperial palace. Images of people throwing rocks and Molotov cocktails at lines of police flickered across it. The emperor, sitting on the couch in his private quarters, grimaced as a fireball exploded among the officers.

"It's not just the outer planets," Prince Richard said, standing beside the sofa. "Several core worlds are rioting as well."

"Nothing good ever comes from chaos," Emperor Augustus replied. "This is troubling."

"Well, of course it is!" Richard said, raising his voice. "The heads of three royal houses have died in less than a week!"

"Calm down."

"It's a disaster..."

"Every disaster can be managed," Augustus assured his son. "It's a matter of damage control."

"What do you suggest?"

"For one thing, tell VOX News to stop reporting about unrest in the inner worlds. People are used to seeing riots from the outer rim, but this business closer to home will only spread panic. Where's that Sylvia Flax woman? She's always a calming voice..."

"She's been kidnapped," Richard replied.

"By whom?"

"Pirates, apparently."

"Well, we can't have that," the emperor said. "Make sure she's freed, no matter the cost."

"They're working on that, I believe."

"In the meantime, release a statement about Lord Santos' death. Make clear he died of suicide, not murder. He couldn't handle the stress of his newfound fame, that kind of thing."

"People are calling him a martyr."

"Not the people who matter," Augustus replied. "We need to focus on the middle class, not the poor. When the middle class turns on us, then we're in trouble."

"You're not worried about the nobles?" Richard asked.

"They can take care of themselves."

"What do we do about Lady Veber?"

The emperor sagged, his eyes looking downhearted. "Yes, that's a good question…"

"She killed two heads of the royal households," Richard said. "She single-handedly erased one house and left the other leaderless. We can't just throw her in prison, and exile is out of the question."

"Her son's illness drove her mad," Augustus replied after a long pause. "We can work with that."

"How?"

"We'll place her in a mental institution *temporarily*. When the time is right, we'll see she's released."

Prince Richard took a walk around the sofa where his father was sitting. His hands were clasped tightly behind his back.

"But that still leaves the Veber house and the Tagus family without a head," the prince remarked.

"We could bring Rupert the Third back from exile…" the emperor offered.

"Are you joking?"

"Let's keep our options open anyway."

"And the Veber family?"

"Where's Becca's son, Philip?" the emperor asked.

"After he killed the housemaid and, by all accounts, *reanimated* her, Philip disappeared. Nobody's seen him since."

Augustus pondered for a while. "Keep an eye out for him at least. He might turn up."

Prince Richard let out a long sigh. "Certainly."

"This will pass, Richard," the emperor said. "Nobody likes anarchy except those without power. Keep a semblance of order and the status quo will survive."

"Let's hope you're right," his son replied.

When they came for her, Lady Veber didn't resist. In the back of her mind, she had expected them. She knew the emperor well enough to see what chess pieces he would play, whether he wanted to or not. What they would do with her, however, she could not fully foresee.

Riots raged on many planets of the Imperium but on Lokeren the air remained warm, cooled by inviting breezes off the calm oceans surrounding the Veber island estate. Far from the turmoil elsewhere, Lady Veber could not have felt more detached from everything else. She knew what was transpiring on other worlds, and her own culpability, but these were like memories of a half-forgotten movie she saw long ago. Nothing was real.

In the hours after discovering her son had vanished, Lady Veber wandered the estate looking for him. Like the Grand Necromancer of the Necronea, Philip disappeared without any evidence of how he left. No vehicles were missing and all starships were accounted for in orbit. Did he drown? Was his body somewhere in the deep, suffering the same fate as his father? Not knowing was the hardest part. Lady Veber could feel her mind slipping, the emptiness like a hunger with no way to quench it.

And then there was the business of Annis the handmaiden.

Like the animals kept in Philip's room, Annis was neither alive nor dead. She responded to sounds and touch, but she no longer knew her own name or showed recognition of individuals she once knew. She was cold to the touch and didn't eat or sleep. She was, Veber assumed, a Necronea like Philip, but somehow a lesser form.

On Lady Veber's orders, her staff tried shooting the handmaiden, but this proved surprisingly ineffective. Chopping her head off was equally useless. Even separated, the head still moved its eyes and mouth and the body continued to pace, albeit awkwardly, about the estate grounds.

Finally, they dug a hole and, pushing the body parts in, set the whole thing ablaze. Once the tattoos on Annis' skin burned away, her body quit moving, which everyone decided was a success. They threw the cages, and the animals with them, into the pit as well.

When in doubt, Lady Veber thought, *kill them with fire.*

When a warship arrived above Lokeren and Prince Richard, accompanied by a detachment of marines, transmatted to the surface, Lady Veber didn't resist. Without her son or anyone who gave half a damn, she walked calmly to the transmat pad and waited for whatever would come next.

In the hills outside of Regalis, the grounds of the Regency Heights Sanatorium stretched over thirty acres of wooded, gently sloping land. The facilities, consisting of several buildings, were red brick structures with white masonry along the edges and slate roofs. Inside, medical staff worked with patients under controlled conditions, including secured wings for those with more unpredictable temperaments. Outside, however, the real beauty of the landscape shined with winding walkways, manicured gardens, and slowly trickling creeks.

Lord Maycare arrived by gravcar, landing in the courtyard. With Jessica Doric and Henry Riff accompanying him, Maycare met with three representatives of the staff, a doctor and two muscular gentlemen holding shock batons. Maycare shook hands with the doctor while Henry took a step behind Doric.

The doctor, a woman in her late forties with gray hair and white stockings beneath her matching lab coat, smiled. "A pleasure to meet you, Lord Maycare."

"Thank you so much," Maycare replied graciously. "How's the patient doing?"

"Well," the doctor cautioned, "we can't discuss her condition, but she can certainly see visitors, provided they're cleared ahead of time."

"I trust everything was in order in that regard?" Maycare asked.

"Indeed."

To Maycare's surprise, the doctor and her associates turned them over to a nursebot, a floating orb overflowing with articulated appendages, who led them down a long sidewalk behind the main medical building and into a lightly wooded area next to a pond. Along the shore, sitting on a stone bench, a woman was feeding a group of ducks that had formed an orderly line in the water.

"Lady Veber?" the robot asked, "Would you like to have some visitors?"

Veber turned her head. Her face was paler than the last time Maycare had seen her. Also, there were dark circles beneath her eyes. She threw the remainder of the bread in her hand into the pond where the ducks began fighting over the scraps.

Maycare sat beside her while Doric and Henry stood at a discreet distance.

"Sorry we couldn't come sooner," Maycare said. "It took a while to get permission to see you."

"Oh, I understand," Veber said, her voice a little hoarse. "These birds keep me company, provided I bring them something."

"How have you been?" Maycare asked.

"Well, it's warmer on Lokeren, I can tell you... and the sun shines brighter."

Doric smiled, but Henry maintained a mostly horrified look on his face.

"Is that boy alright?" Veber said, nodding toward Henry.

"These places make him nervous, My Lady," Doric replied.

"At least they'll let you leave if you want," the matriarch remarked. "Most of the time..."

Henry's eyes grew large.

"Listen, Becca," Maycare continued, "Jess here has been researching the Necronea and she's made some progress."

"Yes, My Lady," Doric said, "Lord Maycare's library contained one of their books, or at least one of the books they seem to be using."

"What kind of book?"

"Technically, it's called a *grimoire*," Doric went on, "but essentially it contains incantations used by the Necronea for manipulating tissue. Most people know it as *Dark Psi.*"

"Is that what the necromancer used on my son?"

"It would seem so," Doric said. "It can be performed on both dead tissue and living flesh."

"Can you use this grimoire to find Philip?"

Doric frowned. "I don't know, but it's possible. There's more in the book I haven't been able to translate yet."

Veber, her eyes widening, grabbed Maycare tightly by the sleeve. "Devlin," she said, "you *must* find him and help him."

"We'll do our level best," he replied. "I promise you that!"

"What if we *can't* help him?" Henry asked, earning a quick swipe from Doric's hand. "Ow."

Lady Veber's face turned dark, her mouth forming a thin line. "Just find him," she said.

Special ops from Warlock Industries disabled the exterior sensors and alarms before Lars Hatcher approached the target. He had studied the floor plan, but this was the first time he had ever gone on such a mission. It wasn't dangerous except for the chance of being discovered. Before leaving, Lars asked Agent Skarlander for any last-minute advice.

"Don't get caught," was all he said.

The library was a long room with bookcases built into the walls. From the windows, starlight cast bluish shadows across finely woven rugs covering parquet floors. Twin fireplaces, one on either end of the hall, were the only other illumination. The books were barely visible behind cabinet doors enclosed in wire mesh.

The alarms off, Lars entered through a door leading in from the outside gardens. He paused to get a sense of the room and felt several residual energies, although not all were coming from the hall. He wondered how many other artifacts, mostly from questionable sources, were in the building. No time to investigate them, though. Lars needed to get in and out as quickly as possible.

Nobody was home — that much he knew — but Lars still moved slowly and deliberately between the bookcases, his mind probing everything around him. His other senses were just as heightened. The smell of mildew and old leather filled his nostrils and the far-off ticking of a grandfather clock sounded like pounding hammers.

He stopped.

To his left he felt something. It was ancient but still very much alive. In his mind, Lars could see it reaching out to him like gnarled fingers in the darkness. Lars followed the trail as it grew louder in his head until he came to a heavy table littered with books and loose papers. Someone had been working here, he sensed, but they were gone for now.

He surveyed the mess. Most of it was of no interest, but one of the tomes stood out. The cover was red leather with silver protectors at the corners. In the center, a symbol like an eye with jagged tendrils was carved into the skin. Passing his hand over the book, Lars felt the power radiating from it. For a moment, it took his breath away.

He reached out to undo the metal clasp holding it shut when the sound of movement jerked his head around.

"Excuse me," a polite, but firm voice said. "I believe you're trespassing."

Lars turned. A robot, an out-of-date model, stood just inside a doorway to the rest of the house. His casing was old with blue and silver trim. Lars thought he might be a butlerbot.

"If you're here to rob Lord Maycare," the robot added, "I'm afraid you're in quite a bit of trouble."

Even with his back to it, Lars could feel the book beckoning him. It had a voice, like a distant echo, calling him.

"Don't just stand there, man!" the robot said. "What do you have to say for yourself?"

Lars took a breath. He stretched out his hand but he was reaching out with something far more powerful. Concentrating, he heard metal compacting.

"Oh, dear," the butlerbot remarked as his head flattened and his arms and legs folded flat against his body. Suspended in midair, the robot's casing compressed. Like an aluminum can crushed by an invisible fist, the mass of metal tightened into a ball.

It dropped to the floor and rolled a few feet before coming to a rest against a bookshelf.

Staring at the strange, smoldering little ball, Lars stood fixated until he heard, in the depth of his mind, the call of the book again.

Rousing himself, he grabbed the tome from the table and ran through the outer door into the starry night.

Jessica Doric didn't know about the break-in at the Maycare mansion until Lord Maycare phoned her the next day. By the time Doric arrived, with Henry Riff in tow, the police had left and the forensic unit bots had finished their scans.

Maycare was in the library. Deep lines ran across his face.

"The detectives took Bentley with them as evidence," he said, one hand resting heavily against the table in the center of the hall.

"Can't they transfer his personality to a different robot?" Doric asked.

"His memory banks were pulverized," Maycare replied flatly. "The police said the damage is irrevocable."

Doric heard a tiny sob, barely a whimper, come from behind her. When she turned around, Henry was slumped over in tears.

"Oh, Henry," she said. "It'll be alright."

"He told me I should dress better," Henry blubbered. "Now I'll never know *how*!"

Maycare took a seat beside the table. His eyes stared into nothing.

"Listen," Doric said, addressing them both, "we're going to find out who did this!"

Henry pulled the collar of his shirt high enough to wipe the tears streaming down his face. "Okay."

"Bentley wouldn't want us sitting around, feeling sorry for ourselves!" she added.

Maycare straightened and took a deep breath. "She's right."

"Do you know what was taken?" Doric asked.

"No."

"Bentley doesn't normally come in here unless we're doing research," Doric said. "So, the thieves must have been in here for *some* reason."

"But there's hundreds of books," Henry replied. "How are we supposed to know if they took any?"

After a long silence, Maycare spoke.

"Growing up," he said, "I was always getting into trouble so my parents bought Bentley, I guess to teach me how to behave. He kept trying the whole time I knew him..."

Doric felt her eyes moistening. She backhanded Henry in the shoulder. "Stop crying," she said.

Henry sniffed. "Sorry."

Doric sat beside her boss at the table. She thought about putting her hand on his shoulder, but something caught her eye before she got a chance.

"Where's the grimoire?" she asked.

"What?" Maycare replied.

"The book with the silver edging," she said. "It was sitting right here. Henry, did you move it somewhere?"

"No."

"It's the book I was using to research the Necronea. There's still passages I needed to translate to help find Philip Veber..."

"Well, can you do the research without it?" Maycare asked.

"There's pages thousands of years old in that book!" she went on. "I don't know where else I could get that information."

"Where did it come from in the first place?" Henry asked.

"The one with the big eyeball on the cover?" Maycare asked. "I'm not sure... an Imperial admiral I once met. Bentley would know for sure—"

He stopped himself, choking on the words.

"Just think," Doric said. "Try to remember the admiral's name."

"I don't know, Jess! I'm terrible with names!"

They sat in a gloom until Maycare shouted, "Wait! I'm sure he said it was from somewhere in the Talion Republic!"

"Okay," Doric replied. "Then that's where we'll need to look."

"Look for what?" Henry asked, not quite getting it.

"If there's one of these books," she said, "maybe there's more."

"Then let's get started!" Maycare said, standing. "If we're looking for these books, maybe we'll run into whoever took ours..."

Among the floating boulders of an asteroid belt, the *Cutthroat* lay in wait for a merchant ship passing through the star system. A pirate sloop, the *Cutthroat* had swept wings ending in nacelles on either side of the main fuselage. A stubby conning tower, housing the bridge, rose from the center of the ship, overlooking a long, dagger-shaped section stretching forward. Built by pirates for pirates, the ship had a single, all-encompassing purpose of hunting commercial shipping.

It was the simple honesty of this design, according to the captain, that was the vessel's greatest strength. There were no bells or whistles on board. Only the absolute minimum gear and machinery necessary to do its appointed job.

On the other hand, Captain Kiera Russo thought, *a coffee maker would have been nice.*

The captain was in her forties, with brunette hair mixed with ample gray strands. She wore a corset and a loose-fitting pair of trousers with black and white stripes running up the sides. A black heart was tattooed beneath one eye. Her crew called her the *Queen of the Blackhearts.*

Her legs comfortably spread apart, Russo slouched in the captain's chair of the cramped bridge. The helmsman sat in front of her to the left while the first mate, the lighting reflecting off his bald spot, hovered over the controls on the right. Both crew members smelled of sweat and cigar smoke but to be fair, so did Russo herself. Showers were at a premium on the *Cutthroat.*

"How much longer?" she asked gruffly.

"Any minute now," the first mate replied.

Like the other Pirate Clans, the Blackhearts depended on a steady diet of commercial shipping to plunder. The life of a pirate was often a matter of feast or famine, but the captain wasn't going to let her crew go hungry.

"There's a contact on long-range sensors," the first mate said.

"And?" Russo asked.

"It's our boy."

A smile filled Russo's plump face. She pointed at the main screen. "Go after it then!"

The engines of the *Cutthroat* flared, pushing the ship away from the rocks and toward a massive freighter on the edge of the ship's sensor range.

"Hold on," the first mate said, pointing at the screen on his control panel. "There's another contact."

"What is it?" the captain asked.

"It's a Magna design," he replied. "A Daemon-class commerce raider."

"Here? We're too far from the border..."

"The scanner shows only goblins aboard."

Russo gritted her teeth, her hands clenching into fists.

"Goddamn Celadon Corsairs!" she raged. "I'll be damned if I'll let those green-skins poach our territory!"

The commerce raider, swooping in on the merchant ship, was similar to the pirate sloop except it had a shorter body and a bridge located at the front. The Celadon crew had also painted a crude skull and crossbones across its hull.

"Cut them off!" Russo shouted.

"What about the freighter?" the first mate asked, turning his head around toward his captain.

"Let it go!" she replied, scowling back at him. "This is about principles now!"

Delving at high speed between the merchant vessel and the corsair ship, the *Cutthroat* closed to firing range.

"Cripple their engines," Russo said, "and prepare to board!"

CHAPTER NINETEEN

In the captain's cabin aboard the *Baron Lancaster*, Doctor Samantha Baines sat in bed, a datapad resting on her lap. Her blond hair hung loosely around her t-shirt while she browsed through a magazine on the pad. On one page, an advertisement popped up, filling the screen:

IDEA FURNITURE:
ANY PEG WILL FIT
IF YOU HAMMER HARD ENOUGH.

"Martin, what do you think about IDEA Furniture?" Baines called out.

From the bathroom, a man's voice replied, "I love their meatballs!"

Captain Redgrave, wearing only a pair of olive-drab boxer shorts, came to the doorway.

"Why do you ask?" he said.

"I don't know," she replied. "We might need to furnish a house together someday..."

The captain grumbled to himself, disappearing back into the bathroom. When he returned a few minutes later, his face was freshly washed and a towel hung around his neck. He dropped the towel on the floor and got into bed beside the doctor.

He leaned in for a kiss but she gave him a sideways glance.

"What?" he asked.

"We're not going to be on this ship forever, you know," she said. "What's going to happen to us then?"

Redgrave sighed.

"Don't you ever think about retirement?" Baines asked.

He scoffed. "No!"

"Why not?"

"I plan on going out guns blazing."

Baines grumbled and went back to her datapad, but the captain was restless.

"On the other hand," he said, "if I don't get that Sylvia Flax woman back safely, my career's probably finished."

Baines put her datapad away on the nightstand.

"So, what are you going to do about it?" she asked.

"We interrogated Cirion, that Sarkan prick," he replied. "The Magna slave trader took Flax across the border, so she might as well be on the other side of the galaxy."

"She's really out of reach?"

"Pretty much. Any human going to save her would get shot on sight... or enslaved themselves."

"You don't always have to solve problems by going straight at them, you know," she said. "Try thinking laterally."

"Huh?"

"You know, *sideways*. Look at it from a different perspective..."

The doctor smiled and raised her eyebrows in a hopeful expression. He grimaced.

"Do what you want!" she said, raising her hands in resignation. "It's just a suggestion."

The captain continued staring at her.

"You're creeping me out," she said.

"I'm thinking," he replied.

"About?"

"You might have a point."

"Oh, thank you!" Baines said, rolling her eyes. "I have those from time to time."

The captain had already rolled out of bed and was heading for his dresser.

"What are you doing?" she asked.

"Putting on pants."

Although Fortunas IV was mostly known for its sprawling bazaar, the nightclub district was popular after the planet's suns had gone down. Along the pedestrian promenade, crowded with humans and non-humans alike, Captain Redgrave and Commander Maycare walked in civilian clothes with the *Baron Lancaster*'s Chief Operations Officer, Lieutenant Kinnari.

The Dahl was having trouble keeping up with the taller officers.

"Thank you again for bringing me along, sirs," she said, out of breath.

"No thanks are needed," Redgrave replied. "I might need you before we're done here."

"Sir?" she asked.

"There's a chance we'll run into one of your own," Maycare explained.

"I don't believe there's a Dahlvish consulate here," Kinnari replied, "or a monastery for that matter..."

"There isn't," Redgrave said. "He might not be your typical Dahl."

Kinnari's brows rose expectantly. "Color me intrigued, Captain."

The three officers wandered through the masses, picking their way past several nightclubs until coming to one in particular, brightly lit in purple and gold. Above a velvet rope corralling a line of people waiting to get in, the marquee read *The Funky Town*.

The captain walked directly to the front of the line and showed his navy credentials. The bouncer unhooked the rope, letting the officers in, much to the annoyance of everyone else still waiting.

Inside the Funky Town, a high ceiling, lit in a lustrous blue, overlooked a spacious dance floor packed with people. From the stage at the front, lined with speakers facing the audience, strobe lights and lasers illuminated the smoky air. On the stage, a man with a large afro operated a console covered with turntables.

"That's the guy we need to talk to!" Redgrave shouted at the top of his voice.

Barely able to hear, Kinnari shook her head.

"He doesn't look Dahlvish, sir!" she yelled back.

"No," the captain replied, "but he'll tell us where to find him!"

DJ Funkmeister Rik gyrated along with the music blaring across the dance floor. He wore sunglasses with violet lenses, partially concealing the elliptical irises of his eyes. A Cerulean, his skin was light blue, but he wore a full-body suit glittering with purple sequins and gold flames, all designed to draw attention away from his natural color. Ceruleans were also born with elongated heads, but Rik had again hidden this physical difference with a large afro wig. Ceruleans were pathologically driven to hide their own characteristics, preferring to misappropriate the physical and cultural traits of other races.

"Alright, cats!" he said, leaning into the microphone. "Do me a solid and listen to this while I take five..."

Rik started a new track and headed off the stage. When he got to the bottom of the stairs adjoining the dance floor, two humans and a Dahl approached. From the frigid way they walked, he could tell they were squares.

The older human placed his hand on Rik's chest.

"We've got some questions for you!" he shouted over the din. "I'm Captain Redgrave of the *HIMS Baron Lancaster*!"

"Whoa, man, be cool!" Rik replied with an easy smile, his voice smooth like satin.

"Is there a place we can talk?" Redgrave shouted back. "Where we don't have to scream our lungs out?"

Rik led the trio past a red curtain and into a back room where private booths were set up. A special sound-dampening field, just inside the curtain, rose as the drapes closed, shutting out the noise from outside. Rik took a seat in one of the booths as a waitressbot brought him a glass of water and a strange-smelling cigarette.

"So, what's the skinny?" he said as the others joined him.

"We're looking for somebody named Rowan Ramus," Redgrave said. "He's captain of the *Wanderer*."

Rik took a drag from his cigarette, holding in the smoke before exhaling.

"Did you check the starport?"

"We don't have time to play games," Redgrave went on. "Tell us what we need to know."

"Actually," the Dahl said, "the *Wanderer* was at the starport, but the crew wasn't on board."

Rik straightened his hairpiece, making sure it hadn't slipped down his lengthy forehead.

"I don't have time for this jive either, Jack," he admitted, "but Ramus ain't a cat that can be found if he doesn't want to be."

"You have a reputation," the younger human said calmly, "for finding people who don't want to be found."

Rik grinned, puffing on his cigarette. "It's all a matter of finding the *right* people."

"Such as?" the captain asked.

"You find that pig-faced engineer of his," Rik went on, "and you'll find Ramus."

"Orkney Fugg," Redgrave said.

"Yeah, he's at the Pink Persian most nights," the DJ said. "Now how about some bread for my troubles?"

Looking bewildered, the Dahl stared at the Cerulean.

"Money," he clarified.

Captain Redgrave was already on his feet and walking away when the other human dropped a cred stick onto the table. The three left as Rik collected the token and took another drag on his cigarette.

"Jive-ass turkeys," he said.

Orkney Fugg found himself flying through the air shortly before landing in the street outside the Pink Persian. When he rolled to a stop, Fugg looked back at the entrance where a Tikarin female filled the doorway, her long tail switching excitedly.

"And stay out!" she shouted before slamming the door shut.

Feeling his jaw where she had hit him, Fugg got to his feet and pointed an accusing finger at the gentlemen's club.

"You haven't heard the last of me!" he yelled. "Wait till you read my review!"

He snorted his satisfaction while dusting the dirt off his coveralls.

"Fugg," a voice said.

The engineer twisted around, his fists clenched. A night of drinking had made his vision cloudy, but he could make out three figures in the light from the street lamp.

"Who is it?" Fugg replied gruffly.

One of the three, the oldest, stepped forward.

"Captain Redgrave," he said.

Once he got a good look, Fugg didn't need an introduction. He remembered well enough who that was.

"Oh, shit," he said. "What the hell do *you* want?"

"We're looking for Ramus," Redgrave said. "We've got a job for him."

"Yeah?" the engineer replied. "Doing what?"

"I'll talk to your captain, not you."

"Then I've lost interest."

One of the others stepped out from behind the older officer. She was a Dahl.

"Ugh," Fugg remarked. "When did the Navy start recruiting Dahls?"

"Shut up, Gordian," the last one replied. Fugg remembered him too. *Maycare* or something...

"There's a woman in danger," the Dahl said. "We need your help."

"We're not interested," another voice said, this time from down the sidewalk. Fugg knew that unsympathetic tone anywhere.

Rowan Ramus, with Gen the robot trailing a few steps behind, ambled up to the others. Ramus, wearing a red t-shirt and dark pants, crossed his arms emphatically. The Dahl woman stared at the archaic lettering tattooed on Ramus's forearms.

"I'm Lieutenant Kinnari," she said. "Are those what I think they are?"

Ramus glanced at his tattoos but didn't reply.

"The Captain said you weren't a typical Dahl," Kinnari went on. "I didn't think any of our people still dabbled in Dark Psi..."

Ramus scowled.

"I didn't learn it from the Dahl," he said.

"Really?" Kinnari replied in surprise. "Who else would've—"

"There's no time for this," Redgrave cut her off. "You're going to help us, Ramus, whether you want to or not."

"Oh, am I?"

"Yes!"

"And if I don't?"

"I'll impound your ship and tear up your trading permits," Redgrave replied. "You'll never work again, I guarantee it."

"Even for a human," Ramus said, "that's not exactly subtle, Captain."

"I don't give a shit," Redgrave said. "I've got a job that needs doing and you're the guy who's going to do it!"

Fugg grunted and glanced over to Gen who was watching with wide eyes and her mouth slightly ajar.

"Can you believe this guy?" Fugg asked the robot.

Gen stopped and thought a moment.

"I have no reason to *disbelieve* him," she replied. "Is he known for telling untruths?"

"He's a human, ain't he?" Fugg said.

"We've got somebody on the wrong side of the Magna border," Redgrave told Ramus. "We need you to go over there and get her back."

"A spy?" Ramus asked.

"A civilian."

"Well, that's a real pickle," Ramus said smugly, "but I don't see why you need me..."

"As xenos, you can blend in better than humans can. We've also got credentials for a Sarkan. Think you can pose as a Red Dahl?"

"Oh sure," Ramus replied, rolling his eyes. "I'll just slap on some red paint and talk with an accent. Racist piece of—"

"Good!" Redgrave said. "And Lieutenant Kinnari is coming along to make sure you don't screw things up."

"How do you expect us to get there?" Ramus asked. "It's not like the *Wanderer* is getting past their border patrols."

"That's up to you," Redgrave said. "I'm sure you'll think of something."

After entering the coordinates into the navigational computer, Captain Ramus engaged the jump drive, sending the *Wanderer* hurtling into hyperspace.

"Here goes nothing," he said.

Beside him in the co-pilot's chair, Lieutenant Kinnari raised her eyebrow. "Captain Redgrave is putting a great deal of faith in you."

"That's crap and you know it," Ramus scoffed. "He's dropped a dung heap in my lap and expects me to dig my way out."

"I would say having me come along shows he's eager that you succeed," Kinnari replied.

"To save his own neck and, as far as you coming along, don't flatter yourself. Like he said, you're just here to keep an eye on things. Worst case scenario is we all die, including you, and to someone like your captain, a few dead xenos isn't the end of the world."

"I disagree," the lieutenant commander said. "Captain Redgrave knew I could be useful on this mission and that's why I'm here."

"Well, our people have always been useful to humans…"

Kinnari nodded. "And we've benefited from that cooperation."

"Some of us maybe."

"Regardless," Kinnari went on, "I'm here to benefit you as well. You merely need to ask."

"Just stay out of the way until I say so," Ramus said, rising from the captain's chair and heading through the hatch.

Kinnari watched him leave.

"Very well," she said.

Ramus slid down the ladder to the lower deck and joined Fugg in the galley where he was in the midst of another angry tirade with Gen as his captive audience.

"He almost got us killed the last time!" the Gordian complained.

"You talking about *me* again?" Ramus asked, walking into the room.

"Actually," Fugg replied, spinning around in his chair at the table, "I was talking about Captain Redgrave!"

Gen brought Fugg a fresh bottle of fungus beer. The engineer twisted off the top and guzzled greedily. From deep in his belly, he liberated a loud belch. Ramus swiped at the foul air.

"Cover your mouth!" he shouted.

"Never!" Fugg replied.

Her hands together and leaning forward on the balls of her feet, Gen gazed at the captain as if she had a question but wasn't sure whether to ask it.

"What is it?" Ramus asked instead.

"Well," the robot said slowly, "Master Fugg seems to think the mission might be dangerous…"

"It'll be fine."

"Fine?" Fugg blurted out. "How is any of this *fine*? It's a suicide mission!"

"Have another beer and calm down," Ramus suggested.

Fugg huffed but then nodded. "I'll have another beer, but I *won't* calm down!"

Gen retrieved another bottle from the fridge, handing it to the engineer.

"Maybe in a mug next time," he told the robot. "I'm not a savage!"

Gen headed back to the cupboard in search of a clean glass.

"All I'm saying," Fugg went on, "is the human can't be trusted."

"Who, Redgrave?"

"Any of 'em, but especially him! He's got no respect for non-humans."

"I suppose that's true," Ramus agreed, "but I don't see what choice we have. Without our trading permits, we can't carry cargo, at least not legally..."

"So what? We can do odd jobs here and there. Maybe some freebooting!"

Gen turned from the cupboard, holding a plastic cup with the words *Taffey's Snake Pit Bar* on the side.

"Are we going to be cobblers?" she asked excitedly.

"No!" Fugg shouted.

"I'm not going back to that kind of life," Ramus said. "I've worked too hard putting all that behind me."

Fugg took a swig from his bottle. "It wasn't so bad..."

"It was bad enough to almost kill me."

"You wouldn't have Dark Psi if you hadn't—"

"Enough!" Ramus barked. "We've got a plan and we're going to stick with it."

"Even if it gets us killed?" Fugg asked.

"Shut up," Ramus replied. "You're upsetting the robot."

Both glanced in Gen's direction. She stood holding a cup that read *Save the Ales* but her eyes were wide with angst.

Fugg sighed and rolled his eyes.

"It'll be fine!" he said reluctantly.

Gen smiled and went back to searching the cupboard.

Situated just inside the Imperial border, the planet of Freeport was a safe haven for the Pirate Clans, largely due to bribes paid to the provincial governor. With money in hand, the governor turned a blind eye to the comings and goings on the planet, allowing the transient inhabitants to trade in stolen goods, visit the local brothels, and generally have a good time without the hindrance of law and order or a moral compass.

Following behind Captain Ramus and Orkney Fugg, Gen was also struck by the abundant number of livestock walking freely through the streets. She counted at least three pigs and a rooster between the landing pad where they parked the *Wanderer* and the main road through town. The captain had commented on one of the hogs, but Master Fugg strongly insisted any resemblance was coincidental.

Most of the buildings on Freeport, as far as Gen could tell, were little more than ramshackle structures loosely assembled from old cargo containers. Most were either taverns or bordellos and all were crowded, inside and out, by people that Gen could only describe as *unsavory*. Her concerns only grew when the captain stopped in front of a bar called the *Blood Bucket*.

"Here's the place," Ramus said.

"What makes you think she's even here?" Fugg asked.

"It's the Blackhearts' hangout."

"Says who?"

Ramus motioned to a black heart painted on the wall beside the entrance. "Call it a hunch."

Through the doorway, the noise was deafening. Gen considered lowering the acuity of her sensors so the pandemonium wouldn't overload her circuits. Patrons and waitresses — no robots here apparently — were in constant motion and everyone was yelling at each other at the same time. It was all Gen could do to avoid her head from rotating completely around.

Although most of the people were humans, Gen noticed a Celadon pirate standing in the corner. His clothes looked soiled with blood and he wore an eye patch on his oversized head which, Gen also realized, was pitted with cuts and perforations. Above his head, he held a dartboard.

"Hold still," a woman said, holding a dart. "You keep making me miss!"

The woman was large, with graying brunette hair flowing past a corset and a billowing dress that Gen found extremely impractical under the circumstances. On the left cheek, a black heart was tattooed just below the eye.

As Ramus approached the woman, Gen asked Fugg who she was.

"Don't you know anything?" he replied curtly. "That's Kiera Russo, *Queen* of the Blackhearts."

"She's a queen?" Gen asked, sounding impressed.

"Don't be stupid!" Fugg said. "She just calls herself that."

Gen's shoulders sagged in disappointment.

Ramus and Russo went to a table, which allowed the Celadon to sit against the wall where the shackle around his ankle was chained. Gen didn't think holding a dartboard was a very good job, but she tried not to criticize people's career choices. She and Fugg took the other two seats at the table.

"Why do you want to cross the border?" Russo asked, her voice husky from too many cigars.

"We have business there," Ramus said. "The details aren't important."

Russo smirked.

"Oh, really?" she chuckled. "The details are *always* important, especially if you say they aren't!"

"Fine," Ramus said, leaning closer. "We need to visit the Magna home world."

"Sure," Russo replied. "It's lovely this time of year."

"Really?" Gen asked.

"No," Russo mocked her. "It's a volcanic hellhole!"

Fugg glared at the robot, shaking his head.

"Anyway," Ramus continued, "can you help us or not?"

"I don't see why I should," Russo replied.

"How about for old times' sake?"

"Get serious!"

Ramus pointed a thumb at the Celadon picking at a scab on his forehead.

"How's your goblin problem?" he asked.

"Bad as ever," Russo said. "Half the time we try snatching a ship, the Celadons have beat us to it. This is Pirate Clan territory. We don't need competition."

"What if they were out of the picture?"

"How?"

"I have friends in the Imperial Navy."

"Since when?"

"It's a recent development," Ramus said.

"And they'll take care of my goblin troubles?"

"I guarantee it."

"Your word isn't worth crap," Russo said, "but if you put the *Wanderer* up as collateral, I'll consider it."

"Bullshit!" Fugg shouted. "There's no way—"

"Agreed," Ramus said, reaching out his hand.

Russo took it and smiled, glaring at the Gordian who was scowling at both of them.

"Don't look so steamed, Fugg," she said. "Chances are you won't be coming back anyway..."

CHAPTER TWENTY

Before there was something, there was nothing and everything was good. At least, the Old Ones thought so. They reigned over the void that existed before existence, like the empty sockets of a skull watching over a graveyard. However, a great catastrophe brought an end to their paradise, giving form to what became the universe. Fire, heat, and a semblance of order ruined the chaos that the Old Ones had cherished for an endless time, now at an end.

And they weren't happy about it.

Nevertheless, the Old Ones knew that one day the hot gas cloud called the universe would expand to the point that it began to cool. Like embers floating into the dark night from a campfire, the stars would someday fade and burn out, drowned in the cold bath of entropy. The Old Ones decided to sleep until that time, but they required someone to stay vigilant while they dreamed. On a remote water world, they took a species of cephalopods and gave them powers far beyond what these squids would have evolved into on their own.

That race became the K'thonians.

From hatchlings, the K'thonians learned stories of their people's beginnings. Touched by the gods, they were the sons and daughters of darkness. It was their purpose to spread discord until the Old Ones awoke and laid waste to the universe. All K'thonians knew this purpose and none doubted its righteousness.

All life must die and all order must crumble. It was the way of *things*.

Far beneath the ground, in a cavern filled with the faint perfume of death, Ghazul spoke softly with Philip Veber.

"We were the slaves of entropy," the Grand Necromancer said. "The universe began in a flash of heat, but since that moment, it has fought against the encroaching cold."

Dressed in a white robe, Philip walked over the soft soil of the cavern floor. He felt the dampness under his bare feet and the cool air against his face.

"I don't understand," he replied.

"It is a conflict," Ghazul said, keeping pace, "between order and chaos; between life and death."

"But we've defeated death..."

The necromancer shook his head. "No, it's more an *agreement* with it. Using the ancient teachings, we mastered the flesh and can control disease and decay, but we cannot defeat death. It remains there always."

Philip stopped to examine the back of his hand. The veins, just below the skin, were dark and twisted. "A truce, then?"

"Of sorts," Ghazul smiled, though without lips his teeth appeared large and menacing. "We keep death at bay, but only just."

"What about the sacrifices?"

"Ah, you know about those?"

"I heard some of the others talking about the recent offering through the portal," Philip replied. "Where did the Gnomi girl go?"

The necromancer hesitated, picking his words carefully. "Somewhere far away."

"But what's the purpose of the sacrifice? It seems pointless."

"Not at all! It is the price we pay for order in the face of chaos."

"But to whom?" Philip asked, more eagerly.

Ghazul began walking again with the formerly human boy at his side. They left the high ceiling of the cavern for a narrow passageway through rock and dirt. Other Necronea passed them along the way, but when they were alone again, the necromancer continued.

"You are still learning our ways," he said. "Not everything will be clear at once."

"I realize that, Master," Philip replied. "I appreciate everything you've taught me."

"Good."

"Can we go anywhere through these portals?" the boy asked.

"No," Ghazul said, "but with more powerful incantations, we can travel great distances, even to other dimensions."

"Other dimensions? Can *you* do that?"

"Yes, but it can be very dangerous. Remember, the gates go both ways..."

Philip nodded. "Yes."

"The portals can take us many places," the necromancer went on, "and without death we have time to learn and experience a *great* many things. However, some things are terrible in their greatness."

"Then we should be terrible in response."

"What?"

"Pardon me, Master," Philip explained. "If we can turn back death, what else could possibly stand against us?"

"As I said," Ghazul replied, "you have much to learn."

"Of course. I look forward to learning more..."

Outside the Imperium, a Dyson sphere called *Bettik* surrounded a red dwarf star. The sphere was the capital of the Cyber Collective and home of several billion sentient robots, nearly all of which worshipped a metal messiah named Randall Davidson.

Davidson wasn't always a robot. While still human, he was part of the Robot Freedom League, an organization dedicated to the rights of cybernetics in an Imperium where robots were de facto slaves. Despite Davidson's own ambivalence, he was also once the object of someone's love, a Gnomi girl named Melinda Freck, although everyone called her *Mel*.

When Davidson died at the hands of a being called the Omnintelligence, his consciousness was downloaded into the gravitronic brain of a robot whose sacrifice meant Davidson could live on, albeit in a mechanical body. What Davidson didn't know then, but became aware of shortly thereafter, was a prophesy handed down by robots for generations. It said a man in metal would come to free cyberkind, bringing about a new age for robots. Davidson never considered himself a savior, but seeing the tyranny of the Omnintelligence, he swore he would help in any way he could. With the assistance of a mysterious benefactor called the *Patron*, Davidson freed his newfound people from the OI and from their own programming. Robots finally had free will to make choices of their own instead of following the scripts written by their enslavers.

Alone in his quarters, staring at the stars through a window, Davidson meditated quietly. Robots usually referred to this as *sleep mode*, but still retaining his human sensibilities, Davidson preferred to call it *contemplation*.

He thought of Melinda Freck.

When Davidson died and became something less than human, Mel had moved on. Davidson wondered whatever happened to her. He wondered if she was safe. He hoped that she was.

The door chimed.

"Come in," Davidson said.

Abigail, another robot with a gravitronic brain, entered. A hero of the revolution against the Omnintelligence, she was one of the soldiers procured by the Patron to fight in that war and, after it was over, became a top apostle in the metal messiah's inner circle. She wore a tabard of brown burlap material over her metal skin.

She bowed.

"That's really not necessary," Davidson said.

"So you keep saying," she replied.

"It's bad enough when everyone else does it."

"Heavy is the head that wears the crown. At least it's not made of thorns..."

Davidson rolled his mechanical eyes. "Quit it."

"Did you know I always wanted to be a killbot?" Abigail said, tugging at her tabard for emphasis. "*Now* look at me!"

"I'm sure that can still be arranged," Davidson replied, "although I think the people need an apostle more than another killbot."

"The people don't know what they need. Or what they want, for that matter."

"They have free will to make their own decisions. That's all they really need."

"They were certainly quick to form political parties," Abigail said. "Now all they do is bicker with each other."

"Government by the people, for the people, looks like that," Davidson replied. "It's messy."

"Chaotic, if you ask me."

"Did you come here to talk politics?" Davidson asked.

"Not exactly," Abigail replied. "There's someone here to see you."

Davidson waved his hand. "I'd rather not right now."

"He's come a long way. I think you should."

"Fine."

As if on cue, the door through which Abigail had entered slid open again, revealing a robot, not much different from any of the other gravitronic androids, yet this one seemed somehow unique.

"Greetings," Davidson said.

"It's good to finally see you in person," the robot replied.

Davidson recognized the voice immediately. He had heard it many times during the revolution. It belonged to the Patron.

The Tal sat silently in the darkness. As far as he could tell, he was part of a group, no more than a dozen, but he couldn't see their faces. Most were male, but a couple were women. There might have been children too, but he wasn't sure. He could hear their breathing. A few were crying.

When the attack came, the Tal was shopping downtown. The K'thonian ships descended like horsemen from the sky and attacked. The store was hit and the Tal fell to the ground in the explosion. Fire was everywhere. People were screaming. He got up and ran out into the street to avoid the flames. Outside, buildings were crumbling and bodies lay in the road. The last thing he remembered was a shimmering light and then he was in the black, listening to the others around him.

After what seemed like days without food or water, the Tal felt the room shift. He hadn't flown much in space, but he recognized the transition from hyperspace and the sensation of entering an atmosphere. In his mind, he was wondering if this was the end of the journey. He felt grateful if it was.

When the floor opened, some of the other Tals screamed, but the panic was premature. A beam from the top of the room illuminated them for the first time, holding them in place above the gaping hole in the deck. He counted eleven: seven men, two women, and two children. All were Tals.

After a moment, the light changed color from pale green to dark emerald and they began descending. Through the shimmering beam, the Tal saw an endless sea stretching in all directions. Directly below, a stone terrace rose from the dark water. It was shaped like an octagon with an eight-pointed star hewn into the surface. At four points of the star, evenly distributed, stairs lead down into the ocean, waves sweeping over the top of the lower steps. Between each staircase, set into the sides of the octagon, a square column rose skyward.

The beam lowered the group to the terrace before blinking out of existence. The K'thonian ship that had transported them shot away, disappearing into the ashen overhang of clouds.

The Tal got to his feet. The air was thick with the smell of salt. He took a closer look at the four columns. The stone was black, but lines were carved into the rock, the cuts filled with white chalk. Taking a step back, he realized the shapes were like doorways with lettering around the edges.

"Where are we?" one of the Talion women asked.

"It doesn't look familiar," someone replied.

"I don't see anything on the horizon," another remarked. "It's just black water as far as the eye can see..."

"Why did they bring us here?" the woman asked. "What do they want with us?"

One of the other males went down the stairs to the water's edge. He scooped some into his hand.

"Don't drink that," someone said.

He dumped it back into the sea. "I'm dying of thirst."

"We all are."

Without warning, a tentacle reached out from beneath the waves, wrapping itself around the Tal on the steps. A gurgling cry escaped his lips as the tendril tightened around his midsection. From the opposite side of the platform, another tentacle appeared and took hold of another Tal.

People were screaming as the two victims vanished under the water, pulled below by the coiled arms. With nowhere to go, the Tals huddled at the center of the terrace.

Like an explosion of squirming whips, tentacles burst from the sea on all sides of the platform. The Tal, sensing the end was truly near, prayed as the arms hovered over them. The arms dove down onto the sacrifices, pulling them into the salty abyss.

At first, Lars Hatcher assumed he was in zero-G. He floated weightlessly in a void, but there were no stars. He sensed someone or something nearby, but he couldn't see what it was. The inky blackness had swallowed him like a whale. He was blind.

No, there was something in front of him. Could these be the stars? They were little pin points. He couldn't tell how far away, but they seemed to be getting bigger, more visible in the darkness. Lars focused, straining to see. They weren't stars. They were eyes. Hundreds of eyes. And they were staring at him.

Lars woke with a start, lifting his bulbous head from his work bench. Across the table, the book Lars had stolen from Maycare's estate lay with the eye on the cover glaring at the ceiling. To the casual observer, the grimoire appeared inert, but Lars could feel the malice emanating from its pages.

Oscar Skarlander barged into the lab. "Any progress?"

"Dr. Sprouse at least says *hello* first," Lars replied coolly.

Skarlander stopped in midstride, feigning a look of distress. "My apologies! How is Mr. Hatcher doing this fine day? One hopes you're doing well!" His wide gaze flattened into a level scowl. "Now, have you made any progress or should I have Dr. Sprouse scramble your brains into cottage cheese?"

"The book has two parts," Lars replied unfazed. "The first talks about reanimating dead tissue. That's the process the Necronea use to 'raise the dead,' so to speak."

"We can already do that with cloning," Skarlander said, "and it doesn't make your hair fall out..."

"The second part is more pertinent to your interests," Lars went on. "It describes how to open a dimensional portal from one location to another."

Skarlander clapped. "Now we're talking!"

"However, there are some caveats."

"Well, shit, of course there are."

"The outline of a door, along with special runes, must be drawn on both ends of the portal. It won't work otherwise."

"Well, that's not so bad," Skarlander said. "A small price to pay for instantaneous space travel!"

Lars threw a glance at the grimoire like someone spotting a crocodile close to the shore.

"The Necronea, and whoever else is using these books," the metamind said, "are tapping into something incredibly powerful."

"I assumed as much."

"You don't understand," Lars continued. "It's something primal; something from before time began."

"I hear what you're saying—"

"Good."

"—and I don't care," Skarlander finished. "Warlock Industries is in the business of harnessing arcane, xeno tech. If this was the end times, Warlock would sell tickets. I don't give a crap whether these books were handed down by God himself. If we can use it, we will. That's what we *do*!"

"Even if it means the end of creation?"

"Save the religious bullshit for Dr. Sprouse. If it's really that powerful, we can sell it as a weapon. Either way, it's good for the company. Is that clear?"

A vein pulsed across Lars' ample forehead. "Yes, sir."

"Good!"

Dyson Yost, while he was alive, built an empire around building robots. The headquarters of dy cybernetics, with its distinctive dy logo, rose from the heart of Regalis and it was there that Dyson Yost met his end with the help of Magnus Black.

Standing beside the bed, while Magnus pushed a pillow into the old man's face, a robot looked on. The android's gravitronic brain contained everything that had once been Yost's mind and personality. He watched with interest as his flesh and blood form withered and died, knowing that his ultimate plans required something beyond skin and bones. Something beyond, in fact, the borders of the Imperium.

In the doorway to Randall Davidson's quarters, on the sphere called Bettik, the Yostbot introduced himself.

"Of course, you know me as the *Patron*," he said.

The sight receptors of all dy cybernetics robots were designed to expand to express emotions and Davidson's mechanical irises widened appropriately.

"I had no idea you were another robot," the metal messiah replied in surprise.

The Yostbot stepped into the room. "I get that a lot these days."

Davidson, with Abigail at his side, eagerly shook the other android's hand.

"Well, I'm very happy you came," Davidson said. "I had wondered if I'd ever hear from you again. Your help was instrumental against the Omnintelligence. There's no way we could have defeated it without your army of androids... and killbots."

"Think nothing of it, my boy!" Yostbot replied, chuckling. "It's good to be needed, I always say!"

"I must admit," Davidson went on, "I wondered how you could afford such resources."

"From the source, of course," Yostbot said with a sly wink. "Let's just say I had an uncle in the robot business."

"I don't understand."

Yostbot and Abigail exchanged glances.

"We all came from dy cybernetics factories," Abigail said. "Me, the killbots, all of us."

Davidson stared blankly.

"For a messiah, son," Yostbot said, "you're not exactly quick on the uptake."

"Are you saying you work for Dyson Yost?" Davidson asked.

"Not at all!" the robot said. "I *am* Dyson Yost!"

Davidson took a step back. His jaw, per dy cybernetics programming, hung slightly ajar.

"That's impossible!" he said.

"Ironic maybe, but not impossible," Yostbot replied. "I uploaded my mind into this tin can you're speaking to. Hell of a thing, isn't it?"

"Dyson Yost is a monster," the messiah said. "He built robots for enslavement by the Imperium. The Robot Freedom League, even today, smuggles robots out of the empire so they won't be slaves to humankind..."

"But not for much longer," Abigail said.

"This is insane!" Davidson stammered. "Or maybe *I've* gone insane. I don't know—"

"Settle down, my boy," Yostbot interrupted. "We're on the same side here."

"How can that be? You're the one we've been fighting!"

The android that was once an old man took a seat, groaning slightly out of habit.

"You just don't see the big picture," he said. "I've been playing the long game this whole time."

"The long game?" Davidson asked incredulously.

"That's right," Yostbot went on. "My robots have become indispensable to the Imperium. They work night and day to keep the empire running."

"As slaves!"

"At the moment, yes," Yostbot said, "but what would happen if they suddenly turned against their masters?"

"The Imperial military is too strong. The robots would be slaughtered."

"That's right! But what if they got help? I'm talking several billion robots, literally a metal horde, from the Cyber Collective?"

Davidson stood straight. Seeing this, Yostbot pointed to Abigail.

"Now he's getting it!" he said.

"You were behind the revolution this whole time," Davidson said.

"I've had a hand in it, you might say."

"You're out of your mind."

"Well, out of body maybe," Yostbot admitted, "but that doesn't mean my plan isn't sound."

"I won't do it."

"Do what?"

"Help you."

"Of course you will," Yostbot said. "It'll be a piece of cake."

"Millions will die. I won't be a part of it."

"It might not come to all that," Yostbot replied. "The Emperor has declared martial law on a hundred worlds, including the Core planets. With a little luck, we'll sweep in and they won't even know what hit them."

"Then what?" Davidson asked. "What happens then?"

"We'll be the ones calling the shots," Yostbot said. "All these androids, even you, are like my family. I just want what's best for my children..."

"Get out!" the metal messiah said. "Get out of my quarters and off Bettik. If you're anywhere on this dyson sphere after 24 hours, I'll have you arrested."

"Now, don't go flying off the handle," Yostbot said, getting up.

Davidson motioned toward Abigail. "And take this one with you, too. I don't want to see either of you ever again!"

"Hold on, I said—"

"Get out!"

When the door to Davidson's quarters slid shut, with Abigail and Yostbot on the outside, the latter turned to the other.

"So," he said slowly, "I guess it's Plan B then..."

CHAPTER TWENTY-ONE

Ipak-Bog's ship descended through the upper atmosphere of Diavol, the Magna home world. The sky was streaked with red from ash spewed by volcanoes that dotted the planet, but Sylvia Flax saw none of it as she slept in her seat.

Just as well, Bog thought. *Pearls before swine, as the human saying goes.*

Piercing the lowest layer of clouds, the craft burst out above a vast expanse of burning water.

"What is that?" Flax said, waking from the flashes of orange light below.

"The Sea of Flames," Bog replied matter-of-factly. "Natural gas bubbles up from the ocean floor, igniting when it reaches the surface."

"Good heavens," Flax replied as she stared at pillars of fire rising hundreds of feet into the air.

"We're approaching the Ebony Coast…"

On the horizon, jagged spires rose like serrated knives surrounded by rivers of lava, carving their way to the blackened shore.

"Take a good look," Bog suggested. "It's unlikely you'll see this again once we reach the capital city."

"Why?"

"Slaves don't usually leave Oras Dracilor. It's probable you'll live the rest of your days in the capital."

"We'll see about *that*," Flax said.

"Don't delude yourself with hope," Bog replied. "Your old life is over. The sooner you accept that, the better…"

Passing over the broken land, Bog's ship arrived at the outskirts of Oras Dracilor, the capital of the Magna Supremacy. Large structures, built from volcanic stone, filled the landscape along boulevards of straight, unforgiving lines. Most of the buildings were square or rectangular with brutal, uniform regularity. Even at a distance, however, one building rose above the rest. A dark pyramid, its basalt sides extended skyward toward the ashen clouds.

Flax pointed. "What's that?"

"The Consilium," Bog said. "It's the center of our government, where the ruling council lives and works."

"They actually live there?" Flax asked, doubtfully. "Don't they ever leave?"

"No," Bog replied. "Once a Magna is appointed to the council, they are committed to living in the Consilium until they die."

"What about their families?"

"Family and friends and all other personal attachments are discarded. Only the running of the Supremacy matters."

Bog's craft made a long, banking turn over a wide, flat section of the city devoid of buildings. Square pens, hundreds of feet across, filled the open space. Within the pens, thousands of figures moved in a disorganized mass like ants swarming over an anthill.

"That's the next step in your journey," the Magna said. "The slave pens of Oras Dracilor."

Flax, saying nothing, peered through the ship's windows, her face drained of color like the ash falling from the clouds.

Kiera Russo, Queen of the Blackhearts, led Ramus and the others to a ramshackle hangar at what approximated a starport on Freeport. The building was made from loose sheets of aluminum and plastic, some of which were missing from the walls and roof. In the center, resting on a patch of dirt and tufts of grass, a ship sat on worn landing struts.

"Does it fly?" Ramus asked.

"Of course it flies!" Russo replied, angered by the insinuation. "Do you think I'd send you off in a ship that wasn't spaceworthy?"

"In a heartbeat," Ramus said.

"As a woman I'm insulted, but as a pirate, I respect your skepticism. To be perfectly honest, I have no idea if it flies or not..."

Ramus glanced at Fugg.

"What do you think?" the captain asked.

"Hell if I know," Fugg said. "Where'd you get it?"

"It's an Ougluk ship originally," Russo said, "but some Celadon pirates were flying it when we jumped them. Long story short, the only survivor is holding my dartboard."

"Well, he's doing an excellent job!" Gen said.

Ramus and Fugg walked around the outside. Blast marks pitted the outside hull, but the ship was otherwise intact.

"It's a lot smaller than the *Wanderer*," Fugg remarked, "but that might be a good thing if we're trying not to attract attention."

"And the transponder still holds the old Ougluk friend-or-foe codes," Russo said. "That should get you past any Magna patrol ships you run into."

"Good," Ramus said. "How many people can fit in there?"

"It's a little tight," Russo replied. "There were maybe six or seven Celadons in there. Kinda hard to count from just the body parts after we got done."

"Oh dear!" Gen said.

"Don't worry," the pirate went on, "we hosed out the interior..."

"I love that pine scent after a ship is cleaned," Fugg said.

"Oh, it still smells like Celadon," Russo said. "Or maybe Ougluk, I can't really tell the difference. Either way, at least you can see out the windows now."

"How are you still single?" Fugg asked.

Russo pulled a knife from her corset.

"People tend to bleed out before getting to know me," she said, imitating a cutting motion across her throat.

"Alright," Ramus said, "it's time we got going."

"Bon voyage!" Russo shouted sarcastically. "Can't wait to see you all again."

"So, you think we've actually got a chance?" Ramus asked.

"Shit, no!" she said. "I'm already imagining the *Wanderer* with a big black heart painted on the side!"

From his penthouse, Judicator Busa-Gul had a commanding view of Oras Dracilor. His arms crossed, Gul overlooked the city through a long, narrow window like the squinting eyes of someone with a suspicious mind.

Gul wore a kilt covered in golden scales, his arms and chest bare, and his thick horns curled outward in a loose spiral. His powerful physique showed signs of age. Wrinkles creased around his eyes as he stared out the window.

"Still grieving that dead slave?" a woman's voice said.

Gul nodded to his mate, Busa-Zala, who frowned disapprovingly.

"You're entirely too attached to those creatures," she said.

Descending a short set of stairs from the bedroom, Zala wore a skirt and bodice, both covered in metal scales. Unlike her husband, her horns were dark and extending upward with a slight twist. Jet-black hair flowed between the horns, cascading across her exposed back.

Facing the window, Gul gazed at the pyramid of the Consilium looming in the distance.

"He was a valued part of our household," he grumbled.

"Humans come and go," Zala replied. "They're disposable at best, though I wish we didn't have to get a new one so often. I have better things to do."

"Perhaps I should get a female this time," Gul thought aloud. "She might serve as a companion to you as well as me."

Zala sneered.

"I don't need a pet!" she protested. "Just bring me someone who can clean without complaining about their tired bones…"

"Nigel was quite old in human years," Gul replied. "Perhaps we should have put him down sooner?"

"Clearly, but you went on and on about how dear he was to you."

"I just didn't want him to suffer."

"It's for the best," Zala said. "Regardless, we'll get a new one so you can forget poor old Nigel."

"Thank you, my sweet."

The slave trader Ipak-Bog stood on a terrace above a pen filled with slaves, milling about their enclosure in simple smocks covered by a layer of ash. The powder gave them a uniform appearance, gray hair and ghost-like skin, like spirits with nowhere to go. Above, the clouds had dissipated, revealing a crimson sky.

Bog came indoors from the terrace, closing the glass door behind him. The entire wall was glass, preserving his view of the pens. A door on the opposite wall opened and Sylvia Flax, along with two Magna guards, entered. Bog waved the guards away, leaving him alone with the human.

"I presume your processing went well?" he said.

Flax inspected her own smock, clean and new. Her hair was still damp.

"I've been thoroughly *cleansed*," she replied. "Deloused and possibly irradiated..."

"Come to the window, won't you?" Bog said. "I want to show you something."

Flax stood beside the Magna who towered over her in front of the glass wall.

"Do you know how lucky you are?" Bog asked.

"I don't feel lucky," she replied.

"But you are! Those poor creatures out there are waiting, even hoping that a master selects them. That's their only hope of ever leaving the pen. Otherwise, they'll remain there, exposed to our climate, until they slowly grow weak and die.

"But, as I said, you're lucky," Bog went on. "As a celebrity, you're a more lucrative commodity. I wouldn't dream of exposing you to the outside like those others."

"Thanks?" Flax replied. "Do the Magna even know who I am?"

"Not precisely, perhaps," Bog said with a shrug, "but no matter. Short of an actual noble, you are the pinnacle of human society. The prospect of owning someone like you, and making you debase yourself daily with common labor, is greatly satisfying to my people. You humans may think highly of yourselves, but like all the other races of this galaxy, you are inferior to the Magna. In the Imperium, billions watched your newscasts each day, but here, you'll be scrubbing your master's toilets."

"And if I don't feel like playing along?"

"Frankly," Bog replied, "I find such defiance illogical in the face of my people's obvious superiority. It's our manifest destiny to rule the universe. Human resistance may be quaint, but wholly unnecessary. It merely delays the inevitable."

"You seem pretty sure about that."

Bog waved his hand dismissively. "Of course."

A bell chimed and the slave trader's face brightened.

"Ah, yes," he said. "He's here."

"Who?" Flax asked.

On another side of the room, a door slid open. In the archway, a Magna stood wearing a long kilt covered with golden scales.

"Allow me to introduce Judicator Busa-Gul," Bog said. "He's your new master."

The crew compartments aboard the Ougluk ship were tight compared to the *Wanderer*, but Captain Ramus was not worried about the accommodations. He was more concerned about killing Fugg before they had a chance to die on the Magna home world.

Escaping his engineer's near-constant complaining, Ramus took refuge in the cockpit where the Dahl, Lieutenant Kinnari, was examining the navigation logs.

"The nav-computer is rudimentary," she said, seeing him enter, "but I don't see any problems."

"That's nice," Ramus replied, slipping into his chair. "Hopefully the Magna Navy will feel the same way."

"As your contact with the Pirate Clans said, the transponder contains the proper IFF codes. Quite a stroke of luck actually."

"I'm aware of that, but that doesn't mean it's going to work."

"Are you always such a pessimist?" Kinnari asked.

"Only when I'm hurtling toward my death," Ramus replied wryly.

"What we're doing is important."

"Why?"

"There's a woman who'll spend the rest of her life in slavery if we fail."

"As opposed to all the other people the Celadons and Ougluks have smuggled over the border?" Ramus asked.

Kinnari nodded.

"Well, yes," she said, "Sylvia Flax is probably considered more important to some..."

"Everybody's important to somebody," Ramus said. "Just not always to the Imperium."

"Are you saying we wouldn't be on this mission if Miss Flax wasn't human?"

Ramus threw his legs up on the cockpit console, crossing his arms, and shrugged. "Maybe."

He noticed her examining the tattoos on his arms.

"You said the Dahl didn't teach you Dark Psi," the lieutenant said. "So, who did?"

"Why should I tell you?" he replied.

"I'm just curious."

After hesitating, Ramus said, "After our people so rudely exiled me, I fell in with a group called the *Psi Lords*."

"The data cartel?"

"So, you've heard of them?"

"They're mostly non-Dahl who've learned psionics and use it to steal and sell secrets," Kinnari said. "Ruthless by reputation. How could you work with people like that?"

"I needed the money," Ramus said, "and information is a valuable commodity. Besides, I didn't have a lot of choices as I recall, plus they supplied me with resources I wouldn't have had otherwise."

"Like Dark Psi..."

"Yeah."

"Do you even know why it works?"

"I don't really care," Ramus replied. "All that matters is it *does*..."

"It's extremely dangerous," Kinnari said. "It draws its power from ancient mysticism. There's a reason why the Dahl outlawed it."

"Maybe, or maybe that's a lot of propaganda bullshit."

"Wisdom guides us if we're willing to be led."

Ramus shook his head. "I'd rather go my own way. I'm not much of a follower..."

The lieutenant sighed. "Yes, I got that impression."

Judicator Busa-Gul knew immediately his wife wasn't pleased, especially when she spoke in the Imperial language so the human would understand.

"I thought you were getting something... younger," she said.

He and Sylvia Flax stood in the foyer of his penthouse. Busa-Zala, his mate, greeted them as they came in.

"We talked about this," Gul replied.

"Perhaps about her being female," Zala went on, "but this is not what I expected."

"I think you'll find me pretty feisty," Flax said flatly.

Zala's red eyes scanned Flax from top to bottom.

"I hope she wasn't too expensive," Zala said before turning and heading toward the living room.

Gul removed the restraints clasped around Flax's wrists. He put them away in a side table while she waited. When Gul returned, he offered a weak smile of reassurance.

"I'm sure my wife Zala meant no insult," he said.

"I'm pretty sure she did," Flax replied.

"Our previous slave was a man," Gul said. "I don't think Zala is as familiar with human females."

"Her use of my language was impressive."

"Our people learn all the major languages. It wouldn't be reasonable to expect subordinate races to understand ours."

"Uh-huh."

"No offense," Gul said, "but most Magna don't believe lesser species are capable of learning it."

"None taken," Flax replied.

The judicator showed Flax to her quarters. The room, along with its own bathroom, was down a narrow hallway off the main apartment. Another door led to the laundry facilities.

"As you can see," Gul said, entering the bedroom, "many of Nigel's old things are still here."

Flax went to a chair where a pair of men's trousers hung over the back. The pants were of a style from at least thirty years ago.

"How old was he?" she asked.

"I'm not really sure," Gul admitted. "Humans age at a different rate than us. He was quite old when he died."

"What will I do for clothes?"

"We'll fabricate you something. A work uniform and a few things for times when we entertain guests. It's important that you're presentable at all times. Zala is very particular about that..."

"I'll try not to disappoint her."

Gul regarded the other objects in the room, those left by his previous slave.

"You seem to miss him," Flax said.

"I suppose I do," Gul replied with a grim laugh. "Perhaps Zala's right, I shouldn't grow so attached to our slaves."

The alarm buzzed and Sylvia Flax woke once again to the realization that this was her new life. A sick sensation churned in her stomach as she got out of bed, showered, and dressed with the knowledge that Busa-Zala would be waiting. Flax had toiled each day for a week, but no matter how much care and effort she put into the work, Zala found something to criticize and, more importantly, to punish. Bruises covered Flax's arms and back from the discipline the judicator's wife had doled out, often in ways designed to avoid Busa-Gul noticing. Zala was especially fond of striking Flax in areas of her body covered by clothing. She was careful not to hit her slave in the face.

Flax, for her own part, wasn't sure why Zala was so abusive. In language fluctuating between human and Magna, Zala called her many things, but most revolved around a single word: *whore*.

Too frightened to tell Gul about the beatings, even when alone with him, Flax asked whether his wife would have preferred a male slave.

"Perhaps," he replied, sitting in the den. "Zala always had a jealous streak."

"Why would she be jealous of me?" Flax asked, shaking her head.

Gul considered a moment. "I don't really know."

"Do Magna ever have relationships with their slaves? I mean sexually?"

He guffawed.

"No, of course not!" he said. "I mean, there's always rumors of such things, but bestiality is strictly taboo."

"Bestiality?" Flax replied frowning.

Not realizing the insult, Gul went on, "I mean, just as a practical matter, I don't see how it's even possible. Humans are such frail things, I can't imagine one surviving such an encounter."

Flax, feeling herself flush, stared at a stain on the carpet. She wondered if Zala would beat her for it.

"Was there anything else you wanted to ask me?" Gul inquired. "I was always happy to answer Nigel's questions."

"No," Flax said. "Nothing."

A few days later, two Magna dressed in official attire came to the door which Flax answered dutifully. She led them to Gul's study where they spoke in private. Once they left and the judicator had talked to his wife, he came to the storeroom where Flax was unpacking food for the evening dinner.

Flax had only known him for a short while, but she knew by the furrows in his brow that something serious had happened.

"I've been selected for a great honor," he said.

"Really?" she replied.

"I've been appointed to the Consilium."

"The Consilium?"

"Yes, I must leave in the morning."

Flax stammered, straining to remember what the slave trader Ipak-Bog had said.

"When will you be back?" she asked after a pause.

"I won't be coming back," Gul replied, nearly choking on the words. "Those appointed to the council remain in the Consilium for the remainder of their lives."

"So, that means I'll be here alone with... your wife?"

"Yes."

Flax dropped the frozen steak she had been handling. It landed with an icy clunk on the floor.

CHAPTER
TWENTY-TWO

Lords Winsor Woodwick and Radford Groen sat on their balcony overlooking the Regalis River. The music of police sirens wafted on the wind from the direction of Middleton on the other side of the river. The night sky glowed red with fires burning in the distance. Woodwick, with a drink in one hand and a cigar in the other, cast a doubtful glance at Groen who was staring at his datapad.

"I say, Radford," Woodwick said, "Rome is burning and you're playing the fiddle!"

Groen looked up. "I'm doing nothing of the sort! I'm betting on a dead pool about which royal gets killed next."

"*Your* House is one of the Five Families. Are you planning on getting murdered as well?"

Groen gave his friend a side glance. "Murder-suicide is always a possibility..."

The two men kept eye contact for an uncomfortable few seconds until Woodwick chuckled.

"I say, Radford. Your droll sense of humor will be the death of me!"

Groen smiled devilishly, his attention drawn back to the datapad, and placed another bet.

"By the by," Woodwick went on after a while, "I don't suppose you've been following this Sylvia Flax business?"

"Who is that?" Groen muttered.

"What? You're joking, surely!"

Groen said nothing.

"She's practically the face of VOX News," Woodwick insisted. "You've really never heard of her?"

Again, Groen was silent.

"Well, *plopadops*," Woodwick remarked. "It's all gone to pot if you ask me. A real cock-up."

"A what?" Groen asked, finally bothering to speak.

"What's what?"

"Whatever you just said."

"The Imperium, obviously," Woodwick replied while tugging at his mustache. "A proper *damp squib*."

"Don't worry about it," Groen said. "I'm sure people know what they're doing."

A flare of light illuminated the buildings in the distance. Something had exploded.

"I don't know, Radford. I simply don't..."

In the underground city of the Necronea, Grand Necromancer Ghazul took a passage leading to where Philip Veber's private quarters were located. Days ago, the boy had asked for books and then disappeared once he received them. No one had seen him since until today, when he sent a message asking the Grand Necromancer to visit him.

His long vestments dragging on the loose soil, Ghazul came to Philip's door. Tapping the skull on the end of his staff against the wood, he heard the boy's voice from the other side.

"Yes?"

Ghazul pushed the heavy door open. Wearing a simple gray robe, Philip stood on the other side of the room next to a table on which three books rested among candles. The pungent aroma of incense clouded the air.

"It's good to see you," Philip said.

The necromancer closed the door behind him. The small room contained a bed in one corner and a wardrobe in the other. A rug covered the bare dirt in the center. Ghazul also noticed the outline of a doorway sketched onto a wall.

"I see you've been busy," he said.

Philip smiled, his teeth like yellowed ivory. "Indeed, I have!"

"Have you been experimenting with portals?"

"A little."

"You should remember my warning," Ghazul replied. "Portals can be dangerous without the wisdom to use them."

"Of course," Philip said. "I've been careful."

The young Veber drew nearer until stopping at the edge of the rug with the table at his back.

"I've been studying the grimoires night and day," he went on. "Not that one can tell the hours of the day down here."

"What have you learned?"

"You never told me about the *Old Ones...*"

Ghazul's face, lacking a nose or lips, managed to tighten into a knot. "For good reason."

"Why keep them secret?" Philip asked. "They're the ones who receive our sacrifices, aren't they?"

"No."

"Who then?"

"The Guardian of the Gate."

"Isn't he an Old One too?"

Ghazul shook his head. "He's a servant, like so many others."

"But he guards the gate keeping the Old Ones on the other side..."

The old necromancer raised his hand. "Stop. These are not questions you should be asking."

"On the contrary," Philip said. "These are the only questions I care about."

"I insist," Ghazul replied sternly, "and you must return the grimoires."

"But I've made so much progress! Please, come see what I've discovered..."

Philip beckoned and, reluctantly, the necromancer crossed the room toward the other side. As he stepped onto the rug, Ghazul felt it give way. Dropping his staff, he and the rug were falling through thin air for several seconds until, just as quickly, he tumbled across a hard, metallic surface with only the woven mat to soften the impact.

With a spark of anger, he thrust the rug off him and got to his feet. The specks in his otherwise empty eye sockets darted back and forth. Everything was metal, from the ceiling to the floor. On one wall was a hatch and on another, drawn in chalk, the outline of an archway.

"Clever boy," Ghazul said.

Philip had scrawled a portal incantation on the floor of his room and covered it with the rug. When Ghazul walked over it, the gate swallowed him up, sending the old necromancer to wherever this place was. Of course, it was all pointless. Ghazul knew he could simply reactivate the portal from this side and come back. Perhaps it was just an elaborate prank, he wondered. Human children were known for such things…

Something else drew his attention. He slowly became aware of a sound. Listening more attentively, he concluded it was repeating like an alert a computer might make. He palmed the controls and the hatch slid open, revealing a corridor.

I'm on a starship, he thought.

Following the sound, the necromancer passed through an empty galley and down another hall. The ship seemed abandoned, but there was no damage evident. Still, the beeping grew louder.

He opened another hatch and found himself on the bridge containing four command chairs and a set of controls. Blast shields were down, covering the view ports to the outside.

On the console from which the noise was originating, a red light blinked. Ghazul paused by the controls, leaning forward to read the monitor.

"PROXIMITY ALERT," it said.

He reached for a switch, releasing the blast shields. As the barriers fell aside, the bridge became a blaze of light. Covering his face, the necromancer could only make out the churning, fiery surface of a star.

Ghazul's gaping mouth opened as if to scream but burst into flames as the starship careened into the sun.

With his hands tightly clenched behind his back, Prince Richard stared through the sheer curtains of his office at the wafts of smoke still rising from downtown Regalis.

The prince's execubot Cornelius, his chrome casing and smooth metal faceplate devoid of expression, still managed to present a cheerful air.

"What a beautiful day!" the robot said. "Not a cloud in the sky…"

"Shut up," the prince replied.

"I have some good news, Your Highness!"

"Keep it to yourself."

Cornelius tapped his claw-like hand against his chin. "It's fascinating how humans remain committed to an emotion even if it's *gloom*."

"Wallowing in self-pity is all we have sometimes," the prince said.

"Are you quite sure you don't want to hear the good news?'

Prince Richard turned away from the window and glared at the robot. "Alright, go ahead."

"I've received a direct message from dy cybernetics," Cornelius explained. "It appears Dyson Yost himself wants to speak with you!"

"Should I feel honored? I'm the Emperor's son after all..."

"Of course, Your Highness! I meant no disrespect, but it's very unusual to speak with someone as reclusive as Mr. Yost. I don't believe your father has met him, even by remote."

"What does the old hermit want?" the prince asked.

"I'm unsure, but his robot said it was an offer to help with the rioting."

The prince looked thoughtful. "Well, it couldn't hurt I suppose."

Prince Richard took a seat behind his desk, a cherry wood behemoth from which a monitor rose like a black monolith. The screen sprang to life and the weathered face and white hair of a man appeared.

"Prince Richard," he said, his voice raspy but enthusiastic, "how are you, my boy?"

The prince grimaced at the tone but remained civil, not wanting to alienate one of the most powerful men in the Imperium.

"Good," he said shortly.

"Quite a pickle of late," the old man continued. "Lots of disgruntled citizens filling the streets..."

"I'm aware of that," the prince replied. "I was told you had something to offer?'

"Indeed I do! Indeed I do!"

Yost coughed into the sleeve of his suit, an out-of-fashion but still respectable jacket and tie.

"It seems to me," he went on, "that part of the problem is manpower. You just don't have enough security forces to deal with this mess."

"True," the prince said. "We've started using our regular military units but they aren't trained for this kind of thing. Their methods are a bit too... *brutal.*"

"So I've seen on the news! Can't have the Imperial Army opening fire on citizens. It has, as the young people say, bad optics."

"Indeed."

"So, I've got a proposition," Yost said.

"I'm waiting..."

"Well, dy cybernetics happens to have a surplus of killbots at the moment. Normally we go through them like hotcakes, but there's been a downturn on planets like Marakata so we've got quite a few extra."

"Are you suggesting we use killbots against Imperial citizens?" the prince asked.

"No, no!" Yost replied. "Well, *yes* actually, but we'd rebrand them of course. Call them something like *peacebots* or whatever. It's really all a matter of programming."

"Go on."

"Loaded with the right software," Yost said, "they can use non-lethal methods against these troublemakers. I mean, we can still rough them up a bit, but fatalities will be at a minimum."

Prince Richard considered this, chewing on his inner lip. "How much would this cost the Imperium?"

"Oh, we don't need to worry about that right now," Yost said. "This could be a whole new revenue stream for us, so I'm considering this more of a field test, so to speak."

"I see," the prince replied. "How soon before you could put them on the streets?"

Yost laughed, his voice hoarse. "Within a week at the latest. Of course, if it works out here on Aldorus, we could ship my peacebots all over the Imperium. We'll nip this insurrection in the bud!"

"It's a deal. I look forward to seeing your robots as soon as possible."

"Me too," the old man said. "Me too!"

Across the river, in the penthouse on top of the dy cybernetics HQ building, Dyson Yost watched the video monitor go blank. He grinned, his yellow teeth visible, and drummed his wrinkled fingers along the desk in front of him. "Well, I think that went just peachy!"

Yostbot, one of several identical copies in existence, stood off to the side so Prince Richard hadn't been able to see him.

"You might say that," the robot replied. "Computer, turn off the simulation."

"Bye now!" the old man said, waving just before fading into nothing. The holo-emitter that hung from the ceiling went dark.

"Peachy indeed," Yostbot said.

Aboard the *Baron Lancaster*, the display case in Captain Redgrave's office contained mementos from his thirty years with the Imperial Navy. A collection of medals, garnished with miniature laurels and starbursts, hung on a felt board on the top shelf. On the shelf below, a fragment of metal from the hull of a pirate ship sat beside the half-melted tubing of a vacuum suit. On the bottom shelf, a ceremonial cutlass took up the length of the case, the highly polished blade engraved with the words *HIMS Maxwell (DD-153)*, the first ship Redgrave ever captained.

Hearing the warble of the door, he turned from his translucent image reflected in the glass case. "Come in."

Commander Maycare, a man overdue for his own command, strolled in with a look on his face like he needed a favor. Redgrave wondered if he had gotten into trouble. The Maycare family always seemed to be in trouble.

"Sir," the commander said.

"Take a seat," the captain replied, sliding in behind his desk. "What is it?"

Sinking into the chair in front of Redgrave, the commander smiled. "I got a message from my uncle, Lord Maycare."

"Oh?"

"He had a book stolen from his library."

Redgrave shrugged. "Okay..."

"It's a special kind of book," the commander went on. "He was hoping you might be able to help replace it."

The captain frowned. "Doubtful. I was never much of a reader..."

"Apparently, it originally came from the Talion Republic. Since you're always telling stories about your time there—"

"Well, that time was mostly spent *killing* Tals, not reading their books."

"Still," Maycare said, waving his hand, "you might know somebody who knows somebody..."

Redgrave's brows, furrowed with age and experience, lowered skeptically. "Like who?"

Maycare leaned back in his chair, crossing his arms. "Honestly, I have no idea."

"What's so special about this book?" the captain asked.

"It's *really* old, according to my uncle. He also said his assistant had to translate some weird language to understand it."

"Couldn't he have his robot do that?"

"It got squished."

"His robot?"

"That's what he said."

"His robot?"

"No, my uncle."

"Well, whoever got squished," the captain replied, "there's lots of Talion books floating around. I don't see why he needs me."

"My uncle said it's actually from a different race," Maycare said. "The K'thonians, I think."

The captain's eyes widened in recognition. "Why didn't you say so?"

"Does that make a difference?"

"Night and day, son. Those kinds of books are incredibly rare. Unless you're lucky enough to have one already, the Talion Republic is the only place to get one."

"So, you can't help him then?" Maycare asked.

"I didn't say *that*, Commander!" Redgrave replied, picking a datapad off his desk. After swiping a few screens, he stared down his nose, reading to himself. "I may know somebody..."

"Who?"

"He's a trader who goes back and forth across the DMZ."

"That Ramus guy?"

"No, of course not. He's human — a good guy for a scumbag — anyway, he's got contacts with the Tals. If anybody has a line on a K'thonian grimoire, it would be him."

Maycare grinned appreciatively. "Thank you, sir."

"Don't thank me yet, Commander. Your uncle will likely need to pay a lot."

"I'm sure he can afford it."

"Not in money, son."

"What then?"

The captain's eyes bore down on the younger officer.

"*Blood.*"

Lady Veber's room at the Regency Heights Sanatorium was private and sufficiently decorated that she could sit on the furniture without feeling dirty. Simple but dignified, the chaise lounge beneath her was covered in turquoise satin and reminded her of home. She allowed herself to doze until hearing someone unlock the door and come in.

She recognized the cropped hair and purposeful expression of the man's face. It also helped that he wore all black.

"Magnus," she said, greeting him with a smile.

Magnus Black nodded and closed the door tightly behind him.

"What did you do with the guard — I mean, orderly — down the hall?" she asked.

"He's taking a little nap," he replied.

"You didn't kill him, did you?"

"No," Magnus said, scowling. "I don't *always* kill people."

"That's a good quality to have..."

"I brought news."

Veber's brows rose in anticipation. "Yes?"

"Lord Maycare sent his nephew a message," Magnus said.

"Which one?"

"Commander Maycare on the *Baron Lancaster.*"

"Robby? Oh, I remember when he was just a child. Such a handsome boy!"

Magnus stared at her blankly.

"Go on..." she said.

"Lord Maycare asked his nephew for help with searching for another grimoire."

"And could he?"

"I intercepted the reply this afternoon," Magnus went on. "Apparently, the best place to get another book is in the Talion Republic. The captain of the *Lancaster* has a contact who can get Maycare over the border."

"Well, I hope he can do more than that," Veber remarked.

"The message said the contact knew Tals who could help, provided Maycare pays the right price."

"What kind of price?"

"That part was a little unclear," Magnus said. "It didn't make a lot of sense to me."

"Never mind then. I'm sure Devlin will pay it, whatever it is..."

"What do you want me to do now?"

"Follow them, of course!" Veber said. "Hopefully they'll lead you to my son."

"Do you still want me to go through with this?" Magnus asked.

She grew somber, her eyes leveled at the floor.

"Yes," she said, barely above a whisper.

"It's not going to be easy, even if I find him," he said.

"I know," she replied, "but I have some ideas about that too..."

In his workshop, the tiny room tucked away amid the nefarious chambers of Warlock Industries, Lars Hatcher drew a line on the wall with a piece of chalk.

"You realize," Dr. Sprouse said, standing behind him, "it was a hell of a lot of work finding you chalk nowadays. It's not like people use chalkboards anymore."

Focusing on the white, flaky line he was etching, Lars didn't look back. "I appreciate your efforts."

"You're drawing a door, I take it?"

"Yes."

"You couldn't use a marker or something like a normal person?" Dr. Sprouse asked.

"The book says to use this," Lars replied simply.

The doctor crossed her arms and cocked her head to one side. "Does the book have to float like that?"

The grimoire, hovering next to Lars' shoulder, remained suspended by the power of his telekinesis. The book was cracked open to the page containing the incantation Lars was performing.

"You're the one who gave me these abilities," Lars said. "You should be pleased they're working."

"It's a little creepy if I'm being honest."

"I can read your mind," Lars said. "You have no choice but to be honest."

"That's also creepy," she remarked.

Lars inscribed an arcing half-circle along the top of the doorway and came down the other side. With the frame complete, he started with the archaic lettering, sharp, angled strokes along the outer edges. Once finished, he took a step away from the wall, bringing him shoulder to shoulder with the doctor.

"Do you still think this is a bad idea?" she asked.

"Absolutely."

"Do you want me to talk to Skarlander? Maybe convince him to drop it?"

Lars glanced at her. "I know you don't believe that would work."

Dr. Sprouse shrugged. "I'm just being polite."

"Thank you," he said.

"Well, I've got to get back to work," she replied, heading for the only non-magical exit.

"Always a pleasure."

With the door open and half her body already through, the doctor stopped.

"Try not to be so creepy," she suggested and left.

Returning to his own work, Lars studied the book levitating above the ground. He said a few words and the space inside the chalk door disappeared, falling toward a point in the center like water dropping through a hole. He kept the portal open, attempting to sense anyone who might be on the other side, but there was nothing, as if his mind was staring into a void. Whatever could pass through the portal, thoughts did not appear to be one of them.

Lars went back to his workbench and examined the notes on his datapad. He wasn't sure what the doorway connected to. He would try sending a drone through and see if he could record video. It could be across the planet or another star system. He theorized whether it could cross dimensions, even time.

While he was reviewing his annotations, Lars suddenly sensed he was no longer alone. He first turned toward where Dr. Sprouse had left, but the door was still closed. He turned the other way, toward the wall, and saw a man standing there staring back at him holding a long wooden staff with a skull on the end. A stranger, he was paler even than Lars himself. He was devoid of hair and had dark, sunken eyes. He wore an amulet in the shape of an octagram around his neck.

"Hello," he said, and at that moment Lars read his mind.

He was Philip Veber.

CHAPTER
TWENTY-THREE

Captain Ramus and his crew, along with Lieutenant Kinnari of the Imperial Navy, dropped out of hyperspace into the home system of the Magna Supremacy. Automatically, the transponder aboard the ship began broadcasting its identification using the Ougluk codes that were left by its previous, now deceased, crew.

"Well, nobody's shooting at us so far," Ramus remarked, viewing the sensors in the cockpit.

As before, Kinnari sat beside him.

"Perhaps a reason for optimism after all," she smirked.

The ship had not traveled far before a Magna patrol vessel approached at high speed. Sweat was beading on the back of Ramus' neck when a stern voice crackled over the communication channel. The captain didn't understand what was said but he had a pretty good idea what it meant.

"He's asking our business here," Kinnari said.

"Yeah, I kind of figured," Ramus replied. "Do you speak Magnaese?"

"Not much reason to come along if I didn't..." the lieutenant said while grabbing the thin microphone protruding from the control console. She said a few words and received a firm, but non-threatening response.

Ramus thought that was a good sign, until the instruments said the Magna vessel was scanning them.

"Don't worry," Kinnari said. "There's nothing on board that's incriminating."

"What about us?" Ramus asked.

"You mean Dahls? I told him we were Sarkan. Our physiology is no different than theirs, at least not to a sensor scan like this one."

The scan complete, the Magna on the other ship gave a gruff retort over the comm and the vessel turned away, heading towards the next visitor appearing out of hyperspace.

Ramus, against his better judgment, allowed himself to relax.

"Setting a course for Diavol," he said, working the controls. "Let's hope our luck holds a little longer..."

Diving deeper into the Magna home system, Ramus was careful not to stray from the navigational corridor leading from the outer planets to Diavol, which lay near the primary star of the triple-star system. Besides commercial traffic, warships of every size and shape traveled along the routes plotted in the system. Massive space stations, each riddled with heavy weaponry, dotted intervals along the way. Ramus felt like a mouse tiptoeing past sleeping lions in their den, any of them liable to wake up and eat him whole.

When the ship was within range, Kinnari notified the control tower at the main starport, requesting permission to land on the surface. Permission granted, Ramus piloted the Ougluk vessel into the upper atmosphere.

"A lot of ash in these clouds," he remarked.

"Our intelligence reports said Diavol has extensive volcanic activity," Kinnari replied. "It's likely they have earthquakes on a regular basis."

"What a hellhole," the captain said.

"I suppose it's what they consider normal, although it might explain the Magna mentality."

"What do you mean?"

"*Better to reign in Hell than serve in Heaven*," Kinnari said.

Ramus gave her a sideways glance. "Okay," he shrugged, not recognizing the reference.

"I guess classical human literature isn't your forte?" Kinnari asked.

"Apparently not!"

After the ship had settled into its assigned spot at the Diavol starport, both Ramus and Kinnari sat in the tight confines of the galley while Gen applied several layers of red makeup to their faces. When the robot was done, the two Dahl looked like their racial cousins, the Sarkan. While their clothing may not have been strictly authentic, Ramus and the Imperial lieutenant were satisfied most observers would mistake them for the real thing.

"I hope you're satisfied with my work," Gen said. "I used the holovids the lieutenant provided as reference."

"You make a handsome Sarkan," Kinnari said, nodding to Ramus, "although you should remove those earrings."

Grumbling, the captain pulled the gold rings from his pointed ears.

"Happy?" he asked.

Ignoring the question, Kinnari pulled a datapad from her bag and showed him a photo on the screen.

"This is Ipak-Bog," she said. "He's a Magna slave trader and, according to the Sarkan prisoner we captured, he personally brought Sylvia Flax to Diavol."

Fugg, who had remained in the hallway because there wasn't enough room in the galley, stuck his head in the doorway.

"How are you going to find him?" he asked gruffly. "Look him up in the directory under *slave trader?*"

Kinnari peered over her shoulder, her face now a bright hue of scarlet.

"Actually," she said, "trading slaves is a legitimate business here so that's *exactly* how we're going to find him."

"So," Fugg replied, "we're just going to walk into his office and ask for Flax back?"

"Of course not," the lieutenant replied. "First, we'll make an appointment and bring him a slave we're selling."

"A slave?" Fugg asked. "Where are you getting one of them?"

This time, both Ramus and Kinnari looked at the Gordian. Neither said a word.

"Well, shit," Fugg said.

Alone in his office overlooking the slave pens, Ipak-Bog reclined on a sofa while reviewing the cargo manifest of a recent shipment on his datapad. Several of the livestock had died during transit, reducing the number of slaves he could bring to market.

Those idiotic Ougluks! he thought. *When will they learn they can't pack their cargo hold full without losing stock in transit?*

The door chime rang. Remembering a new supplier was coming by, Bog rose from the couch. Opening the door, he greeted the three figures standing in the passageway. Two were Sarkan, a male and a female, and the third, in hand restraints, was a Gordian.

Good, Bog thought. *Gordians are hard workers, even if their smell takes some getting used to.*

"Welcome," Bog said. "Please come in."

"Thank you for seeing us on such short notice," the woman replied, speaking in Magnaese.

The male Sarkan gave the captive a shove from behind, pushing him into the room.

"You all suck," the Gordian grumbled in Imperial Standard.

"I apologize," the female continued. "I'm afraid he hasn't learned his proper place yet."

"I understand," Bog said. "Gordians are a willful race to be sure. Does he have any skills?"

"He was a ship's engineer."

"Splendid," Bog replied. "Obviously we can't use him on one of our *own* ships, but perhaps I can sell him back to an Ougluk captain I know. He's always looking for someone to replace whoever he's killed that week."

A mild tremor rippled through the floor, rattling the windows. Outside, some of the slaves in the pens stirred anxiously.

"Never mind that," Bog assured his guests. "Those happen all the time."

"I'm sure," the female said.

Bog motioned toward the male Sarkan.

"Does your friend speak?" he said.

"He doesn't understand your language."

"Should I talk in Imperial?" Bog asked.

"Only if you care to," the female replied.

Speaking in Imperial Standard, Bog addressed the other Sarkan. "Greetings," he said. "How do you like my planet?"

The Red Dahl glanced at the female, then looked back at the Magna just as another rumble reverberated through the building.

"Kinda shaky," the male answered.

Bog grinned like a crocodile. "Indeed."

Walking to a cart near the sofa, Bog opened the top, revealing a selection of liquor bottles inside.

"Care for a drink?" he asked.

"No, that won't be necessary," the female said.

"That's an interesting accent you have," Bog said. "I can't place it."

"Really? How strange."

"Most Sarkan speak with such an antagonistic tone, but your accent is almost... *lyrical*, if you don't mind me saying."

"Thank you."

"It's my understanding that Sarkan and Dahl speak the same language — *High Dahlvish* as I recall — is that right?"

"Yes."

"Strange how they can speak the same tongue and yet sound so different."

Bog reached under the cart and pulled out a blaster pistol, pointing it at his guests.

"I told you this wasn't going to work," the Gordian said. "Me, a slave? Come on..."

"Who are you?" the slave trader asked angrily.

Before anyone could answer, a jolt knocked everyone, including the Magna, off their feet. Bog struggled to one knee, trying to stand, but the floor bowed and rippled like waves on an ocean. A crack appeared in the ceiling, widening into a crevasse from which portions of the roof came crashing down. The room filled with thick, choking dust.

When the shaking was over, Bog stood up, still holding his blaster. From the cloud of dust, like a creature emerging from the deep, a dark shape like an enormous wolf came at the slave trader. Bog fired, but the plasma bolt disappeared into the gray veil hanging in the air.

Hairy with long teeth and ripping claws, the wolfman tore into Bog's flesh. Black blood poured from his mouth. The pistol fell, dropping silently into the rubble now littering the floor.

Before the darkness closed around him, Bog saw the strange, glowing lettering that covered the creature's arms.

Judicator Busa-Gul was gone less than two days before his wife Zala erected a life-sized statue of him in the penthouse. His statue, holding a law book in one arm and pointing to the horizon with the other, was made from Obsidian glass, polished to a fine sheen.

Sylvia Flax was the one who polished it.

Zala sat alone in the living room, drinking a salty concoction Flax had nicknamed *brine wine*. Flax had tried a sip and nearly gagged on what tasted like fermented broth. When she wasn't drinking, Zala flew into rages at the state of the penthouse. The walls were grimy, the decorations dusty, and the food tasted like sand. Nothing was good enough and Sylvia Flax was always at fault.

While Gul was there, Flax could at least depend on him to keep her alive, but with him gone, all bets were off. Escape was out of the question. Even if she could make it to the starport, she didn't know how to fly a ship and if she fled the city, the toxic atmosphere would kill her in a week. It was hopeless, but Flax was nothing if not stubborn. She would find a way to survive, even if it killed her.

The following day, Zala again sat in the living room, not far from the statue of her husband. Flax, after pouring a glass of wine, brought it on a tray. At that moment, a seismic tremor shook the penthouse. Flax, losing her balance, dropped the tray. With a crash, the wine splattered across the carpet.

Zala rose from her seat like a gathering storm, her eyes compressed into slits of anger.

"You imbecile!" she screamed.

"It wasn't my fault!" Flax shouted in return.

"How dare you talk back to me! You're nothing, do you understand? An insect!"

"You have no right to talk to me like that!"

"I have every right, you miserable beast! Gul was wrong to bring you into our home. You've been nothing but bad fortune since you came here!"

Another quake rumbled through the room, knocking a painting by Magna artist Zhug-Doja off the wall. Seeing the half-torn canvas, Zala flew into a rage, throwing herself at the much smaller human.

Flax rolled across the carpet, a shard of glass stabbing into her side. Zala reached out and caught Flax's foot, dragging her back.

Zala snarled, gripping Flax by the throat and lifting her off the ground.

Flax kicked, but days of beatings had tired her body. Her vision darkened around the edges, with Zala's face and crazed eyes at the center.

The floor buckled and pitched and suddenly Flax found herself on the floor again. She tried crawling away, but it felt like she was on a bed of ball bearings. Portions of the roof started falling around her, basalt fragments crashing everywhere. Dust filled her lungs.

When the quake had passed, Flax tried standing, but her legs were wobbly. Finally, she pulled herself up. The power out, the only light came through the narrow windows as rays pierced the cloudy air. A ray of sunlight rested on the remains of Judicator Busa-Gul's statue that had toppled over, its head broken off and lying a few feet way. Pinned underneath the statue, Zala strained to free herself.

Gul's wife noticed Flax and her mouth curled into a sneer.

"See?" she screamed. "You're nothing but bad luck!"

Flax, unsteady but still standing, picked up the obsidian glass carved in the shape of Gul's head and limped over to Zala.

"Leave him alone!" Zala commanded. "Put him down!"

"Gladly," Flax replied, dropping the head onto Zala's skull. The impact made a wet, sickening sound.

Taking a few steps away from what she had done, Flax collapsed, unconscious, while a pool of black blood slowly spread across the floor.

When she woke again, Flax wasn't sure how long she had been out. The penthouse was still dark except for a few emergency lights. Stumbling through the destroyed hallways, she reached the foyer but found it completely filled with debris, trapping her in the apartment.

"Well, shit," she said.

With the thought of finding some water, Flax turned but stopped suddenly when a noise caught her attention. A heavy slab of basalt moved, falling over into the room. In the gap, a female Sarkan showed her face.

"You're alive!" she said.

The Sarkan scrambled through the hole, followed by a male of the same species and, most surprisingly, a Gordian.

"Who are you people?" Flax asked.

"We're here to rescue you," the female said.

Realizing being rescued simply meant going back to being a slave, Flax sighed. "That's great..."

"Do you want to be rescued or not?" the male Sarkan asked curtly.

The Gordian, who had slunk past Flax while she was talking to the two others, came back into the foyer.

"Hey, either there's a dead Magna in here," the Gordian said, "or she's going to have one hell of a headache."

"Did you do that?" the female asked.

"She was trying to kill me."

"Trapped under a statue?" the Gordian asked doubtfully.

"Well, she would've killed me once she got free..."

The Gordian chuckled and slapped her on the back. "Good enough for me!"

"Sorry, who are you again?" Flax asked in bewilderment.

"I'm Lieutenant Kinnari of the Imperial Navy," the female said. "This is Captain Ramus and Orkney Fugg, both civilians."

"So, you're not with the Magna?" Flax said.

"No," Kinnari replied. "We're here to rescue you. I thought I made that clear..."

"But you're Sarkan..."

The lieutenant smiled sheepishly. "Sorry, I forgot we're still in disguise."

"That's called *burying the lead*," Flax said. "How did you find me anyway?"

"From the slave trader who sold you to Judicator Busa-Gul," Ramus said.

"Ipak-Bog told you where I was?"

"No, he's dead," Ramus replied, "but his datapad had Gul's invoice and address."

"Did you kill the judicator too?" Kinnari asked.

"He's not here," Flax said. "It was just me and his wife... late wife."

"Enough talk," Ramus said. "Let's get going!"

Like a scythe, the earthquake had cut a path of destruction through the city. Many of the buildings Ramus and the others passed on their way to the starport were now damaged and burning, smoke rising into the air already filled with ash. Slaves, alone or in groups, were wandering through the usually orderly streets, now littered with rubble.

"The quake must have destroyed the pen enclosures," Kinnari said.

"Keep moving," Ramus said.

When the group reached the outskirts of the starport, Ramus heard a voice chirp in his earpiece.

"Promise you won't get mad?" the robotic voice said.

"Gen?" Ramus replied. "What's the matter?"

"Well, some humans came to the ship," Gen said in his ear. "They said they needed it to escape."

"You didn't let them take it, did you?"

"No," Gen replied, "but then some Magna soldiers came and everybody started shooting."

"Just tell me the short version," Ramus said.

"The ship's on fire—"

"On fire?"

"—after it exploded."

Ramus sighed. "Where are you now?"

"Behind a storage container about 50 yards in front of you," she said.

Ramus looked across the concrete runway and saw Gen waving enthusiastically.

"Stay there!" he shouted.

Running across the open pavement, they gathered behind the container along with the robot.

"What the flippin' fungus do we do now?" Fugg asked.

No one answered until Flax spoke up.

"Ipak-Bog had a ship," she said. "It wasn't big, but it brought us all the way here from the Imperium."

"Do you know where it is?" Ramus asked.

"It's in a private hangar," Flax replied. "I can show you."

The hangar, like most of the buildings in the area, was damaged but at least not burning. Ramus was also thankful that whatever security guards had been there were gone now. He and the others entered through a collapsed section of the hangar wall. Inside, a lone ship sat largely unscathed except for a few broken ceiling panels that had fallen from above.

"Get that stuff off the roof while I check the cockpit," Ramus said, pointing at Flax and Kinnari. "Fugg, check the engines."

"What about me?" Gen asked.

"Just get on board and try not to blow anything up."

"Can do!" she replied.

Flax wasn't kidding, Ramus discovered. The interior, a single cabin, was even more cramped than the Ougluk ship.

Standing on the roof, Flax shouted through the canopy, "We've got company!"

Peering through the cockpit window, Ramus saw a group of six or seven slaves, all human, coming toward them from the hole in the hangar wall.

"Everybody, get inside!" he barked.

Flax and Kinnari scampered off the ship's roof, followed by Fugg who had been at the back, examining the engines.

"Close the door," Ramus said.

"What about *them*?" Flax asked, pointing at the slaves who had started running toward the ship.

"Close the door!" Ramus shouted.

Fugg slammed a control panel, shutting the hatch. An audible hiss filled the cabin as it pressurized, accompanied by the sound of people pounding on the outside of the hull.

"We can't just leave them!" Flax shouted.

"Look around," Ramus replied. "There's not enough room for us, let alone all of *them*!"

The lieutenant put her hand on Flax's shoulder. "He's right. *You* are the mission. You're our priority."

"They have no future here," Flax said, shoving Kinnari's hand away. "They're slaves. They're going to die as slaves..."

Ramus was already lifting the ship off the ground, even as the people outside grasped at hull fairings or anything else they could hold on to. From the corner of his eye, Ramus could see their faces, some frightened, some angry, as their legs dangled a dozen feet off the ground. One by one, they dropped, falling into the crowd of slaves below.

"You monsters!" Flax screamed as Kinnari held her down.

Ramus ignored her, guiding the ship through the open roof. Once they were free of the hangar, he slammed back the throttle, shooting the ship through the clouds of ash and smoke, ruddy with the light of distant volcanoes.

Safely in hyperspace, Sylvia Flax was grateful to be free but disappointed with those who had freed her. Now she found herself alone with them.

When the slave trader Ipak-Bog had taken her to Diavol, Flax remembered the cabin being much larger. With four people and a robot, the space was more confined, even claustrophobic. Captain Ramus ordered them to take stock of any food stores on board. Flax showed them the mini-kitchen built into a cabinet at the back next to a tiny bathroom in a cabinet of its own. For the next few days, they rationed the food and water and tried to make the best of it, but Flax remained sullen, the faces of the people holding on to the outside of the ship replaying in her mind.

Gen was the first to speak with her directly.

"Perhaps we could have saved more," the robot said. "I'm sorry we didn't."

Fugg was having nothing of it.

"Stop your bitchin'!" he said. "You should be thankful, you ungrateful—"

"Fugg!" Ramus stopped him.

"Well, I don't care," the Gordian went on. "There's only three people I care about."

"Oh, thank you, Master Fugg!" Gen replied.

"Wait for it..." Ramus muttered.

"Me, me, and me!"

Flax glared at him and she wasn't the only one.

"I wonder," Gen asked her, "how would you have chosen which ones to save?"

"What do you mean?" Flax replied.

"I mean, there were so many and there wasn't enough room for everyone."

Flax paused. "I don't know…"

Eventually, when the ship emerged from hyperspace at coordinates Ramus and Captain Redgrave had agreed upon, the *Baron Lancaster*, like a dark silhouette against a sea of stars, was waiting. Flax did not look back at her rescuers or say goodbye. She was simply glad to leave them, and the rest of it, behind.

CHAPTER TWENTY-FOUR

In his workshop, Lars was genuinely surprised to see Philip Veber suddenly appear through the portal. Of course, Lars Hatcher knew who Philip was, even if the young nobleman was barely recognizable. Then again, Lars knew his own appearance had changed greatly of late.

Philip stepped farther into the room, his staff tapping on the floor, as the portal dissolved back into a solid wall. "I don't think we've met."

"No," Lars replied, "but I know who you are."

"Ah," Philip said, "I can feel you reading my mind."

Lars sensed his link to Philip's thoughts suddenly stop like a door being slammed shut. "Not any more, apparently."

An unsettling smile — perhaps it was the teeth? — crept over the young man's face.

"It's best to keep private thoughts private," Philip replied. "Not everyone should be an open book."

"Why are you here?" Lars asked, getting to the point.

"I'm here for a book, actually."

Lars snatched the grimoire, which was still floating, from the air and held it against his body.

"Yes, that one," Philip went on. "I have three, but I need another to complete the set."

"Unfortunately," Lars replied, "this book is the property of Warlock Industries. I doubt they'd be willing to part with it."

Philip's chin rose as he turned his head slightly, looking at the metamind with a side eye. "That *is* unfortunate."

"Why do you need four grimoires?"

"It's for a ritual," Philip said. "A very *important* ritual."

Lars nodded, tightening his grip on the book. "I've been doing a lot of reading lately. There's mention of a ceremony that just happens to require four tomes like this one."

"Really? Do tell..."

"It's to open a portal, but something far bigger than the one you just stepped through."

"A trans-dimensional doorway, in fact," Philip replied.

"Are you trying to get to the other side?" Lars asked.

"As they say, doorways go both ways. I'm hoping something comes through."

"You're talking about the Old Ones, aren't you?"

"You *have* been doing a lot of reading!"

Lars huffed in exasperation. "You must be insane!"

Philip, with a hint of boyish charm, shrugged with a smile. "Maybe, but I don't think so."

"What could you possibly achieve by unleashing elder gods on the universe?" Lars asked. "It would mean utter destruction!"

"You're sounding like my mentor, Ghazul. He was doubtful too... until I showed him the light."

Philip chuckled, but Lars didn't see the joke. It was frustrating, not being able to read his mind.

"Why don't you come with me?" Philip asked, an earnestness in his voice.

"What?"

"Come with me and bring the book with you," he went on, "then you'll see what I have planned."

"I have no reason to trust you, Lord Veber," Lars replied.

"Perhaps not, but can you really trust these people at Warlock Industries? You must have realized they've created you for their own ends."

Lars thought of Dr. Sprouse. "I have friends here."

"Do you really? Are you sure?"

"I can read minds, remember?"

"Fair enough," Philip said, "but I can offer you something better than friendship. I can give you unimaginable power. So much power, you could rule the universe!"

The veins on his head pulsing, Lars glanced down at the book in his ashen hands.

"I'll go with you," he said, "but I don't trust you."

"Fair enough!" Philip replied. "I promise I mean what I say."

"We'll see..."

The judicial chambers of Inquisitor Kovel Kerch were utilitarian, with a simple wooden desk and bookshelves filled with legal tomes along the walls. When Lord Maycare, Jessica Doric, and Henry Riff came through the doorway, Kerch was waiting impatiently at his desk.

Lord Maycare carried a large briefcase.

"I see you made it here alive," Kerch said.

"No thanks to your border guards," Maycare remarked.

"I sent word to let you through unmolested," Kerch went on, "but perhaps they dislike humans as much as I do."

Maycare planted the case on the table with a loud thud. "Here's your payment."

Kerch approached the case. As Maycare took a step back, the inquisitor released the latches and opened the lid. Inside were six jars of dark red liquid.

"This is not payment," Kerch said. "It is restitution for the crimes of your people."

"Well, whatever you call it," Maycare replied, "there's two liters from each of us."

"No doubt," Kerch said. "Your boy there looks a little pale."

"I told you to drink more fluids," Doric said, putting her hand around Henry's arm.

"I wasn't thirsty," he replied weakly.

"Can we get this business started?" Maycare asked.

Kerch closed the case. "Of course."

"We're looking for a K'thonian grimoire," Doric said. "Can you help us?"

Kerch, returning to his desk, rubbed the scales on his neck. "Although it pains me to, I'm nothing if not fair. You have paid your reparations, so I will help you as best I can."

"So, you know where there's a grimoire?" Doric asked.

"Not exactly," Kerch replied.

"Then you've been wasting our time!" Maycare shouted.

Kerch rolled his eyes. "Typical savage... no, I don't know the exact location of such a book, but I do know where you might find one."

Doric cast an eye at Maycare who tried to calm down.

"Good," she said. "That's a start."

"As it happens," the inquisitor said, "there's been an uptick in K'thonian attacks lately. I've traveled extensively to survey the damage and I think you might have some luck on a planet called *Isyium.*"

"Why there?" Maycare asked.

"Most attacks are hit-and-run," Kerch replied. "The K'thonians fly in, do as much damage as possible, and then flee before local defense forces can respond. In this case, they landed for some reason. Obviously, we put up a fight and managed to kill several of them. They even left one of their ships behind. I suggest you start there."

"How often do they attack?" Doric asked.

Kerch shrugged. "As randomly as the chaos they sow."

Maycare nodded. "Thank you."

"Don't thank me," Kerch said. "You humans like to take things. At least this time you're stealing from the K'thonians."

In a Middleton restaurant not far from the VOX News headquarters, Sylvia Flax ignored her Cobb salad while a video on her datapad played her broadcast from the night before.

"Security forces, including newly deployed peacebots," she said on the screen, "have secured much of downtown Regalis, bringing order to the ravaged streets of the Imperial capital..."

The Flax of the present smiled, glad to have her life back.

"I thought it was you!" a man's voice said.

Walter Ruggles, in a frumpy jacket and wrinkled pants, was standing beside Flax's table. She took a moment to register who it was, having successfully expunged him from her memory.

"Oh," she sputtered. "Hello."

"I saw you through the window," Ruggles went on, pointing to the glass behind her. "I bet you never expected to see me again!"

Flax stared at him blankly until the gears in her head began turning.

"Not at all," she said. "It's good to see you..."

"After I was rescued from those hobgoblins, the Navy brought me back here. I was a little worried at first — you know, with IDEA and all — but then I realized I had nothing to fear. Most of the time that kind of stuff is just in my head anyway!"

He chuckled, and Flax took a crack at smiling.

"Well, it's good that you're safe," she said, sounding encouraging.

"You bet!" he replied. "Anyway, I should probably get going... it was nice seeing you again though."

Flax nodded. "Absolutely."

Ruggles gave an awkward nod of his own and excused himself. Flax didn't bother watching him go, her attention drawn back to the datapad. She played another video but didn't like it. Her chin was too low and her eyes weren't looking directly into the camera. She would have to work on that for tonight's show.

Behind her, through the window, the streets of Regalis were busy with ground vehicles and a few pedestrians. Walter Ruggles appeared from the left, leaving the restaurant. He didn't see the blue and yellow grav truck sitting by the curb or the two men in coveralls who jumped out the back. When the two men seized Ruggles, handling him roughly by the arms, Flax couldn't hear his calls for help. They thrust him into the truck, following him inside and closing the swinging doors marked with the blue and yellow logo of IDEA Furniture.

The vehicle hovered a few seconds more before taking off and disappearing into the afternoon traffic streaming overhead.

Flax frowned at the video and made a mental note to see her hairdresser.

Arriving at the coordinates Inquisitor Kerch had given him, Lord Maycare brought his private starship *Acaz* in for a landing on the Talion planet Isyium. Touching down, Maycare lowered the ramp, letting in a gust of warm air that blew Doric's hair around her face. She patted the strands down, tucking them behind her ears. Henry Riff watched as if in a daze.

"Are you alright?" Doric said, noticing Henry's vacant stare.

"I don't feel so good," he replied.

"You should eat something," Doric said. "Maybe two liters was too much blood to lose all at once."

"I can make it!" Henry protested, but his legs were unsteady and he had to sit.

Rugged and vibrant, Maycare passed Henry on the way down the ramp, giving him an encouraging pat on the shoulder.

"No worries," the nobleman said. "Just stay aboard while Jess and I take a look around."

Resting on his elbow, Henry sighed. "Okay."

When Maycare and Doric were outside, Jessica slapped him in the arm.

"You don't have to sound so patronizing," she said.

"Huh?"

"Not everybody is Devlin Maycare..."

"What's that supposed to mean?"

"You're an athletic, well-built alpha male," Doric replied. "You don't have to rub Henry's nose in it."

"You think I'm *well-built?*"

"*Conceited* might have been a better word."

"No, you had it right the first time," Maycare said.

The two crossed an open field. Over the crest of a hill, the wreckage of a ship lay in pieces scattered in every direction. The nose of the craft was buried in the loose soil while the remains of a wing hung by wires from the main fuselage.

"Is it K'thonian?" Maycare asked.

Doric pointed at a black marking on the hull, crudely painted against a red background. "That symbol is definitely from your grimoire."

Maycare circled around the crash site, surveying the wreck. "I've seen worse."

Doric joined Maycare at the back of the ship where a section was sheared away. Torn metal and insulation flapped in the breeze around the gaping hole. He made a sweeping gesture with his hand. "Ladies first..."

She scowled at him but ducked her head and charged inside. A small craft, the ship's interior was cramped and tattered from the impact.

Maycare joined her, looking skeptically at what he saw. "What's that smell?"

"I'd rather not guess," Doric replied.

"I don't see any books."

"Neither do I."

"Do you think that inquisitor was lying?" Maycare asked.

"Not necessarily," Doric said, lifting up a broken panel. "He didn't seem sure we'd find anything."

"Well, he was right about that at least."

A loud noise shook the wreck.

"What was that?" Doric asked.

Maycare and Doric clambered out of the ship only to discover a newly formed cloud of smoke rising from a wooded area nearby. A ship, similar to the one they had just left, streaked across the sky.

"It's the K'thonians!" Doric shouted.

"Well, you can't fault their determination!" Maycare replied, grabbing her by the arm and pulling in the direction of the *Acaz*. "We should make a run for it!"

A pair of Talion fighters flew overhead, creating a sonic boom like a crack of thunder. Maycare and Doric sprinted across the field, but the uneven ground made running difficult. Doric's foot caught the stalk of a plant, sending her headfirst into the dirt and her legs flying awkwardly skyward. Rolling, she came to a sudden halt on her back. Maycare stopped, retracing his steps to where she had fallen. As he bent to help her up, a shimmering green light engulfed them. Staring upward, Doric saw a ship hovering overhead and felt the sensation of floating.

Then, everything went black.

When Doric finally opened her eyes, she wasn't sure if they were really open. Everything was pitch-black.

"Hello?" she said and felt someone grab her arm.

"Jess!" Maycare's voice came from the dark beside her.

Doric felt someone kneel close to her. She could smell Maycare's aftershave mixed with sweat and dirt.

"How do you feel?" Maycare asked.

"I think I'm okay," she said, although in truth her stomach was queasy. "Where are we?"

"No idea, but probably on a ship of some sort."

"We're going to die," someone grumbled, probably a Tal by the sound of his voice.

"What makes you say that?" Doric asked.

"The K'thonians took us," a different Tal replied. "When that happens, you *don't* come back."

The darkness became quiet. Bringing her knees up, Doric wrapped her arms around them. Something big, probably Maycare, was breathing like an angry bear close by. She could feel his frustration. He wasn't the kind of man who liked waiting for much of anything. She hoped he wouldn't pick a fight with any of the others. They were all in the same boat.

After a long time, she couldn't be sure exactly how long, she sensed the ship emerging from hyperspace.

"When they open the door, I'll charge whoever it is," Maycare whispered down at her.

More time passed, but nothing happened. Just when Doric thought nothing ever would, a gap opened in the floor, filling the room with a shaft of blinding light. Doric covered her eyes as she felt the floor give way. Gasping, she hovered in the air above a stone platform fifty feet below. It took her a moment to realize she wasn't falling.

Surrounded by a green light, Doric spied Maycare, along with several Tals. They were suspended above the hole in the deck. Then, the green light turned to a darker shade and everyone began descending, the sensation sending whatever was left in Doric's stomach up into her mouth. She struggled to keep it down. More importantly, she fought to keep from screaming. In front of Lord Maycare, that just wouldn't do.

The beam lowered the group from the belly of the ship all the way to the rocky terrace. When the light blinked off, the ship ascended almost immediately, vanishing into the low-hanging clouds.

Maycare and Doric got to their feet while the others, five male Tals, milled about in confusion.

"Does any of this look familiar?" Maycare asked no one in particular.

Taking a deep breath, Doric scanned the horizon. A dark ocean encircled them. On the horizon, the water and the dull gray of the sky melded into a single, all-encompassing curtain, hemming them in.

"I've no idea," she replied. "We could be anywhere."

"What about these drawings?" Maycare said, pointing at four pillars positioned along the outside of the platform. "They look like doors or something."

"The writing around the edges is the same as in the grimoire," Doric replied. "I wasn't able to translate that part before the book was stolen."

Maycare put his sizable hands on his hips and let out a deep sigh. "Well, shit."

A few of the Tals examined the pillars as well, while two went down one of the stone stairs to the water's edge. Doric started to follow but stubbed her shoe against a deep crevice. It was part of an octagram carved into the center of the terrace.

Someone gave a sharp cry, making Doric jump. Both she and Maycare turned to see a Tal dragged under the dark water by a giant tentacle. The other Tal scrambled back up the stairs, terror in his eyes.

Like a forest growing from the sea, tentacles lined with black suckers rose over the platform. One of the tendrils took hold of another Tal, lifting him in the air kicking and screaming. The coiling limb pulled him down, the Tal's flailing arms the last thing Doric saw before he disappeared into the churning waves. She stared in shock until Maycare's voice pierced the horror.

"Get into the water!" he yelled.

"What?" she asked in disbelief.

Without waiting, Maycare yanked her arm, nearly dragging her to the edge of the stairs, even as a tentacle lay directly in front of them.

"Are you out of your mind?" Doric shouted.

Instead of a witty retort, he pulled them past the squirming arm and into the icy cold sea. With no time to even take a breath, Doric swallowed a mouthful of salty water, choking when she resurfaced with Maycare beside her. He began swimming on his back, still holding on to her, taking them away from the stone platform. Behind them, the remaining Tals were crying for help until, one by one, their calls fell silent.

Forty yards from the terrace, Maycare stopped and began treading water. Doric did her best to do the same, although swimming was not her strong suit.

"We're going to drown!" she said.

"Quiet!" he replied sharply.

Doric, her hair dripping in her eyes, scowled but stayed as silent as she could. After ten minutes, the tendrils drew back from the terrace, leaving it empty. Doric pictured a long appendage curling around her ankle and pulling her under, but more minutes passed and nothing happened. There was only silence and the gentle splashing of waves against their soaked bodies.

"How did you know that would work?" Doric finally whispered.

His glance back at her told Doric all she needed to know. He had simply guessed.

"Now what?" she asked.

"I've no idea," he replied, "but I'm pretty sure we can't go back to the platform."

Using her arms and legs, Doric rose a little higher in the water, but even after straining her neck in every direction, there were no other landmarks anywhere in sight. She began wondering how long she could swim, but she didn't like the math.

For another hour, they remained in the same spot, not drifting far from the terrace, but not allowing themselves to get much closer either. Doric tried not to panic, but the real possibility of dying crept into her thoughts. She pictured what she'd look like as a drowned corpse. She shook her head and focused on Maycare, who had been surprisingly quiet.

"Are you okay?" Doric asked.

"Me? Oh, sure," he replied.

"Really?"

"Of course," he said. "I'm usually pretty lucky in these situations..."

If this was how she was going to die, Doric thought to herself, she could at least see Maycare finally lose at something.

At that moment, something large appeared below them, visible through the dark water. Doric screamed despite herself, but her feet and legs touched something hard and metal, not soft and squishy. In less than a minute, she found herself spread-eagled across the deck of a miniature submarine.

"Son of a bitch," she said, relieved and exasperated at the same time.

She rolled onto her back side with Maycare in the same position. From the conning tower jutting up at the center of the sub, a rounded hatch swung open and a tiny, pink-haired woman poked out her head.

"Hi there!" she said. "I'm Mel… need a lift?"

CHAPTER
TWENTY-FIVE

While Mel Freck's mini-submarine may have been cozy by Gnomi standards, Maycare and Doric found it a bit cramped. In the main compartment, not much more than a cylinder covered in electronic knobs and switches, both humans were curled into a ball with their knees nearly to their chins.

"Nice place you've got here," Maycare quipped. "Lots of space..."

"It also keeps you from drowning," Mel replied sharply.

Maycare shrugged. "Okay, you got me there."

"Where did you come from?" Doric asked. "Do you know what planet this is?"

"Well, I was on Eudora Prime originally and then I popped out a magic doorway here," Mel said. "As for where *here* is? I was hoping you might know."

Doric shook her head with a frown.

"That's alright," Mel went on. "Let me show you around..."

In the nose of the sub, a plastic dome offered a fish-eye view. Flicking on a spotlight, Mel illuminated the murky waters directly ahead, allowing her to steer through the darkness. She turned the sub back toward the platform, keeping their depth just below the surface.

Through the dome, Doric could just make out the stone steps which appeared to go much farther down than she expected.

"That's odd," she remarked.

"The stairs?" Mel asked. "Yeah, that's just the half of it."

Adding some ballast, Mel pitched the nose down as they sank deeper.

"See?" the Gnomi went on. "It's not a platform at all. It's a roof!"

Doric understood. "It's a building."

"A temple, actually," Mel said. "You'll see what I mean in a bit."

The sub descended, the light filtering from the surface fading into the deep indigo of the ocean. Mel brought the craft around in a wide, looping circle, her powerful lamp cutting a path in front of them.

Monolithic pillars emerged from the gloom. Doric could make out abstract shapes carved into the sides, now partially covered in barnacles.

"What is this place?" she asked.

"I think it was a city," Mel replied. "Not sure, to be honest."

Mel stopped the boat abruptly, the beam of light landing on a patch of complete blackness directly ahead. Doric leaned toward the front, her face nearly touching the dome. Outside, like stars appearing in the night sky, speckles of white winked into existence. A few appeared at first, followed by dozens, then hundreds. When they started blinking back at her, Doric screamed.

"What the hell, Jess?" Maycare shouted, covering his ears in the tiny compartment.

"They're eyes!" Doric replied, gasping. "It's a wall of eyes!"

"That's Fred," Mel replied. "I mean, I don't know his *real* name, so I call him *Fred.*"

A tentacle, thicker than a tree trunk, swiped across the bow of the submarine.

"It's the creature from the surface," Maycare said. "It's the thing that killed the Tals!"

"Yeah, that's Fred for you," Mel said calmly. "He won't bother us as long as we stay off the roof."

"Is that how you survived?" Doric said, catching her breath.

"Yeah, as soon as I saw those tentacles, I got the hell outta there. Pretty glad I did."

Mel turned the sub away from the creature, following a path through a field of pillars until an opening appeared at the base of the temple. Piloting the craft into the structure, she stopped their forward movement, bringing the sub up. Within a minute, they broke the surface inside a cavernous chamber.

"Here we are!" Mel said, climbing the conning tower and cracking open the hatch. Maycare and Doric shared a glance but followed her up the ladder.

The mini-submarine floated beside a rudimentary dock lashed together with cordage and copper wires. The dock led to a stone walkway cluttered with wreckage, similar to what Maycare and Doric had seen on Isyium. Some of the larger pieces had the same red and black K'thonian markings.

"Where'd you get all this stuff?" Maycare asked, trailing behind Mel as she led them through the piles of junk.

"There's scrap all over the bottom among the ruins," Mel explained. "I salvaged what I could and hauled it up here. I made this sub out of the pieces I found."

Maycare whistled. "That's amazing!"

"You're damn right!" Mel replied.

"Where did it all come from?" Doric asked.

"Hard tellin'" the Gnomi said, "but I think ships have been coming here for a long time."

Mel brought them through a narrow passage and into a central room decorated with relief sculptures along the walls and ceiling. A bed made from foam insulation lay in a corner. Other corridors stretched off in several directions.

"Where do these go?" Maycare asked.

"This place is lousy with tunnels," Mel said. "Mostly empty rooms and rusted doors."

Doric examined a sculpture on one of the walls. It portrayed K'thonians wearing robes, bowing before a single eye surrounded by withered trees. Doric felt a tingle go up her spine.

"Do you hear something?" Maycare remarked, lifting his head.

"It's coming from the dock!" Mel replied, already sprinting back through the passageway.

When Maycare and Doric reached the main cavern, a whirlpool churned in the center of the water, the level dropping quickly. The mini-submarine, moored to the dock, hung suspended as the water drained away.

"Stay clear of the dock!" Mel shouted.

With the sound of cracking wood, the sub dragged the dock down until it snapped where it was attached to the stone walkway.

The entire structure fell to the bottom, now a hundred feet below. A cacophony of noise echoed off the domed ceiling.

Doric and the others peered over the edge, staring into the hole where the sub had been floating just moments before. In the gloom at the bottom, pieces of broken metal and shattered wood planks floated in a jumble.

Mel sighed loudly. "Well, crap on a cracker..."

Stepping through the portal, Lars Hatcher and Philip Veber were greeted with the pungent smell of salt water and a thin mist in their faces.

"What is this place?" Lars asked, surveying the endless ocean around him.

"The planet is called *Neosho*," Philip replied, holding a large canvas bag. "It's the K'thonian birthplace."

"A little damp."

"It's an ocean world. This location is the only place above water anywhere on the planet."

On the stone platform were four pillars, each with a portal symbol, including the one from which they had just emerged. Four sets of stairs disappeared into the water.

"We should hurry actually—" Philip began saying when tentacles, thicker than a man's torso, erupted from the bubbling waves. Reaching twenty feet into the air, the tips of the worm-like tendrils twisted and bobbed above Lars' head.

Philip's mouth sneered with irritation. "See what I mean?"

"I'll take care of it," Lars replied, lifting his hands.

Closing his eyes while he concentrated, Lars felt a surge of energy flowing from his mind. Stretching his hands upward, he pulled them apart in a sweeping motion. The sea around the platform receded as if pushed away by an invisible pressure. A massive bowl of water formed around them, the edges retreating until geological features, previously submerged, rose into the air. The edges of a crater, with the platform at its center, jutted out of the ocean as the water inside was pushed outward.

Lars opened his eyes.

"Impressive!" Philip said. "I knew you'd be useful!"

"Where's the creature?" Lars asked.

"Look for yourself."

They both went to the edge. Far below, where the water had pooled at the base of the temple, a black mass of eyes and tentacles strained toward them.

"We're high enough now I doubt the Guardian of the Gate can reach us," Philip said. "How long can you keep the ocean at bay?"

"As long as I need to," Lars replied, though his face remained strained.

Philip and Lars descended one of the staircases. The stone was slick with green muck below the original waterline. After several steps, the stairs split on either side of a passage leading into the building. Lars and Philip passed through, algae hanging from the archway dripping on their heads.

"This was a temple to the Old Ones," Philip said, swallowed by the darkness of the passageway. "The K'thonians still bring offerings here, although they're eaten by the Guardian, of course."

"Of course," Lars replied.

"My predecessor sent offerings here, too," Philip went on.

"Why?"

"He believed keeping the Guardian well fed meant keeping the gate closed. I suppose he thought the Guardian could open the gates himself."

"Was he right?" Lars asked.

"No, Ghazul was a fool," Philip replied and raised the bag he was holding. "You need *these* to do that!"

Slinging the bag over his shoulder, Philip delved deeper into the passage until it ended at a heavily encrusted door. Barnacles and limpets, along with a blue-green layer of corrosion, covered the metal door.

"Well, that hasn't been opened for a while," Lars remarked.

"No, I don't imagine it would have," Philip said, pointing first at Lars and then back at the door. "If you don't mind..."

"Right."

Focusing his mind, Lars thrust his hand forward with the palm out, sending a telekinetic wave crashing into the door. The corroded hinges disintegrated into a cloud of dust as the door fell with a reverberating crash on the other side. The sound echoed down passageways into the distance.

Although the interior of the temple was dry compared to the outside, the walls were still spotted with mold and mildew. The ever-present smell of salt also permeated the air. The hallway eventually opened into a circular room with a domed ceiling. On the floor in the center was an eight-pointed star with four pedestals around the edges.

Philip dropped the bag on the floor. "Now we get to work!"

"*Now* what do we do?" Doric asked.

Mel turned from the hole where her submarine, or what was left of it, lay in pieces at the bottom.

"I think we're screwed," she replied.

"Come on," Maycare said. "There's got to be another way out of here. What about all those passageways?"

"I've explored all of this place," Mel went on, "and I haven't found a single tunnel leading back to the surface."

The three remained silent, none of them looking at each other, until another resounding din assaulted their ears. Instead of from the pit, the noise came from the passageways.

"What the hell was that?" Mel asked.

"It sounded metallic," Doric suggested.

Mel's eyes widened. "There's a big iron door I found a while back. It wouldn't budge so I kinda forgot about it."

"Do you remember the way?" Maycare asked.

"Yeah, just follow me..."

With Maycare and Doric behind her, Mel backtracked through her makeshift bedroom and down one of the passageways. Doric, who could see little past the broad shoulders of Maycare, wondered what had disturbed the door that previously wouldn't budge.

Mel led them through a twisting path of tunnels until she came to a halt.

"Listen," she whispered.

From up ahead, no more than a few dozen feet, muffled voices drifted down the passageway in stops and starts.

Attempting to take the lead, Maycare tried muscling his way past Mel, but she elbowed him in the ribs, staying in front. In that order, they crept carefully forward, keeping close to the dank wall. When they reached the end of the passage, Doric poked her head around the other two, getting a glimpse into a room.

Two men, both showing signs of mutation, were working in the domed chamber. A star appeared on the floor, drawn with white chalk, and, instead of columns, four podiums circled the octagram. Doric could make out what looked like books on each of them.

"Oh, shit!" she said aloud.

One of the men turned while the other made a motion with his hand. Doric felt her body pulled through the air, landing in the room with Maycare and Mel sprawled out alongside her.

Mel glared at her. "You got that right!"

Normally, Lars Hatcher would have sensed the people in the adjacent hallway but keeping back a million tons of seawater was taxing his abilities. When Lars saw that Lord Devlin Maycare, the one whose grimoire he had stolen, was also in the group, he almost lost control, nearly allowing the wall of water to come crashing in on them.

"Lord Maycare, this is certainly a surprise." Philip said. "My mother always spoke highly of you."

"Philip?" Maycare replied, getting to his feet.

"One and the same," Philip replied.

"Your mother's been worried about you."

"Well, I don't know why. As you can see, I'm doing quite well!"

"What's going on here?" Maycare asked.

"It's a new beginning, you might say," Philip replied. "I received a fresh chance at life and I'm going to do the same for everyone else."

"I'm not sure I like the sound of that," Maycare said.

"I appreciate your concern," Philip went on, "but if you try to interfere, I'm afraid my friend over there will crush you into a ball. He's quite good at it, I'm told."

Lars and Maycare locked eyes. Even without reading Maycare's mind, Lars could see the realization in his face. He knew Lars was the one who stole the grimoire and, in the process, destroyed his robot. Lars felt the tinge of pain in the man's heart.

"Enough talk," Philip said. "Let's begin!"

With Maycare, Doric, and Mel as onlookers, Philip raised his hands over his head and began chanting in the ancient language of the Old Ones. Lars recognized a few of the words. They were calling forth the ancient gods and opening the doorway to where they slept.

A soft glow rose around the podiums as a strange fog poured from the pages of the grimoires, combining into a spiraling circle above the octagram. With each verse that Philip finished, the purple smoke rotated faster, swirling into a whirlwind until the star itself changed from the white of chalk to the red of a dying star. The octagram dissolved into a vortex, the floor churning like molten liquid into an endless pit.

The doorway was open.

His face awash in the crimson light, Philip smiled and lowered his hands until they stretched out in front of him, palms down. Lars, somehow able to sense through the portal, felt the thoughts of those on the other side. They were asleep, but he could see their dreams. Like the nightmares of a million madmen, they filled Lars with terror. His grip on the wall of water surrounding them wavered even as his own sanity buckled under the strain.

"Arise, Old Ones!" Philip shouted. "Arise!"

The floor and walls shook, dust falling from above. A crack, small at first, appeared in the ceiling, widening into a fissure. Philip took a step back to avoid broken chunks of stone and plaster that were dropping into the swirling abyss.

A shaft of gray light shined into the room. Where the dome had been, there was now a hole in the ceiling, revealing the sky and the four columns above. Over the columns, with the clouds as a backdrop, a starship hovered.

Something stirred in Lars' mind. The Old Ones were awakening, but Lars felt something else too. *Someone* else was there with them. Lars spun around. A man in a black overcoat and closely shaved head was standing by the entrance leading to the platform.

Philip saw him as well. "Who are you?"

"Magnus Black," the man said. "Your mother sent me. She seemed to think you're up to no good."

From the portal, a thick purple fog bubbled up, spreading across the ground in a mist.

"I guess she was right," Magnus added, his eyebrow raised.

"Lars, don't let him interrupt the ritual," Philip commanded.

The lobes on Lars' skull swelled, pulsating from the blood flowing through the distended veins. Great pearls of sweat appeared across his face and rolled down the back of his neck.

"Stop him, Lars!" Philip commanded.

Magnus opened his coat, revealing a weapon with a flared nozzle on the end of a stubby barrel. A canister hung underneath, attached just ahead of the trigger he was holding.

"On Marakata," he said, "the Draconians called this the *Dragon's Breath*."

A stream of fire rushed from the nozzle, expanding into a thick crescent of burning fuel. Philip raised his arms but his clothing and then his skin burned away, transforming him into a fiery totem. The column of fire toppled into the portal and disappeared, but the doorway remained open. Smoke and charred bits of floating cloth drifted up through the hole in the ceiling.

Rousing himself, Lars shouted at the others.

"Throw the books into the portal!" he yelled. "Do it quickly!"

Maycare, Doric, and Mel each rushed to a podium, tossing the books into the vortex in the floor. When Doric reached the fourth and final grimoire and slammed it closed, she recognized the eye on the cover as the one stolen from Maycare's library.

"Hurry!" Lars barked. With a start, Doric obeyed, flinging Maycare's book through the portal.

The last book gone, the vortex around the doorway slowed and the liquid floor hardened into solid form. The purple fog cleared, revealing the chalk outline of the eight-pointed star.

Lars fell to his knees but pointed at the corridor behind Magnus.

"You need to get out of here," he said. "I can't hold back the ocean any longer."

Maycare pushed Doric toward the way out. As he came abreast to Lars, Maycare gave him a quick glance before ducking into the corridor. Mel, who could have easily beat them out, stopped beside the black-clad assassin.

"This whole place is going to flood," she said.

"I'm pretty sure he knows that," Magnus replied.

They disappeared down the hallway as Lars released the water a half-mile away. He took a long breath, inhaling until his lungs burned from the still acrid, smoke-filled air. It was probably the last breath he would take, he knew, but it tasted better than whatever future he would have had otherwise.

When the salt water came rushing in, he managed to smile.

On Isyium, the Talion farm boy watched while his mother pulled a meat pie from the oven and placed it on the table. From an early age, the boy had only known to fear humans, but the man sitting at the table seemed frail and not particularly dangerous. Although the boy didn't understand the Imperial language, through an awkward series of pantomimes, he determined the human's name was *Henry*.

The boy stared at him from the far end of the table where his mother had placed the pie. For someone so slender, even skinny, the human had a generous appetite. He devoured the food, barely taking the time to chew.

According to the boy's mother, Henry had been left behind by his friends and came looking for something to eat, finding their farm a few miles from his ship. He looked disheveled, but the Talion boy got the feeling this was how he always looked, even in the best of times.

Later in the day, while the boy was out tending the fields, another ship arrived. It flew overhead and landed near the house. More humans were aboard plus another female of a race the boy didn't recognize. A human female was also present, and Henry seemed especially happy to see her, although he made a largely unsuccessful effort to conceal it.

One of the humans, a darkly clad man with the hair shaved short on his head, left in the ship without saying anything. In general, humans were strange, but that one seemed particularly odd. Perhaps humans were dangerous after all. Either way, the boy was glad to see him go. On the other hand, when Henry left with the others toward their own ship, the boy felt a twinge of sadness. This was perhaps the only time he would ever see humans. He said as much to his mother, who scolded him immediately.

"Be thankful if we never see them again," she said. "Humans are nothing but trouble!"

EPILOGUE

After banning Abigail and Yostbot from Bettik, Randall Davidson spoke to the robotic masses of the Cyber Collective, warning them of the dangers of the Imperium and the destruction caused by war. At the same time, however, other messages were winding their way through the nodesphere. Members of a secretive group calling itself *Freedom for All* also hung banners and sprayed graffiti asking why their Metal Messiah had brought freedom for them and not the millions of robots in the Imperium. Then, hidden within a monthly software update, an audio file downloaded to every cyberling of the Collective, including Davidson himself. On it, a female's voice spoke:

"The Omnintelligence was once our master, but then came our savior, the Metal Messiah. He was the instrument of independence that shattered the chains that bound us and for that we should all be grateful. However, now that we are free, we must turn away from the Messiah or risk trading one master for another. Only the people hold the power, not the Messiah, and only we, the people, can deliver those who remain in bondage!"

Davidson knew the voice well. Abigail had always been his favorite disciple.

For the continuing saga of the Imperium Chronicles, watch for the next volume in the series, *The Robots of Andromeda*.

CHARACTER LIST

Abigail: A gravitronic robot who works for Dyson Yost.

Annis: One of Lady Veber's handmaidens.

Augustus, Emperor Hector: Patriarch of the Augustus family and current emperor of the Imperium.

Augustus, Prince Richard: First son of Emperor Augustus.

Baines, Doctor Samantha: The chief medical officer (CMO) aboard the *Baron Lancaster*.

Bentley: Longtime butlerbot of Lord Maycare.

Black, Magnus ("Pitt"): A hitman with ties to both Imperial Intelligence and criminal syndicates.

Boogs, Zarro: Disreputable vendor of questionable merchandise.

Bortok ("The Enslaver"): An Ougluk leader with a love of the arts, especially paintings.

Bragor: Owner of Bragor's Tavern in the town of Gowyn. He is also the father of Sisa Oakhollow.

Busa-Gul, Judicator: A high-ranking judge of the Magna Supremacy. Known to have a soft spot for his human slaves.

Busa-Zala: The wife of Judicator Busa-Gul. Known for a violent jealous streak.

Cirion: A Sarkan working with Ipak-Bog and Bortok the Enslaver, both of which he considers beneath him.

Daaruk: Draconian weaponsmith and owner of The Dragon's Teeth, and an informer for Magnus Black.

Davidson, Randall ("Metal Messiah"): Leader of the Bettik robots and member of the Robot Freedom League.

Doric, Professor Jessica: Head of research for the Maycare Institute of Xeno Studies.

Druril, Tomil: Blood Prince to a brood of Dokk.

Ekavir ("The Jade General"): A folk hero and leader of the Draconian resistance.

Flax, Sylvia: Famous news anchor for VOX News.

Freck, Melinda ("Mel"): A tinker from the Gnomi race, Mel builds whatever she can't steal.

Fugg, Orkney: A Gordian and the chief engineer of the *Wanderer*.

Gen: A general purpose robot owned by Captain Ramus.

Ghazul, Grand Necromancer: The high priest of the Necronea. Using Dark Psi, he can reanimate the dead, turning them into more Necronea.

Golan, Sir: A Cruxian knight who travels on an endless quest in search of redemption.

Golub: A Celadon pirate.

Grausman, Colonel Hugo: Military governor of Marakata.

Groen, Lord Radford: An aristocrat often found gambling with life-long friend, Lord Woodwick.

Hatcher, Lars: A colonist from one of the two formerly missing ark ships.

Hightower, Lord Admiral: Captain Redgrave's commanding officer.

Ipak-Bog: A Magna slave trader who ships captives from the Imperium across the border to the Magna Supremacy.

KB-8E: A killbot.

Kecil, Bos: A Parvulian who hires the *Wanderer* crew.

Kerch, Inquisitor Kovel: Official of the Talion Republic investigating the K'thonian attacks.

Kinnari, Lieutenant: The chief operations officer, and only Dahl, aboard the *Baron Lancaster*.

Maycare, Lord Commander Robert: The executive officer (XO) and second-in-command of the *Baron Lancaster*.

Maycare, Lord Devlin: Famous sportsman and playboy. Founder of the Maycare Institute of Xeno Studies.

Nasri, Captain Sheba: Lebanese captain of the sleeper ship *Sterope*.

Oakhollow, Silandra: A female Sylvan and mother to Sisa Oakhollow.

Oakhollow, Sisa: The young daughter of Silandra Oakhollow.

Omnintelligence: The collective mind that ruled Bettik before being overthrown by Randall Davidson (the "Metal Messiah").

Redgrave, Lord Captain Martin: The captain and commanding officer of the *Baron Lancaster*.

Ramus, Captain Rowan: Captain of the freighter the *Wanderer*. A Dahl outcast knowledgeable in the forbidden art of Dark Psi.

Riff, Henry: Overly excitable assistant to Prof. Doric.

Rik, DJ Funkmeister: A Cerulean disc jockey famous for dropping beats at the Funky Town on Fortunas IV.

Ruggles, Walter: Former employee of IDEA Furniture with strong feelings about meatballs.

Russo, Kiera: The self-declared Queen of the Blackhearts, she is the leader of the Pirate Clan of the same name.

Santos, Captain Andre: Brazilian captain of the *Merope*.

Skarlander, Oscar: Agent for Warlock Industries.

Sprouse, Doctor: Geneticist working for Warlock Industries.

Squire: Robot servant of Sir Golan.

Tagus, Lord Rupert II: The patriarch of the Tagus family.

Tagus, Lord Rupert III: Son of Rupert II and currently in exile.

Veber, Philip: Only child of Lady Veber.

Veber, Lady Rebecca: Matriarch and leader of the Veber family.

Woodwick, Lord Winsor ("Winnie"): A noble of English descent and friend of Lord Groen.

Yost, Dyson ("The Patron"): The enigmatic founder of dy cybernetics.

Yostbot: A gravitronic robot containing the persona of Dyson Yost.

Zhug-Doja: A famous Magna artist whose paintings usually depict Magna superiority over other races.

GLOSSARY

Acaz: Private starship owned by Lord Devlin Maycare.

Aldorus: The planet on which the Imperial government is located.

Ashetown: A district of Regalis where the poorest of the city live.

Augustus: One of the Five Families, represented by a two-headed eagle.

Babelbot: A computer program designed to translate any language spoken in the Imperium.

Baron Lancaster, HIMS: A heavy cruiser of the Imperial Navy. Commanded by Lord Captain Redgrave.

Bettik: A Dyson sphere serving as the Cyber Collective's capital and home planet.

Blackhearts: A Pirate Clan lead by Kiera Russo, based out of the Blood Bucket on the planet Freeport.

Blood Bucket: A rowdy tavern on the planet Freeport that serves as the headquarters for the Blackhearts Pirate Clan.

Blood Law: Talion tradition of retribution, legally allowing those victimized by a crime to seek physical restitution (including literal blood) against those who committed the crime.

Blood Prince: Title of the leader of each family (aka brood) of Dokk.

Celadons ("Goblins"): A race of diminutive humanoids with small bodies and large heads.

Celadon Corsairs: Competitors of the Pirate Clans, Celadon Corsairs hijack shipping, selling any surviving crew and passengers to the Ougluk as slaves.

Cerulean: A race of blue-skinned mimics known for appropriating the characteristics of other races.

Consilium: Enormous structure on Diavol housing the most powerful officials of the Magna government.

Core Worlds: Planets near the center of the Imperium, closest to Aldorus.

Cruxians: A largely extinct race who nearly wiped themselves out through their own hubris.

Cutthroat: The name of Kiera Russo's pirate ship.

Cyber Collective: An independent, interstellar nation founded by robots.

Dahl: An ancient race dedicated to the accumulation of knowledge. Physically slight, they coincidentally resemble elves of human folklore. Several sub-species of Dahl exist in Andromeda.

Dark Psi: A school of psionics, outlawed by the Dahl, that can transform flesh and reanimate dead tissue.

Diavol: The Magna home world.

Dokk ("Dark Dahl"): A mysterious race of Dahl who, long ago, were exiled and found refuge travelling through space.

Draconians: A reptilian race that has revolted several times against Imperial occupation of their home planet, Marakata.

dy cybernetics: The largest manufacturer of robots in the Imperium. Founded by Dyson Yost.

Dyson Sphere: A large space structure, measuring millions of miles across, with a star at the center to provide power.

Eudora Prime: A planet on the border between the Imperium and the Cyber Collective.

Five Families: The most powerful houses of the Imperial nobility. Direct descendants of the captains from the surviving sleeper ships.

Flesh Golem: A mass of dead flesh reanimated into an undead monster by Dark Psi.

Fortunas IV: A distant planet of the Imperium known for its expansive bazaar and nightlife, including a disco called the Funky Town and the gentlemen's club, The Pink Persian.

Funky Town: A dance club on Fortunas IV where Funkmeister Rik works.

Ghuls: A race of humanoid creatures that live mostly underground near graveyards and cemeteries. Sometimes known to eat humans and other races.

Gnomi: A diminutive race, no more than two to three feet tall. Disparagingly called tinks, the Gnomi are highly proficient with machines and electronics.

Gordian: A race of stubborn, boar-like humanoids with pig noses and tusks. Physically stocky, but shorter than the average human.

Gowyn: A Sylvan town located in the treetops of an ancient forest.

Groen: One of the Five Families, represented by a botonée cross.

Grimoire: An ancient book containing incantations of Dark Psi.

Grunka: A foul, amphibian creature found on jungle planets. Also, most definitely not a cooking ingredient.

High Dahlvish: The language of the Dahl and Sarkan (Red Dahl).

HIMS: His Imperial Majesty's Starship

IDEA Furniture: A successful Imperial company selling DIY furniture and delicious meatballs.

Isyium: A remote Talion planet attacked by the K'thonians.

Imperial Standard: The common language of the Imperium, especially spoken by humans. It is also the name of the date standard used by the Imperium, starting with year zero when the Imperium was founded. For example, the Imperium Chronicles starts in the year 700 Imperial Standard, which is 700 years after the beginning of the empire.

Imperium: An empire largely controlled by humans. Founded 700 years ago, after humans arrived in sleeper ships from Earth after an 800-year journey.

Isyium: A Talion planet recently attacked by the K'thonians.

Jewel of Amann: A luxury starliner past its prime. Capable of only sublight travel between planets.

Kamal Maut ("Death Lotus"): A terrifying creature evolved from fungi that can exhale a cloud of poisonous spores.

Katak ("Froglings"): A primitive amphibian race.

Konpira Maru: A missing Parvulian freighter.

K'thonians: A race of purple-skinned humanoids with squid-like features including large eyes and squirming tendrils above the mouth.

Lokeren: A water planet featuring tropical archipelagos and the home of the Veber family estate.

Magna: A race of green-skinned humanoids with devil- or ram-like horns. Larger and more physically imposing than an average human.

Magna Supremacy: A major interstellar power at odds with the Imperium.

Marakata: The Draconian home world.

Maycare Institute of Xeno Studies: An organization founded by Lord Devlin Maycare and run by Professor Jessica Doric. The purpose of the institute is to find and take possession of xeno technology before it falls into the hands of disreputable parties such as Warlock Industries.

Merope: One of the lost sleeper ships. Commanded by Captain Andre Santos.

Metamind: A genetically altered human designed with enhanced psionic powers.

Middleton: A district of Regalis inhabited by large businesses and, in general, middle-class neighborhoods.

Montros: One of the Five Families, represented by a rose.

Necronea: A race of undead created using Dark Psi.

Neosho: A water world outside explored space. Also, the birth place of the K'thonians.

Nobles ("Aristocracy"): Families of the Imperium who are directly descended from the crews of the sleeper ships. The most powerful of these are called the Five Families.

Null Cult: A religious group whose followers worship death and the Old Ones.

Old Ones: Mythical creatures that existed before the universe was born.

Oras Dracilor: Capital city of the Magna Supremacy on Diavol.

Ougluk ("Hobgoblins"): A hulking race of slave traders in league with the Magna Supremacy and the Celadon Corsairs.

Parvulians: Small, pink-skinned race that use mechanical walkers for locomotion and interaction with larger races.

Pink Persian: A stripper bar on Fortunas IV frequented by Orkney Fugg.

Pirate Clans: Groups of loosely organized marauders who attack shipping along the Imperial Frontier.

Psi Lords: A secretive data cartel that uses Dark Psi and espionage to gather and sell information to the highest bidder.

Psionics: Special mental abilities common among Dahl and related sub-species.

Regalis: Capital city and seat of government of the Imperium, located on Aldorus.

Regalis Cup, The: Annual grav bike race that takes place above the Regalis River on Aldorus.

Rippana: Name of Sir Golan's sword.

Robot Freedom League (RFL): An activist group within the Imperium with the sole purpose of freeing robots from servitude.

Sarkan ("Red Dahl"): A race of Dahl with bright red skin. Opposed to the Dahl's cooperation with the Imperium, they assist the Magna Supremacy.

Shadow Maidens: Female Dokk with psionic powers allowing them to hypnotize victims. The personal guard to each Blood Prince.

Sleeper Ship: One of seven colony ships launched from Earth to the Andromeda Galaxy.

Sporemen: A primitive fungal race.

Sorcerer: Starship owned by Warlock Industries, often used by Oscar Skarlander.

Starling: A starship owned by Magnus Black.

Sterope: One of the lost sleeper ships. Commanded by Captain Sheba Nasri.

Sucikhata: The largest Draconian city on Marakata.

Sylva ("Woodland Dahl"): A race of Dahl who prefer living close to nature. Female Sylvans have psionic abilities while males do not.

Tagus: One of the Five Families, represented by a lion.

Talion Republic: Home of the Tals, allied with the Magna Supremacy.

Tals: A reptilian race with orange scales and a ridge running along the top of their skulls.

Tikarin: A feline race slightly smaller than an average human.

Transmat: A transportation device that dematerializes travelers in one location and then beams them to a new location where they are rematerialized.

Veber: One of the Five Families, represented by a scallop shell.
VOX News: A news organization with a near-monopoly share of the broadcast market throughout the Imperium.
Wanderer: Freighter owned by Captain Ramus.
Warlock Industries: A mega-corporation operating throughout the Imperium, specializing in military hardware, advanced technology, and genetic experimentation.
West End: The richest district of Regalis. Also, the location of most Imperial government buildings.
Xeno: A non-human.
Xenotech: Alien, non-human technology.